Dear Reader:

I first heard about the murder that inspired *What's Left of Me Is Yours* on the radio over breakfast in 2010. You may have heard about it, too. At the time, the crime was a short-lived international media sensation, as salacious as it was mystifying: a love triangle, a covert industry in the underbelly of Tokyo laid bare, and a woman found brutally murdered, her lover the only person at the scene of the crime. I still remember thinking to myself, "I bet that's a book one day." But I was not an editor at the time, so I promptly turned back to my toast and forgot about the whole thing.

Elsewhere in the world Stephanie Scott was reading an article about the same crime, and she didn't forget about it. In fact, she spent the next nine years researching the book you have in your hands, wherein a version of that article is on the very first page. She spent years traveling in Japan, interviewing experts and citizens, and visiting the cities and towns she describes in intricate detail in these pages. As a result of her studies, she is now a member of the British Japanese Law Association and was awarded a British Association of Japanese Studies Toshiba Studentship for her work on this novel—an anthropological prize for postgraduate research that has never before been awarded to a novelist. Her goal was not only to portray the Japanese legal system and marriage breakup industry in all its complexity, but also to explore an overarching question about the human capacity for darkness: Is it possible to love someone and kill her?

When this manuscript arrived on my desk almost a decade after I'd finished eating that piece of toast, I couldn't believe the story had found me twice. I'll warn you: *What's Left of Me Is Yours* offers no easy answers. It is enthralling and unsettling, gorgeous and relentless, and it has found you now, too. You won't forget it.

**Margo Shickmanter**
***Editor***
***mshickmanter@penguinrandomhouse.com***

# *What's Left of Me Is Yours*

A NOVEL

**Stephanie Scott**

Doubleday
*New York*

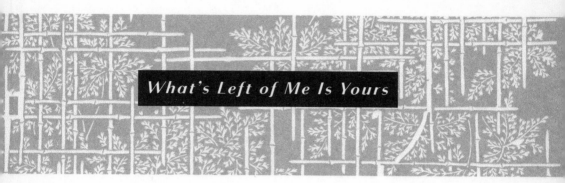

This is a work of fiction. Names, characters, places, and incidents either are the product of the author's imagination or are used fictitiously. Any resemblance to actual persons, living or dead, events, or locales is entirely coincidental.



www.doubleday.com



[Permissions, if any]

Book design by Maria Carella
Jacket photograph TK
Jacket design TK

Library of Congress Cataloging-in-Publication Data
Names: Scott, Stephanie, 1983– author.
Title: What's left of me is yours : a novel / by Stephanie Scott.
Description: First edition. | New York : Doubleday, [2020]
Identifiers: LCCN 2019022477 (print) | LCCN 2019022478 (ebook) |
ISBN 9780385544702 (hardcover) | ISBN 9780385544719 (ebook) |
ISBN: 9780385546331 (open market)
Subjects: GSAFD: Love stories.
Classification: LCC PR6119.C683 W47 2020 (print) | LCC PR6119.C683 (ebook) |
DDC 823/.92—dc23
LC record available at https://lccn.loc.gov/2019022477
LC ebook record available at https://lccn.loc.gov/2019022478

MANUFACTURED IN THE UNITED STATES OF AMERICA

1 3 5 7 9 10 8 6 4 2

First Edition

For Subhashini, Roger, and Tom,
*with all my love.*

It matters not how strait the gate,
How charged with punishments the scroll,
I am the master of my fate:
I am the captain of my soul.

—WILLIAM ERNEST HENLEY

*What's Left of Me Is Yours*

# *Prologue*

Sarashima is a beautiful name; a name that now belongs only to me. I was not born with it, this name, but I have chosen to take it, because once it belonged to my mother.

It is customary upon meeting someone to explain who you are and where you come from, but whether you realize it or not, you already know me and you know my story. Look closely. Reach into the far corners of your mind and sift through the news clippings, bulletins, tabloid crimes tucked away there. You will see me. I am the line at the end of an article; I am the final sentence ending with a full stop.

*WAKARESASEYA AGENT GOES TOO FAR?*

*By Yu Yamada. Published: 6:30 p.m., 05/16/1994*

**The trial of Kaitarō Nakamura, the man accused of murdering Rina Satō, began today at the Tokyo District Court.**

**The case has attracted international attention due to the fact that the defendant, Mr. Nakamura, is an agent in the wakaresaseya or so-called "marriage breakup" industry, and has admitted that he was hired by the victim's husband, Osamu Satō, to seduce his wife, Rina Satō, and provide grounds for divorce.**

**Nakamura claims that he and the deceased fell in love and were planning to start a new life together. If convicted of murder, Nakamura faces a minimum 20-year prison sentence; the judges may even consider the death penalty.**

**Rina Satō's father, Mr. Sarashima, told reporters: "A business such as this which destroys peoples' lives should not**

**be allowed to operate in Tokyo. Rina was my only child and the heart of our family. I shall never get over her loss, nor forgive it."**

**Rina Satō is survived by a daughter of seven years old.**

Can you remember when you first read this? Were you at home at your breakfast table or in the office, scanning the morning news? I can see your face as you read about my family; your brows drew together in a slight frown, a crinkle formed above your nose. Perhaps the smell of coffee was strong and reassuring in the air, and eventually you shook your head and turned the page. The world is full of strange things.

Wakaresaseya was not common in Japan when Kaitarō was drawn into my mother's life. The industry emerged out of a demand for its services, a demand that exists all over the world today. Look at the people around you: those you love, those who love you, those who want what you have. They can enter your life as easily as he entered mine.

Do you know now when we first met or where? Was it in the *Telegraph, New York Times, Le Monde, Sydney Morning Herald*? My story stopped there in the foreign press. Later articles focused on the marriage break-up industry itself and the agents who populate it, but none of them mentioned me. Lives to be rebuilt are always less interesting than lives destroyed. Even in Japan, I disappeared from the page.

# *Part One*

When you look at the world with knowledge,
you realize that things are unchangeable and at the
same time are constantly being transformed.

—MISHIMA

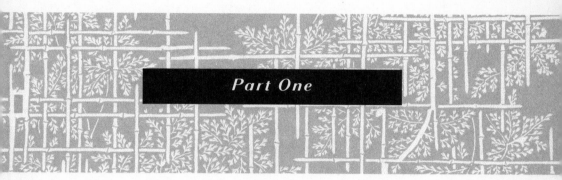

## *Sumiko*

## *WHAT'S IN A NAME?*

For the Sarashima, the naming of a child is a family matter. For me, it marked a bond with tradition that would govern my life. The names of my maternal relatives have always been chosen at Kiyoji in Meguro. You can just about glimpse the temple from the park at the end of our street. It sits at the base of a hill in the very center of our neighborhood; the green peaks of its roof tiles gleam in the sun and the red pillars of the portico peer out over the surrounding buildings.

As I grew up, my grandfather told me that our family had worshipped there since coming to Tokyo. He said that they remained at prayer during the firebombing of the city and that after the war they restored the temple. For him, it is a symbol of regeneration.

This is why, as soon as Mama had recovered from my birth, instead of gathering around the kamidana in the northern corner of the living room, my family went to Kiyoji and my mother carried me in her arms beneath the gates and into the heart of the temple complex.

As we climbed the stone steps leading to the main hall, my mother glanced up at the sprawling wooden roof, at its curved eaves stretching out beyond the building—shutting out the sunlight—resulting in the cool, dark shadows within. Inside, we proceeded through the sweet smoke of incense to the altar. All around us the wind blew through in gusts and the air swirled, while outside the bronze bells of the surrounding temples began to toll.

I don't remember this journey, but I can see it quite clearly: me in my cream blanket, my father carrying Tora, the toy white tiger Grandpa had given to me, and my grandfather himself, grave in his three-piece suit. I have been told this story so many times it has seeped into my memory.

One of the monks, pale in his indigo robes, bowed to my grandfather and took from him a pouch containing a selection of names. My mother had prepared these names, first consulting the astrologer and then choosing her favorite three, counting the strokes of the characters to ensure that each first name, combined with our surname, would add up to an optimal number.

I can still see her sitting at our dining table in her house slippers and jeans, an oversized T-shirt covering the bump that was me. The blinds are open, the sun slanting across the marble floors of our home, while in the kitchen the rice cooker bubbles and the washing up dries on the draining board. My mother lays the sheets of rice paper out in front of her and turns to the inkstone by her side. I can see her dip her brush into the ink, smell the rich scent of earth and pine soot rising into the air, as using the very tip of the bristles she presses down, the horsehair bending to create the first fluid stroke.

The monk bowed once more and placed the names in a shallow dish upon the altar. Then, kneeling before them, he selected a delicate wooden fan and, in unison with the breeze that drifted through the open screens, unfurled it, whipping up currents of air. Everyone was silent. The gray smoke of the incense drifted towards the rafters as one by one the names painted by my mother flew towards the ceiling. Eventually, one remained, alone on the teak surface: 寿美子

Grandpa knelt and picked it up from the altar and a smile broke out on his face as he read the characters of my name: celebration, beauty, child.

"Sumiko," he said. "Sumiko Sarashima."

My father had been silent throughout the proceedings. In the weeks leading up to my birth, plans for an "adoptive" ceremony had been discussed. Under Japanese law, both people in a marriage must share the same surname, but in certain circumstances, a husband may take his wife's surname and join her household, so that her name and her line may continue. My father was a second son and his family, the Satōs, readily agreed. However, that day, as the priest took out a fresh sheet of paper and began to write out my name, my father spoke:

"Satō," he said. "She is a Satō, not a Sarashima."

## *WHAT I KNOW*

- I was raised by my grandfather, Yoshi Sarashima.
- I lived with him in a white house in Meguro, Tokyo.
- In the evenings he would read to me.
- He told me every story but my own.

My grandfather was a lawyer; he was careful in his speech. Even when we were alone together in his study and I would sit on his lap tracing the creases in his leather armchair, or later, when I sat on a stool by his side, even then, he had a precision with words. I have kept faith with that precision to this day.

Grandpa read everything to me—Mishima, Sartre, Dumas, Tolstoy, Bashō, tales of his youth and duck hunting in Shimoda, and one book, *The Trial,* that became my favorite. The story begins like this: "Someone must have been telling lies about Josef K."

When we read that line for the first time, Grandpa explained that the story was a translation. I was twelve years old, stretching out my fingers for a world beyond my own, and I reached out then to the yellowed page, stroking the written characters that spoke of something new. I read the opening aloud, summoning the figure of Josef K.: a lonely man, a man people would tell lies about.

As I grew older, I began to argue with Grandpa about *The Trial.* He told me other people fought over it too, that they fight about it even today—over the translation of one word in particular—*verleumdet.* To tell a lie. In some versions of the story, this word is translated as “slander.” Slander speaks of courts and accusations, of public reckoning; it has none of the childhood resonance of “telling lies.” And yet, when I read this story for the first time, it was the translator’s use of “telling lies” that fascinated me.

Lies, when they are first told, have a shadow quality to them, a gossamer texture that can wrap around a life. They have that feather-light essence of childhood, and my childhood was built on lies.

═

The summer before my mother died, we went to the sea. When I look back on that time, those months hold a sense of finality for me, not because that was the last holiday my mother and I would take together, but because it is the site of my last true memory.

Every year, as the August heat engulfed Tokyo, my family piled their suitcases onto a local train and headed for the coast. We went to Shimoda. Father remained in the city to work, but Grandpa Sarashima came with us. Each time, he stopped at the same kiosk in the station to buy frozen clementines for the train, and in the metallic heat of the carriage Mama and I would wait impatiently for the fruit to soften so we could get at the pockets of sorbet within. Finally, when our chins were sticky with juice, Mama would turn to me in our little row of two and ask what I would like to do by the sea, just she and I, alone.

Our house on the peninsula was old, its wooden gateposts warped by the winds that peeled off the Pacific. As we climbed towards the rocky promontory at the top of the hill, the gates, dark and encrusted with salt, signaled that my home was near: Washikura—Eagle’s Nest, the house overlooking the bay, between Mount Fuji and the sea.

Our country is built around mountains, and people are piled up in concrete boxes, cages. To have land is rare, but the house in Shimoda had belonged to my family since before the war, and afterward my grandfather fought to keep it when everything else was lost.

Forest sweeps over the hills above the house. I was not allowed up there alone as a child, so when I looked at my mother on the train that summer she knew immediately what I would ask to do. In the afternoons, Mama and I climbed high on the wooded slopes above Washikura. We watched the tea fields as they darkened before autumn. We lay back on the rocky black soil and breathed in the sharp resin of the pines. Some days, we heard the call of a sea eagle as it circled overhead.

Grandpa knew the forest but he never found us there. At four o'clock each afternoon, he would venture to the base of the hillside and call to us through the trees. He shouted our names: "Rina!" "Sumi!" Together, we nestled among the pines, giggling, as grandfather's voice wavered and fell.

I often heard Grandpa calling before Mama did, but I always waited for her signal to be quiet. On our last afternoon in the forest, I lay still, feeling the soft and steady puff of my mother's breath against my face. She pulled me against her and her breathing quieted and slowed. I opened my eyes and stared at her, at the dark lashes against her cheeks. I took in her pallor, her stillness. I heard my grandfather begin to call, his voice thin and distant. I snuggled closer, kissing her face, pushing through the coldness with my breath. Suddenly, she smiled, her eyes still closed, and pressed a finger to her lips.

We no longer own our home, Washikura, on the outskirts of Shimoda; Grandpa sold it years ago. But when I go there today, climbing up through the undergrowth, I can feel my mother there beneath the trees. When I lie down on the ground, the pine needles sharp under my cheek, I imagine that the chill of the breeze is the stroke of her finger.

# Rina

# *ATAMI*

Rina stood in the garden of Washikura and looked out across the slopes and mountains stretching towards Mount Fuji, at the deep shadows forming on the forested hills. She thought of how the plates that created this peninsula had converged at Fuji-san millions of years ago, causing a land of volcanoes, earthquakes, and hot springs to rise from the sea.

The volcano was still active, she knew. On a clear day one could see vapor and smoke curling above the snow-covered peak, hinting at the new islands, plateaus, and peninsulas waiting within. But that summer, as Rina watched the slopes before her turn gradually from lime green to pomegranate to rust, she did not think of what was to come; she thought about her daughter kneeling beside Grandpa Yoshi in the garden, digging into the dark soil of the azaleas with her trowel, her face turned sullenly away from her mother. Rina looked up at the mountains watching over them, and beneath their quiet gaze she climbed into her red Nissan and drove to Atami.

At the crowded beachfront Rina stopped and looked for a space to park. Atami had become a place for pleasure-seekers. Salarymen flocked to its beaches, eager to supplement their existence in Tokyo with summer condos, shopping malls, and karaoke. Hotels capitalized on the natural hot springs, and buildings long ago replaced the trees. The forests of camphor and ferns that once surrounded the town were all cut back until little trace of them remained. Rina left her car at the end of the beach and walked back along the waterfront, shading her eyes against the glare of the sun as it glanced off the concrete.

"You came!"

At the sound of his voice, Rina turned. Kaitarō was walking across the beach towards her, barefoot in the sand. She smiled and watched his slow, loping stride.

"I was afraid you'd stood me up," he said as he reached her.

"You weren't afraid."

"I am when you're not with me," he replied.

Rina laughed and they began to walk towards the yachts bobbing against the blue of the sea. She stopped by an ice cream stall advertising azuki, red bean flavor. At her side, Kaitarō passed his sandals from one hand to the other and reached into his pocket for some change.

"Just one, please."

Rina smiled at him. "My daughter loves these," she said as she bit into the ice cream, savoring the caramel sweetness of the beans. She felt Kaitarō's eyes on her and lowered her gaze.

"We can bring Sumiko here," he said.

"Impossible." Rina shifted as he stepped behind her. She felt the warmth of him at her back, his breath at her ear.

"Yoshi will not notice if we take her out for an afternoon."

"What will I tell her when this ends?"

"It won't end, Rina."

He drew her back against his chest and she dug her toes deep into the white sand, feeling the tiny grains sift between her red sandals and her skin.

"I shouldn't be here," she said, but her sentence ended in a shriek as he lifted her up into the air and over his shoulder.

"Oh my god!" she hissed, hitting at him with her fists. "What are you doing?" Rina gasped as her ice cream fell into the sand.

"There are too many people here," he said. "We can't talk."

"What are you, a child?"

Kaitarō grinned against her. "You bring out the worst in me."

"People are staring."

"I don't care," he said. And it was true, she thought, he really didn't.

They reached his car and he put her down. Rina could feel the blush rising in her cheeks; people were still looking at them. Kaitarō placed his palms on either side of her face. "Rina," he said, "you're with me today. Try to concentrate."

She took a deep breath and looked up at him. "I don't have long."

Rina caught glimpses of the view as they drove up into the hills above the town, following a narrow road that wove between the pines. The sea was a deep blue against the concrete of the bay, and along the slopes she could see the cypresses and cedars settling along the fringes of Atami, as though they would one day reclaim it.

They drove to a parking spot where a stone path led up onto the hillside. Rina tied her bobbed hair back with a handkerchief to protect it from the wind and then she joined Kaitarō on the slope. Together they climbed up into an orchard of natsumikan trees; the summer oranges hung low and heavy against the dark green shells of their leaves. Kaitarō found a spot for them in the grass and spread out the raincoat he had brought from the car. It was beige in the style of New York detectives, and Rina smiled; she liked to tease him about it. A few minutes later, however, as the cool of the breeze settled against the back of her neck, she felt a thread of unease. She had committed herself by coming with him. He wanted more from her, a great deal more, of that she was sure. Rina shifted away from him, pulling her skirt down over her knees. She sat further back on the coat as he dug into his satchel.

Kaitarō looked up at her; he must have seen the nerves on her face but he just smiled, his right hand reaching to the bottom of the bag while Rina pressed her nails into the flesh of her palm.

"I brought this for you," he said.

She turned towards him to look at what he held in his hands: a Canon EOS 3500. Surprise pushed through her anxiety. She'd seen one in the back streets of Akihabara, looked at it in catalogs, but she had never held one.

"Go on," he said. "Take it. I thought we could do some work while we're up here."

"Work?"

"Don't you think it's time?"

Rina turned away. He brought this up persistently—the possibility that she might return to the photography career she'd once planned, but she was afraid: if you neglected something for long enough didn't it die?

"I found your essay, Rina," he said. "The one you published in *Exposure*?"

Rina bit her lip. "That was experimenting."

"It doesn't read that way."

"I wrote it just before I left the law program at Tōdai. Father threw every copy out of the house."

"I can get you a copy."

"No need," she said, and she looked at him then. "I remember it."

Silently, he handed her the camera.

They moved through the orchard and lay down on the sheets of leaves. Rina watched him, her eyes following the speed of his movements, his fingers nimble as they slid across the bevel of the lens, selecting apertures to accentuate the natural palette of the hillside. For half an hour she remained still beside him, enjoying the rapid click of the shutter, feeling the weight of the camera in her palm. Then, slowly, she lifted the viewfinder of her Canon to see what he could see.

They finished photographing in color and then, gauging the light and shadows of the afternoon, switched to monochrome film, drawing the shapes of the leaves out through the filters of black and white. She turned to find Kaitarō propped up on his elbow watching her; he was waiting for her to take her shot. Rina narrowed her eyes at him and he grinned as he twisted the lens off his camera. She leaned towards him, watching as he reached into his satchel and drew out a new lens, holding it out to her, describing how he could capture the light drifting down to them.

Later, sitting barefoot on the grass, Rina reached out and plucked an orange from a branch. Kaitarō settled beside her as she split the bright skin and pith of the fruit open with her thumbnail, releasing tiny droplets of zest into the air. She pulled it apart and handed half to him, sucking the sour liquid off her palm. As the sun sank lower on the horizon, Rina leaned back against his shoulder. She rested her cheek on the ridge of his collarbone and watched the light flickering between the trees.

A droplet of water fell onto Rina's hair followed by two more. It was not until the shower broke through the leaves that she rose to her feet. The storm had crept up on them. It was that way in the mountains; the undergrowth beckoned to the moisture in the air. Kaitarō threw his coat over both of them and she grabbed her sandals as they scrambled down the slope, awash with wet leaves, to his car. Streams of water cascaded down the windows and a white fog materialized over the hills, flattening the mountains into two dimensions before rendering them invisible. Neither of them turned the radio on; they sat in the silence as Kaitarō took her hand, interlacing his fingers with hers.

"I came third in the Fukase-Isono Photography Prize," he said. "They're going to feature one of my pieces in an exhibition. Will you come?"

"Where is it?" Rina asked, turning her head to look at him.

"A warehouse in Akihabara. If the art isn't to your taste I can always take you to Yabu Soba."

Rina smiled; he was so cunningly aware of her obsession with food.

"Don't mention the duck soba," she said, warning him off with her hand.

"It would mean a lot to me if you would come."

She looked at him and the laughter faded from her eyes. "Then I will."

The rain slowed to a drizzle and stopped as the evening drew on. They got out of the car and approached the rails lining the road; they could see the sea emerging through the wisps of mist that lingered on the hillside.

Kaitarō put his arms around her and rubbed her shoulders to ward off the chill. "I should go," she said, but now she was reluctant to leave. "Kai"—she turned towards him—"about today . . ."

"You don't have to say anything."

"Thank you."

He brushed her hair away from her face and untied the damp

handkerchief that held it in place. Rina watched as he put it in his pocket and she let him take it.

"I love you," he said.

Rina shifted in his arms. She tried to say something, but he shook his head, placing his fingers over her lips; his skin was rough where it touched her mouth.

"I do."

# *Sumiko*

## *TOKYO*

My mother was a photographer, before she became a wife. Each year when we went to the sea, Mama would play with me on the beach, taking roll after roll of film. Grandpa would send them off to Kodak to be made into Kodachrome slides. In the autumn, as the leaves darkened and we returned to Tokyo, my mother would open a bottle of Coca-Cola at Grandpa's home in Meguro and we would watch the slides all at once on the projector.

I still have them, these home movies of sorts; they are in the basement of the Meguro house, filed away in narrow leather boxes. Sometimes I go down there to look at the slides. They are beautiful, each one a rectangular jewel encased in white card. I can see my mother in miniature biting the cone of an ice cream; me in the sand with my red bucket, my swimsuit damp from the sea; Grandpa sheltering under an umbrella, even though he is already in the shade.

I have other memories too, but they are not of Shimoda. These appear to me as glimpses and flashes. In my mind's eye, the line of the coast straightens, the rocky inlets of Shimoda are replaced by an open harbor, and I hear the slap of my feet on concrete as I run and run. There are moments of clarity, liquid scenes: I see a yacht on the waves, its sails stretched taut; I feel strong arms lifting me into the air; I turn away from the bright sun glinting off a camera lens; a man's hand offers me a cone of red bean ice cream, a man with long elegant fingers that do not belong to my father.

I have never found these images in my grandfather's basement, nor have I seen that harbor in any of our photographs. But sometimes, I wake in the night to the caramel scent of red beans. A breeze lingers in the air and there is an echo of people talking in the distance, but perhaps it is only the whir of the ceiling fan and the scent of buns left to cool in the kitchen, which Hannae, Grandpa's housekeeper, taught me to make.

I asked Grandpa once about these memories of mine. He said I was remembering our summers in Shimoda. When I continued to look at him, he laughed and motioned for me to sit beside him on the stool by his chair. He reached for a pile of books stacked on the edge of his shelves, his fingers tracing the hardbacks, paperbacks, and volumes of poetry. "Which one will it be today?" he asked.

Years later, I was standing in my grandfather's study when the lies that had wrapped around my life finally began to unravel. I was due to give a talk to the final-year law students at Tōdai, and I was dressed in a navy suit, my hair pulled back in a sleek ponytail, immaculate but late, for I had lost my notes.

I remember that I was leaning over Grandpa's desk, casting the papers into disorder. I had passed the Japanese bar a year before and my legal apprenticeship with the Supreme Court in Wakō City was drawing to a close. I had just completed the final exams, so all my cases from the long months of rotations with judges, public prosecutors, and attorneys were stacked across every surface. Grandpa had gone to stay at an onsen with friends, but long before that he had ceded his office to me, too delighted by my professional choices and the job offer from Nomura & Higashino to question the invasion.

Crossing to the leather armchair in the corner of the room, I leafed through the files I'd left on the seat. Following my long daily commute home from Wakō, I often fell asleep reading there. In the past year I had taken on extra cases in an effort to stand out from the other trainees, and I'd worked hard to build up my network among the attorneys and prosecutors, but the lack of sleep was finally catching up with me.

I was kneeling on the floor, my hand outstretched towards a sheaf of papers that might have been my notes, when the phone started to ring. My life was in that room: certificates from childhood and university, the framed newspaper article on Grandpa's most famous case, the folder on current events that he kept for me. Each morning before work, Grandpa would sit at the breakfast table, sipping his favorite cold noodles and cutting clippings from the day's news so I would not get caught out. I had read every article, every story in that room, except mine. I was so caught up in the paraphernalia of my life that I almost didn't hear it.

"Hello?" I said, picking up the phone.

"Good afternoon," the voice said. It was hesitant, female. "May I speak to Mr. Sarashima?"

I was distracted so I mumbled into the receiver, glancing around the room. "I'm afraid he is in Hakone at the moment. What is this regarding?"

"Is this the home of Mr. Yoshitake Sarashima?"

"Yes," I repeated. "I am his granddaughter, Sumiko. How can I help?"

"Is this the household and family of Mrs. Rina Satō?"

"My mother is dead," I replied, focusing on the phone and the person at the other end of the line. There was silence. For a moment I thought that the girl with the hesitant voice had hung up, but then I heard her take a breath. Over the earpiece she said, "I am calling from the Ministry of Justice, on behalf of the Prison Service. I am very sorry to disturb you, Miss Satō, but my call is regarding Kaitarō Nakamura."

"Who is that?" I asked.

As my voice traveled into the silence, the line went dead.

## *BELLS*

People say that you can't unring a bell, that words once spoken hang in the air with a life of their own. In the last year of my mother's life, Grandpa started taking me to a temple in the city. The hum of the crowds surrounded us as we made our way towards Sensōji. As we walked I took a deep breath, inhaling the scent of burning leaves and incense, and I tugged at Grandpa's coat. He looked down and lifted me into his arms, continuing to walk through the market. It was a new ritual of ours, this weekly visit. He lifted me higher onto his hip, tucking my yellow skirt around my legs. I chattered to him as we walked, pointing out the things that caught my eye. There were over a hundred stalls stretching between the beginning of the avenue and Sensōji, and there was another arcade running east to west, but he always chose this approach because I liked it best; it contained my favorite treats.

"Manjū!" I demanded, pointing to a stall selling deep-fried jam buns in yam, cherry, sweet potato, or chocolate. I loved them all, but I lived for the red bean. "Manjū, Grandpa," I repeated. Already a large queue was forming, spreading out beyond the store several lanes wide. People jostled one another, trying to get closer, as flavor by flavor the hot buns were lined up beneath the counter. A stocky middle-aged woman stood in the center of the crowd moving sales along; she pushed people forward and then would shove them away again as soon as they collected their buns, almost in one fluid motion.

I pointed at a tray of golden manjū, but Grandpa shook his head. "Red bean!" I squealed.

"Later Sumiko," he said while I pulled at his hair in annoyance.

"Did you bring Mummy here?"

"Yes, when she was small," Grandpa replied, shifting me on his hip. I was perhaps getting too big to carry, but he didn't seem to mind. He said he wanted to remember me at this age.

"Where is Mummy?" I asked.

"She's shopping."

"Why didn't she take me?"

"I wanted to spend time with you."

"I want—"

"Your mother and I started coming here when she was just as old as you are now," he continued as I began to lean away from him again towards the bun stall.

"Sumichan!" Grandpa put me down on the ground. "Temple first," he scolded, and held out his hand for me to take. In the midst of the crowds, I pressed against his legs and my fingers tangled with his; I did not like to be surrounded by the other people and tourists. I was quiet as we passed beneath the Thunder Gate, but as we approached the red pillars of the inner gate with their giant hanging sandals made of straw, I stretched to see if I could catch a glimpse of the great bell. It was one of the bells of time. My mother said that even the poet Bashō, hundreds of years ago, had heard it tolling through fields of flowers. For back then, when Tokyo was still Edo, the whole city was governed by these chimes, which told the people when to rise, eat, and sleep. Now the great bell was heard only at 6 each morning and on the first midnight of the New Year when it was rung 108 times for each of the 108 worldly desires that are said to enslave mankind. Grandpa had taken Mama and me to see it. His friends on the local board had secured us a place very near the bell, and even now I could feel each reverberation in the air, the silent pause while the cedar beam was drawn back and then released, followed by the mellow vibrations of the bronze.

Weaving through the throng, Grandpa made his way towards the incense burner in front of the temple. As we walked he told me that the smoke emanating from it had always reminded him not of purification, but of my mother when she was a child, washing herself in the waves while he held her up, her hair tied with white satin bows, her petticoats showing through her Sunday dress.

"Are you ready to go in?" Grandpa asked, and I nodded, contrite. He lifted me onto his hip once more and I smiled at him as he found a place for us in front of the huge burnished cauldron billowing smoke into the air. I leaned in and Grandpa wafted the incense towards me as I pretended to wash in it, scrubbing my face and hands.

"Are you pure now?" Grandpa asked. "Are you sure?" he teased. "No more naughty little girl?" He laughed when I smiled sweetly at him. "I know what you would like to do," he said. "You would like to see your fortune."

This too was a ritual of ours. Every time we came to Sensōji, before Grandpa said his prayers in the main temple, he would take me to the bureau of the one hundred drawers. He gave me a coin to throw between the slots and together we listened to the metal as it tumbled and fell into the donation box. Then he handed me a cylinder filled with long, slender sticks and let me shake it back and forth until one fell out.

Lifting the stick, I looked at the writing carved into the wood and we searched for the matching symbol on a drawer. When I found it, Grandpa reached inside and took the first sheet of paper off the pile. Then he handed it to me.

Grandpa watched as I shaped the words in my mouth, reading the fortune aloud. I loved these predictions. Even in the mountains I would ask Grandpa to buy them for me from the vending machines by the ski slopes, but that day, when I had finished reading, I was not sure what the fortune meant so I held out the paper to my grandfather. He smiled, giving me a slight bow, and murmured that he was glad to be of service. "What do we have here?" he asked, scanning the symbols, looking for the scale of luck in the top right-hand corner. He lifted the paper higher and I heard his intake of breath. He turned away from me and I could see him looking at the wire that hung above the drawers, the wire where all the fortunes he would not explain to me were hung. There were several there that day, idly flapping in the wind.

I stepped forward as he tried to fold the fortune into a strip so he could tie it around the wire, but as he fumbled with the paper I snatched it from his hands.

"What does it mean?" I asked, peering at the symbols and characters again.

"We don't want this one," he said. "Let's tie it up, so the wind can blow it away."

"I want to know," I said, stepping back from him, holding the fortune in my hands.

"Sumichan, give it to me. This one belongs to the wind."

"Tell!" I said, crumpling the thin sheet in my fist.

Grandpa reached for my hand and began to pry my fingers open. "Come on, Sumiko, I'll get you another," he said, but his eyes widened in horror as I shoved the wisp of paper into my mouth and began to chew. Words may be buried, some are even burned, but over the years they re-emerge, ringing out like temple bells, rising above the din.

# *Rina and Kaitarō*

## *A NEW CASE*

Kaitarō sat in his shirtsleeves, his tie neatly folded on the desk beside him. Steam from a cup of coffee curled into the air as he flippedthrough his latest case file. The subject was a housewife: aged thirty, brown eyes, brown hair, medium build. She liked cheesecake.

As he pulled out a map of Tokyo and located her home address, he glanced over her daily schedule, noting her preferred transport routes and mapping out how long it would take him to move between locations. He knew that weeks of tailing would follow as he collated her interests and favorite places.

The husband had filled out a case form and his answers stipulated the number of properties and family assets that were at stake in the divorce. There were two residences in Tokyo: the marital apartment in Ebisu and a further home in Meguro, as well as a holiday home on the coast in Shimoda, all registered under Sarashima, the wife's maiden name. There was a further list of figures: bank accounts, shares, estimated net worth. Kaitarō added a separate column next to this and began to make notes of his own. Clients often lied about their assets or at least exaggerated; he had no doubt that Osamu Satō would have as well. Certainly, he had not told them everything.

Putting down his pen, Kaitarō pinched the bridge of his nose between thumb and forefinger; a headache had begun to build behind his eyes and he shook his head to clear it. He scanned the details of the file once more: the main assets were the properties owned by the wife or her family, and there was also one child, a girl. He'd seen it before, this method of acquisition. His clients used whatever they could to gain an advantage, and some found purchase within the law itself, for only sole custody of children was ever awarded; joint custody was illegal. And so a child could become a point of leverage. Of course, there were some situations in which a separation was best for all involved, including the children, but the cases he saw did not often revolve around welfare. He was no longer surprised at the lengths to which people would go to secure what they wanted, but then he didn't have to approve of his clients, only manage them.

Glancing up from the file, he caught sight of his business cards in their clear plastic box on the desk in front of him. They were plain white, necessarily discreet, detailing only his name, current telephone number, and fax. For some reason in the harsh light of the office, the characters of his name seemed to stand out in sharp relief, the name his parents had chosen for him with such hope: Kaitarō, composed of the characters for "sea" and "firstborn son." For a second he could almost feel that he was back home in Hokkaido, walking through the tall grass with his uncle, the weight of a camera heavy and steadying on his neck, and all around them the wheeling of the gulls and the roar of the ocean.

Once, in a rare quiet moment, after no more than two or three beers, his father had told him how his parents had chosen his name, how they'd sat at the kitchen table in their tiny bungalow and debated between two versions. His father had been pensive when he told this story, recently home from a stint on the trawlers and strangely mellow. He liked "son of the sea" and had insisted until it was chosen. He hoped that his boy would follow him onto the boats, or perhaps get a job at the fisheries; the family had lived off the ocean for so long that to his father the choice had seemed inevitable.

But his name had always meant something different to Kaitarō; it meant the vastness of the open water by his home, the sand glinting silver as it melded with the waves; it was the feel of his uncle's camera in his hands as he learned to capture the vibrant world around him. His uncle visited only sporadically, but when he'd been able to secure photography jobs that would pay enough for both of them, he had taken Kaitarō with him and together they'd traveled Hokkaido, falling into narrow beds at rural guesthouses or hostel bunks in towns at the end of long days, exhausted, but free. What was inevitable was that Kai would eventually disappoint his father, so he learned quickly to read his moods, analyzing his face the moment he came home for signs of drink or temper.

His mother preferred the alternate version of his name, the combination of characters for Kaitarō that contained the one for "mediator." She liked the agency and capability this implied, arguing that their boy could get onto a managerial track at the local seaweed plant or go into business. Staring at his card in the tiny office in Shibuya, Kai doubted this line of work was what she had in mind. She'd had other hopes too, of course, other mediator roles for him to fill, but he had failed her there as well. He had not been able to smooth over the rough edges of her marriage, had not been able to protect her or even himself. He had survived to become a mediator indeed, though not the kind anyone would necessarily aspire to. Kaitarō reached for his coffee but a thick skin had formed on the top and it was lukewarm on his tongue. He shook his head, trying once more to clear it and dislodge the headache gathering there. There was no point thinking this way; he was none of those once-hoped-for people and he could not go back.

His eyes felt raw in the dry fug of the office and he rubbed a hand over his face before returning to the case file in front of him. The job before him was lucrative, not merely a "survey," the swift surveillance of an errant boyfriend or spouse, but a relationship job, a breakup. A survey might take no more than a couple of weeks, but it was quick work, more in the line of what a private eye does, involving tailing, photographs of infidelity, and a report to the client who could then decide what to do with their spouse. This job could take months and the fees would be worthwhile to whomever his boss, Takeda, chose to undertake it; it might even buy him some time for himself.

The case itself looked fairly simple. Kaitarō sketched out a "bait and switch" over a period of two months: one month to engage the subject and another to collect the evidence—perhaps photographs of him and the woman exiting a love hotel or, if it would do, a kiss in the street. After that, he would disconnect the phone number he'd given her and rotate to work in another ward of Tokyo; the firm might even move him to a different prefecture for a while. But, as he looked over the file and flipped to the back, one detail began to bother him, a detail barely relevant for the seduction of a housewife. It was her photograph, a passport shot, the only one they'd been given. The lighting was harsh and she wore no makeup. She was looking at the camera straight on, but it was the way she stared at the lens that struck him, as though she were more interested in the camera than anything else in the world. Her eyes and the look within them lifted off the page and into his head.

He was still holding the photo in his hands when Mia swung around the door to his office. Takeda had her managing the company calendar, but Kaitarō had asked her to meet the husband in this case. Mia was sharp and subtle, she was patient and could break through personal barriers with ease, but when she knocked on his door that afternoon she looked openly annoyed.

"He won't talk to me," she said. "He wants to meet the agent he'll be working with."

Kaitarō looked up from the file. "What did Takeda say?"

"He'd like you to go in."

"What do you think of him?"

Mia handed him a single sheet of paper. "Your call," she said as he glanced over her notes.

Kaitarō put on his tie, smoothing it down over his shirt, and followed her into the conference room. He bowed low to Satō and handed him a business card, holding it in both hands. As Mia poured ice water into two glasses, Kaitarō sat down and assessed his new client, measuring the man he'd read about in the file against the one before him now.

"My colleague tells me you're not interested in reconciling with your wife?" he said.

"I've told the young lady I would like a divorce," Satō replied, gesturing at Mia, who sat beside him picking lint off her stockings.

"We can certainly offer you some preliminary investigations before you decide," Kaitarō continued. "Mia could take your wife"—he glanced down at the sheet—"Rina, out for a drink? See how she feels about your marriage, perhaps gauge her reaction to the two of you separating."

"She doesn't believe in divorce."

"Why is that?"

"It doesn't matter."

"Mr. Satō," Kaitarō leaned forward, "if we are going to undertake this case, there is a great deal we will need to know about you and your wife, and the majority of it will be highly personal."

Satō remained silent.

"Has your wife been unfaithful to you?"

"No."

"She's had no lovers, flirtations, close friendships?"

"No."

"She doesn't have any friends?"

"She isn't very interesting; it's why I want to be rid of her."

"But you would like custody of your daughter?"

"For the moment."

Kaitarō looked away and Satō laughed. "I was told you were discreet," he murmured, "I didn't realize that meant squeamish."

"These are emotional matters," Kaitarō said, meeting his gaze. "We try to minimize the pain experienced by all parties, at least until the papers are signed. The most successful separations are the ones with the least resentment." He smiled almost imperceptibly at Satō who narrowed his eyes; clearly he did not like to be challenged.

"I'll try another agency."

Kaitarō shrugged, relieved in spite of himself as Satō rose to his feet, but Mia stopped him, bowing low.

"We understand your impatience, sir," she explained, urging him to sit down once more. "These are big decisions and they cannot be taken lightly. We have to make sure that you really know what you want."

"I'm not getting a fucking abortion," Satō muttered. "I want to separate from my wife."

"Then let's do it," Mia said with a cute lift of her eyebrow as she snapped open her notebook. "How much time do we have?" she asked.

"As long as you need," Satō replied. "But you have a reputation for efficiency?"

"We do." Mia nodded. "I can't stand long attachments," she said, giving him a wink.

Kaitarō took a deep breath and raised his eyes to the ceiling.

"I want to be clear," Satō said. "Your boy here—is he up to it?"

Mia bowed. "Mr. Nakamura is one of our best. Whatever you need, he will accomplish it."

"I don't want any fuss."

"You are aiming for a private settlement?" Mia asked.

Satō looked at her, the answer evident in his eyes. Slowly, he turned to face Kaitarō. "My wife has to want to leave our marriage and she has to be willing to sacrifice everything to do so. Can you do that? Can you make a woman love you?"

Kaitarō returned his look with an impassive stare until finally Satō laughed. "Let's hope he's better with the ladies."

"Do you have another photo of your wife?" Kaitarō asked.

"Why? Do you only take on the sexy prospects?" Satō looked at Mia and they shared a small smile.

"There will be a preliminary fee for research carried out before the assignment," Kaitarō said. "It would be good to have a picture of her in her everyday life."

Satō smirked, something he would do continually in the meetings to come. "Don't get too excited."

"Could we trouble you for some additional information now?" Mia asked. "There are some remaining questions about her background and education, her hobbies, her relationship with your daughter. Perhaps you and I could go for a drink?"

Satō looked away. "Send them to my office. It won't take long." He rose and walked to the door. Mia bowed, low and appreciative, and Satō looked over her bent head at Kaitarō. "I did bring another photo—to pique your interest," he said.

Later that day, Kaitarō stood before the window in his office. In front of him the streets of Shibuya glowed in the gathering dusk. In his hands was a picture of the woman he was being paid to seduce, the photograph Satō had brought him.

He leaned his shoulder against the glass and examined the

print. He saw a woman with bobbed hair wearing a cardigan that was too big for her—the material enveloped her, framing her face. He looked at her posture, the angle of the shot. It was black and white, the frame precise, cropped close to her face and torso, with the room behind her out of focus. It was possibly a self-portrait. Kai was pondering this when he saw the tiny detail that confirmed his suspicions, for nestled in her palm, almost hidden by the folds of her cardigan, was the black bulb of an air balloon and a wire trailing out of the shot that would trigger the camera's shutter. She was a photographer or she had been one, once.

Tilting the photograph towards the light, Kaitarō traced the line of her brow with his thumb. He thought of her name. Rina. She had large dark eyes framed by delicate lashes, but there was no joy in her expression, no exuberance, only the seriousness that he had noted before, the intensity with which she stared at the camera. Rina looked into the lens with concentration, perhaps even aggression, and there was something else there as well: the look of a life cut short.

# *SILVER HALIDE*

There was a time when she had been visible, Rina was sure of it. It wasn't physical attention that she wanted or even romance; it was contact, for someone to see her, to prove that she was still there.

In the mornings she shopped for dinner and for the household. She wore knee-length dresses and a coat that she could wrap around herself. There was barely a stir in the air as she moved through Ebisu. She knew, had known for months now, that she could walk down a street and no heads would turn, no eyes would lift in recognition or curiosity. As her life began to unravel, fewer and fewer people saw her.

When she was a child it had been impossible not to notice Rina—she had been vibrant not just with youth but with a quiet confidence that was hers alone. She made friends easily. Tokyo spoke to her in its teahouses, bookshops, and on the streets. People watched her because she had something they wanted: her happiness.

Rina was lucky. Growing up, her desires had coincided with those of her family. She was close to her father and had followed him into the study of law. But, as her articles on photography began to be published and she was offered her first shared exhibition, Rina had left her law degree to focus on new possibilities. She imagined another life.

This went well at first, as new ventures often do. Still, as one year turned into two, the question of how she would live and support herself remained, as did who would take over Yoshi's legal practice. Her classmates graduated and qualified; others married. She saw them become useful to their families, accepted. In the city she had once loved, each new street corner and junction confronted her with a reality she could not ignore. She saw it in the faces of those around her; even strangers seemed to judge her and to know that she could not survive on her own. Her father's hurt, explosive at first, blossomed in silence. When he approached her about a match with Osamu Satō, a fellow student at Tōdai and the son of a friend, the pressures surrounding her had suddenly eased. She had leapt at the respite. It was a weakness within herself that she would never forgive.

Once she moved to Ebisu and settled into being a wife, Rina found that her college friends had drifted away to other towns, other cities, lives abroad, and soon her peers from the photography group and the journal *Exposure* spoke to her less and less as she left their world and her husband's colleagues filled their places. For a time, Rina enjoyed the entertaining; she enjoyed the business parties, the hosting, and excelled at them. But the more people he brought to the apartment her father had purchased for them, the more he used their crystal decanters and entertained at the ebony dining table that was yet another wedding present, the more Rina began to see why Satō had married her.

When Satō wasn't entertaining his clients and his bosses, he began to stay out late. Often, he crawled into bed after a night of beer in some izakaya, pulling her to him, his skin reeking of nicotine.

Gradually, as she should have foreseen, the things she loved slipped from her life and the imaginative world Rina had built for herself also began to disappear. She stopped looking at the sky and gauging the light meters. She no longer walked through the streets and saw exposures, angles, and new projects at each turn. Day by day, the house overwhelmed her. She began to move more slowly, to think slowly.

After a time, her fingerprints, so clear and sure on the surface of her old Canon T90, faded, leaving only faint smudges of oil. Eventually, these too lifted away, until it was as though they had never been. Her collection of lenses glazed over with dust; the bottles in her darkroom crystallized around the tops, stuck fast with granulated chemicals. The baths of solution dried out till only a thin layer of grime remained and spiders began to make nests in the corners of her room. Satō moved boxes into her darkroom. He used it as a place to store his files, his skis, a broken tennis racket. More items filled the space: Satō's clothes, old running shoes unwanted gifts from his friends. When Rina peered around the door and looked in she saw other people, another marriage, another life. Inside her darkroom, like film abandoned to the light, Rina vanished.

═

Near Kaitarō's apartment was a series of shops. On Saturdays and Sundays, this small alley became a street market. In the winter, the homeless set up shelters there; their lodgings were neat, uniform boxes of plastic sheeting and tarps, but in the spring they were moved on and new stalls for pirated videos, manga comics, and Nintendo games filled the plots they had left.

At the far end of this alley was a family business, a photography shop that opened at 8 a.m. every morning and closed in the evenings at 7 p.m. But sometimes, late at night, the security gate remained up above the entranceway and a light could be seen at the back of the shop as Kaitarō Nakamura made his way home through the alleys behind the train station.

"Evening, Jinsei," Kaitarō murmured, as the old man unlocked the front door of the shop and motioned him inside. "Thank you for staying up so late."

Jinsei smiled and nodded. "It's no problem. Thank you for the photographs of my niece. My sister likes them very much."

"It was a pleasure."

The older man offered him a stool. "Have you had dinner? My wife has left some chicken yakitori and beer for us if you're interested?"

"That is very kind but I don't want to keep you from your bed."

"Busy day?" Jinsei asked. "Is it interesting this detective work, an important case?"

"I think so. Challenging."

Jinsei laughed. "I don't know how you bear it, looking so closely at other people."

"They're not all bad," Kaitarō said as Jinsei pulled open the curtain that separated the shop from the stairs to his apartment.

"Good night, son."

"Good night, sir."

Kaitarō made his way to the darkroom at the back of the store, checking the warning light out of habit to see if anyone was developing. Inside, he breathed in the familiar alkaline scent of the chemicals and removed his camera from his rucksack, ejecting a single roll of film. Then he flicked on the red safety light and beneath the ruby glow began to organize the equipment around him, turning on the tap in the corner for the water baths.

When the chemicals had been measured and set out, Kaitarō switched off the lights and began to unspool the film in his hands, winding it tightly onto the spiral reel, his fingers fluid and skillful. This was the part that he loved, the intimate, tactile nature of photography. Kaitarō's eyes swiftly grew accustomed to the dark, the deep, rich blackness of it. He loved its silence. He could easily have outsourced this side of his work, but there were times when he liked to do it himself, when he needed to. There was something about bringing an image into focus and burning it onto a page that linked the man he was before, to who he was now in Tokyo.

With a metallic snip of the scissors he cut the film from the cassette and placed the loaded reel into the portable development tank, soaking it first in water to swell the gelatin. Turning on the red light once more he added the developing agent, agitating the tank from side to side in his hands and counting out the seconds, soothed by the familiar timings and rhythm, before tapping it sharply on the table in front of him to dispel any air bubbles. For a few moments he let the film sit, the tiny images within converting to latent silver. Then he drained the tank and added the stop bath, flooding the room with the scent of vinegar. Finally, he applied the fixer and began to agitate the film once more, thinking of all the photographs he had taken that day and how they would look once developed, when invisible silver halide finally transformed into pure black and white.

Once the film was rinsed and dry, Kaitarō selected a clip of five shots and stretched the images over an enlarger. He could see her now, Rina.

The photos were not evidence of any kind—they would not prove anything in court—but already Kaitarō had extracted his loupe from his pocket and was looking closely at the negatives. He knew which one he would print even through the shocking reverse of dark and light.

As he looked at her, picturing her face as it would soon appear, Kaitarō wondered if the lens had truly captured what he had seen as he watched her in the market: Rina in a dark dress pausing before a fruit stall; Rina suddenly smiling and tossing an apple into the air; Rina looking about her and listening, as though at any moment she might turn towards him.

Kaitarō selected the last shot and placed it in the enlarger, turning the dial until he had the size he wanted and the image was in focus. Then he placed the photographic paper on the baseboard and flicked on the white projector light for eight seconds.

Under the red glow of the safety light once more, Kaitarō lowered the slip of paper into a development bath. There was no image yet, but slowly, slowly, it emerged, darkening from the center into sharp reality. He could see the curve of her cheek, a wisp of her hair as it blew in the wind. He lifted the paper out and applied the fixer, washing it next in a pure bath to ensure that the clear black and white of the image would not fade or yellow with time. Then he stood, swirling the picture beneath the water, looking at Rina through the ripples and waves.

## *NIGHT MARKET*

Rina browsed beneath the heat of the lamps. It was warm for spring and muggy. The stench of stagnant water from the pavement rose into the air along with the bittersweet scents of chargrilled squid and corn on the cob. She paused beside a toy stall selling multicolored trolls with their bright puffs of hair and bought two, a purple one and a green one, for Sumiko's collection. Yoshi had taken Sumi out for dinner so that Rina could have a break, but once alone she hadn't known what to do with herself, so she'd come here, to the market. It appeared in Ebisu each year when the cherry blossoms began to flower, selling fast food and toys but also fruits and vegetables. That day there was a stall with specialty produce flown in from Gifu. Rina stopped in front of the display of nashi pears, their golden skins shining bright beneath the lamps. They were enormous and beautifully wrapped, each one placed in its own pouch of webbed Styrofoam. She was reaching into her purse, counting out the notes, when he approached her.

"Excuse me. Do you know where I could find a good cheesecake?"

"Cheesecake?" Rina looked up. He was tall. Taller than the usual salaryman and slender, and there were crinkles around his eyes, perhaps from laughter. Rina smiled a little, fumbling with her purse.

"I'm addicted," he replied.

Rina gestured to a stall behind her. "There are some over there," she said.

"Are they any good?"

Rina considered this. "I'm not sure." She was aware that she was frowning as though this were a grave matter. "The slices don't look right. I think the cream is too light."

"Oh no!"

"Hmm," Rina nodded, biting back a smile.

"Can I buy you a coffee?" he asked, smiling with her.

"I'm married."

"I know," he said.

"You do?"

"Your wedding band."

"Oh." Startled, Rina felt a flush of embarrassment creeping into her face. It must be clear that no one has approached her this way for quite some time.

"Thank you," she said, "but I am happily married." When he didn't turn away she added, "And I have a daughter."

"Well," he reached into his pocket for his card, "if you change your mind and ever want a coffee or a slice of cheesecake."

She took it from him, nodding politely, but as her eyes glanced over his name, she felt the corners of her mouth curve up. "Son of the sea," she murmured.

"I'm sorry?"

"Your name," she said, looking up at him. "Isn't that what it means?" She shook her head, embarrassed again; he must think her quite strange. "Sorry, I—"

"Yes," he said, "that's what it means." His eyes were warm and intent on her face as he considered her. "Not many people notice,"

"Does it say a lot about you?" Rina asked, emboldened in spite of herself. "What do you do, Kaitarō Nakamura?" she asked

"Have coffee with me and I'll tell you." He smiled again. "Go safely home."

Rina watched him walk away through the crowds. He moved with grace, stepping around people. A cool breeze blew through the market. Rina looked at the cherry trees surrounding the square, their blossoms opening, turning from pale pink to white. There were blue plastic mats beneath the trees set out by avid blossom viewers. All around her, people were smiling, enjoying the picnics and celebrations of spring. Rina could feel the joy, the expectation in the air; she watched him turn towards the fast-food stalls and made her decision.

He was walking fast, perhaps a little embarrassed by her rejection. He had seemed nice, Rina thought, genuine and not at all pushy. She watched him pause by an onigiri stand and buy a rice snack from the vendor. He walked on as he ate, careful of the people around him, courteous. He wove through the women choosing vegetables, their arms laden with brightly colored plastic bags, and around the teenagers eating deep-fried curry buns or chocolate bananas covered in sprinkles. He was stepping around a group of hawkers, nearing the edge of the market, when she quickened her pace.

"Wait!" she called. To her surprise, Kaitarō stopped and turned, almost as though he had been expecting her to come after him. But when his eyes met hers, she could see that he was shocked.

Rina felt her courage waver. "Hi," she said. "I do have time for a quick coffee, if you'd like?" She smiled and stood in the wake of his silence. "I'm Rina," she said. "Rina Satō."

She watched for a moment as the surprised expression on his face turned into something like distaste. He stepped away from her. "I think you should go home, Mrs. Satō. Your first instincts were right."

Rina frowned as he turned and walked swiftly away from her. She waited until he had reached the edge of the market and crossed the street, but he did not look back.

## *Sumiko*

## *EVIDENCE*

My mother died at the end of my first year of school. It was March, on the last day of term before spring break. During my parents' divorce, I had gone to live with Grandpa in Meguro. Mama came too initially, but after a time she left to find us a new apartment of our own. She was getting it ready for me, she said, and soon I could move in. We were only meant to be apart for a little while. She was very busy in those last weeks, I know, but she still made sure to see me every day. As I walked home from school with the other kids, beribboned badges on our hats signifying which route we should take so locals could help us if we got lost, I would think of her. I imagined her opening our gate with one hand and holding a clear plastic bag of steamed pork buns or some other treat for me in the other. Once at home, I would look out the window for her, staring down the driveway to the small white gate at its end, every day, until the day she died.

I scarcely remember the weeks that followed; they are hollow with a pain I have never known how to express. I know that I left Tokyo, that Hannae took me away to see some of her family in the south, but I do not recall much of it, as though after the loss of my mother my brain shut down and was unable to take in anything else. I know that Grandpa handled everything, that he didn't want me exposed to the full horror of her death, but in a way this only made it more surreal, more incomprehensible. For years I would ask him to tell me again how she died, why she had not come to meet me in Meguro as she had promised, and he would always say the same thing: a car accident on a busy road. When I was older, I asked him to show me the spot where it happened and he took me to Shinagawa. I had been told that my mother was the driver at fault, and as I stood staring at the curved stretch of motorway, I asked if anyone else had been hurt in the accident, but he said no, only her.

When Hannae and I returned to Tokyo, Grandpa thought it best that I go back to school as quickly as possible. In those weeks, he came to collect me himself. When he could not come he sent Hannae and she held my hand all the way home. I was not to go with anyone else, Grandpa told me, not even a friend. I was therefore surprised when my father walked into the classroom one day. I had not seen him since the divorce, and even before then, his mercurial presence in my life had always been measured in sporadic appearances. Like so many salarymen he worked long hours and my school was not his domain; it was yet another place where he was defined by his absence, by the groups my mother socialized with before and after their separation. Before it, she had chatted with the married mothers at school functions, and after it, she joined the single mothers who talked of having to be both "Mum and Dad," who lifted their kids onto their own shoulders at Disneyland because there was no man to do it for them. But Mama had always been the one to lift me in any case.

My father took a while to locate me. His eyes scanned the circular tables and the children seated in the small blue chairs and he frowned when he could not find me, for I was not sitting at a table; I was standing in a corner of the room, alone.

That morning we had been given a test. It would evaluate how our minds worked, they told us. This exercise replaced our usual calligraphy lesson, and I had felt surprisingly energized and curious. We took our places at the tables, and I squirmed and fidgeted trying to get comfortable. I put my knees on the chair and knelt, leaning over my sheet of paper. I looked with interest at the other children, at the tests that would map out our minds, but I gasped as the teacher hauled me off my seat, lifting me by the hand. She accused me of cheating.

At the midmorning break I was allowed to tidy the school with the others. We worked in pairs to sweep the halls and empty the bins before collecting our cups of juice from the cafeteria. Still people stared at me, and after the break I was told to stand in the corner once more. From that day on, rumors spread around the school that I was becoming a difficult child. It was my first experience of being judged.

I watched as my father spoke with the teacher and wondered if she had been the one to call him. I wondered if Grandpa knew how bad I had been. I had seen other parents of naughty children bowing repeatedly in such a manner, and I grimaced. My father glanced at where I was standing in the corner of the room and snapped his fingers at me, gesturing to my bag and coat. He did not speak as he led me outside to his car.

"I wasn't cheating," I whispered.

"What?"

"I didn't cheat," I said more forcefully.

My father sighed and turned the car keys in the ignition. "Try to behave yourself, Sumiko."

I was quiet as we drove through the city and into a residential area of low condominiums. We stopped outside a large building with cream walls and brown glass windows. It reminded me of the place they took us for juku, the cram school I now attended so that I would get into the right secondary school. All the children I knew came to juku—we called it "Future Club"—and every day we gathered together in the sports hall for the afternoon chant. We stood in rows, hundreds of us, red and white bandannas tied tight around our heads, shouting the same statement into the air: "I will get into Myonichi Gakuen!" This gakuen was everyone's goal, the best secondary school in Tokyo; the name means "School of Tomorrow." So inside a cavernous hall, throughout the year, we shouted every afternoon as though force of will was all it would take. What I learned is that people rely on reiterative ideas and statements; they ask the same questions and repeat the same thoughts, as though comfort might be found there.

My father entered the building and I followed closely behind him. A model of Peepo, the mascot for the Metropolitan Police force, stood on the main desk. Peepo is a tubby orange fairy from a family of orange fairies. He has large ears so he can listen to the populace, big eyes to see around every corner, and an antenna to sense the mood of the city. This one was stuffed and covered in felt. I was reaching up to touch him when the officer bowed to my father and opened a panel door in the main desk to let us through.

The room we were taken to contained a grayscale map of Tokyo that spanned one wall. Before he left, my father took me by the shoulders, "Just tell the truth, Sumiko." He looked at me closely; his hands gripping me hard through the cotton of my blouse. "The truth," he said.

Alone, I studied the map above my head, following the sprawl of the city as it spread out over the bay, the skein of streets stretching out like a tracery of my mother's palm. I wondered where she was on that map, where her body might be. When Grandpa first told me she was dead, I had refused to believe him. When I was not permitted to see her, this suspicion only grew, and it blossomed when Hannae and I went away and my mother's funeral took place without me.

I started as the door to the room opened and I was joined by a woman in a white silk blouse and black skirt. She carried an oversized jacket stuffed with shoulder pads. Chunky gold earrings hung from her ears, and as she moved I smelled a sweet, cloying perfume that intensified and stuck in my throat.

The woman put her arm around me and smiled; she spoke in a high chivvying voice. She drew me towards a low table and placed a file in front of me. It was made of brown card and it contained pictures of my parents. She began to ask me about my mother. I moved away from her and sat cross-legged on the floor, but she joined me, awkward in her high heels. Had I met anyone new at my home? I shook my head. She began to ask me about my grandfather. Was he a good grandpa? Did I like living with him?

When I remained silent, she began to flick through the photographs. She showed me an apartment I did not know and a small bedroom, partially decorated and painted pink with a border of stars on the two finished walls. There was a single bed and a white bookshelf, empty except for a copy of *Where the Wild Things Are;* my mother used to read it to me when I was small, but I had not heard it for some time.

The woman showed me a photograph of a man I did not recognize and one of a man I did—he was a friend of my mother's. She leaned towards me and the scent of her perfume struck up a throbbing pain in my head. I said nothing. I hated her.

After a time, the woman fetched some paper and crayons from a cupboard in the corner of the room and placed them before me, watched as I began to draw the things my mother had taught me: circles for faces, petals for orchids, the things her own mother had taught her. The woman knelt once more, looking at my drawings, but when I began to sketch the plants in our greenhouse in Shimoda, her impatience returned. She started to lay out the photographs again, one by one, asking me if I had seen the pink bedroom. In the end, she pulled out a final photograph, one of the man I recognized. He was standing next to my mother with an arm around her shoulders. She pointed at him, jabbing at his face with her manicured nail. "Do you know this man, Sumiko? Do you?"

I looked at the photograph, at the two of them smiling together with dabs of pink paint on their faces. I stared at the picture and wondered if my mother could truly be dead. It was hard to believe that she would leave me; indeed, I have always felt her with me, throughout my life. Always there, just out of reach. Grandpa took me to our family tomb and said that Mama was resting inside, but I could not imagine my vibrant mother in a ceramic jar, reduced to ash. The woman kept on asking, stabbing at the photo with her finger. Eventually, I pulled it into my mouth and bit her, feeling the crunch of flesh between my teeth.

I was left alone after that. They didn't even move me to another room. A young woman came in with a glass of water and I asked if I could see my father, but she only smiled at me and left. As the afternoon drew on, I curled myself into a ball on the floor and thought of my mother. I remembered her voice and the very last time I had heard it. She had called me at the house in Meguro. She was speaking quickly over the phone, rushed and breathless, but still my mother.

I had been waiting for her since I got back from school and I remembered holding the receiver beneath my chin, listening to the warm timbre of her words. "I'm coming, Sumichan," she said. "I will pick you up and we will go to Shimoda."

I thought about the homework I still had to do for juku and the written kanji exercises I'd been given, but I didn't care; I was tired of living with Grandpa. "Will you stay with me, Mummy?"

"Yes, Sumi," she said. "I promise. I am coming to get you." She paused. I could hear her fumbling with her keys. "Tell Grandpa to expect me. I'll be with you in an hour, okay?" I nodded and then gasped, "Yes," into the phone. I was so excited. "I'm coming, Sumi," she repeated. "I'm coming!"

I lay on the floor beneath the grayscale map as the minutes ticked past. I was cold and they had taken my coat. I wondered if my father had left a bento for me. Eventually, another woman entered the room. She was dressed in a simple black trouser suit and she held a briefcase in one hand and a large leather handbag in the other. The woman paused at the threshold of the room and her pearl earrings caught the light as she turned her head and quickly shut the door.

She approached me slowly. "Hello there," she said. Her voice was soft. "Has anyone brought you lunch?" I shook my head. The woman looked at my bare arms in my light school blouse, at my legs in their thin white stockings and plaid skirt. "Are you cold?" She went outside for a minute and returned with my coat.

"This is nice," she said as she wrapped me in the camel-colored wool, admiring the black bows down the front. "Did your mummy buy this for you?"

I nodded.

She slipped off her high heels, placing them by the wall, and sat on the floor beside me. "Here," she said, reaching into her handbag and pulling out a small box. "You can have my bento. I brought it from home." She opened the lid to reveal barbecued eel and pickles on a bed of rice with sesame. "Is this all right?" she asked and I nodded. She handed me some chopsticks. "These are a bit big for you," she said, "but we'll manage." I took them from her, feeling the smoothness of the lacquer between my fingertips, and bit into the eel, smiling as it melted in my mouth.

She did not ask me any questions as I ate my lunch, and her

briefcase remained closed. When I had finished, she opened her handbag and brought out a portable Shogi set. "This is no way to spend time away from school, is it?" She opened up the box and I looked at the flat white tablets inside with fine black characters imprinted on them. I liked this game; it was like chess. I thought it was strange that she would carry it around, so I looked up at her in question. "It's magnetic," she said, lifting up the board to demonstrate, shaking it slightly so I could see how the pieces adhered to the plastic. "My husband bought it for me—so I can practice on the train home."

She set it down in front of me and waited. I did not really feel like playing, but the lady had been kind to me. She looked at me and smiled, and when she did there was something so illicit and fun about our being together that I did not want to refuse her. She glanced towards the door and it occurred to me that she had somewhere else to be, that she might not have time to play with me. I began to set out the pieces, choosing my side of the board. She settled down to play, although for a time she remained distracted, alert to the sounds that passed outside. In the end she played the first game so badly that I actually laughed.

As the afternoon drew on she relaxed and we chatted about my life, what I'd been learning at school, the activities I liked to do, my favorite dinner at Grandpa's house. Gradually, I began to answer her questions and we spoke about my home in Meguro. She asked when I had last lived with my parents. She asked about my parents' friends—did any of them visit us? I shrugged and tried to answer as best I could, but I was closest to Grandpa and Mama. I grew quiet as I mentioned my mother. "When did you last see her, Sumiko?" she asked. I shook my head and the silence stretched between us. "When did you last speak to her?" she continued. I was quiet as she looked at me. When I refused to say anything more she moved closer to me on the carpet and placed an arm around my shoulders. Eventually, I allowed her to pull me against her and rest her cheek against my hair. I could smell the scent she wore, a light musk, like my mother's. "The last time you spoke to her, Sumi, was it on the phone?" she asked softly.

"She didn't come," I whispered, as the pain in my chest began to swell and spread. "She didn't come."

The woman picked me up, drawing me half across her lap. She held me tight, rubbing my back. "It's okay, baby, everything is okay," she murmured as I gasped in sharp, wet sobs, leaning into her neck, soaking the collar of her shirt. She was still holding me when my grandfather opened the door. I have never seen him look so angry.

## *TIES THAT BIND*

I remember exactly where I was standing in Grandpa's study when I received the phone call from the Ministry of Justice. I can still see everything just as it was, in the home I had lived in nearly all my life. For a long time after that call, I remained very still, staring at the carpet. There were twists of white twine dotted here and there and in tangled piles beneath Grandpa's armchair. My fingers tingled. I rubbed their tips together reflexively as though to soothe myself with movement.

The twine was made from very thin, tightly wound paper, which writhes against your fingers as you try to tie it. During the final exams for the Supreme Court all our handwritten essays have to be bound together neatly with this string. Every lawyer I know, anyone who has ever practiced law, will have spent hours and hours tying and retying twine, for if you cannot bind the exam papers correctly, you fail the year. No one writes until the end. In the final flurry you can hear the slide and tap of papers being stacked and then the silence as everyone in the auditorium bends to secure their answers with loops and knots, pulling the string taut.

These events were so recent that coils of twine were still scattered across the floor of the study, yet that phone call had jarred me from my present life. It had mentioned my mother, dead for twenty years.

Standing at my grandfather's desk, I picked up the receiver again. I returned the call to the Ministry of Justice and was put through to the prison service. My name was not on their records, they said; they could not release any information about the prisoner. I mentioned the phone call I had received and that the caller had hung up, but they were skeptical. "Our staff are extremely professional, Miss Sarashima. If there were an accident with the line, they would have called you again."

It was true that the Ministry of Justice was precise in its communications. Their caller had asked for my grandfather so she should have spoken only to him. For a moment I thought of phoning him myself, but then, as I pictured him at the onsen sitting with his friends in the heated rock pools, white washcloths resting on their heads as they retold stories and jokes, I realized that I could not ask him. He had never mentioned anything like this to me; he had never implied, even for a second, that there was a connection between my mother and a man in prison.

Slowly, I walked towards our bookcases, looking at the bound ledgers of Grandpa's favorite legal cases placed next to my own small white textbooks. I ran my hands over the shelves of novels, poetry, and plays, before finally stopping at a row of box files. These contained our family birth certificates, health insurance, bank accounts: a paper trail of our lives running straight from my grandfather to my mother to me. Everything we were was in that room, yet I had never seen a trace of Kaitarō Nakamura there.

Kneeling on the floor, I located the file for my mother. There was only one. Through all these years it has remained on the shelf, still there, beneath the layers of current life: "Rina 1965–1994." The leather veneer was slippery to the touch as I rested the box on my lap. Inside were my mother's certificates from school and her acceptance letter from Tōdai, formatted in exactly the same way as mine. This was followed by her marriage certificate and a copy of the deed to the apartment in Ebisu where she had lived with me and my father. Next was a rental agreement for a two-bedroom flat in Shinagawa; it had my mother's seal and my grandfather's at the base of the lease. He had helped her secure the new apartment. Even after the divorce. He helped her as he has always helped me.

That apartment in Shinagawa was meant to be my home yet I never saw it—it contains the last hidden moments of my mother's life. I cannot even remember the sound of her voice, but I do remember the last time I heard it. I believe she was standing in that apartment when she called to tell me she was coming to fetch me, when she said we would go to Shimoda.

For hours after speaking to my mother I had waited and waited. Later that night, Grandpa went out to look for her while I remained on the stairs, holding my stuffed white tiger. He was gone for so long that I feared he too had been swallowed by the darkness. When he returned, Hannae told him that I had refused to eat my dinner or go to bed; he could see from my face that I had been crying with fear. Grandpa sat next to me and drew his arm around me to hold me tight. His touch was warm and familiar; the amber and ginger of his cologne prickled in my nose as I leaned into the heat of his skin. Grandpa rested his chin on my head. He told me that Mama had tried to keep her promise, that she had been driving home to us from Shinagawa when her car had gone off the road. Driving home, to me.

At the bottom of the file was her death certificate. I paused before reaching out to touch it. To this day it reads:

Place of Death: Shinagawa Ward.

Cause of Death: Cerebral hypoxia.

Everything was consistent with what I'd been told of how she died in the car crash. Nothing has changed. Those facts have not altered in twenty years. That afternoon, alone on the floor of my grandfather's study, looking at those words, I realized that of all the lies we are told, the very best ones are close to the truth.

# *FORGOTTEN PARTIES*

A few hours later I walked through Shinagawa, with the road twisting ahead of me in the fading light. The neighborhood was quiet; only the leaves stirred. A detached cobweb floated in the breeze as I walked past the low condominiums and an abandoned soccer field, bare of sand. I had read once that hundreds of years ago there was a site of public execution near here, that even when the site moved on, kegare remained in the earth—the soil foul with spiritual corruption, polluted by blood and crime. Now, of course, the very knowledge of this is buried. There is only the steady influx of everyday life: new people, new homes, new families. And no one to give a thought for what lies beneath the dust. I wondered if my mother had known about this when she moved to Shinagawa. I wondered if she had walked here in the early evening as I did, if she had ever come here in search of help.

The police station had retained its cream cement walls and brown glass windows, but at only seven stories high, it looked squat in comparison to the towering modern architecture by the bay. Through the glass doors I could see the model of Peepo, though he too looked smaller.

I walked towards the main counter, noting the officers sitting behind their desks in their loose blue jackets and face masks to keep out summer allergens and pollution. These are the faithful omawari-san, "Honorable Mr. Go Around," the keepers of our peace. As I walked across the hard gray tiles, several officers noticed me. Was

I all right? Could they help? They were anxious, but also surprised that anything requiring their attention should have happened.

I handed over my birth certificate and the document confirming my surname change from Satō to Sarashima. I needed to speak with someone regarding a closed case, I said. The man behind the main counter hesitated and bit down on a yawn. It was difficult, he said. Perhaps I could come back on Monday?

I looked beyond him, to the very back of the room and the metal grill and velvet curtain that shielded the inner corridors and departments. I had visited several police stations in the service of learning about the law, but I had entered this one only once before, when I was a very small child.

I believe that a crime against my mother occurred in this neighborhood, I explained. I would like to see any records you have relating to Rina Satō. The man behind the desk was reluctant. If I could come back, he suggested, there might be someone on duty next week who could help.

I thought of the aborted phone call, of how the prison service had asked for my grandfather, how they had mentioned my mother as though she were still alive. I could feel anger rising inside me. I looked at the police officer, an administrator with his bored Friday afternoon face, and said a word rarely used in daily conversation.

"No."

He looked at me as though he had not heard. "Ms. Sarashima, if this is an old case the files will be in the archives."

"No." I repeated. He smiled as though I had said something amusing. I leaned towards him over the desk.

"You will find someone," I said. "Anyone who is aware of a case involving Rina Satō—you will find them now."

"Miss—"

"I received a phone call from the Ministry of Justice about my family. A crime against my mother occurred in this ward," I persisted. "A record of it will be here."

To my slight gratification, my voice filled the sad little hall. People were staring at me as I stood next to Peepo. I thought of the photographs Grandpa had shown me of my mother at university, of her laughing over her shoulder, fierce and young with ocher dyed hair in downtown Tokyo. I think she would have smiled.

The man hurried away, brushing aside the velvet curtain and disappearing deep into the station. He left me standing by the desk for an age. The other officers would not look at me. I was sitting alone, cold in my anger, when an older woman appeared before me. "Ms. Sarashima," she said, "please follow me." She held the curtain for me and then walked up the staircase ahead. "You would not have had any luck with the archives," she said as we climbed. "The files you need have not been transferred. Everything before 1995 is no longer considered necessary."

I followed her in silence. Through the walls I could hear the thud of feet and limbs on tatami mats, the daily judo practice that was compulsory for every officer in the force.

"I will skip mine today," my guide said with a smile.

"You are not an active officer?" I asked.

"I am nearing retirement."

We continued down a corridor to an open-plan office. The woman held the door for me and I followed her inside, taking the spare seat by her desk.

"Thank you for your help," I said as she sat down beside me. I looked at the file in front of us. It was impossibly slender, as though it contained nothing at all. "Could you please confirm for me what Kaitarō Nakamura was charged with in relation to my mother?" She looked slightly startled by my question, as though she could not imagine that I did not know. "There has been some debate in my family as to the exact charge," I added.

The woman nodded and opened the file, turning over the first page. "According to the notes, the public prosecutor did not charge him for a long time," she said, "but eventually they filed for homicide."

"Homicide?" I asked. I could hear a dull pounding in my ears, the beat of my blood.

"Ms. Sarashima, can I get you some water?"

I looked up at her and shook my head. "Is this the only charge against him?"

The woman nodded, but still I watched her, waiting for her to contradict me, to tell me that my mother had died in an accident while driving alone.

"I'll just be a minute," the woman said, leaving me with the file open on the desk. I could see the charge sheet clearly. There was his name, Kaitarō Nakamura, and beneath it his occupation: Wakaresaseya. As I read the word and mentally traced its origin, I began to understand how he had become involved with my parents and the role he had played in their divorce. I looked at the characters again: wakaresase—"to split couples up" and ya—"professionally." It is hard to believe, but such services exist all over the world today in honey trappers, hustlers, con artists, friends and family for hire. Where there is a desire, there are people willing to fulfill that desire for a price. Consequences are not necessarily part of the deal. My hand shook as I held the piece of paper. At the bottom of the sheet was the official charge: homicide of Rina Satō.

My throat closed. The fluorescent light was too bright for my eyes. I thought of my grandfather and all the stories he had told me, the family stories that everyone has that eventually transcend into myth. I thought of my mother, who had been taken from me not by accident, but by another person.

I swallowed, wanting to ask the officer if there was any more information on the case, but I knew that all the documents would have been sent to the Tokyo Public Prosecutors Office in preparation for the trial. Nothing of the investigation remained with the police, only the names of those involved and the charges.

The policewoman returned with a glass of water and I sipped it slowly. "Do you have the name of the prosecutor who handled the case?" I asked. "Or the opposing counsel?" The woman pulled the file towards her and flipped to the back. There were two business cards stapled to the final page and, beneath them, a newspaper article. The one cutting my grandfather had never given me. The police woman apologized and moved to tuck it away, but I asked to see it, holding out my hand.

She watched me as I read over the paragraphs. There were scarcely more than two hundred words there and yet they defined me and my family so completely. "Please keep it, if you like," she said, before turning back to the file and noting down for me the names and office addresses of the prosecutor and the defense attorney.

"They will have moved on, I expect," she said, handing me the slip of paper.

I nodded. "Thank you, I am very grateful." I rose and gave her a deep bow. She bowed in return and would have spoken, but I shook my head and stepped away. "Please do not trouble yourself. I can find my own way out," I said, turning and heading for the doors, unable to bear the sympathy in her eyes.

In the corridor I leaned my head against the cold tinted glass of the window. Night had fallen over the city and the ward of Shinagawa lay sprawled out before me. I could see my reflection sharply delineated by the fluorescent lights, and beyond it the expanse of Tokyo prickling in the darkness. I looked at my face in the glass, a young woman with large dark eyes and high cheekbones. Around my neck was a string of pearls that had belonged to my mother. Under the glare of the lights the opalescent orbs gleamed as I touched them.

For so many years I had not known what I was, that there is a term that defines me, even today. I had first seen it while studying in the library at Tōdai, not realizing at the time that I was studying myself—a "forgotten party."

During the investigation of a crime, the family of a victim may be questioned repeatedly by police and prosecutors preparing their cases for trial. At the time of my mother's death, the legal system determined that after the interviews, these people and their descendants should be "forgotten," so as to protect the criminal defendants. Families were not informed of court proceedings so they could not attend. They were not told the outcome of sentencing or even the perpetrator's date of release from prison. My grandfather and others like him were required to bury their dead and continue with their lives with no knowledge of what befell the people who had harmed them.

Today the newly bereaved are still known as forgotten parties, but they have more rights. Families can access trials and even hire a lawyer, such as myself, to defend them in court or influence sentencing, and there is one final privilege that is also available to them.

In the Imperial district, where mirrored offices and skyscrapers surround the royal park, and the palace that nestles shrunken at its center is the Public Prosecutors Office. On the ground floor, set back from the reach of the sun, is a room filled with single desks and chairs. For up to three years after a criminal has been sentenced, case records and court judgments, even redacted trial documents, can be accessed there by a victim's family. I reviewed several cases there during my training with the Supreme Court. But as I stood alone in the corridor of the police station in Shinagawa, I knew that I would never be granted access to that room on my own account. For those of us who live in the past, whose loved ones were murdered years ago, old cases cannot be reopened or their content released. Everything I needed to know—who Kaitarō Nakamura was, what he had meant to my mother, how she had died—would remain filed away out of reach, and nothing, neither emotional nor legal appeals, would retrieve them.

I am a forgotten party. That day I realized that I had been forgotten twice: once by the law and once by my grandfather, who had taken away my history and erased it from view.

Alone in the corridor, I shivered; the adrenaline of the afternoon had left a film of sweat on my skin that had cooled in damp patches beneath my clothes. I was tired of stories. I wanted the facts themselves, unadulterated and clear. I wanted to get as close to my mother's life as possible. I wanted to witness the events that had led to her death.

Looking across the city, I knew that there was one person who would still have the case files, but I would not find them in the Public Prosecutors Office and I could not appeal to the state, the police, or my grandfather. If I wanted to know how my mother had really lived and how she had died, I would have to contact the last person I wanted to see—the woman who had defended my mother's murderer at his trial: Yurie Kagashima, attorney at law.

## *A LEGAL DEFENSE*

The morning was bright and clear; the wind had stilled and the air was like glass, refracting each ray of the sun. In the business district, buildings shone ocher against the dawn and a haze of heat shimmered on the tarmac. As the sun rose higher, the wide avenues and overhead expressways filled with traffic and the lanes roared with noise, but deep in the city, where the office blocks huddled together separated only by tiny alleys strung across with telephone wires, was the office I sought. Walking through the shadows, I stopped outside a building faced in pale gray tiles and took the lift up to the third floor. A young girl led me from the firm's reception into a boardroom. Inside was a round table, a white bookcase, and an ikebana of paradise flowers in a narrow window. "Ms. Kagashima will be in shortly," the girl said, placing a bottle of tea from a vending machine in front of me. The bottle was warm to the touch and the heat soothed me as I took a sip, willing myself to calm and focus on the confrontation ahead.

When she finally came in, I rose to my feet and smiled, but in spite of all my rehearsals I could not control my shock at seeing her. There were things about her that galled me: she had laughter lines at the corners of her eyes and dimples in her cheeks. There was no gray in her hair, which glistened under the lights, jet-black and professionally set. When she reached out to me, she had a warm, firm handshake that belied her thin frame. She wore a spotted scarf around her neck and a golden phoenix broach on her lapel—license to dress up now that she was partner.

Few attorneys choose to work in criminal defense. The government will usually appoint counsel but, even for those who are chosen, this work takes up a fraction of their time. Prosecutors ensure that each year 99.9 percent of those brought to trial are convicted and sentenced. If only the guilty should be charged, then by that same logic the charged are almost certainly guilty. Thus, the lawyers who defend these criminals are viewed with suspicion, poorly paid, and shrouded in shame, but I saw none of this as I looked at the prosperous Yurie Kagashima. She had matured and thrived since I saw her last, that much was clear.

She motioned for me to sit and unscrewed the lid on her bottle of tea. Setting a leather portfolio in front of her she leaned forward to look at me. "Ms. Mizuguchi," she said, using the false name I had given her, "how can I be of assistance? My secretary said you wanted to consult with me about a divorce?" She smiled. "You look very young, if I may say so."

"I wanted to talk to you about my mother."

"I see. Are you here on her behalf?"

"Yes," I replied.

"Please," she said, gesturing to my tea, "make yourself comfortable."

"My mother's name is Rina." I paused before I said her married name—her last name. "Rina Satō. She died in 1994."

Yurie Kagashima looked at me and the warmth faded from her face.

"You defended the man who killed her," I continued, "Kaitarō Nakamura."

She looked down at the portfolio in front of her; she spread her fingers across it, the flesh bulging around her wedding ring.

"You realize," she said, "that I cannot talk about my clients."

"But you remember the trial?" I asked. "Do you still have the documents relating to it?"

"I am not at liberty to discuss them."

"But you do have them?"

"I do." She lifted her chin and looked me straight in the face. I admired that.

"Do you still represent Kaitarō Nakamura?" I asked.

For a moment she studied me, glancing at my hair crammed into a tight chignon, wisps already escaping, and then at my eyes and the dark shadows beneath them. "I no longer represent him," she replied.

I reached for the bottle in front of me and took a sip of my tea. "I recently qualified as an attorney," I said, looking at her closely. "I have just finished the apprenticeship in Wakō."

She nodded and leaned back in her chair, stretching the distance between us.

"I have always wanted to be a lawyer," I continued, "like my grandfather." I watched as her right hand clenched on the tabletop. "Did you know him?" I asked. "Did you meet with him? You certainly must have spoken to him."

She hesitated and glanced towards the door. "Ms. Satō, I cannot help you."

"Were you a good broker?" I asked. "Did you manage to negotiate a jidan?" She was striving for calm, but she flinched when I mentioned the solace money that can be offered to a victim's family, financial reparations paid in exchange for forgiveness and, sometimes, an appeal to the courts for a lighter sentence.

"Your grandfather refused," she said.

"To accept the money or to write an appeal?"

"Everything."

I leaned towards her, holding her gaze. "I just want to know what happened."

"Please—I cannot assist you in this."

"Did he kill her?" I asked.

She frowned and looked down at her hands now clasped in front of her. She was not immune to emotion or to me, and I was glad.

"I do not care what happened to him," I said slowly. "His fate was determined a long time ago. I will not do anything further to Kaitarō Nakamura. But I do want to know what he did to me; I want to know why he came into my life."

This time she leaned towards me and for a moment she reached out, taking my hand in hers. "It is still privileged information," she said softly. "I cannot break confidentiality."

Her words infuriated me, the smug hypocrisy of them. "You know me," I said, enveloping her fingers with my own. "We've met before." I tightened my grip and pulled her across the table. "Don't you remember? You cradled me on your lap?"

"Ms. Satō, please—"

"Sarashima," I said, releasing her hand. "I changed my surname."

She withdrew into her chair. Her gaze dropped to the leather portfolio, unopened in front of her, and the small badge pinned to its rim. My eyes followed hers to the golden sphere, noting the carved individual petals and the tiny device that lay encircled at its center: the Sunflower and Scales.

Upon qualification, each attorney receives this pin with their personal number engraved on the back. Mine had not yet arrived. I imagined it in a store room at the Japanese Federation of Bar Associations, gleaming gold in its black velvet case, waiting in the dark.

In the beginning these badges are shiny and bright, their gold plate untarnished, but over time the gold wears away, fading first over the central scales, to reveal the plain silver beneath. Friends of mine planned to store their badges in coin purses to accelerate the aging process and acquire a veneer of experience—in that moment I did not know if I would ever use mine—but the badge on the table in front of me, however it had begun its life, was now tarnished only by age: the sunflower signifying freedom, and the scales, justice for all men.

Yurie Kagashima looked at me and she did something that I hadn't expected then; she smiled.

"The case is closed," I said. "If I do not care what happens to him, what does it matter if you help me?"

She said nothing.

"I know the risks you face in sharing your knowledge, but I will not expose you."

She glanced at her fingers, the skin still pink where I had gripped her hand.

"You must know how difficult this is for me," I said. "To ask you for help." At this last I could not keep the vehemence out of my voice. "Is he such a monster that he would deny me the truth of what happened?" I asked. "Would he want me to live like this?"

For a moment she looked down at her portfolio and then she drew it towards her, her fingers closing over the badge at its edge. "Come with me," she said.

We left the meeting room and crossed the open-plan office to her cubicle. Files were stacked against the flimsy walls and her desk was covered with papers and notes, like mine. In the corner was a wheeled gray suitcase. The law is still very much paper based. Information is rarely transferred or even available online, and so, if we are taking work home or meeting a client, we use these bags to transport our files. At her desk Yurie Kagashima opened a small box and drew out a key. "Follow me please," she said.

We walked across the office and she nodded to those she saw, stopping to murmur a few instructions to her secretary. As we passed the reception desk, I picked up the black roller bag I had left there. She raised an eyebrow at my confidence and preparation and I smiled.

At the end of the room was a painted screen that concealed a set of double doors. She unlocked one and gestured for me to precede her. The room that I entered was so dimly lit it was almost sepia. At the end of it, rows of rolling stacks, like the ones you might find in a library, rose to the ceiling. Breathing in the cool, musty air, I looked from them to the cabinets resting against the walls.

"Do you remember the case well?" I asked.

"I do," she said, turning on the main lights.

I walked forward, my footsteps muffled by the dark brown carpet. There were so many files in that room, decades of them, everything arranged by year and in alphabetical order: 1994 A-J, K-R. S.

"What you need is here," she said, moving to stand in front of a series of cabinets lining the wall. "These deep trays at the bottom." She separated a key from the ring in her hand and unlocked one of the drawers. "They contain the tapes."

"Tapes?"

"Kaitarō Nakamura refused to sign his confession," she said. "For days after his arrest he did not even speak. In the end they filmed him."

She held my gaze, daring me to look away. Upon arrest, a suspect can be held for twenty-three days without charge or recourse to an attorney.

"How many days before he was charged?" I asked

"Twenty- three," she said, and I did the calculations in my head: 552 hours, 33,120 slow minutes in the power of the state.

"Is there . . ." I paused. "Is there anything I should be prepared for?"

She turned back to the drawers.

"Did he sign it?" I asked. "The confession?"

"See for yourself," she said, extracting several VHS tapes and placing them on the counter. For a moment I stood staring while she walked to the end of the room and rolled out the stacks to reveal a narrow corridor filled with paper files. "Don't read any of this here."

"Can I take the videos?" I asked, and she nodded, her eyes on my face.

"I will give you two weeks," she said. "But I must have everything back."

"May I take a quick look at the papers?" I asked. "Just for a minute?"

She nodded and in my sudden relief I smiled, the tension easing out of me for the first time since I'd entered her office. I stepped forward, allowing my gratitude to show through. "Thank you," I said.

"You should know what happened."

"Thank you," I murmured again.

"And you cannot harm Kaitarō."

I flinched at the sound of his name and the sentiment behind it.

"Sumiko," she murmured, looking over me as though seeing the child I once was in the woman I had become.

I glared at her as she walked back towards the exit.

"Yurie," I said, and she turned. I can still see her face beneath the glowing brightness of the strip lights. "Did it help him, whatever you found out from me?"

She considered for a moment and then opened the door. "You decide," she said. As the latch clicked behind her, I turned towards the rising stacks and all the files they held.

I could not stay long, and I would take the papers with me, but before I left there was one document that I had to see. Having lived for so long without my mother, without true knowledge of her, I needed to know how she had died. I wanted the facts. So I searched for the procedure derived from the Greek "to see with one's own eyes": her autopsy.

It would not be the first that I had seen. During Supreme Court training, each and every aspiring lawyer spends months in court, assists prosecutorial teams, and investigates crimes. We sat with judges and drafted custodial sentences, and in each homicide case we attended the post mortem. I will always remember my first—standing in a hospital basement, my nostrils coated in the sharp menthol of Vicks VapoRub and seeing my pallor mirrored in the faces of others as we waited for the medical examiner in our white latex gloves.

The MEs were careful and diligent, eager to explain human anatomy and announcing discoveries as they made them. They encouraged us to participate. On one occasion the doctor beckoned to me and the other apprentices moved aside as I joined her. She had deviated from the traditional Y incision across the body and focused instead on dissecting the larynx and throat in order to investigate the damage sustained there. I leaned forward as she showed me the ligatures, the musculature and bone, the fabric of the person we were fighting for. I had read the files on the case, but I understood it differently when I was invited to touch the body, pressing down through the open flesh to the white of the mandible.

It is a crucial element of our training: to look life and death in the face. From all sides of the courtroom—as a judge, a prosecutor, or an attorney—every lawyer must know what is at stake and each of us must decide what is just. These lessons made us appreciate our lives and our families. They were designed to give us courage to do what was right, to assess the people who did the unspeakable and be fair to them and those they had harmed.

Standing in the archives of Yurie Kagashima's firm, I wondered if she had attended my mother's autopsy, if she had looked at her on a slab and understood, in the clearest terms, how my mother had come to be there. I wondered if she had touched her with a gloved hand and felt in her limbs the life she had lived and lost. I believe that she had. I believe that finally, when the forensic assistants were done and each mark on the skin had been analyzed, she stood beside my mother and watched as they opened her up and cut down to the bone.

## OFFICE OF THE TOKYO METROPOLITAN POLICE DEPARTMENT

**Takanawa Police Station, Shinagawa Ward, Case # 001294-23E-1994**
**Autopsy performed by Hiroshi Matsuda, MD**
**Fuminori Asao, PhD, Chief Toxicologist.**

Date: 3/27/94 Time: 0830
Name of Deceased: Satō, Rina Date of Birth: 3/28/65
Age: 30 Race: Japanese
Sex: Female Date of Death: 3/23/94
Body Identified by: Yoshitake Sarashima, father of the deceased

### PRELIMINARY REPORT

The body is that of a normally developed Japanesefemale measuring 160 cm, weighing 53 kg, and appearing generally consistent with the stated age of thirty years. The eyes are open, irises are dark brown, pupils 0.3 cm, corneas are cloudy. The hair is brown, undyed, layered, and approximately 25 cm in length at the longest point. The body is cold and unembalmed.

There are several scars present on the body. An incision found over the McBurney point of the abdomen suggests an appendectomy (confirmed by absent appendix in internal examination). Surgical scarring is also present on the lower abdomen, which, in combination with the extended pelvic girdle, indicates that the deceased was delivered of a child by cesarean section. Residual burns are present on the right and left ulnar forearms and wrists in addition to superficial scarring on the thumbs and index fingers of both hands. Interviews with family suggest these injuries resulted from cooking and domestic work.

Rigor mortis is discernible in the muscles of the face, neck, upper body, and extremities. There is also lividity in the tissues of the lower back, buttocks, and distal portions of the limbs. This white compressed tissue and corresponding dark purple discoloration—a result of blood settling in the limbs—indicate that the body lay flat for some hours after death, before being moved or held in an upright seated position. Injuries to the head include bruising and swelling to the scalp above the occipital bone and a contusion to the base of the chin. There is also substantial discoloration and congestion in the face of the deceased with petechial hemorrhages present in the conjunctivae and sclera of the eyes as well as the mucosa of the lips and interior of the mouth. These injuries manifest most commonly in cases of strangulation where the pressure within the veins of the neck, face, and eyes rises suddenly and forcefully.

In the tissue of the deceased's neck two horizontal ligature furrows are present, which encircle and cross just below the laryngeal prominence. The angle of these grooves forms a shallow V shape on the anterior of the neck and indicates that string or twine was slipped over the deceased's head and pulled taut. Internal examination revealed that hemorrhaging from the ligatures had penetrated the subdermal tissues of the neck. The width of these furrows varies between 0.3 cm and 0.5 cm and matches that of the suspected ligature used—a sample of household string found at the crime scene. Several white fibers also thought to originate from the string are embedded in the furrows of the skin.

Although these injuries point to the manner of death being ligature strangulation, there is evidence to suggest that manual strangulation occurred as well. The neck is covered in a combination of severe contusions, namely, diffuse round bruises on either side of the trachea and deep crescent-shaped nail marks found at the sides of the neck. Internal examination of the body revealed bleeding into the muscles of the neck from this assault and also that the hyoid bone and thyroid cartilage had fractured in response to trauma.

There are a number of defensive wounds on the body including bruising to the left and right forearms and wrists, abrasions across the back of each hand, and a torn fingernail on the right hand that are thought to have occurred as the result of a struggle.

Samples of blood and epithelial cells were taken from beneath all the fingernails of the deceased and sent for testing in addition to swabs from the face, neck, torso, and genitals.

Examination of the genital system reveals evidence of recent sexual activity (fluids removed for analysis). However, there is no trauma present in the genital tissue nor any indication that the sexual contact was forcible and coerced. The deceased is not pregnant.

## OPINION

Time of Death: Body temperature, rigor and livor mortis assessed at the crime scene indicate an estimated time of death between 1700 and 1900 on 3/23/1994.

Manner of Death: Strangulation

Cause of Death: Cerebral hypoxia

Remarks: Blood samples taken from the deceased tested O positive. Further samples of blood found beneath the victim's nails tested as AB positive (uncommon, found in only 20 percent of Japanese males). Initial DNA profiling has identified this blood sample as matching that of her alleged assailant. Further skin swabs taken from the body have revealed the saliva of a second male. The viability of these samples suggest contact with the victim near the time of death. Further tests are awaiting approval.

## EVIDENCE COLLECTED

1. Twenty autopsy photographs of the body clothed and unclothed
2. One white turtleneck T-shirt, size Small
3. One pair navy blue denim dungarees stained with pink paint, size Small
4. One pair white underwear
5. One white bra
6. Two white socks

7. Two smooth-textured gold stud earrings 0.5 cm in diameter
8. One gold wristwatch with braided metal band measuring 1.7 cm in width, 16 cm in length
9. Set of fingerprints taken
10. Ten fingernails clipped, scraped, and sent for analysis
11. Fifty head, eyebrow, eyelash, and pubic hair samples taken
12. Twenty swab samples collected from the body and sent for DNA analysis
13. Five vaginal and anal swabs retained and tested for semen
14. Samples of blood, bile, tissue (heart, lung, brain, kidney, liver, spleen) retained
15. Right pleural blood and bile submitted for toxicologic analysis. Stomach contents saved
16. One postmortem CT scan
17. One postmortem MRI

**// Hiroshi Matsuda, MD**
**Tokyo Prefecture Office of the Coroner**
**April 27, 1994**

## *HOME*

That evening in Meguro, standing outside the white metal gate of the house I still shared with my grandfather, I realized I had not seen my home clearly in quite some time. The image I had created in my mind had been generated years before, while in front of me reality had shifted. We see what we expect to see; I am proof of that.

When my mother was alive, the front garden had been full of glossy white pebbles, and tiny shrubs bordering the tiled driveway. As I opened the gate, I saw what time had done in her absence. The small green tiles were still swept clean, but the magnolia that used to reside in a corner beside the gate now threatened to burst onto the drive itself. The walkway, once polished, glistened with mold, and the pebbled borders were shrouded with a layer of speckled gray film.

I unlocked the front door and stepped into the hallway. For a second, I caught myself listening for Hannae in the kitchen, for the clatter of cooking utensils as she prepared the evening meal, but she was not there. She had left us when I turned twenty and had gone south to live with her family.

The house was silent as I put on my slippers and padded down the dimly lit stairway to the basement. There the familiar smell of my family home gave way to a damp chill. The basement was our safe haven during earthquakes. The walls and floors were reinforced concrete, secured by thick pillars in each corner. My grandfather's passion for filing continued there. All those things he did not need but could not throw away were shelved and boxed by category. Once a year, Grandpa would employ a cleaning company to dust everything, and then he himself would go down to make sure that nothing had been stolen. Taking a deep breath of the cold air, I walked towards the section labeled "Electronics."

With the VCR in my arms, I paused in the front hall to collect my bag with the videos and case file. The overhead lamp cast a shaft of light into Grandpa's study, illuminating the books within. I had spent so much time in that room that I had begun to think of it as mine, but this too had proved to be an illusion.

From where I stood, I could see the shelves that I had colonized while studying for my degree and training with the Supreme Court in Wakō. When working with the judiciary, I had drafted several custodial sentences. Those that were approved were carried out. I had collected manuals on prisons in Tokyo and the surrounding prefectures. Most of them were academic, but others were published for the curious reading public and filled with cartoon drawings of summer and winter uniforms, men sitting in the seiza position awaiting cell inspection, or kneeling with their rice bowls in regulated rows. I had read them all, but that night I viewed them differently from the books I had studied. They would feel different too, if I picked them up. They would feel personal.

Looking at those volumes in the darkness of my home, I was sure of one thing: I did not want to know the fate of Kaitarō Nakamura; I only wanted to know what he had done to me and mine.

Upstairs in my bedroom, I set everything down in front of the small brown television in the corner. This at least was just the same, although I had not watched it in some time. I remembered how in the evenings after school when Grandpa returned home from work, he would run upstairs to see me and then place his hand on the back of the TV. If it was warm he knew that I had been watching soaps all afternoon instead of completing my homework. I learned quickly about timing and the benefits of giving the machine an hour to cool down.

As I set up the VCR, I saw my room reflected in that same small screen. My bed, neatly made, the gray coverlet with white flowers folded on the end. The dry-cleaned suit I had picked up that morning hung on the door of my wardrobe while novels, magazines, an old textbook were piled up on the window seat, next to my battered white tiger, Tora. By the window, the white mirror and dresser, at which I applied my makeup and brushed my hair each morning, looked as it always had; only that night I could see the years of dress-up, summer festivals, and school concerts in its lacquered surface. That bureau contained layers of my childhood, memories that had gathered at the bottom of my life, like silt.

I sat down before the dressing table and began to sift through the first of the drawers. It was filled with lipsticks and dried nail polish from the drugstore, a high school archery certificate, and, finally, a baseball team photograph. I was sitting next to Kimiko, whom I hated for all of fifth grade; even looking at her now made my childhood irritation resurface.

In the next drawer was a photograph of my parents at a party. They were dressed as pirates in bohemian chic; my mother was wearing a beaded necklace across her forehead. All of my pictures of her were in the family album downstairs, and there were very few of my father, so I was stunned to find this one. My parents looked glamorous, impenetrable, but no matter how much I stared at them, I could not tell what they were thinking. I tucked the photograph away and turned to a pile of notebooks topped with my "stress" ball in the shape of a globe, which I used to squeeze and toss from hand to hand when revising. I remembered the thud of the foam against my palm as I memorized fact after fact. There was a replica Roman coin that Grandpa had bought me in Italy along with pictures from our trip. I had just started at the juku that would prepare me for applying to Tōdai, and as a treat Grandpa decided to take me abroad. I smiled at a photo of Grandpa ecstatic on the steps of the chapel in Assisi and one of me, constrained by my adolescence, tired and bored, leaning against the bus.

In the final drawer, I found a copy of the national anthem, a flag from a school parade, and a stack of birthday cards from my mother. At the base of these, beneath the last card she had given me, was an envelope.

We erase events from our lives, experiences that do not fit in with the stories we tell ourselves. Still, there are some memories that hover on the periphery. They reach out to you from another time and transform a moment of joy into one of shame. From then on these recollections stay with you. They linger on the edge of your vision and say, "Look at what you are."

Inside the envelope was a photograph. I picked it up, feeling the waxy texture of it between my fingers. The print was grainy and old, and it depicted a group of three on a beach in late summer. The sun had a soft, filtered quality to it and the air was tinged with heat. In the background the waves curled crisply on the shore, edged in white foam, and yachts floated in a small open harbor. In the foreground was a family.

The woman was wearing a light cardigan over her cotton dress; the collar was high and narrow framing her slender neck. She was laughing at the pair beside her—a little girl in red shorts and a T-shirt was kicking her heels in the air and sticking her tongue out at the man holding her aloft. He grinned back at her. The sun was setting behind them, and apart from the flash of his smile, the man's face was in shadow. But if you looked closely at this picture, if you focused in on the man and the little girl, you could see that their eyes were looking into each other's and that they were happy. Standing by my bed where I had tucked myself in night after night—alone for all the nights of my childhood—I let the photograph slip from my fingers.

The case file must have been beige originally; in the light of my bedroom I could see that it had been smudged gray over time by fingers stained with cheap ink. Inside were forensic tests, interview notes, and witness statements, all of them carefully typed and official, but there were handwritten notes as well, some on Post-its or scrawled on sheets of lined paper. As I read them, they began to shift and coalesce. An image began to form, providing a glimpse of the man my mother loved. For she must have loved him; surely she could not have left me for anything less.

Once in police custody a person may be held for up to twenty-three days without charge or legal counsel, and during that time the state will decide when they eat, sleep, or bathe. Interrogations can be endless, conducted with fresh relays of police officers. Mild violence such as a slap is accepted, though kicking is a step too far.

I knew from Yurie Kagashima's notes what the detectives thought of Kaitarō Nakamura—they viewed him as a monster and a murderer. They judged his reticence as defiance, his rejection of their confession as a lack of remorse. I could understand their attitude and in that moment I shared it, for if he was the man who killed my mother then he deserved no quarter.

Prosecutors have a mandate to solve a crime and to get to the whole truth of the matter. Often, this is achieved by obtaining a full confession, and, once it is signed, a confession is transformed into legal evidence: the key to a swift and easy trial. I saw several versions were drafted for Kaitarō Nakamura, first by the police detectives and finally by the lead prosecutor himself. For a long time Kaitarō Nakamura refused to sign them, but he did sign the last. That night in my bedroom, I could not imagine the reason he would do so.

Beside me on the floor were the interrogation tapes given to Yurie Kagashima at the prosecutor's discretion. He was not required to share the tapes, so he must have thought them robust, yet I wondered what Yurie Kagashima had seen there for she had marked three of them with an asterisk in red pen. Towards the end of the investigation, the prosecutor conducted all the interviews of Kaitarō Nakamura himself. His interrogation began on April 12, 1994, the date of the first marked tape. Slipping it into the VCR, I rose to switch off the lamps around my bedroom. Then I sat before the screen, alone in a pool of light; beyond me there was darkness.

The film flickered with black-and-white dots and then suddenly the image stabilized. He was sitting in a chair, looking away from the camera as though refusing to acknowledge it. His head was tilted down towards his lap. His hair was long and unwashed. I could see bruises on his face through weeks of stubble. There was a livid scratch on his cheek, purple and raised, yet probably older than his confinement because the edges were already healed. And then there beneath it all, like a shadow, his former self: dark, young, and vital. The man my mother would have known. The opening of the interview was lost on my intake of breath as suddenly Kaitarō looked up at the camera and smiled.

"I love my job. I'm good at it."

"Answer the question, Mr. Nakamura."

"There is no one-word answer."

"She was a job? A target?"

Kaitarō laughs. "She was my life," he says, glancing at the room around him, from the gray walls to the opaque glass and the police officers behind it and finally back to the man sitting opposite him, "and she'll have it in the end too."

"When did you first encounter the victim? Mr. Satō has told us that you first met his wife at a market in Ebisu. Is this true?"

Kaitarō leans over the table. "Have you met people like me before?"

"No, you are the first."

Kaitarō clasps his hands in front of him, long elegant hands that might hand a child a cone of ice-cream.

"Your questions are ridiculous," he says, looking over his interrogator, taking in his manicured nails, his suit. "You are all ridiculous."

The interviewer's lips twitch but he doesn't say anything. The room must be hot under the lights for a sheen of sweat has developed at Kaitarō's temples and above his chapped lips, but he does not move to wipe the moisture away. For a second, he flicks a glance at the portfolio on the table between them and the badge pinned to its corner. It is a white chrysanthemum with golden leaves surrounding a red sun—the climatic extremes of autumn frost and scorching sunlight—designed to remind its bearer of the constant principles and harsh judgments expected from those who enforce the law. Kaitarō may not understand the badge, but the man before him is no simple detective and Kaitarō knows it.

"Mr. Satō supplied you with information about his wife. Was he very involved in the case?" Kaitarō lifts his chin; his eyes gleam in response.

"Did he intend for you to kill her?"

"Fuck you." His voice is soft and low, but his face has paled beneath the bruises on his skin. "I know what you think of me," he says. "You and your nameless flunkies."

"My name is Prosecutor Hideo Kurosawa."

"You won't listen either."

"I want to understand."

"Prove it."

Beneath the white heat of the lights the two men assess each other. Kaitarō's eyes flicker to the stapled papers on the table in front of him, the prepared confession. Kurosawa follows his gaze and then reaches for the typed sheets, tucking them back into his portfolio and returning it to his briefcase, out of sight. Only his notebook is left on the table, open at a blank page. He looks back at Kaitarō. "How did it begin?" he asks.

Kaitarō straightens a little in his seat, considering. Then he takes an uneasy breath. After a moment his voice filters out through the tape. "I followed Rina to the market," he says. "I had a photograph of her from your pal Satō, but she looked very young, very . . ." he pauses as though the word eludes him. "I thought it might have been taken a long time ago." He glances up to see if Kurosawa is taking notes, but he isn't.

"From Satō's description," Kaitarō says, "I had expected someone older—a bit more homely. He made it sound as though Rina was a lonely woman, bored with her life. My boss expected a quick result and, to be honest, so did I. When you have worked in this industry as I have, it becomes rather formulaic—love, that is." Kaitarō smiles as though daring Kurosawa to interrupt him, but the prosecutor doesn't, and the silence stretches between them.

"People think that what I do . . ." Kaitarō says, "what I did, for a living is strange. They cannot imagine themselves in such a profession. And yet everyone goes through the motions of my job every day. It is as natural as breathing. We read those around us, their wants, their needs, and we make our move."

"Isn't that a bit cynical?" Kurosawa asks.

"There isn't a child on earth who doesn't read his parents," Kaitarō replies. "Every toddler will gauge the emotions of those looking after him and act accordingly to get what he wants. That is the skill of living with others. We spend our lives in training, Prosecutor Kurosawa. You just use your knowledge differently."

"How?"

"You investigate criminals and their crimes, but you can see what they need. You know what to do to elicit their help. You are capable of all manner of things to get what you want—either outside this room among the bureaucrats or at home with your wife. I think we operate very similarly." Kaitarō leans forward. "May I have a glass of water?"

"No. Go on with what you were saying."

"When I came to Tokyo I had nothing, not even a camera. What else was I going to use but myself?"

Kurosawa nods, waiting.

"What do people want? Approval? Praise? Affection? That is all attraction is: I like you because you like me and that's how it's done. You turn yourself into a mirror for each person. You pretend interest in their problems, radiate approval, and you reflect back to them the things they want to see."

Kurosawa reaches for his Styrofoam cup of tea and takes a sip; the liquid within is dark and thick as tobacco. "How many of these jobs have you worked on?" he asks, but Kaitarō ignores him.

"I watched Rina for weeks. She was always in a hurry, a mother running errands so she could get home to her child. But one night there was something about her, something in her expression, a sadness I had not seen before. She seemed lost, and I sensed an opening.

"She was in the market, looking at a selection of nashi pears, reaching into her purse. Her hair had fallen over her face when I approached her, but I already knew that she was not the dumpy housewife her husband seemed to think her. Not some simple, lonely woman. When she looked up at me I saw that she possessed a confidence I had thought she would lack. She raised her eyebrow, challenging me. I asked her if she knew a good place to buy cheesecake."

Kaitarō looks up startled as Kurosawa laughs.

"I know, right? Because dessert is sexy?" Kaitarō grins. "Rina laughed too. She gestured to a stall behind her. . . . She was still laughing when I invited her out for coffee."

"Did she go with you?" Kurosawa asks.

Kaitarō shakes his head, the smile fading from his lips. "She was married, she told me. She said she had a child. That was meant to warn me off, to appeal to my decency." He swallows. "She was decent," he says, "and all I could think, after reading about her, following her, photographing her, was that I knew her. I knew her as I had no right to, and I knew what she was going home to.

"I gestured to Rina's wedding band and said that I knew she was married. This startled her. It was clear no one had flirted with her for a long time. I cannot believe how blind people can be.

"I handed her my card, told her to contact me if she changed her mind, but when she shook her head, I walked away with relief. I was crossing the market, thinking about my boss, how I could persuade him to let this one go, when something awful happened. She followed me.

"She stood before me looking so composed, both shy and alluring, and said that she did have time for coffee if I was still interested. 'I'm Rina,' she said with a small smile. 'Rina Satō.' It was the hope in her eyes that undid me. I told her to go home, that her first instincts had been right. I remember the look I gave her and the hurt on her face as I turned away, but I did not look back. It took weeks to approach her again."

"But you did?" the prosecutor asks. "You did approach her again?"

"I had to," Kaitarō replies.

"Was there pressure from work?"

Kaitarō shakes his head. "That's not why I went back."

"Was it the other agent, Haru?"

"I wouldn't have let him touch her."

"So what happened?"

Kaitarō looks down at his hands. "I returned to her neighborhood, but she was always busy. I tried turning up at places I knew she would be, but I couldn't approach her. I thought about her constantly. I had been in a relationship when I was young. I liked the companionship, enjoyed sex—even when I moved to Tokyo and took this job—but after a while, with all those people, I started to keep myself at a distance. With Rina, even looking at her file, I felt this pull towards her as though I wanted to be caught. I wanted to tell her about Satō. No more jokes, no mirrors. I could have suggested we go to a love ho and have a photo taken or she could have divorced him on her own terms. Then we could have met as real people and started again."

"Why didn't you?" Kurosawa asks.

"Chemistry is a powerful thing," Kaitarō says, "but it can shatter. If I told her what I had been hired to do, the life that I sensed was there waiting for us would never have come into being."

"You still could have walked," Kurosawa says, but Kaitarō ignores him.

"When I met Rina again she could sense my indecision. Emotions were always quite tangible between us. She could feel what I was thinking, but she took my reluctance for shyness, perhaps that decency she was hoping for. I knew then that our friendship, fragile as it was, would not survive my profession. There would be no starting again. She would have been disgusted with me, and all the hope, the feelings between us, would mean nothing." Kaitarō pauses. "And I couldn't leave her to Haru and Satō."

Kurosawa is silent, then he gestures at the tinted glass panel. Soon afterward a young man in police uniform enters with a plastic cup of water. He sets it down in front of Kaitarō whose mouth curves into a smile, but he does not drink.

"I never had to act with Rina," Kaitarō says quietly. "None of the professional roles that I used on other women attracted her. Rina would call me on them; she could see through them. She observed other people more closely than they did her. We were alike that way."

"So you told her about yourself?"

"I was myself."

"Did you tell her about your childhood? Where you grew up? Where you're from?" Kurosawa persists. "Why risk it and have an abandoned target, a mark turning up in your hometown?"

"I didn't abandon her," Kaitarō says.

"No," Kurosawa replies quietly, "you didn't."

"She knew me," Kaitarō says, looking straight at his interrogator, "not my job, but the real me, and she wasn't horrified by what she saw." He sits back and his gaze lifts beyond Kurosawa. For the first time there is a lightness in his expression, a memory of hope. "What I felt for Rina—she was my home, a woman who not only understood me, but liked me. She was like me."

"Did she want to get divorced?"

Kaitarō's gaze shifts. "Not at first, no."

"Is that common?"

"Most people are selfish; they love to have the distraction of a new romance in their lives, particularly when they're bored and frustrated. Some are so desperate for attention that they latch on to an affair quickly without pausing to question it. Even those of us who think we are good can be ruthless when survival or our happiness is at stake. Rina was different. She valued the promises she had made to her family. She balanced everything: the needs of her father, her husband, her daughter. She prioritized them above herself, and she did not break with this lightly. One of her greatest strengths was that she was kind, but her way of living was stifling. She needed to make room for herself and so we did it together. We never did anything she didn't want to do."

"What happened after the divorce?"

"Rina moved to Meguro for a time and then she came to live with me," Kaitarō says. He looks at the camera and for a moment there is joy in his face.

"Did you continue to work as an agent?"

"No I"—Kaitarō shakes his head—"I found work at a photography shop. Rina met with some of her old contacts and she was close to exhibiting again. She had a series she was working on. One that she'd started that summer. We just needed a nest egg." Kaitarō pauses as Kurosawa looks at him in question. "Sumiko was living with her grandfather," he explains. "It was one of his conditions, that the child live with him until Rina could provide a stable home. Sumiko knew me as a friend. I didn't get to see her much. Rina said her father was testing her and me, but we wanted Sumiko so we did everything he asked."

"Did you usually work with children?" Kurosawa asks.

"No."

"But you involved this child, you knew her?"

"I liked her," he pauses and smiles to himself. "She was precocious. She had these large dark eyes and a knack for getting her own way. I appreciated that."

"How did Rina die?"

The smile slides from Kaitarō's face and for a time he is silent. "Do you know what it is like to find the one person who completes you?" he asks. "Wherever you are, whatever your choices, they complete you? That is how I felt about her."

"How did she die, Kaitarō?"

"String," he says. "It was on our bedside table. Kitchen string."

His image blurred as I paused the tape. My nails had left crescents in the flesh of my palm. Prosecutor Kurosawa sat frozen in action, his hand paused over his notebook, although I could not remember when he had started to write. At the very edge of the page was a sketch of a parcel neatly tied with string. I closed my eyes. I could still see Kaitarō's face behind my eyelids. I could hear his words, clear and sure. I wanted to reach into the interview and stop him. I wanted to press my fingers to his mouth and stop time.

In some homicide cases, there are security videos from shops or convenience stores that record the last moments of a person's life. When you watch these, you want call out to the figure on the screen and warn them not to take the path they're already heading down. When I paused Kaitarō's interview, I thought that if I did not let him finish speaking, if I did not listen to what had happened, then it would not be real. When I pressed play again he was sitting still in the silence, looking straight at the camera.

"I loved her," he said. "I love her still."

## *PEARLS*

That night I stood in my bedroom holding my mother's pearls. They have always been a talisman for me. I turned them over in my hands, enjoying the gentle click of them between my fingers, watching my reflection in each curve. The pearls are old and heavy, something that should be passed down from mother to daughter. On my twelfth birthday, Grandpa drew these pearls from his pocket and gave them to me. He lowered them into my palm and told me of how once I had nearly lost them altogether.

We were at a party and I was sitting on Mama's lap near a shallow pool. Mama had been chatting and entertaining some of my father's colleagues. My grandfather told me that as a baby I had loved attention and wanted to be at the center of things, so I had tugged on her pearls and, feeling the glossy orbs between my small fingers, tugged again. The thread snapped, and the pearls flew everywhere, rolling towards the pool. Mama stood up and ran after them, laughing, with me clasped in her arms. Together we scooped them up, one by one, lifting the last few out of the pool. When they had all been collected, my mother had pointed to our reflections in the shimmering water. Two heads close together, large dark eyes and pale cheeks. The images wavered, diving into each other—two women, where now there was just one.

# *Yoshi*

# *BUTSUDAN*

Yoshi Sarashima stood alone in his home in Meguro, looking down at a photograph of his daughter, Rina. It was his favorite picture of her. She was on the beach in Shimoda and she was looking straight at the camera, the sun shining down on her face. He could see the girl she was and the woman she would become, the mother she would be to Sumiko.

Candles flanked the photograph where it sat within an open rosewood cabinet, a butsudan, the family altar in the tatami room. The scent of incense lingered in the air, although that morning's sticks were now nothing more than gray powder in the trays.

In the months since his daughter's death, Yoshi would come downstairs each day to find fresh flowers upon the altar, the candles and incense already lit. Hannae was very attentive. But lately he had found Sumiko kneeling on the carpet, her back to him as he stood in the doorway; she did not notice him as he turned and walked quietly from the room. Hannae was usually in the kitchen packing Sumiko's bento, but when the clock struck 7 a.m., she would go into the tatami room with a fresh handkerchief to wipe Sumi's face before school.

Yoshi lifted the photo from its shrine and gazed down at Rina. He had never thought to see those eyes again, those high, delicate cheekbones. There was a cry from the garden, a shriek, and he looked outside. Sumiko was playing with Hannae. She ran into the sunlight, leaping into the air, her white cotton dress flying above her knees. She jumped again, her fingers snatching at the Frisbee. Yoshi watched her play, her eyes wide with excitement and joy. Her face was upturned to the sun and she was swift as she ran over the grass. He saw her for what she was—a child, just a normal child; he wanted her to remain that way. Slowly, Yoshi bent to the candles on the altar and, using a small folding fan, extinguished them one by one. He removed Rina's photograph from the family shrine and did not put it back.

# *Part Two*

There may be more beautiful times,
but this one is ours.

—SARTRE

# *Rina and Kaitarō*

# *RAZOR FISH*

A woman is born with all the children she will ever carry, all those tiny souls, like shells embedded in the coral of her womb. In a hospital room, astringent with antiseptic and starched sheets, Rina was shown a picture on a screen, an underwater cave flickering with phosphorescent light. And then, at the center of this space, swept clean, a knot of cells like a new world beginning: the child she had prayed for.

They communicated differently, Rina knew. Not through scans and blood tests, but through marks and skin, the push and pull of one life inside another. There was the first stretch mark that appeared on her stomach and grew, broad and deep, like a vein. Her pelvis widened and you, she thought, you tumbled within me, stretching me, carving a home for yourself out of my core. *You.* There was no need to say it aloud.

In the early months, Rina would lie awake in the night waiting for the shift and drop of liquid in her belly, the pull of currents within a pool, but soon she was awakened by a curl within her like the crest of a wave, and suddenly a bump on her stomach. You, she thought. Kicking. Tap, tap, tapping your way out of me.

These were moments Rina would never forget, the hours of gestation. Waking each dawn, Rina would lie very still to feel her. If there was no movement she would grow afraid, worried that something had happened to the baby, but then there would be a deep pulse within and Rina would fold her hands over her stomach and smile; movement meant that they were safe, they were alive.

In these moments too Rina thought of her mother, who'd died of cancer when she turned fifteen and now lay in the family tomb. There was never a time when Rina did not miss her, did not wish for her. But it was here, in the physical experience of new life, that it seemed if only for the briefest of seconds that her mother was there, as she needed her to be.

In the silence of her home, as she felt her child inside her, Rina looked around at the world she had created. She thought of the choices she had made and her early courtship with Satō. He had taken her to Tokyo Disneyland. From those months, their short time alone together, all she could remember was the theme park: his warm hand on her arm as he tugged her into Cinderella's castle; the light glinting off the colored towers and costumes; the chatter in the air as they stood in line with other couples, waiting to buy milk-chocolate popcorn, which came in plastic fairy-tale carriages with handles so that you could carry them like a purse. It was such a popular destination for dates that adults outnumbered the children. She remembered the rides and the whirlwind, the sugar on her tongue, and behind it all the clamor of expectation: fear drowned out by a smile, the sudden foreign taste of a kiss.

As the child inside her strengthened and grew, Rina began to consider what in her and Satō's relationship was real, and when the pains came she could not conceal her panic. As she staggered for the phone, she placed a hand to her belly, telling the baby inside to stop, to wait, but the force within her was relentless; it took over her whole body and deepened, the pain like a razor fish shooting down, down, through the sand of her skin. I'm coming, it said, I'm coming, and Rina wondered how such a small thing, unshelled, could be so unafraid.

Later, at home, Rina held her daughter. Satō had returned to the office, leaving behind an opulent bunch of winter roses, and so it was just the two of them. Her arms around her child, Rina looked at the tiny head cradled in the palm of her hand, the whorl of hair on the baby's crown as big as a fingernail. Her breath lingered against the powder-soft skin, the new-washed, newborn hair. It's you, she thought, *you,* and we've been together all along. The picture they had given her had never felt quite true. This being was not a photograph or a captured image; she was what Rina had been born for.

As the sun lowered in the sky, Rina stood by the window with the baby in her arms, her burgeoning fears replaced by resolve. She bounced the blanket-wrapped bundle and pointed to the horizon. The child's eyes remained closed, but Rina nuzzled her head and pointed again, telling her daughter about Tokyo, of the world she would inherit. Around them were gifts, a bassinet, a changing table, white romper suits strewn across the sofa, a new set of diapers, and, in a colander by the sink, fresh gooseberries, plump to bursting, their skins an expensive glossy green. Days later, Rina would write her thank-you notes, but in that moment there was only her daughter. Silhouetted against the city, Rina breathed in the scent of Sumiko. She kissed her head and thought of all the things she would become.

## *STARTING AGAIN*

The photography group and journal known as *Exposure* does not exist today. The studio that housed the quarterly seminars cannot be found. The narrow side street in Ginza on which it once operated is like so many others in the vicinity with thin yellow brick buildings that huddle together, blending into one another, squashed by their newer glass counterparts into dull uniformity.

Kaitarō stood beneath a streetlamp on the corner, a cigarette between his fingers; he lit it and inhaled, watching as people approached the recessed door beside the ramen bar and climbed the stairs within. Haru was inside and so was Rina, but still Kaitarō waited, wanting to slip in at the last minute and sit at the back.

He had asked to work alone that night, but Takeda had not permitted it. After the debacle at the night market it had been difficult for Kaitarō to remain on the case. His tentative suggestion that they pass on this job had been met with disappointment, even suspicion, a matter not helped by the fact that the agency's latest recruit, Haru, was establishing a track record that grew more impressive by the day. Only Kaitarō's previous rapport with Takeda, his insistence that he was perfectly suited to the target, had saved him. But his role in the case and whether he would be allowed to do the rest of the job alone—all of it depended on tonight. The last few people filed up the stairs and Kaitarō followed them; their young, high voices filled the stairwell, echoing around him, drowning out his footsteps.

He found a seat in the last row and glanced quickly to his right, spotting Haru and then Rina. She was sitting to the far side of the room, out of view of the speaker. She was nervous, he realized. This was not the sort of place she frequented, not anymore. He watched as she set her bag on the floor and adjusted the red strap of her sandal where it rubbed against her heel.

The speaker, an acolyte of the seascape photographer Shōmei Tōmatsu, approached the podium. Looking out over the crowd of assembled students, amateurs, and professionals, he nodded to his assistant by the slide projector and with the first image the seminar began.

In those first moments, Kaitarō leaned back in his chair; it had been a while since he'd been to a talk like this, a while since he had used his nights for anything other than working or snatched hours of sleep. He did not like being alone in his apartment, but he preferred it to socializing with his colleagues. In any case, none of them would have accompanied him to a talk like this. Still, as he listened, he felt the tiredness ebb from him and the freedom he witnessed, the possibility of working with nothing but yourself and the camera, began to lift his mood. He looked over at Rina; she had started the evening cross-legged and wrapped in her coat, but she had taken it off now and was leaning forward in her seat, her gaze following the speaker as he pointed out something on the projection. There was a small reluctant smile on her face, like the feeling of surprise.

For the rest of the evening he tried not to watch her, glancing at her only during the question-and-answer session at the end. It was hard though; she drew his attention. She was sitting up and listening. He could see her turning questions over in her mind; it was there in the bend of her head, the delicate curve of her cheek, her slow smile. It was infectious, that smile; it made him smile too, and so he looked away.

Haru had fallen asleep in his chair. Kaitarō wanted to prod him but he was too far away; he could only hope that his sleeping was an act, part of a new boorish persona. The problem was that Haru was a bore, a stud who spent his free evenings playing pachinko. Even looking at him now, Kaitarō could hear the blaring music of the parlors, the flashing rainbow lights, the click of the silver balls and the cacophony of noises emitted by the machines as each player struggled to win. He was the last person Kaitarō would have chosen to accompany him tonight, but he was quick on his feet, apparently a natural, and Takeda had insisted.

Eventually, the speaker gave his closing remarks and a few of the students approached him for autographs. Haru opened his eyes and looked around yawning, making sure Rina saw him. He registered the look of distaste on her face and smirked at her. He waited for Rina to put on her coat and collect her bag, before rising and making his way over to the entrance. Haru jostled people on the way out, causing them to tut and glare at him. At the door to the street he pushed past Rina, knocking her bag to the floor. Rina gasped as the contents of her purse spilled out onto the pavement, her lipstick and wallet rolling into a puddle left by the recent rain. She called after Haru but he walked swiftly away, leaving her to collect her things as people stepped over and around her.

Kaitarō joined her on the pavement, kneeling down in the damp grit. He collected the few items that had rolled beyond her reach and a book she'd been carrying. Carefully, he dried it, blotting the paper on his sleeve before handing it to her.

"It won't stain," he said.

"Thank you." Rina was still looking at the pavement, checking for anything she might have missed. "What a jerk! You know, I think he fell asleep in there?"

"I'm sure of it." Kaitarō offered a hand to help her to her feet, and that was when she finally looked at him.

"Hi . . ." she paused for a moment. "It is you, isn't it? I'm not going—"

"Yes." He smiled. "Hello."

"You like photography?"

"Yeah," Kaitarō laughed, self-conscious now. "I'm not stalking you."

"Oh I didn't mean—" Rina stammered.

"No no," he was quick to reassure her. "I know," he said, holding her gaze. "Look, now that I have you here, I want to apologize for my behavior the other night—at the market."

"Oh," Rina shrugged and shook her head. "No it's—"

"It's just that I could see you didn't really want to have coffee with me. I was embarrassed."

"You don't take rejection well," she supplied.

"Something like that."

"Oversensitive," she said, grinning at him.

"I'm not good at this."

"At picking up women?"

Kaitarō laughed. "Talking to people," he said, and Rina smiled with him.

"So, Rina . . ."

"You remember my name?" she asked and her smile widened.

Kaitarō nodded, still looking at her. "Do you have to get home to your daughter or do you have time for a coffee?" He watched as she glanced up at him, perhaps surprised that he had remembered her child. He waited as she looked off down the street and then at the watch on her wrist. "You have to get home," he said, stepping away from her.

"Sumiko is with her grandfather," Rina said, finally. She narrowed her eyes at him. "Are you going to walk me to the café or will you run away again?"

"Not this time." Kaitarō smiled, shifting the portfolio he was carrying under his arm.

"Is that work? Are you a photographer?" Rina asked.

"No—I mean, it's just some of my photos . . . I was going to show"—he gestured up at the seminar room—"but I decided not to."

"Will you show them to me?"

"If you let me buy the coffee."

"Okay," Rina said.

Standing beside her in the evening light, Kaitarō thought about offering her his arm. He wanted to draw them together, to feel the touch of her, light over his clothes, the pressure of her hand as she placed it in the crook of his elbow. But it was too soon. He could not rush her, and looking at the small, hopeful smile on her face, he did not want to. Instead, he gestured for her to precede him on the pavement while he walked through the puddles in the street. Together they headed towards the lights at the end of the alley.

## *SLEEPLESS TOWN*

It was late evening and Kaitarō could just make out the sound of Tokyo's cicadas snickering in the trees as he walked through the streets of Kabukichō, the "sleepless town" at the heart of the pleasure district. The air conditioners from the bars blasted out gusts of warm air while hundreds of vertical neon signs reflected off the glass buildings, infusing the dusk with oppressive heat. As he passed each club, some of them barely distinguishable from each other, Kaitarō tried to ignore the mockery implicit in Satō's choice of locale, and entering one of the venues, he wove between the tables until he found the man he was looking for.

"How long is this going to take?" Satō was sitting on his own cradling a chilled Asahi beer, fumes pouring off him. Smoke filtered through the air, and from the shadows at the back there was a flash of thigh as a girl entertained a customer.

"These things take time, Satō." Kaitarō took a seat.

"Any problems so far?"

"No."

"What was it that happened at the night market, exactly?" Satō smiled. "Takeda wouldn't say."

"It's a staggered approach," Kaitarō said, "piques the subject's interest," he added, using one of Satō pet phrases.

"So what's the story? Who have you said you are?"

"No story, just a man about town."

"Well, at least you got her to go out with you," Satō took a long pull on his beer, "and thank you for these," he said, tapping the receipts on the table in front of him. "You've been taking her coffee? How sweet. What's next, fucking cheesecake?"

"Are you seeing anyone?" Kaitarō asked, his expression calm, neutral. "Don't tell me there isn't a girlfriend . . ."

Satō narrowed his eyes. "What's it to you?"

"Is she 'the one,' this girl? You've thought it through."

Satō leaned back in his chair and took a sip of his beer. He sat in silence for a moment, assessing Kaitarō. Gradually, his eyes lit up in realization.

"Rina's not giving it up, is she? She won't put out?" He laughed then, a high phlegmy sound. "And I thought you were such a player, the finest stud in Tokyo." He was shaking with laughter, sloshing beer onto the floor.

Under the table, Kaitarō's fingers tightened into a fist and he felt the blood pulse in his palm.

"It's that difficult then?" Satō smirked and took another swig of his beer. "Just a couple of kisses, Nakamura, if that's all you can manage. Get them photographed."

"I'd prefer to do the photography myself," Kaitarō murmured.

Satō smiled, all equanimity. "As you like."

One of the girls behind the bar had finished her break and approached them. She was wearing a tiny skirt and shiny black cat ears à la Michelle Pfeiffer. She ran her nails through Satō's hair and rubbed his scalp as he pulled her into his lap.

"Give me something real, mind—she doesn't need a playmate." Satō grinned as Kaitarō continued to watch him. "Don't worry, Nakamura, you don't have to fuck her."

The girl was nibbling Satō's earlobe and he turned to her, putting his hands on her waist. After a moment he looked back at Kaitarō, his eyes shrewd. "You're not in love with her, are you?"

"I need two months," Kaitarō said, barely bowing as he got to his feet. He could hear the man's laughter behind him as he shoved through the dancing figures and the people crowding the bar to exit the club. Outside, Kaitarō leaned against a wall and took a deep breath of the heavy evening air. The concrete at his back felt solid and cool. It's a job, he thought, just a job, and walked out into the night.

# *EBISU*

There are some experiences, even small ones, that hit you like a blow to the gut. Their force can linger for months, even years. One morning, Rina awoke slowly. Still safe in the cocoon of sleep, she let her thoughts drift to Kaitarō and their last meeting. She thought of the light in his eyes as he'd looked at her and how those same eyes had lingered on her face. How she could feel within her even now the warm glow of desire, of being desirable. She turned amid the tangled sheets to find her husband still asleep beside her. She pressed her face into her pillow and his scent rose from the bedding—cigarette smoke and tea and sweat—but beneath it all the faintest trace of him alone, the musk of his skin after a bath. Rina moved and rested her head on his chest. Her hand grazed his belly and moved down over his shorts, feeling the hardening ridge there. Idly, she began to stroke it and play with the tip, feeling it respond to her. She sensed Satō stir and she smiled, but just then his hand covered hers and stilled it. Rina lay very still while a trail of shame smoldered within her. Eventually he pushed her off him and left the bed. As he dressed she raised an eyebrow at him, questioning, but he did not bother to reply.

That afternoon Rina stood in her apartment and waited. She watched the shadows lengthen across the floor of the living room. She listened for sounds of her family, but Satō was at the office and Sumiko had started school. There was no one else in her home. Nothing. Only the cool feel of the marble beneath her feet, the silence of the walls. She walked to the door of her bedroom and leaned against the white doorjamb, taking in the windows that overlooked Ebisu. That day, the sheets of glass no longer seemed cold; they lead to another city, to another world.

He had asked her to meet him at a nature reserve, one of the oldest and most beautiful parks in the city. She wasn't sure if she should go, although she wanted to. Now she held the decision in her hands. Rina walked farther into the room, noting the conservative furniture, the taupe walls, the neutral shades she had chosen all those years ago on the eve of her marriage. By the windows, amid the restrained palette of her bedroom, was a ficus that Rina loved. That afternoon, as the sun shone into the room, the plant's bright green leaves were reflected on the walls, rippling in a blend of shadow and light, flickering faster and faster as though the world itself were speeding up.

## *TOUCH*

Rina noticed him the moment she arrived at Meguro station, and he seemed to know at once that she was there, for before she had even started to walk towards him, Kaitarō looked up and smiled. He nodded in welcome, folding his paper beneath his arm. There was a warm, playful light in his eyes that Rina could not resist; she smiled too.

"I'm sorry I'm late," she said, apologizing automatically, but he shook his head. "I was early," he replied, and the honesty of this small point pleased her.

Across the road from the station were the gates of the nature reserve. Next to them was the ticket booth with a small electronic sign and the number 295 lit up on its black screen. "We should hurry," Kaitarō said, glancing around, making sure it was safe for them to cross. She felt the shadow of his arm at her back, the thrill of his nearness, although he didn't touch her at all, simply shielded her from the people around them.

Straight ahead, rising beyond the gates and the white ticket booth, was the green forest of the park, an ancient woodland of dogwoods and zelkovas in the middle of the metropolis, preserved and protected, even now. The number on the sign changed to 296 as they joined the queue, and ridiculously Rina felt her pulse speed up. Only three hundred people at a time were allowed into the reserve, and though it was near her childhood home, though she had seen it many times, that day she desperately wanted to be allowed in.

Kaitarō smiled at her and nodded in reassurance but he too seemed tense, repeatedly looking over his shoulder and surveying the crowd. Rina wondered if he was worried that they might be recognized by people they knew and followed into the park. His concern for her was touching, and perhaps, like her, he simply wanted them to have some time alone, together. There was only one couple ahead of them and Rina forced herself to take a deep breath. Still, she leaped forward as soon as the attendant was free. Embarrassed by her eagerness, she glanced up at Kaitarō, but as they reached the front desk and the number on the sign changed to 298, he too took a triumphant breath and smiled, no longer anxious, but excited.

Inside, they walked in silence beneath the shade of the trees. Rina watched the dappled shadows as they played across the leather of Kaitarō's jacket, softening its lines and cut. As the path curved, they paused to let a jogger and then a young mother with her children pass them. Kaitarō relaxed completely once they entered the park, and Rina found it harder to steal glances at him, now that he'd returned his full attention to her. Instead, she glanced up at the sprawling branches of the giant "Fabled Pine" and caught a glimpse of her reflection in the small hyotan pond at its base, the remnants of an ancient pleasure garden where once lovers used to meet.

"So you grew up near here?" Kaitarō asked, and Rina nodded.

"Just up the hill, in Meguro. My father still lives there, actually."

"Should I have chosen somewhere else?" Kaitarō asked. "Is it too . . . familiar?"

"No!" Rina shook her head and smiled. She paused to take in the abundance of greenery all around them, the sweet scent of late spring. "It's perfect," she said. "A good choice." Beneath the canopy of the trees she eyed his leather jacket and dark jeans, his city loafers. "Don't you like nature?" she asked. "A real city guy?" she teased when he looked ruefully at her. Rina smiled and began to walk up the path, but he put his hand on her arm and she turned, surprised by the intensity of his gaze.

"Actually, I'm not from the city," he said.

"No?"

"I'm from Hokkaido." Kaitarō said it slowly and without inflection. He watched her, waiting for a reaction. "From a small fishing village, north of Sapporo."

Rina stood still while the breeze lifted the lace edge of her collar, causing it to rise up her neck.

"I worked at a seaweed plant," Kaitarō continued, "my father at the fisheries."

"So you don't belong in Tokyo?"

"No."

"So this Kaitarō," Rina smiled slightly, "with his leather jackets and town polish he's—"

"Fake."

"I see," she said. "So who are you really?" Rina looked at him for a moment, her eyes grave. "Are you still a photographer?"

Startled, Kaitarō laughed. "Yes—I mean it's not my day job—but yes. At heart that's what I want to be."

Slowly, Rina's lips stretched into a grin. "Phew!" she said, delighting at the look in his eyes, and started off again up the path, quickening her pace. Rina smiled as she walked along the track. She could feel the warmth of his gaze as he watched her, her own rising elation. Finally, she left the main path and started towards a swathe of forest. When he continued to hang back, as though uncertain of what she might do next, she turned to face him. "Come on!" she called, laughing as he ran to catch up.

Later, they sat together outside a small café by the edge of a pond. There was a breeze blowing, and sunlight caught on the water as it flowed into the reeds where brown ducks swerved and dived, searching for food. Rina could feel the sun at her back; she could see her shadow stretching out to the side. She closed her eyes and smiled. The café was not large, no more than a kiosk with some tables beside the water, but she felt at peace there, more so than she had in a long time. When they had first arrived, they headed straight for the glass cabinet of cakes. Rina had felt a flutter in her stomach as she spotted a raspberry cheesecake. She looked up to see Kaitarō's eyes, equally bright and focused on her. "Shall we?" he asked, and she had smiled at his timidity. "I don't want to force you," he said. "I mean, if it's only my obsession," he added until she turned to him. "I love it too," she said, and he ordered two slices.

Now with their empty plates stacked to one side, a black folder lay open on the table between them. It was her portfolio, a silly thing, a sample of her work from long ago, but still, she had brought it to show him. Kaitarō was holding one of her photographs in his hands. She could see him following the lines of the landscape, analyzing the angle of the light as it settled in the bay. This was Rina's favorite photograph, the last to be exhibited before she left her career for good. The print run had been small, only five exhibition-size pieces and all of them had sold. This one small version was all she had left.

The picture had been taken early in her marriage, in secret, on a winter day trip to Shimoda. She had caught a taxi from the station and climbed down the rocky embankment in front of her home to the beach. Kicking off her shoes, Rina walked on the freezing sand all the way to the edge of the sea. She watched the waves curl, icy and languid, beneath a stormy sky, and as the water unfurled she pressed the shutter, capturing the light as it pierced the clouds and hit the waves. It was at this moment, as she stood on the beach, staring through her lens, registering all the gradations of black and white, the power of the natural world, that she first felt Sumiko leap inside her, jumping out of the monochrome picture like a silver fish.

It represented so much, this photograph: all she had wanted to achieve and what was left. She still remembered printing it—the alkaline scents of her darkroom, how she'd experimented with variations of dodging and burning, her hands flying between the light source and the photographic paper to create the perfect accentuation of luminescence and shadow. She didn't expect Kaitarō to see any of this there, but she liked how careful he was with it, the attentiveness with which he looked at the composition, the way he wiped the table surface brushing away stray crumbs before he set the photograph down so that it would not get dirty. Something about the way he held the very edges of the picture, so that the oil on his fingers would not soil it, made her smile. And perhaps he did see what was there, for she watched as his finger traced the lines she had created, hovering over the space where her own hand had hovered as she let the light in through her fingers, drawing out the exposure, burning the details of the waves onto the paper.

"You stopped working after this?" Kaitarō said. It was more of a statement than a question, but Rina nodded in assent.

"I had completed a series on Shimoda, taken part in a few shared exhibitions, but after this photo was shown I—"

"Focused on your marriage," he supplied. Rina nodded once more, biting her thumbnail in silence, but she did not object to what he had said. There was no judgment in his tone, only a statement of fact.

"You never included Sumiko in your work?" he asked.

At this Rina smiled, "I have wanted to. Sometimes when I'm in Shimoda with her and we're in the forest above our house or down by the bay, I catch the light glancing off her figure or illuminating her face as she turns to smile at me, but I—I don't know how to bridge the gap. I can't imagine a new project; my ideas have dried up." Rina looked down at her hands, twisting them in her lap. After a few moments she felt Kaitarō lean towards her and she lifted her eyes to his.

"Rina, you can do anything," he said, "anything at all." It was a grandiose statement, probably a platitude, but there was something about his expression, the energy in his eyes, that made her want to believe him. His hope and encouragement kindled something within her.

"Perhaps," she said with a small smile.

Drawing her portfolio across the table she closed it and returned it to her bag. "What about you?" she asked. "Have you ever included anyone you loved in your work?"

Kaitarō grimaced and Rina laughed, happy to turn the conversation towards him.

"No," Kaitarō said quietly.

"No one?"

Kaitarō shook his head, wincing once more at the determined look in her eyes.

"There's not a single person in the whole—"

"Perhaps my uncle."

"Your uncle?"

"He taught me photography," Kaitarō said, looking away and rubbing at the back of his neck. "The pictures I showed you—I was with him when I took them."

Rina was silent for a while, watching him. She thought of the first coffee they'd shared together after the lecture in Ginza. He had told her of a mentor, a photographer he worked for, but she had not realized he was family. She thought too of the photos he had shown her then, of the sun rising above the fields, golden rays coating translucent stems of rice, of giant greenhouses stuffed with chrysanthemums for trading, a single dragonfly gliding on the wind with wings clear as cellophane. They're just postcard shots, he had said, but they weren't like any postcards she had ever seen. She thought they were perhaps experiments in landscape from a trip to the far north; she had envied him his mentor and their ability to travel for work. She hadn't realized that he'd been showing her his home or noticed that there were not, not in any of the photographs, any people.

"When were they taken?" she asked. "The pictures you showed me?"

"Just before I moved to Tokyo."

"You haven't seen him since?"

Rina waited, watching him as he glanced at her tentatively, not wanting to push too hard.

"I haven't been home," he said finally. "I doubt my uncle has either; he wouldn't be welcome."

Rina felt her forehead crease into a frown and swiftly smoothed it. Kaitarō lowered his gaze to the mottled gray surface of the table and his eyelid twitched. She had thought he was merely shy about where he was from. Rina knew insecurity well and she didn't blame him for his, but she realized now that there was a lot more to it and that they were both on new ground, for clearly he didn't talk about this often. She waited once more, hoping he would go on.

"My father blamed him," he said at last. "He liked to blame people."

"I know someone like that," Rina said softly, giving Kaitarō a small smile when he looked up at her.

"So your uncle was a photographer?" Rina pressed. "When did he teach you?"

"On and off, as I was growing up," Kaitarō replied. A grin tugged at the corner of his mouth, and Rina was relieved to see that she had asked the right question, that these memories at least were good.

"He traveled a lot, was a loner at heart, but when he was in the area he took me out with him. I started as his assistant, keeping his cameras loaded, cleaning the darkrooms we used, running endless water baths." He paused. "Of course, there was that time early on when I used the fixer instead of the developer and wiped his film!"

Rina snorted with laughter, but it was the sympathetic kind. "We've all been there," she said, and he smiled with her.

"Eventually, he let me get my hands on his camera, and then it was all he could do to take it away from me." Kaitarō laughed, and Rina loved the note of satisfaction in his voice. "The work wasn't steady by any means, but when he could get it, and when it could pay for both of us, I came along and he taught me what he knew."

"What work did you do with him?"

Kaitarō grinned. "Not high art, that's for sure. We used to set up temporary photography stalls outside the train stations. Sometimes we'd get bigger projects—local festivals, a high school graduation—but mostly it was local matchmakers needing shots of prospects or boyfriends and their girls, smoking cheap cigarettes."

"Motorbikes and leather?" Rina asked, laughing when Kaitarō nodded. "Did you have a bike?" she asked.

Kaitarō smiled. "I did. Took some years, but I saved up the profits we made from those kids and bought my own camera too. Stupid punks, I just wanted their money."

"Money is useful."

"It is indeed," he said, and their eyes met in understanding.

"He sounds like a good uncle," she said.

Kaitarō shrugged, looking down for a moment, and Rina held her breath. She knew, could just feel, that they had reached the part he had been avoiding. She wondered if he would trust her enough to continue. He clasped his hands on the table in front of him and kneaded his knuckles. Then he glanced up at her with such trepidation that Rina wanted to place her hands over his, but then he dropped them to his lap and looked away. It was as though he was deciding something and Rina could only wait.

"I had just finished school when he came back," he said after a while, his voice low. "I'd been drifting since graduation, unable to find work on the trawlers and growing idle with only my evenings at the seaweed plant." Again he paused and Rina could see he was still wary of her.

"My father never liked my uncle," he said. "He tolerated him for my mother's sake, but he didn't respect him. Dad called him a wanderer, but he didn't mean it as a compliment. My uncle didn't really have a home, he would travel for months and then suddenly reappear with a new jacket or flashy clothes. Whenever he did my father would say it was all right to earn a bit extra with a hobby, but it was no way to make a living. That year, I wanted to work with him again, but my father wouldn't allow it. When my uncle came round to try to talk to him, Dad threw him out of the house. He was a good uncle, but there was only so much he could give. In the end he left for the west coast; he never did say exactly where.

"I still went out with my camera though. My mother spoke up for me for a while, but as the weeks passed my father fought with her more and more. I'd hear him shouting from the end of the street. I can still remember the smell of him as I opened our front door—blood and sardines, the stink of kerosene from the boats. He wanted me to be like him. He thought I was like him." Kaitarō glanced up nervously, but Rina was just listening, her eyes on his face.

"I tried to find more acceptable work, I evaded and dissembled, but in the end it—"

"Came to a head?" Rina offered, and he nodded still looking down.

"My father got me a contract on one of the boats, a full-time apprenticeship. It was a good offer, but I didn't want it. When I came home one night he was waiting up for me. The house was quiet. I had thought they were asleep, but when I went into the kitchen he was there. His buddies had told him I turned down the job. He rose to meet me. I was holding my camera in my hand and tried to set it on the table, but he snatched it from me. My mother came in from the bedroom. She reached out for him, tried to calm him, but he turned and smacked her, hard. I remember how she staggered and fell."

Rina swallowed. This was violence like she had never witnessed. Anger expressed through force.

"I did nothing," Kaitarō said, eventually. "Most times, we would both try to dodge or slip out till he slept it off, but that night he really hit her. It's hard to do, you know? Takes effort to knock someone out cold."

"It wasn't your fault, Kai."

"But it was," he said. "I tried to stay out of the house. I came home later and later, but in the end I just made him worse.

"That night—I still hadn't gone to help my mother—I was waiting for him to come at me, could see him building up to it. Mum kept a miso pot on the windowsill. It was too old and cracked for cooking, so she grew herbs in it. He hefted it up and it exploded near my ear, shattering into shards of dirt and old fired clay. As this happened, Mum started to come round and her recovery distracted my father. She snapped at him to stop it and I could see her cheek beginning to swell. She told me to leave, and I did." For a moment, he looked at her steadily as though to emphasize this point. "She told me to get out and I did. I left my camera with them as rent, sold my bike, and crossed the Tsugaru Strait. I haven't been back." He looked swiftly away, but Rina had already seen the anxiety in his eyes, the panic that he had told her too much too soon, that he shouldn't have told her anything at all.

"You chose to look after yourself. That's not a crime," Rina said. She leaned forward across the table, looking at the refined young man sitting opposite her. He was so resilient, contained. "You are nothing like him," she insisted, and Kaitarō lifted his head.

"Rina, I hope not," he whispered. There was so much hope in his face.

"Kai," she said, and his eyes warmed at his name on her tongue, "I know so." Finally, she slid her hand across to cover his. He drew a ragged breath as she touched him, his eyes and hers moving to their fingers intertwined on the tabletop. Rina felt the texture of him through her palm, the slide of skin against skin and the warm grip of his hand as it enveloped her own.

"You haven't been back?"

Kaitarō shook his head.

Rina nodded. "I would have left too, if I could," she said, while his hold on her hand tightened, drawing her towards him so they sat very close. There was such an affinity between them, she thought, that he must know she understood, that she spoke for them both. He said her name and the timbre of his voice stroked up her spine.

"Rina. When can I see you again?"

## *FOLLOW ME*

"What's it like?" Rina asked.

"What?"

"To follow people?"

"You want my job?" Kaitarō took a sip of his coffee, watching her over the rim of his cup. He had told her he was a private detective, and it was close enough. As close as he dared.

"It can't be that hard," she said.

His smile broadened as he looked at her; she was so fascinated by his work. She loved to watch people, was so inquisitive and nosy; it must be the fact that they were both photographers at heart and given to voyeurism. "I'll show you," he said, stepping down from the bar stool. As he waited for her to put on her coat, he checked the bill and threw some notes onto the table.

"Don't you want your change?" she asked, ever frugal. The question made him smile, and as she passed before him he caught—all too briefly—the fresh scent of her hair. "Come with me, Rina," he said, falling into step beside her.

He led her out into the sunshine, the glass doors of the coffee shop swinging shut behind them. "Who should we choose?"

"That one, the pretentious one in the trilby."

Kaitarō laughed. "Too easy, and I don't think he's going anywhere interesting."

"You choose then."

"That one. The woman in the brown coat."

"Do you ever talk to them? The people you follow?"

"Sometimes," he replied. "Sometimes you need information; sometimes you just need to gauge what they're like."

"And you can do that? In a couple of minutes."

Kaitarō looked at her, still smiling.

"First one to talk to her wins," Rina whispered, and she took off down the road after their target.

Kaitarō followed. He caught up with her just as she turned a corner, and she looked so gleeful, so happy that he had to stop himself from reaching for her.

"Slow down, you're getting too close."

"Go away. We're not working as a team."

"You have to wait," he said quietly "until she goes into a supermarket or a shop, engage her by the fruit."

"Or over cheesecake?"

Kaitarō looked over his shoulder up the street. "Something like that."

Rina quickened her step, moving away from him, and Kaitarō returned his attention to her. He caught the scent of her hair once more and his jaw tightened. It maddened him that they were never truly alone, that he could not touch her in public, and with each new meeting that madness grew.

"Let's see how much we can pick up before she notices us," Rina whispered, her eyes meeting his with a slow enticing smile and so they followed, sometimes extremely close, giggling like children.

Towards the end of the road, as they entered the newly built up part of Ginza with its shining department stores, Kaitarō became serious. The woman went into a couple of the designer shops but remained on the ground floor. He tapped Rina on the arm, moving around her so they could pretend to look at a selection of perfumes. They followed the woman out into the street, and Kaitarō picked up a free newspaper, slowing, as she decided which direction to go in next. He signaled to Rina, his movements deft. He wanted to impress her, wanted her to know he was good at his job.

"I want to talk to her," she demanded, and Kaitarō slanted a glance at her.

"We are not doing a 'close follow' today."

"I'll do what I want!" she threw at him over her shoulder and broke into a run, but she shrieked as he caught her and swung her into his arms, dragging them both into a small side alley. The woman they were following must have looked around in shock, but all that remained was the echo of their laughter and the flash of Rina's coat as they disappeared together.

They stood in alley, breathing rapidly. It was cool out of the sunlight and damp underfoot, but Kai didn't care and he didn't think Rina did either. Her eyes darkened as she looked up at him. He reached out and with just one finger caressed her cheek. Rina leaned towards him and he pulled her into his arms, his mouth opening over hers, filling his hands with her hair, with the touch and scent of her. She moaned into his kiss, and he moved his hands down, palms on either side of her face, shielding her. To an outsider, she could be anyone, any girl in the street, but to him she was Rina. He knew who she was and the delight of it was overwhelming. Kaitarō drew her closer, savoring this first taste of her, kissing her as though he might never stop, and for a while neither of them was aware of anything or anyone else beyond the alley. Eventually, he pulled himself away, although his breathing was still unsteady. Rina raised her eyes to his and a smile curved her lips as she leaned in once more, bringing their faces close.

"Follow me," she whispered.

═

She walked away, not looking back. A few hundred yards down the street Rina stopped at a shop window to check the reflection. She couldn't see him but she knew he was there. She looked at herself in the glass, at her smiling face. This was happiness, she thought; she remembered it well.

Rina walked into the shop and asked if they had a ladies room. Finding it and also a back exit she slipped outside and into another alley. Ginza was full of glittering thoroughfares and tiny twisting streets abounding with artisans and small restaurants, her own favorite, Kyubey was near here. She paused as people walked past her, swiftly making their way to the fish market and the eateries there. Couples strolled, tourists stopped. Rina took off her light summer coat and turned it inside out so that she was now dressed in black and the red outer fabric became the inner lining. She walked down the street, turning and turning again. She returned to the main thoroughfare and ducked into another shop. Out of the corner of her eye, she saw a slip of his tan-colored raincoat. Sloppy, she thought, smiling as she exited the further down, racing him to the end of the street, weaving in and out of the shoppers, heedless of their startled glances. She entered the Matsuya department store so fast that the white-gloved attendants barely had time to open the doors and went straight to the top floor, slowing and browsing through the racks of yukata there, stocked for stylish housewives and tourists looking for gifts. She crossed the floor and went up the staircase leading to the roof where she paused, looking out over Tokyo. Her breath caught as she smiled to herself and her hand drifted to the pearls at her neck.

She walked to the Shinto shrine in the center of the rooftop and threw a coin between its wooden slats, bowing deeply and clapping her hands together twice. As the sound echoed in the air, she ran to the staircase on the opposite side of the roof, reversing her coat once more and disappearing down the stairs in a flash of red. She circled the third floor and then went up again to children's toys before taking the elevator to the basement. She entered it just as Kaitarō did, and he grinned at her from the opposite side of the room.

Delighted, disappointed, Rina laughed at him as he made his way towards her, moving around the shoppers and housewives who were stocking up for the week. They met in the center of the food court.

"It's always the food," he said smiling.

"How did you find me? I was so fast and I changed my coat."

"That was brilliant," he said, "a stroke of genius." He looked around them and discreetly lifted her hand to his lips, pressing his mouth to the center of her palm. "You almost lost me."

"Don't be kind," she said.

"I'm not. Really. There was a time on the roof when I had no idea where you would go."

Rina smiled and then punched him in the shoulder. He laughed and she moved closer to him, as close as she could without touching;

she could feel his breath against the sweep of her hair.

After a moment, she stepped back, aware that people might be looking at them. She turned towards a cheesecake display where they had come to a halt. "Kai, look how beautiful they are. Shall we get one?" She scanned the stylish array until her eyes homed in on the one she wanted. "Look at that, banoffee chocolate . . ."

She was aware that he had gone still beside her, saw him glance behind them, but then when he returned his gaze to her face she felt her excitement ebb away as she realized they had nowhere to take the cake. She had to go home.

"Rina, stay with me," Kai said. He moved to take her hand, his lips curving into a playful smile. It was as though he sensed her change in mood, felt her slipping away.

"Let me come with you to Shimoda this summer."

She looked into his eyes and shook her head, suddenly, painfully, aware of Sumiko and all the lives she held in her hands.

"We can still be together there," he persisted, but Rina frowned once more.

"My family will be with me."

"Then meet me in Atami? Rina, look at me," he pleaded, but she would not.

"I have to go home," she said softly. Then she walked away, leaving him standing there, alone before the cakes.

Kaitarō watched Rina leave, realizing that he might never get used to this feeling—this fear of being without her. Out of the corner of his eye he saw a movement at the edge of the food hall, a satchel being adjusted. Kaitarō followed, going up the escalators and into the main lobby. He exited the store and walked for a couple of blocks, pausing on a street lined with telephone poles. In the aftermath of a short rain shower, crows perched on the thin black power lines, scattering raindrops on the unwary and observing the people below.

Haru was at the end of the street in a brown leather jacket; he was still wearing the baseball cap he'd had on in the food court. He stood and waited as the traffic lights turned red. Kaitarō put a hand on his shoulder.

"Kai,"

"Hey." Gesturing for Haru's satchel, Kaitarō took it from his hands and lifted the camera out of the bag, flipping it over.

"Did you get what you wanted?" he asked.

"Yeah—"

Kaitarō nodded, unclipping the back of the camera and ejecting the finished roll within. Then, before Haru could stop him, he tugged on the film itself, pulling it out in reams between his fingers, exposing it to the light. For a second he paused, studying the lens of the camera before driving it into the wall at his side. Heedless of the shattered glass at his feet, he looked at Haru once more.

"Don't follow me again."

# *THE SCENT OF ORANGES*

When Rina awoke she was alone at Washikura in Shimoda. Yoshi had come in to say good-bye just before he took Sumi to Mount Fuji for their overnight trip. She remembered waving sleepily at him from under the covers as he bent to ruffle her hair. He must have opened the wooden shutters too for she could see that the sun was high in the sky, its light filtering down through the filmy summer curtains. She felt the breeze, cool on her skin, and just beyond the open window she could hear the sound of the sea.

Stretching, Rina slid down into the sun-warmed sheets. There was solitude that was unwanted and then there were moments when it was pure bliss. She had not been happy in her own company for some years, but as the summer drew to a close she was beginning to feel whole again, relaxed, and at peace. Satō was in Tokyo, he had never liked Shimoda, and so alone in her family's home, Rina knew that that day she could be herself, without fear of interruption.

She opened her eyes once more and saw the Canon EOS 3500 resting on the windowsill in its new leather case, her gift from Kaitarō. She thought of the photos they had taken together on the hillside above Atami, of the light filtering down to them through the leaves. She could smell the bittersweet scent of the orange as she split its thick skin, hear the rainfall battering the car as they sat within and talked; she could feel Kaitarō's finger rough against her mouth as he told her he loved her. Slowly, she raised herself on an elbow and reached for her camera. She slipped it out of its case, enjoying the weight of it in her palm.

When the phone rang she was out of bed and downstairs in seconds, breathless by the time she lifted the receiver.

"Hi."

"It's me."

"I know," Rina said smiling. "They've gone."

They met in the bay. Tufts of dried seaweed rolled in the breeze as Rina made her way down to the beach, following the rocky path that led from her garden. She had bought a red broad-brimmed hat and she was wearing it with a matching bikini. Lowering herself to the ground, she sat with her back to the hillside and waited for the crunch of his footsteps on the sand.

"You took your time."

"Not all of us have private access to the coast," he replied, settling down next to her.

Rina turned to look at him over her shoulder.

"Hi," she said.

"Hi."

They were both grinning.

Together, they looked out over the sea. The beach was bright and clear; there were no bottles, junk food wrappers or plastic detritus, only branches of driftwood scattered at the edges, some of it white, ossified like bone. Were she alone, Rina would have tied it into bundles and carried it up to the wood burner in the house, but that day she wanted nothing more than to sit beside Kaitarō, their shoulders just touching, while before them the sun danced upon the waves.

Rina tilted her head towards him, savoring his nearness. She could smell the summer on him, warm skin beneath a cotton shirt. He turned to look at her and a smile curved his lips, but his eyes were solemn, intent. She knew suddenly that he was going to kiss her. With a smile of her own, she rose to her feet, discarding her hat on the sand, and ran towards the water.

═

"Rina!" Kaitarō shouted after her, laughing in frustration. He began to unbutton his shirt as she headed into the sea. There was a bank of shingle at the edge of the water, and Rina shrieked sliding down into the waves as a small avalanche slipped away beneath her feet.

"Rina, stop!" Kaitarō shouted. "It will be cold!"

"City boy," she called, turning to face him. The water was up to her waist and it had splashed the top of her bikini, darkening the fabric.

Kaitarō's hand went to the top button of his jeans. Rina was still watching him on the beach, her smile openly taunting. "I'm coming in there," he called. But Rina just laughed. "I'd like to see that!" she shouted, sinking into the clean blue of the bay and striking forward, the water of the Pacific encircling her. Kaitarō watched her swim, admiring her sure, strong strokes. There were a few clouds overhead. The water was gray in the shadows and blue in the sun as Kaitarō anticipated the steep shelf beyond the shingle and shallow dived into the waves, following her. When his head broke through the surface, she was swimming away from him, drawing him into deep water, farther and farther out, until only a wisp of the summer's warmth lingered in the waves. But she didn't flinch at the cold and neither did he. She clearly loved the sea, a woman who was comfortable with the currents and knew the tides. She drifted ahead of him, swimming slowly, underestimating the speed he was capable of. She jumped when he grabbed her ankle, and tried to swim away, but he held her fast, his hand traveling up her calf, her knee, to the top of her thigh. Hooking a finger into her bikini bottoms, he pulled her towards him. "I was born by the sea," he said as the water ebbed and flowed all around them. "This sea. We've been together all along."

Rina was silent as the waves lapped at her shoulders, rising up her neck. She drifted with him, so close he could almost feel the smoothness of her body along his, her long pale limbs treading water in front of him. She licked a drop of salt from her bottom lip and closed the gap between them in the water. "Well that explains it," her gaze drifted to his lips reddened by the wind. "I don't like city boys," she said, before curving her hand around his neck and kissing him full on the mouth.

Kaitarō shuddered and reached up to cup her face, sliding his fingers into her hair. His hands were rough as he pulled her to him. A trail of water ran down her neck and Kaitarō followed it, licking the salt, tasting her skin beneath the taste of the sea. His hands travelled lower and he lifted her, wrapping her legs around him. His breath grew ragged as she gripped him with her thighs, pressing herself against him.

"You're going to drown me," he gasped, holding them afloat in the waves.

"Really," Rina smiled, her grin bright and challenging. "I thought you were born to this?"

Kaitarō flexed his hands at her waist and would have replied but in that moment Rina pushed down on his shoulders, propelling him away from her and shoving him with all her might beneath the waves.

When he resurfaced, choking on surprise and the sea, she was yards ahead of him, swimming away in a fast front crawl. For a moment he treaded water and then he moved to follow, keeping his head above the waves so he could watch her as she reached the beach. Rina swam to the shingle bank and climbed from the water, crossing to his bag, which he'd left on the sand. There was a curve to her lips as she glanced back at him, and then she bent down, rifled through his things and lifted out his shirt. She put it on over her wet bikini, adjusting the collar and doing up the buttons. Then, with a last look at him, she picked up her hat and made her way up the stairs towards her home, knowing he would follow.

The sky had darkened by the time Kaitarō dressed and climbed the stairs to the house. A storm was building on the horizon, turning the clouds the color of mussel shells. Looking at them, he thought that within the hour they would tip forward and pour into the sea, engulfing the peninsula in rain and fog. He entered the house through a side door and crossed the small den. This room had to be Rina's, for her books and magazines were strewn across the floor along with her flip-flops, beach gear, and a child's small red bucket and spade. He walked farther into the house, into the living room, listening for her all the while. To his left he found the kitchen and then suddenly there was she was, still in his shirt. The water from her bikini had seeped through the fabric, molding it to her.

"Stealing my things?" he said.

"What's yours is mine."

"You're lucky I think it's damn sexy," he replied, and Rina laughed.

She left the kettle to boil on the stovetop and turned to the fridge to locate a foil packet of tea. Kaitarō leaned against the door jam and watched her, wondering at the grace of her, the ease of her in this domestic space, but he was unable to read her expression. Rina added two spoonfuls of tea to a small clay pot and as she did so her hair fell forward, obscuring her face. He watched as she poured boiling water into two cups, filling them to the brim and then adding these to the pot in turn, ensuring that the tea would be of equal strength for each cup and that there would be exactly enough for both of them.

When she turned to him he was still lounging in the doorway, and Kaitarō was gratified to see a blush rise to her cheeks. She swallowed and rested her hand on the counter next to the teapot. "I'll leave it to steep while I light the wood burner," she said.

"I can light it," Kaitarō replied, and Rina raised an eyebrow in question.

"We had one at home," he said, stepping back from the doorway and allowing her to precede him into the living room. Together they knelt on the floor by the stove and Rina handed him the kindling and paper. From the basket by his side, Kaitarō selected a pair of small logs and a larger one, positioning each so they would burn to best effect. Then he lit a match and touched it to the twists of paper, watching as the flames stretched towards the wood, singeing and finally engulfing it.

"Told you," he said, turning to face her.

Rina nodded, staring into the flames. "So many skills," she said, rising to her feet. She smiled as Kaitarō reached for her and took an answering step back. Kaitarō paused, amused and infuriated by the teasing in her eyes. She stood before him, still in his shirt, her legs bare all the way up to the pale skin of her thighs. Her lips curved in challenge.

"Keep going," he said with a lift of his chin, and she did, stepping away from him as he matched her step for step, stalking her, until her back was against the wall and there was nothing between them but his shirt.

Reaching beneath the damp fabric, he ran a hand up her stomach to her bikini top, untying it at her neck and back, before dropping it to the floor. Her eyes lifted to his face as his hands found her nipples, pebbled with desire, and pinched them, hard. She gasped and he pressed his lips to hers, swallowing her next cry with his mouth before traveling down, down once more to her breasts so that he could draw her nipple into his mouth, suckling her through the fabric of his shirt. Rina stretched beneath him, her fingernails digging into his scalp as she pulled him up to her, no longer laughing. Their breaths mingled and fused as he pressed her into the wall. Kaitarō kissed her openmouthed and felt her hands leave him. He nuzzled her in rebuke until he realized that she had reached under the shirt to her bikini bottoms, had tugged them off and dropped them, so they now lay on the floor. For a moment Kaitarō forgot to breathe, and then he stepped forward to stand between her thighs, lifting her, pushing himself against her, while Rina licked and bit and kissed at his neck.

Kaitarō slid his hand down between her legs and the slick warmth of her was almost his undoing. For weeks, months, he had dreamed of making love to Rina, he had imagined a slow seduction on fresh sheets, he had imagined the caramel-salt sweetness of her as he licked between her thighs, imagined driving her to such pleasure that she could barely breathe, but now as his fingers slipped into the warmth of her body all he could think about was being inside her, of baring her whole self to his mouth so that there was nothing between them but skin. Trembling, he slipped the top two buttons from his shirt and then the third, before she said something that made his hands still and stop.

"I'm not ready," she murmured.

"Oh gods," Kaitarō leaned his forehead against hers, breathing hard. She was so wet he didn't want to believe her, but he had to and so he stopped, blood roaring through his veins while he felt the warm puffs of her breath against his face.

"I'm joking," she whispered, trailing tiny kisses along his cheek to his ear. "I'm joking! I'm joking."

"Not funny," Kaitarō breathed, tugging roughly at the shirt.

"Careful!" Rina squealed as the remaining buttons went flying, skittering across the floor.

"I don't care," Kaitarō said, pressing himself against her. His hands shoved at the fabric until her bare breasts were revealed, high and taut, her nipples soft, like satin, and dark. Holding her still for his kiss, he lifted her, widening her thighs until she was fully open to him. Rina whimpered and wrapped her legs around him, gripping him tight until he pushed inside her hard, filling her. A tremor of pleasure ran through him as he began to move. He kissed her ear, her cheek, her lips, all the while building a rhythm. At last he tasted her nipples and her sharp moan made him thrust into her harder still. She shuddered against him, and his lips found the soft skin under her jaw where her pulse thundered beneath his mouth. Faintly, he remembered that he'd meant to look at all of her properly, to explore every inch, but the feel of her was already more than he could bear. "Tell me to stop and I will." He sounded hoarse, nothing like himself. "Never," she whispered, and he felt her clench around him, drawing him in deeper, the slide of her against him urging him on until finally he lost control and pounded into her again and again, driving them both to a fracturing climax where their cries became shouts.

═

They lay on the floor in a tangle of limbs and sweat. Rina was curled in his arms, her head on his chest, enjoying the rapid beating of his heart. Slowly, she turned her head and smiled at him, loving the stroke of his hand on her back, the way his fingers smoothed over her bottom and playfully squeezed. She raised herself on his chest to look at him properly. He opened his eyes and a small, wondering smile played on his lips as he reached out to trace the sweep of her brow, her cheekbone, the fullness of her bottom lip. Smiling in return, Rina kissed the pad of his thumb and then gently bit it.

"So you love me, do you?" she asked, delight spreading through her at his slow, confident nod. "Have there been many women, in Tokyo?" she persisted, watching as the light in his eyes softened and dimmed.

"None like you," he said.

"What about in Hokkaido?" Rina asked, her eyes traveling over his face, leaning up to kiss his nose and the crease between his brows where he frowned.

"There was one," he said, "but I couldn't stay, not even for her." Rina lay down on her side in the crook of his arm, facing him. Kaitarō ran his hand along her back, keeping her close. She loved the way he looked at her, loved his concentrated stare that could read her mind, as though they might become one person. He smiled as he watched her. "Go on, ask," he said.

Rina reached up to touch his face, stroking his cheek with her fingers. "This other girl, did she know about your dad? And your mum?"

"Some of it," Kaitarō said quietly. "She knows that I ran away."

"That wasn't your fault," she said. "That was self-preservation," she added, softening his derision with a kiss. "And you had to live as you wanted to."

"I didn't understand my parents," he said slowly. "I let my mother down, but why didn't she leave?"

Rina drew her fingers through his hair as though trying to soothe him with her touch.

"There were times I despised her. . . . Can you understand that Rina?"

Curled against him, she nodded, though she said nothing, waiting for him to go on.

"She should have put herself, both of us, beyond his reach. And then she . . . blamed me." His mouth tightened and he lowered his gaze.

"You loved and hated them," Rina said finally. She raised herself up on her elbow to look at him, and he visibly relaxed when she pressed a soft kiss to his cheek. "That's understandable too," she said, smiling at his doubtful expression.

"I think she set you free, Kai." Slowly, Rina stroked the hair at his nape, and then pulled him to her so that they lay skin to skin. "You didn't belong there," she said, wrapping her arms around him, "and she gave you permission to go. You can still contact her. Make amends?" she added, pressing her forehead to his, sensing in that way they had with each other that she had reached him and his mood was lifting.

"You really have never told anyone else?" Rina persisted.

Kaitarō shook his head with a quiet laugh. "It wouldn't go over well with the Tokyo girls," he said, and Rina smiled at the look in his eyes, the wonder, as he rolled her onto her back, rose above her, kissing his way across her cheek to her mouth. Rina turned her face into his neck, enjoying the slide of his hands down her body, nipping at his ear when he stopped. He was looking at something over her shoulder.

"What's that?" he asked

Rina turned and then smiled. "You know what that is. It's a Polaroid camera."

"When did you—"

"After our day in Atami," she said. "I love the camera you gave me. I wanted to get one for Sumiko, something she can play with."

"And what will you do with the camera I gave you?" he asked, and she grinned at the seriousness of his expression.

"I thought," she said, tentatively walking her fingers up his chest, "that I would take Sumi out to photograph the coastline. We don't have much of the summer left, but we could play in the coves and I could photograph her by the sea."

"A new project?" he asked, his voice low, and Rina nodded in affirmation, enjoying the satisfaction she saw in his gaze.

"Can I come?" he asked, and Rina's heart swelled at the uncertainty in his eyes, how much it would mean to him. How much it would mean to her.

"Yes," Rina said, watching his eyes widen in surprise. "Now, let me up. I have to make dinner."

"Dinner?" he asked, reaching for her, pressing kisses to her neck, the corner of her mouth.

"Real food first," she said, pushing him off and rising quickly to her feet. She felt his hand close around her ankle and stroke up her calf. "Stop that!" she scolded, but without heat. Stepping over him she bent to pick up his shirt where it had fallen on the floor and, pulling it on, walked into the kitchen.

"I'm making something special," she said as he came to stand behind her. She was rinsing clams in a basin in the sink and all the sand had drifted to the bottom. The newspaper the fishmonger had wrapped them in lay damp and unfurled on the side. Rina smiled as Kaitarō pressed a kiss to her nape and then another beneath her jaw. She felt his arms tighten as he hugged her to him, lifting her a little off her feet. Rina laughed. "I'll be ten minutes!" she said, and as he took this as his cue to leave, but instead she grasped his hand. "No . . . no," she said, drawing him back to her, "stay with me." She felt him rest his chin on her shoulder and she turned, kissing the stubble of his cheek. She glanced at the packet of Italian pasta on the side and a mise en place of garlic, chili, and herbs that she had made earlier.

"Let me help you," he said, laughing as Rina quickly shook her head.

"I can do it," he said. "I can cook pasta."

Rina stopped sifting through the clams and held a finger up, her eyes serious. "This is not *just* pasta."

Kaitarō grabbed her outstretched hand. "I know . . . good pasta. I can make good pasta."

"Al dente?" Rina persisted, but he just laughed, palms up, and backed away in surrender. She sautéed the garlic and chili, then left them to cool on the stovetop. She had just placed the linguine in the pan when he returned to the kitchen.

"If you want to eat sometime tonight, I wouldn't disturb me," she warned. "There's white wine in the fridge," she said, still sensing him behind her.

"Come with me."

Turning, Rina saw that he was hiding something behind his back, and taking his outstretched hand she allowed him to draw her to him. When she was close, close enough to kiss, Kaitarō produced the Polaroid camera.

"No!" Rina shrieked, pushing past him and running into the living room. "I'm not ready for my close-up!"

"You look scrumptious."

"Let me go! You beast!" She squealed as he grabbed her wrist, wrestling with him until he reached the large leather chair by the fire and tugged her onto his lap.

"There's sand in my hair."

"You're gorgeous."

"Give me that," she said, reaching over his head for the camera.

Kaitarō clamped an arm around her waist and pulled her down to him. "Sit still"—he brushed his nose gently against hers—"or I'll spank you!"

She was laughing when he brought the camera up and took the shot.

"Give it to me," she said, and he did. "You have to hold it like this," she said, grinning as his arms enfolded her.

Together they looked into the lens and their smiles were wide, happy. They took another and another, laughing, fighting over the camera as blank black squares littered the floor. Eventually, Kaitarō turned Rina into his arms and she smiled against his mouth just as the pasta timer sounded from the kitchen, a sharp triple beep.

"Stay with me," Kaitarō said. His hands were at her waist, but his grip was light. Rina bent down to collect the photos from the floor and then settled back against him. Sitting in his lap, they flicked through them, giggling and debating, until they found the ones they would keep. Rina kept two for herself and put them on a side table.

Kaitarō looked at her suddenly anxious. "You will be careful?" he said. "Don't let anyone see them," he persisted.

"I'll keep us safe."

"Promise?" he said, kissing her once more. He cradled her face in his hands, and she returned his gaze. Then she smiled and he did too.

"I promise," she said.

## *REFLECTION*

Kaitarō stood by the window in his motel room. On the nightstand his pager beeped with a message from the office, but he ignored it. It had been hours since he had left Rina in Shimoda, but he knew he would not sleep. He looked up at the sky, the great ink expanse of it, and opened the window, leaning out. Below him the pavement gleamed like a mirror in the dark wet of the evening. The clouds of earlier had made good on their promise and Kai could hear the gutters of the town overflowing with rainwater. He looked at the buildings on either side of his motel, at the lodges and spas covering the hills, and his gaze followed the streetlights straight down to the bay and the boardwalk, a flat stretch of concrete facing the sea. The yachts in the harbor bobbed on the waves, their taillights glinting in the darkness.

Reaching into his pocket he took out a box of matches and placed them on the desk in front of him. Then he lifted up a small metal bin and set that in front of him too. He was still wearing the fleece Rina had given him that afternoon. There was a lingering trace of her in the fabric, like a touch. In the drawer of the desk was the handkerchief he had taken from her in the orchard days before. Kaitarō raised the material to his face for a moment, before striking a match, lighting the silk, and watching it catch and flame. Slowly, he lowered it into the metal bin. In his pocket were the Polaroids.

He had left most of them with Rina and her promise to hide them away, but he had kept three for himself. There was one of her laughing, squirming off his lap, and another, just her curled before the fire, wearing his shirt. He looked at them for some time, feeling the texture of them beneath his fingertips. They were so precious to him, so valuable, but they were also all the evidence that Satō would ever need. He lifted them in his hands and one by one consigned them to the flames, watching the plastic bubble and peel away from the film, the images crumpling, melting. As he controlled the fire, the heat of it warmed his face. Extracting a cigarette from his satchel, he lit it and inhaled slowly. Rina hated cigarettes so he never smoked around her, was trying to give up, but as the nicotine of this last hit his system he breathed out, watching the smoke dissipate into the air, a rare and final pleasure.

Eventually, he flicked the cigarette into the trash and doused the fire with a bottle of water. The paper had blackened and curled in on itself and he placed the bin outside on the windowsill. Tendrils of smoke wafted up, curling into the air, while above him the moon rose clear over the bay and the summer sky, washed clean by the rain, shone beyond the lights of Atami into the distance.

# *Sumiko*

## *SHOES*

I always struggle to imagine my mother when she was young. When I think of her it is as my mother and I cannot picture her any other way. Do you ever think of your parents like this? Perhaps in their youth when they had just met and were falling in love, two people interested only in themselves with no notion of you; people leading different lives. My mother led a life without me. The difference is that she did this both before and after I was born.

Through the years the idea of her has haunted me. I return constantly to her life. I still feel that if only I could look hard enough at the traces I have left, perhaps see them in a different way, that then I could see her: a young woman at her work, a woman in love, a mother trying to do the right thing. There were so many events in her life that I have no access to, experiences she kept to herself. Still, I cannot help but wonder whether if she had lived, perhaps one day she would have shared them with me, and then we could have seen ourselves in each other as mothers and daughters do.

There is not much left. As a child I hoarded her things, afraid that like her photograph on our family altar, they would be taken away. But I do have something of hers, something she gave to me, a plane ticket from Hokkaido to put in my scrap book. She brought me other things as well. I have a memory of a Baumkuchen, a layered log cake, coated in white and dark chocolate to resemble the bark of a silver birch. It was extraordinary. When I first saw it I thought it was a branch from a tree, but inside were the thin layers of sponge, and I was told that it was so delicious and smooth, like a sunburst on the tongue, because it was made with butter from Hokkaido. I have always had a fondness for Baumkuchen, but I don't know if it started with this cake, and of course we ate it, so now there is nothing left, no trace of what might have been.

When the divorce was finalized, my mother came to live with me and Grandpa in Meguro. She stayed with us only for a few months, but the plane ticket is from that time, from a short trip that she took then. She said it was an adventure, like finding the new apartment for us in Shinagawa, that she was going on ahead to explore a new home for me. She said Hokkaido would become very special for both of us and that she would take me there, but of course she never did.

When she died, Grandpa brought what remained of her life home to me in Meguro. He carried her belongings into the house and put them in the room she had grown up in; the room next to mine.

Even as a child, I could tell there was a great deal missing: there were no books, no photographs, no cameras. There were only a few items of her clothing, her shoes, her formal kimono still wrapped in paper, a small box of jewelry, her calligraphy brushes, and, finally, sachets of her scent—packets of the coffee-colored powder worn by the monks to purify themselves before temple and sold in Ginza for a hundred yen a pack. I grew up knowing that smell on her skin, so I have never associated it with men or temples. Just her. And the pine forest above our house in Shimoda.

For so long these things were all I had, and I treasured them. As I grew older, I visited them in secret, taking care never to let Grandpa see me, for I was convinced that if I did not cry or make a fuss that he would forget they were there and let me keep them.

When Yurie Kagashima first gave me the case file on my mother's murder, its contents obsessed me. I laid out all the documents across our dining room table, filling the space where once my grandfather had eaten breakfast and cut out newspaper clippings for me to read before work. Still, after a time, even as fact upon fact and detail upon detail began to settle in my mind, it was her belongings that drew me. They called to me from her room until I abandoned the case file downstairs and found myself opening the doors to her wardrobe, sinking to my knees on the carpet.

I have always loved my mother's shoes. That day when I looked at them in their final resting place there was a timeless quality to each pair, as though they would outlast even me. The shoes were lined up on metal racks inside her closet in a parody of how she herself would have arranged them earlier in life. Then, they would have been part of an evolving collection as she moved from school to university to young adult life, changing, shifting along the rows as old pairs were moved to the back and new pairs were placed in front. But, as I looked at them then, the collection was static, final. All that remained of her had been left in Meguro, like me.

Even when she was alive, I marveled at her shoes. I wondered where she wore them—the black pumps with the bows over the toes in silver and gold; the white trainers with holes in the heel; navy pumps, thick and stocky, like those a legal intern would wear; and my favorites, low heels of dark red, open at the toes, with thin straps that wrapped around her ankles. These were the shoes that I went for as a child, the ones I tried on. I found that if I stuffed tissue into the toes I could slide my feet inside and secure them enough by tying the straps. The imprint of her foot remains, a pinched crease in the leather; this was a pair that was well loved by both of us.

Kneeling before her closet, I reached for the red shoes once more, our favorites, bought one year before she died. She had worn them out to dinner in Shimoda during our last summer together, and again when she had driven away in her car to Atami. And that autumn, when we all returned to Tokyo, she wore them when she took me to visit Grandpa in Meguro. Sitting on the floor, legs crossed like a child, I pressed the shoes to my face and inhaled the dusty scent of camphor, recalling that afternoon.

As soon as we arrived, Mama left the red sandals on the outdoor footwear rack in the hall, and I snatched them up, running upstairs with them to her old bedroom while she and Grandpa made tea downstairs. I sat on the carpet and spread the skirt of my new dress—white with pink peonies in the fabric—out all around me. Then I lay back on the floor, watching as the dust motes floated down from the ceiling. By the front door were the pink ballet shoes my mother had bought me to match my new outfit, but that afternoon I wanted to be my mother; I wanted to be just like her. I knew that it was my childhood that separated us.

I lifted her red shoes in my hands, tracing the intricate stitching with my fingers, feeling the soft silk of the leather against my skin. Then I stood and slipped my feet into them. My heel only reached halfway up the sole, but if I faced the mirror straight on, the shoes looked like they were mine. I perched first on one foot and then on the other, bending to secure the straps. I liked how I looked in them—I was taller, and my thin legs were elegant, graceful. I could be a lady, I thought, a lady with red shoes and red painted nails.

I heard Grandpa and Mama walk into the hallway. Their conversation had started in whispers but their voices were rising. The doorbell rang as I turned from side to side. Grandpa's voice rose to a shout. I heard my mother move towards the door. She was walking away from him.

"I won't have it, Rina," I heard him say, "not in this house."

"Sumi!" My mother called. "Where are you?"

I looked down at the straps around my ankles, at the bows so neat and symmetrical; they were the best bows I had ever tied.

"Sumi! Take off my shoes and come downstairs. There's a friend of ours here who wants to say hello to you."

I wrinkled my nose at myself in the mirror. Sitting on the floor, I undid my handiwork, unraveling the bows. Thinking of my boring ballet shoes waiting for me in the hall, I came out onto the landing. Grandpa was standing by the front door, rigid in his anger. "Not in my house," he repeated.

"Then we'll leave your house, Yoshi," my mother said. As I came down the stairs, I passed the red sandals to her and she handed my own shoes to me. Then she opened the front door and went out into the sunlight to meet the friend standing in our garden- he had bought me an ice cream that summer. As I followed her, he turned towards us and smiled. I liked his smile.

# *Rina and Kaitarō*

## *DOLLS*

Rina transferred her groceries to one hand and lifted the latch of the gate with the other. Even from the driveway she could hear Sumiko's shrieks of laughter as she played inside the house with her grandfather. Although it was only autumn, Yoshi was already pestering Rina about Girls' Day and how they would celebrate in the coming year. He returned again and again to the collection of Hinamatsuri dolls she still kept at his house, asking when she would move them to her and Satō's apartment in Ebisu. It had started some days before when Rina had allowed Kai to drop by and see them at the Meguro house, and although she'd argued that he was just a friend, Yoshi had not believed her. Since then his disapproval had simmered between them and Rina could only wait for its latest manifestation. Perhaps he had brought the dolls out of storage. It would explain Sumiko's excitement too.

Fitting her key into the lock Rina let herself in and set her shopping down by the door. She was just changing her outdoor shoes for house slippers when she suddenly caught sight of herself in the hall mirror. The mirror had hung in her home ever since she could remember, and it had existed before then, in her mother's house, recording all who entered and left, reflecting the lives of her family. Normally Rina would hang up her coat and walk past without a second glance, but that day there was something she saw that gave her pause: Rina had always been able to recognize herself in the mirror. In every age, every mood, she had been able to see herself clearly, as she really was, but that day as she looked into the glass, her face half in and out of the reflection, she did not resemble herself. For a moment she stood very still, waiting for a glimpse of the person she knew, a woman who was prepared to live with her choices. She shut her eyes and then opened them again, seeking something in the glass, but there was only the vanishing point along the beveled edge—the point where she and all the women before her disappeared into the half-light of the afternoon shining through the front door.

Rina started as the clock on the wall began to chime, and suddenly Sumiko ran into the hall. "Mummy come look, come see!" she said, taking Rina's hand. Sliding into her house slippers Rina followed her child into the living room and saw that it was so; Yoshi had indeed brought out the dolls. He had even hefted the lacquer display of wide black steps up from the basement and set it up in the living room, assembling all the figures along it from the emperor and empress at the top to the ladies, musicians, ministers, and servants at the bottom. Her father was sitting on the floor arranging a fan in the empress's hand and placing tiny swords on the stands before each samurai warrior, everything just so. He sat back to admire the display, and Rina's eye was drawn to the finery: the tiny ceremonial rice cakes her mother had once purchased in pale peach, green, and white, and the intricate betrothal gifts—for not only did the dolls represent the imperial court, they were also attired for a wedding. The dream and duty of all young girls. Rina turned away and caught sight of an anthology of Bashō on a side table that Yoshi had read to her as a child; doubtless he had been showing the same poems to Sumi. Unbidden, one of them came to her mind:

*Behind this door*
*Now buried in deep grass*
*A different generation will celebrate*
*The Festival of Dolls.*

"You shouldn't spoil her like this," Rina protested, glaring at her father. "Now she will talk of nothing else and she will not want to put the dolls away." Sumiko had settled on the floor next to Yoshi. She ignored the rebuke and was counting all twelve layers of the empress's tiny kimono, touching the delicate porcelain hands that extended from the pressed silk.

"You should take them home with you, Rinachan," Yoshi said. "You cannot continue to celebrate Girl's Day with that small set of figures you have in Ebisu. They are nothing in comparison to this." With a glance he took in the assembled dolls, row upon row, collected over generations to celebrate the Sarashima girls.

Rina bit her lip and nodded, as she did when she did not want to take her father on. "There is no space in Ebisu," she murmured, but he did not hear. The trouble was that her father was right; this was Sumiko's heritage. She was always so excited to see the dolls displayed at school and in the houses of her friends. She loved to think of families across the islands setting up displays in their homes, and she treasured the small set that Rina had in Ebisu.

Every year, in the weeks leading up to the third of March, Rina would choose a special day to set the dolls up early. She was very careful to put the whole set away by the end of Girls' Day itself, because otherwise Sumiko would be late to be a bride. But for a few weeks at least, the whole family could enjoy the dolls and Sumi, loved to guess when Rina would put them up. Each morning she would run down the corridor to Rina and Satō's bedroom. They didn't receive much warning, only the beat of small feet in the hallway and the rush of air into the room as a small body catapulted itself onto the bed, lifting the blankets between them and snuggling down. "Mummy! Daddy! Are they ready? Are the dolls up?" she would ask, shrieking as Rina tickled her and pretended to wrap her into a sushi roll. Satō would laugh too, reaching out to stroke Sumi's hair. He had never shared anything like this with his parents. They did not discuss it, but Rina knew, and so the tentative softening that occurred in these moments was all the more precious. She felt it keenly now as she thought of Satō and how their eyes met above their daughter, for it was at times like these when Rina saw most clearly the value of what was between them. Together they looked down at their girl, at her pale skin, the long dark sweep of her eyelashes, the gleam in her eyes, and knew that they would never again create anything so exquisite and pure.

"Girl's Day is not until March, Dad. I will pick them up then."

Yoshi stopped fussing with the dolls and for a moment he looked up and held his daughter's gaze. "You should take them now," he said. "Ebisu is your home; it is where your husband is. Is that going to change?"

## *MAKE-BELIEVE*

Rina could feel Kaitarō behind her on the stairs. The building was a walk-up, no porter, no lift. Her skirt brushed against her thighs as she climbed, and she was aware of the click of her heels on the concrete. She had thought about this so often, where he lived, where he spent the time he was not with her. It was becoming increasingly difficult to be together. Since the episode with the dolls, Yoshi's disapproval had only become more explicit. Now he was refusing to look after Sumiko, so Rina found it nearly impossible to get away. Kaitarō also said they had to be careful in public. He never stood too close, brushed her hand, or touched her face. He had not kissed her since Shimoda. Out of desperation she had suggested that they go to a love ho for a couple of hours, but he had not wanted that; he had wanted to bring her here, to his home.

All through the subway ride Rina thought of what would happen when they reached his apartment and were finally alone together. She remembered his touch, the feel of their limbs as they'd swum together and kissed in the sea. She recalled everything, but she did not turn to him as she held the hand rail on the train. She merely stood still, keeping a careful distance between them, all the way to Asakusa.

Kai reached around her to open the door to his apartment and his jacket brushed her sleeve as he let her enter first. She stepped directly into the kitchen. A gray stove lined one wall with an extraction fan above it. Opposite there was counter space for a kettle and one drawer for pots and pans. The apartment was a long, narrow room, like a corridor, leading to the bedroom. Rina walked past the tiny shower stall, conscious of him behind her, of his eyes upon her as she looked at his home.

The bedroom was more spacious with a double bed, a desk, and a window, which thankfully let in some light. Rina turned and smiled at Kaitarō, who had been watching her from the doorway. There were clothes and books scattered across the bed, and his camera was on his desk along with his portfolio. The closet had been left hanging open, and within it she saw a biker jacket. "From Hokkaido?" she asked, and he nodded

"Just need another bike," he said, but Rina shook her head.

"You'd take Sumi on it. I cannot allow that," she said, and he laughed.

Turning away from him, Rina moved to the window and looked out at the view. She could see a monorail train tilting sharply into a curve, compelling its passengers to look down on the canals, motorways, and junctions of the city below, while on the ground people ran frantically, eyes flicking up to the rails overhead, anxious to catch their trains. For a second Rina shuddered, thinking of the crush of the station, of standing flush to the edge of the platform as the train came in, with hundreds of eyes behind glass doors peering into her life, inches from her face. She took a deep breath and then Kai was there, one hand warm on her back and the other reaching up to close the curtains and block out the world outside. Gratefully she turned to him, conscious only of his nearness, the calming scent of him, the intimacy of his things all around them, the close quarters of the room, and them, finally alone, together.

"Would you like a drink?"

Rina shook her head. As always his proximity was making her dizzy. She remembered the last time he'd held her, his hands and mouth on her body, his shirt still infused with the scent of him and stuffed into the bottom of a wooden box in the den in Shimoda. She reached out and touched him, feeling the pulse of his heart in his chest. "Rina," he murmured, covering her hand with his, "stay with me." She kept her eyes on his face, and as if he knew what she was thinking he said, "We can get a place, somewhere for us and Sumiko." Rina placed her finger over his mouth, pressing down on the soft, delicate skin. He slipped his hands around her waist, sure and possessive. She loved the security of this man, his confidence. She looked around at the life he had built, his hard-won independence.

"You can't rescue me, Kai," she said. "I'm not good for you," she added, and he laughed. "There is so much ahead of you. You should visit Hokkaido and start your photography firm."

"Not without you."

"I shouldn't be here," she continued as he reached up to cup her cheek, the warmth of his palm radiating through her skin. "I'm not strong enough, not brave." He put his hand on the back of her neck and pulled her close, close enough that she could feel his breath on her face.

His hand increased its pressure, stroking, soothing her. "Rina," he whispered, "you're wrong." Then he kissed her, kissed her deeply and so completely that she felt herself being drawn into him, falling further and further into his arms, a woman playing make-believe.

## *KARASU*

It had been many years since Kaitarō had come to Tokyo, and he had been many people since then: many men to many women. But this time, he wanted to stay. This time, with Rina, he had slipped back into his own skin, and the rightness of it, the ease of being his original self, was a balm to his soul.

Since he'd met her he had been able to think more clearly, as though the energy he had once expended in reading other people and fitting around them had been diverted back into his mind. The natural fluidity of being able to express true joy when he felt it and sadness and doubt when he did not was so liberating he could almost be free. Even his guilt about leaving Hokkaido had eased and he had begun to think of making amends. Still, at night he lay awake. Since Shimoda, Kaitarō could not sleep. His pager beeped constantly with messages from work that he tried to ignore. Only Rina's presence could soothe him, and when he was not with her he thought of all the things he had told her—the truth about his home and the lies about his current life—lies that had built up one by one until he could not escape them. At night they encircled him, settling suffocatingly over his mouth.

He could sense her shock at both of them being back in Tokyo. He could feel her withdrawing, her conviction slipping. He needed her to stay with him, to *choose* him, but he could not ensure that unless he told her the truth about Satō, and then she would learn the truth about him. Night after night, he tried to think of a way out that would leave them with each other, but in the darkness of his room, with the glow of neon filtering though the curtains, no solution came. He knew that he could never tell her any of it.

Rubbing his eyes, he rose from his bed. His pager sat at the edge of his desk but he had buried it beneath several sheets of paper, most of them bills and bank statements. There was a summary of his savings. He had enough to last him three months, but no more. The rest of his money had been spent on Rina's new camera and bribes so that Haru would keep his mouth shut at work. Until recently, Takeda had been quite content, pleased with Kaitarō's updates over the summer and all he'd achieved. But now, as Takeda continued to wait in vain for the evidence and the promised report, Kai knew his excuses were wearing thin. He was running out of time.

There was half a cup of black coffee on the desk and he drank it down, welcoming the bitter jolt of it and shivering in the unheated room. Realizing it was probably the same temperature inside as out and stifled by the fears surrounding him in his apartment, Kai fled to the streets, hoping that by walking through the night, perhaps a solution would come. And it was there, staring up into the sky, that he noticed the karasu.

Black and menacing, these birds were a plague on Tokyo and an emblem; on every street corner, by fast-food shops, crawling out of rubbish bins, perching on telephone wires, they dived down upon the populace, swiping at those who passed too close to their young. They were urban pests and harbingers, carrion birds, the frequenters of battlefields. Both real and mythic.

The photographer, Masahisa Fukase, had devoted entire collections to them in the years after his wife, Yoko, left him. The original prints were coveted and hard to find. But recently in a bookstore in the backstreets of Kanda, when Rina had been unable to meet him, Kaitarō had come across a copy of the collected *Karasu* and seen for himself Fukase's homage to the corvids of Japan: the ravens of Hokkaido and the jungle crows of Tokyo.

As Kaitarō flicked through the pages, his fingers sticking to the expensive, glossy paper, he found that he could picture Fukase at the end of his marriage: smoke-stained and balding, awake on a sleeper train to Hokkaido, returning to his birthplace with nothing but a bag of underwear, a camera, and a hip flask of whiskey. Kaitarō looked at the photos and then reached up to touch his hair; he did not care for the comparison.

The pictures were extraordinary though. On each page, the birds appeared in massive flocks from a distance or as black silhouettes against gray wintry skies. The close-ups were monochrome, impressionistic and overexposed, so that huge wings spread out across the page, bleeding into the paper. They were desolate, irresistible. And yet as Kaitarō walked through his neighborhood that night, he wondered if he might photograph them too, if there was a chance he might find something else there: solace, or beauty, perhaps even redemption. The birds around him had eyes that glowed like beads of jet; their beaks gleamed, and their feathers shone iridescent in the moonlight. For a second they were visible and then they were not; they were many things to many people, and they gathered in the quiet of the night.

## *LISTEN*

Satō was mixing a gin and tonic when Kaitarō entered the apartment. He didn't even turn around as the front door opened and closed, focusing instead on adding cubes of ice to a crystal tumbler. Kaitarō stepped forward, looking for signs of Rina. He noted the large pink shell on the bureau and in it only one set of keys. Satisfied that she wasn't there, he took an unsteady breath and, ignoring the stand for his outdoor shoes, walked towards Satō, his boots heavy as he crossed the room.

"What the hell is going on?"

With a smile Satō gestured for him to take a seat. "What a pleasure to see you, Kaitarō. Can I offer you a drink?"

"What if Rina finds me here?"

Satō looked pointedly at Kaitarō's shoes, still on his feet, and then up at his hair, which was mussed and sweaty as though he'd been running. His smile broadened to a grin. "Drink?"

"Thank you, no."

"What do you think?" Satō asked gesturing to the wide open space of his living room from the white marble floor and tall windows to the cream rugs and elegant lacquer cabinets. Kaitarō followed his movements but he saw other things. His eyes were drawn to the items that were hers: there was a bunch of silk needlepoint camellias in a vase on the sideboard, her set of calligraphy brushes in their box gathering dust, and a wooden Buddha that she'd bought in Nara and once described to him. Now that he was there, he could see that the apartment was also surprisingly spare. There were a few photographs of Sumiko on the sideboard and only one shot of them as a family; it looked like it had been taken on a skiing holiday, some time ago. There was nothing more recent.

"Very nice," Kaitarō said, struggling to keep his temper under control. He looked at his watch and then favored Satō with an even expression.

"See anything you like?" Satō asked.

Kaitarō turned and took a seat on the sofa, but as he settled among the cushions he caught the scent of her—just a hint—the cedarwood powder she wore. Rina.

"It's a job to me. What do I care if you want this apartment or her trust fund?"

"You think money is all it is?"

Kai shrugged and tried not to check his watch again. Rina would be picking Sumiko up from school soon. It took her twenty minutes to get there and twenty minutes to return home. He needed to be gone by the time they got back.

"Satō," he began diplomatically, "you didn't call me here to show me your house. Tell me what it is you need and I will get it for you. What were you thinking? Do you want to blow my cover with Rina?" At this last his voice rose; he couldn't help it.

"You're not doing your job."

"I'll get it done," Kaitarō replied, leaning forward, pressing his palms together. "We are too far into this case to assign another agent."

"That's just it," Satō said, sipping his drink and walking towards the younger man. "I've spoken to Takeda. He said there was a great agent available—excellent track record."

Kaitarō swallowed and looked up, registering too late the latent fury in Satō's expression. He tried for a shrug but remained tense; he could taste the metallic tang of fear on his tongue. "You must do what you think best, but bringing in another man now will only muddy the water."

Satō snorted. "Irreplaceable, are you? Yes, your boss said you and this Haru guy were quite competitive . . ."

Kaitarō got to his feet and caught a faint trace of Rina once more. "I just need a little more time."

"You have said that before."

"Sir, I can give you everything you want."

"You were brought in to save *me* time, Nakamura," Satō said. "Time. Money. The painful conflict of a divorce." For a moment he sipped his drink and held Kaitarō's gaze. "There will be no second agent."

Kai inhaled sharply. "Thank you, sir."

"I've decided to stay married."

"What?"

"You're fired. And at the agency too. Takeda will confirm it." Satō paused, relishing the moment and the look on Kaitarō's face. "Now get out of here, before my wife finds you in our apartment."

## *ALL THAT GLITTERS*

When Rina was young she had loved the heat of the streets, the whir of the traffic outside her window. In the evenings as dusk fell, she would sit on a ledge in her bedroom barefoot, listening to jazz, tapping out the beat of the drums with her feet as the moon rose higher.

It must have been her youth that had colored everything. Tonight, the jazz didn't sound the same. It was dull, synchronized. Dusk was falling, but Rina could not hear or sense the traffic below, the footsteps of the people, the rumble of cars; the smoke and steam. Up on the twenty-eighth floor of the latest Hilton everything was silenced by tall walls of shimmering glass.

When she was a child, Yoshi had told Rina about the various transformations of Tokyo and how so many of them had come about in his lifetime. She remembered his tales of the war, a time so full of deprivation that even his cat was collected and skinned to make soldiers' mittens. She thought of the new highways and underpasses of her childhood, the vitality and freedom of her years at Tōdai, and the wealth that had flowed into Tokyo on the eve of her marriage. She wondered what her father thought of the world Satō aspired to, this world of vintage liquor cocktails sprinkled with gold leaf. He saw it for what it was, she was sure, but she also knew that he expected her to take advantage of it. Having raised her in a period of prosperity, he expected her to grasp it with both hands. When she did not, he had to settle for her marriage and, in the end, he had invested in that too. Rina knew that if she left Satō and the life they had built, the life her father believed in, she would be betraying every single member of her family.

The flute of champagne had grown warm in her hand and she put it to one side. On her right, Sumiko fidgeted in her new shoes, fingering the white lace of her dress. This was her first grown-up party, a new world, one that she very much wanted to enter. There were a few children present, but they were older and in their early teens, those that were considered suitable for adult company. Still, when she behaved herself, Sumi was eminently presentable and an asset to her father.

Satō was holding court with his business colleagues. Their wives were smiling at his jokes, crunching on triangles of fois gras toast and laughing as he delivered a punch line. Standing on the outer edge of the circle with her daughter, it was clear to Rina, if not to Sumiko, that the jokes and laughter were not for them, nor were the extensions of charm, the invitations, the promises: "When we go to dinner . . ."

A waiter approached and offered Sumi a glass of lemonade but she refused, shaking her dark head. A drink would mean that she might spill it and need to wash her hands or leave her father, and she wanted to be there when his attention turned to her.

Rina accepted the lemonade in her stead and surveyed the room. She looked at the buffet tables covered in pristine white damask, the chandeliers glinting above the crowd. The more people she was with, the more she felt alone. There was only one exception.

Turning a little, Rina noted the women who watched her, the groups who talked among themselves and turned away as she approached them. These barriers were nothing to Satō; he was good in a crowd, able to judge and infiltrate each little set, adjusting his manner to please. He didn't mind that he was being judged, that these people were pricing them up inch by inch. Satō liked to be on show; it was when he was the best form of himself.

Like her father, Sumiko was at ease in these situations. She was older than her years, as only children often are, and adept at reading adults. Sumi was excited, but she could also stand by herself with ease, happy to watch the other guests and take part in conversations when invited. She had that glorious immunity of childhood, the ability to slip between situations and generations freely.

Suddenly, the moment arrived and Satō turned to Sumiko, drawing her fully into his group. "My daughter," he said, and Sumi gave a polite little bow and accepted a canapé. Rina watched as her child was drawn away from her. She wanted to call her back, but at the same time she felt a flicker of pride as Sumi answered questions and laughed with her father and his friends. Her daughter loved praise and approbation. An easily influenced child, Yoshi said, but watching her, Rina saw only grace in her immunity and exuberance. Looking at Sumiko smiling amid the crush of strangers, Rina prayed that she would always have it.

As the minutes ticked by, Sumiko glanced back at her mother and Rina smiled, raising her glass in a toast. When Sumi was a baby and she was allowed to sit at the table with the adults, she loved to raise her handled cup at each toast, holding it out to her mother's wineglass and waiting for her to say "Kanpai!" Sumiko adored this, and it made Rina and everyone else laugh. The baby's joy was infectious as was her love of celebrating. Rina remembered the concentration of her face as she grew older and wanted to raise her cup to each person at the table, leaning over to tap their glass.

Looking around, Rina decided to give her daughter some room; she would find someone she could bear to talk to. Putting down her empty glass, she took one last look at Sumiko. She was in the thick of the party now, the shoulders of her white lace dress just visible within the group of people. Satō had found an ally and an entertainer in their child. She was confident but polite—just precocious enough.

Rina had been like that once, secure and bold. She had thought that her mother would always protect her; she had not realized that there would come a time when she would be watched by all and feel alone. Above the sound of Satō's laughter, she made a promise to herself that Sumiko would never know such isolation.

The cream of Rina's generation were in the room that night, even some of her classmates from Tōdai. She had introduced Sumiko to them earlier, and though her friends meant to be kind, she could see them measuring her child and her marriage against her potential, the dreams she'd once spoken of. Rina had laughed. Sumiko wanted to be a lawyer, she told them; perhaps there was still time for her to grow out of it. She had beamed at them and turned just as their smiles had begun to fade.

Crossing to the end of the room, Rina decided to head to the ladies' room. Perhaps a few moments of solitude would put her in a better mood. It did not help that she disliked everything about herself, even the dress she was wearing, black, beaded, and fiercely tight, but it was elegant, European, and Satō had insisted. Rina tugged at the collar as she walked.

She had not seen Kaitarō in more than two weeks, had been avoiding him, and the more he called her, the more she retreated into an almost paralyzing silence. Yoshi approved. As the weeks passed he had become ever more critical, even going so far as to remind her of the custody laws. She knew he was only trying to protect her, knew he was trying to protect Sumiko, but she was aware of what could happen just as much as he was; she did not need reminding. Before her mother died, when she was just fifteen, the two of them had spoken of Rina's marriage, packing a lifetime of advice into the months remaining to them. Her mother wanted her to be happy; she would support a divorce, she said, but not once there were children. And that was it. That was what it would always come down to, in the end, her child.

For a second she allowed herself to think of Kai. She loved him, but it could not be. The rush of attraction, the beauty of their friendship, the trust between them, had deepened into something so perfect so fast that it had allowed her to block out all else. But now that she was back in Tokyo and confronted with her life, she could see clearly what was at stake. They had thrived in the shadows, in pockets of time, snatched and secluded. They could not exist in the light.

It was a fault of hers, Rina knew; she could be so set on a course of action that she became almost willfully blind, as though she could sense consequences on the periphery of her vision but she never turned to look. She had employed this tactic at every stage of her life, in trying to make it as a photographer, in marrying Satō, in falling for Kaitarō. Only now there was an inescapable truth and she could not turn away.

There were couples who could arrange things between themselves, who would communicate through all the twists and turns of a marriage. These couples could perhaps go to the local ward office and agree terms for a divorce, but even thinking about it now made her shudder. She and Satō were not like that. There was simply too much at stake, too much to fight for, and Satō would fight, she knew. She could not take him on. She could not risk losing her child.

Behind her the party blared on. No matter how far she walked down the hotel corridor, she could not escape it, and she could not walk particularly fast in the dress anyway. She moved on past the cloakroom and stopped at an alcove overlooking the city. It was a viewing platform of sorts, framed by silk curtains with a heavy swag, private. Perhaps here she could find some peace, just for a moment. Stepping inside she walked to the tall glass window and looked out over her home, the city she had grown up in, and as always it looked right back.

Staring into the darkness, Rina felt a hand at her back as a figure stepped into the alcove with her. He was wearing black-tie and in it he looked beautiful, expensive. Like everything he did, he wore his clothes with ease. His hair, usually soft to the touch beneath her fingers, was slicked back, but his eyes, his eyes were the same; they had that warm glow that she had come to love.

"How did you get in here?" she asked, frowning and smiling at the same time. Now that he was there everything was better. "Has my husband seen you?" she asked and immediately felt ashamed, though she peeked beyond the curtain nonetheless.

He leaned a shoulder against the glass, looking only at her. "I would never let that happen," he said, and as she returned his gaze, she knew it was true.

"You haven't been taking my calls," he said, and her heart sped up; feelings, sharp and fierce at having been suppressed, rose to the surface. But just as quickly, she felt common sense intercede. She could not continue to do this. She wanted to be near him, to be held by him, but with each new touch or caress she was leading him on. She stepped back, resisting contact.

"You know," she said, "you know we cannot do this anymore."

His jaw tightened and she could see that he was struggling not to reach for her, to disperse her doubts as only he could. "Rina," he said, his voice unsteady, "I know you think there's no way out, but we can do this, we can build a life."

Rina looked up at him. She forgot when they were apart, when she was not in his arms, how tall he was. "I have a life," she replied. "There is a man I am married to and a child who is his. We have a home, a future." Rina closed her eyes, remembering the night before when she had lain awake next to Satō, the scent of him all over the sheets, the black tea that seemed to emanate from his skin. He had remained in their marital bed and so had she.

"What about us?" Kai asked, and she flinched at his tone, at the pain she heard there.

"You do not trust me?" he asked.

"I do."

"You will not trust us?"

Rina bit her lip. She could feel the tension rising in him, had felt it these past weeks since they'd returned to Tokyo. It was not right to give him hope. Even in this moment, her indecision was crippling and he could sense it. She took a deep breath and held it, preparing to hear him out and defend her decision, but he came to her then. His palms were warm as they smoothed up her arms, and she shivered at his sudden nearness, at his head lowering to hers.

"Is this all I'm good for?" he whispered.

She blinked and stepped away from him.

"Is it?" Kaitarō followed her, backing her into the wall. His warmth and urbanity had vanished; there was only the man she loved, the man she was walking away from. His hand reached out and took hold of her arm. He was angry, she realized, angrier than she had ever seen him.

"If you are going to throw what we have away, at least look at what you are sacrificing us for." His voice was quiet but filled with rage. "Ask yourself what you really want from this life." His hand came up to the beaded edge of her collar and he hooked his finger beneath it to reach the smoothness of her skin, stroking her there, watching her eyes flicker up to his, the desire she could not hide.

"You do not need these things to be happy; they have only made you lazy."

Rina pulled away from him. "You cannot judge me. You have nothing to lose."

"I have everything to lose," he hissed. "You—your circumstances," he said, lingering over the word, "have made you a coward. You would rather have the illusion of security than the autonomy to lead your own life."

"No," Rina whispered, squaring up to him. "No one depends on you and you need no one." She was shaking as she said this. "What would you do with me and my daughter? You cannot even look after your mother." She pushed at him then, shoving him back with the flat of her palm. Surely now he would go away, and to her horror he did. She felt him mentally withdraw from her, and then he stepped back towards the window and looked out into the night.

"You can throw me away, Rina. You can tell me that you don't want me or anything I have to offer, but I wanted to tell you that I have listened to your advice. I have resigned from my job and I am leaving Tokyo. I'm going home to my family. I will try to repair things there."

He didn't even look at her as he said this, as though unaware of the impact his words would have. Rina closed her eyes. The pain burned in her chest, so searing it should be an end in itself, but it was not. He was looking to the future, a future she could not be part of, and suddenly she wished she had not pushed him away. She wanted to wrap her arms around his shoulders and feel the strength of him, to have the peace she knew when she was with him just one more time, but he was leaving and she could not bear that now he might refuse her touch.

"I go tomorrow," he said, turning to face her once more. "If you want to change your mind, if you want a life with me, now is the time."

Rina stood still, the buzz of the party loud in her ears. If he was trying to make her aware of the desolation his loss would bring, he was succeeding, but still she fought against it. She looked away from him, suddenly aware that anyone could have walked past their alcove and seen them.

Almost as if he had read her mind, Kaitarō's mouth twisted. "You are safe," he said. "Nothing will prevent you from going back in there and returning to your marriage."

Rina swallowed. She wanted to say something to him, something that would communicate all she was feeling, to ask him to at least give her more time, but she could not. "Good-bye," she said. She felt his gaze travel over her, from her powdered skin to her neat chignon, the beads at her neck.

"Good-bye, Rina," he said, and even though she had said it first, it hurt her anew.

She moved to leave the alcove but for a second he grasped her arm, his fingers pressing into her skin. "Listen," he said, looking her in the face, "I want to be with you, but after tonight, if you mean this, do not come looking for me. Do not think about me, because I will not be there for you, do you understand?" He reached up and his fingers uncurled to touch her cheek. She could feel his skin rough against hers, his thumb where it came to rest at the corner of her mouth, almost a caress.

Rina saw the eyes that she loved growing cold; his touch, which she loved, withdrawing from her. She nodded, and before she could do anything more he left her alone in the alcove, with only the faint trace of his cologne to prove he'd been there.

In the car on the way home, Rina held Sumiko tight against her. Satō was silent, as the driver put the Lexus in gear. Rina knew that Sumiko wanted to talk, to relive the party, but Rina covered her small hand with her own and squeezed it. Satō rested his elbow on the window and leaned towards the night air. He did not look at his wife and daughter.

Rina shifted on the leather seat as Sumiko leaned into her. For a moment Sumi lifted her face and frowned as though puzzled; then she returned to snuggling against her mother, closing her eyes.

As they traveled through the brightly lit streets and neon signs, the evening played out in Rina's mind, each moment up until he had found her in the alcove. She did not think that Satō had noticed her absence; certainly Sumiko had said nothing when Rina reappeared at the party, although her eyes were red. She tried once more to block the joy she'd felt at seeing Kaitarō and the reality of the car she was in now. She thought of her fear that they had been seen, that he might jeopardize her reputation, her marriage, but then it occurred to her that what she had chosen was perhaps more frightening.

As always, they had stayed late into the night, past Sumi's bedtime. Satō loved a party, his work never done. But when the silver buffet service had grown cold and the waiters began to talk among themselves, they finally left. As they had walked through the ballroom, the lights seemed too harsh to Rina's tired eyes; the space had lost its soft, romantic glow. The large glass windows looked cold, even dangerous, and beyond them the night was black. Empty plates and glasses littered the tables alongside half-eaten canapés of butterflied prawns, blinis and caviar, chicken teriyaki, and in little piles everywhere there were tiny cocktail sticks, gnawed and abandoned. After such an elegant gathering, this was what remained.

The memory of that room stayed with Rina as they took the lift up to their apartment. She could see that exhaustion had kicked in for Sumi, that her eyelids were drooping. But under the gaze of Satō, Sumiko kept her posture straight. She placed her shoes neatly in the rack by the door and put on her house slippers. Rina moved into the living room, making it ready for Satō, turning on a lamp that cast a warm and familiar glow about the apartment. She walked to the sideboard to fix Satō a drink, her hand reaching for the scotch. But when she looked up, her husband was glaring at her. For a moment she thought he was going to ask her about her absence that evening, her silence among his friends, but then she caught sight of Sumiko's toys cast across the coffee table. She had asked her daughter to put them away before the party, but in their haste to get ready Sumiko must have forgotten. Satō raised an eyebrow at Rina. She saw Sumiko's slinky on the bar cart and palmed it before Satō could notice it, but she could not hide the other things. Satō took the glass of whiskey from her and sat down on the sofa. Rina moved about the room, picking up a pair of trolls and a doll, plumping the pillows that had been flattened earlier in the day, but as she turned towards her daughter she saw the wariness with which Sumiko was watching her father.

Rina wanted to smile and reassure her, to tell her that it was all right about the toys, that there was nothing to be afraid of, but just then Satō turned and snapped at Sumi to get to bed and leave them alone. Swiftly, Sumiko darted forward, scooping up a toy Rina had missed, and hurrying with it into her bedroom. Satō had turned on the news and did not notice, but Rina did.

# *Part Three*

There are two ways of seeing: with the body and
with the soul. The body's sight can sometimes forget,
but the soul remembers forever.

—DUMAS,

# *Sumiko*

# *TEMPORARY RUINS*

The next morning I woke at dawn. There was something in the light filtering through the blinds that reached beneath my eyelids and flicked them open. In seconds, I was wide awake. There was urgency in the air as I rose from tangled sheets. Sleep no longer came easily, and it vanished in the blink of an eye.

Unable to face the tapes and case file, I went to a small café in the city. The presence of other people with their daily routine calmed me. I sat at the counter with my thick slab of white toast and peanut butter, watching the small café buzz with life in a mall on the edge of Tokyo Bay. It was still early, the water beyond the windows a shifting gray, but as it lightened I left my seat, placing a few coins on the bar, and took the ferry across the bay to the island of Odaiba.

On the beach I walked to the water's edge and knelt, running my fingers through the shallows. It was cold and dense, as though lulled by the unexpected chill of the night. Such nights are deceptive in summer; they lead to kiln-hot days, where mist curls into the air, burning off the surface of the sea. I knew that day would be the same.

Walking to the thin strip of parkland that faced the city, I climbed onto a rock to watch the sun rise over Tokyo. It began up over the skyscrapers and the needle point of Tokyo Tower. Then the light spread across the bay, illuminating the white span of the Rainbow Bridge.

Our word for landscape is Fūkei. It combines the characters for "flow" or "wind" with "view"—a "flowing view," something transient and ephemeral that never stops.

The view before me was not what my mother would have seen when she came here as a university student to hang out in the park or at the newly built malls. For her, the water would have been an uninterrupted expanse of blue with the rivers—the Tsurumi, the Tama, the Arakawa—pouring into the bay. There was no bridge then.

Perhaps in those heady months when she was with Kaitarō she might have seen the pylons sticking up into the air and the road in progress, stretching between them. But in the end, she would not have known the "Rainbow" so beloved by our city, for it was completed late in 1994, the year of her death.

The air remained cool as the sun rose in the sky, and for a while a sharp breeze blew across the island, providing a barrier between me and Tokyo. Still, as the hours passed, the city began to shimmer, and I watched the haze rising slowly from the baking concrete until it reached me on the wind: sulfurous heat.

You know that my mother was a photographer. Perhaps, if she had not married and had me, she would have been a great one. She told me once that when she went out with her camera her aim was to capture the essence of a scene, one moment on a particular day. Yet exposure after exposure, her photographs only ever borrowed from nature—they represented one part of the view, a mere fragment of what the eye can see.

The sun was painfully bright, and as I watched the city wavering in the distance, I wondered if one could truly photograph the heat, how my mother might have done it. Some things you can borrow from life and imprint onto film, but surely not what I felt that day, nor the baking fire of my skin, the sweat seeping out under my hair and running down my neck, the glare of Tokyo in August.

I looked out across the water towards the buildings that my mother would have known, the condominiums of the eighties sitting alongside skyscrapers with fanciful Bubble Economyera names like Golden Plaza or Sunshine Tower, from the days when Japan was wealthy.

It was strange to look at my home as she would have known it. The once fancy buildings with their tinted glass windows were outdated now, and the office blocks that filled the city center were crumbling at the edges, encrusted black with smog.

There are traces of the past that linger in Tokyo, but nothing remains for long. If you want to see the vanished rivers, moats, and canals of Edo you must look for the bridges, motorways, and overpasses set into their beds.

It was in my mother's lifetime that the evolution of our city accelerated. When she married my father and shortly after she had me, wealth propelled our home into the future. Land was reclaimed from the silt of the bay, and the ancient fishing posts, once so popular, vanished. The harbor was transformed. Train tracks and highways snaked above ground, and the earth bristled with skyscrapers. Brick apartment blocks and art deco buildings that had survived both the Kanto earthquake and the firebombing of the city during the war were ripped up by the roots. In the fever of redevelopment everything was made new, subordinated to a bright clean world. As the months passed, gradations of history, past and present, were dismantled; there was no time for them to decay. There is nothing permanent in Tokyo, only temporary ruins.

People often think that buildings will exist longer than an individual's life. They seem indestructible, but in truth they are as fragile as people. Relics of a scrap-and-build city that can be torn down and eradicated easily, like a parent.

That afternoon, as the wind blew across my face, lifting the strands of hair from my neck, I saw reflections glinting off the new towers in the bay—one temporary ruin mirrored by another—and I knew that all that was before me would soon be gone.

The wind blew around me in gusts, whipping up the sea until tiny crests of white foam curled on the waves, and I wondered if the transmutations of our world were not visible all at once to the naked eye, then perhaps they could be preserved in a story. The city's sense of memory and my own intertwined. I thought of the tapes and documents waiting for me at home. Only they could tell me what was still standing.

# *PAPER TRIALS*

People like to believe that they are "innocent until proven guilty," but if you are a defendant on trial, do not make this mistake. You are guilty from the moment of arrest. Even the media encourage this view: their articles at the beginning of a case, during the rounding up of suspects, the charging of the guilty, are long and lurid, but once the trial has begun, these same reporters produce little more than a paragraph or two in summary, a sentence on a defendant's likely fate.

Any lawyer, particularly a defense lawyer, will tell you this is so. For if you are taken into custody, the chances of regaining your freedom decrease by the day. Our very language endorses this. Once the police make an arrest, sometimes even before charges have been brought, the polite titles attached to a surname, such as san, the equivalent of "Mr.," are no longer used. In the national press, san is replaced with "yogisha"; in the corridors of power and the interrogation rooms of the police, "higisha." These terms, one colloquial, one legal, mean the same thing. And so, all at once, a person is transformed, no longer an ordinary citizen but Higisha Nakamura: Criminal Suspect Nakamura.

## OFFICE OF THE TOKYO METROPOLITAN POLICE DEPARTMENT

Takanawa Police Station, Shinagawa Ward,
Case # 001294-23E-1994

### INCIDENT REPORT

Date of Offense: March 23, 1994
Time Reported: 2042 (JST)
Name of Victim: Rina Satō
Complainant: Mr. Yoshitake Sarashima
Extent of Injury: Fatal
Relationship to Victim: Father
Time Officers Arrived: 2118 (JST)
Officers in Attendance:
Reporting Officer: Detective Ichiro Soma
Police Coroner: Akihiko Ito
Assisting Officer: Masashi Hikosaka
Forensics Officers: Keigo Miyabe, Natsuo Murasaki & Akio Ogawa
Location: 03-08-20 Takanawa, Minato-ku, Tokyo.

2045 Detective Ichiro Soma was dispatched to the above location.

2118 On arrival Detective Soma made contact with the complainant, the victim's father, Mr. Sarashima, who discovered the body of his daughter, Rina Satō.

Mr. Sarashima reported that his daughter had been due to meet him at his home in Meguro that afternoon. When she did not arrive, his granddaughter, the child of the deceased, who is currently living with Mr. Sarashima, became agitated and distressed. Mr. Sarashima waited for approximately two hours and when he was still unable to reach his daughter by phone, he made the decision to travel to her apartment in Shinagawa. He accessed the apartment using a key his daughter had given him, and, upon entering, he found her home in a state of disarray with furniture and various items strewn across the floor. Mr. Sarashima reported that his daughter was sitting against a wall in the living room but that her posture was limp and unnatural with her head hanging forward. He recalled that her boyfriend, Kaitarō Nakamura, was standing near the body, holding a duffle bag containing some of his and the deceased's belongings. According to Mr. Sarashima, his appearance was also much disordered—his hair was mussed and sweaty, his clothes torn, and he was bleeding from a scratch to his face.

Mr. Sarashima reported that he ran to his daughter to check for a pulse but finding none called for an ambulance and performed a citizen's arrest on Kaitarō Nakamura, who confessed to the murder of the victim.

At 2138 Emergency Medical Technicians arrived and declared the victim to be deceased. The area was secured and photographs of the exterior and interior of the apartment were taken. The contents and positioning of all items within were also recorded. Environmental conditions at the scene were: exterior ambient temperature 60°F, relative humidity 70%, interior ambient temperature 70°F, relative humidity 40%.

At 2200 Police Coroner Ito visually examined the deceased, noting that while rigor mortis was not yet evident, there were early indications of livor mortis in the hands, legs and distal portions of the limbs indicating that death had most likely occurred approximately two to four hours prior. Police Coroner Ito declared that the injuries sustained and markings on the body were consistent with manual and ligature strangulation and determined the case to be a homicide.

At 2230 District Prosecutor Kurosawa arrived on the scene and consulted with Det. Soma and Police Coroner Ito and the witness, Mr. Sarashima.

2245 Mr. Sarashima explained that his granddaughter was waiting for him at home. He asked permission to leave the scene and agreed to come to the police station the following day to give a full statement.

At 2315 The body of the deceased was removed from the scene and transported to Shinagawa District Hospital for autopsy and formal identification.

At 2320 Higisha Nakamura was formally taken into police custody. He did not resist arrest.

## OFFICE OF THE TOKYO METROPOLITAN POLICE DEPARTMENT

**Takanawa Police Station, Shinagawa Ward,**
**Case # 001294-23E-1994**

### CRIME SCENE REPORT

Date of Offense: March 23, 1994
Time Reported: 2042 (JST)
Name of Victim: Rina Satō
Complainant: Mr. Yoshitake Sarashima
Extent of Injury: Fatal
Relationship to Victim: Father
Time Officers Arrived: 2118
Reporting Officer: Detective Ichiro Soma
Police Coroner: Akihiko Ito
Assisting Officer: Masashi Hikosaka
Forensics Officers: Keigo Miyabe, Natsuo Murasaki & Akio Ogawa
Location: 03-08-20 Takanawa, Minato-ku, Tokyo.
Prosecutor: Prosecutor Hideo Kurosawa was advised of a suspected homicide at 2203 and arrived on scene at 2230 with forensics officers in attendance.
Preliminary Analysis by Detective Ichiro Soma

I found the body in a sitting position on the floor of the living room, the torso supported by a wall. The victim's arms hung straight down to the floor, her hands palm up, while her legs had been laid out in front of her. Visual examination revealed that the victim was wearing a white turtleneck shirt and denim dungarees and one white trainer—the other was lying on its side across the room 1.23 m from the body. Several injuries sustained by the victim were visibly apparent; ligature furrows in the skin and severe bruising to the neck and throat imply that she was strangled manually and also with twine or string. I delayed further inspection of her injuries until after the autopsy; however, the abrasions on her arms and hands indicate that what occurred was a physical struggle. Although it is most likely that the victim died at the scene, she was not killed in the position in which she was found.

Part of the assault evidently took place in the living room. The bureau by the front door had been overturned. The complainant, Mr. Sarashima, stated that when he entered the apartment, the household phone was lying on the floor by the overturned bureau and that he used this to call the police. He stated that the phone was usually kept on the bureau. A set of footprints was found on the floor of the living room beneath the window (male, size 9). It has since been established that Mr. Sarashima wears a size 8 and Higisha Nakamura wears a size 11.

The low black coffee table in the center of the living room was askew, and the contents of a salmon and roe bento box were found lying beneath it. One upright bento remained on the table. The victim's handbag was found next to the coffee table, its contents—a coin purse, wallet, handkerchief, notebook, and two sets of house keys—were scattered across the floor. On the other side of the coffee table was an open holdall containing clothes for an adult female, hairbrush, toiletries, one camera, and a child's formal obi. This holdall is separate from the duffle bag containing bundles of photographs that was confiscated from Higisha Nakamura and that has also been taken into evidence. By the entrance to the kitchen, a box of red bean buns was found lying on its side next to a bag of sakura sweets; the receipt indicates both were bought from a local bakery.

There is evidence to suggest that the struggle between the victim and her assailant extended to the master bedroom. Three spots of fresh blood between 3 mm and 5 mm in diameter respectively were found on the bed covers (DNA analysis ordered). I observed that the remainder of the bedroom was in a state of chaos: the closets were open, as was a chest of drawers, and on the floor were three books, a white beside clock with a cracked face, and two cardboard boxes haphazardly filled with clothes.

Forensic analysis has revealed that hand marks and fingerprints belonging to the victim were found on the door frame of the living room. The height, density, and distribution of oil on these prints indicate that at one point the victim grabbed at them, perhaps to avoid being pulled or dragged backwards. There were further handprints from the victim on the floor of the living room. The angle and oil distribution from these prints suggest that during the struggle the victim had either tried to crawl away from her attacker or towards the phone on the floor. A spool of white kitchen twine lay partially unraveled 33 cm from the last recorded handprint.

As of this filing, evidence remanded into the custody of forensics has been transported to the prefecture crime lab for analysis, and an inventory of items taken into evidence will be circulated to the investigating team within five days of this report. Please see Appendix A for the crime scene floorplan, diagrams on the placement of objects, and precise dimensions.

═

As I sat in the low light of our dining room my fingers trembled. I ran my hands over and over the contents of the case file. I read each document again and again, as though I would remain imprisoned at that table until I could make sense of the events. I knew that Kaitarō Nakamura had eventually signed a confession—the final one drafted for him by Prosecutor Kurosawa. I knew too that he had pled guilty to the murder of my mother. But what I realized, sitting in the soft light of my home, was the importance his plea would have given to the documents before me. Where once these reports and accounts would have been debated in open court, suddenly it was the documents themselves, line by line, that would speak.

Kaitarō's confession altered the nature of his trial, shortening it to two days. As he stood before the District Court, his case would have been considered by a panel of three judges headed by a presiding judge—the Saiban-Chō—there was no jury. The prosecutor would have addressed the bench and delivered the case file. He might even have discussed the contents of each document and read out his summation to the court, but once he and the defense attorney had given their opinions on the case, the files and all the documents within them would have been taken away to be considered in private by each judge. They alone debated the case between themselves, and it was the private process of reading—the relationship between a reader and the page—that would play the most important part.

There is only one basic homicide statute in Japan: Article 199 of the Penal Code. It states that "a person who kills another shall be punished." So it was on that day. What kind of murder had been committed, the motivation behind the killing, any remorse felt by the defendant, an appropriate punishment—all of this was decided by a panel of three, alone in their judicial chambers.

They say that a prosecutor's duty is to find the truth, to get as close as they can to the events that have occurred, even if they can never see them perfectly. Prosecutor Kurosawa's written address to the court would have presented his understanding of events, but it was the evidence collected, the files and the video interviews themselves, that would have led each judge to the heart of the case and, ultimately, into the mind of Kaitarō Nakamura.

Our judicial process revolves around the issue of motive. Who, how, where, when are not as important as *why*. The desires that dwell in the deepest parts of the mind must be examined and proven before a sentence can be determined. Even in the most brutal of murders, the emotional state of the suspect comes to the fore. The notion of love is considered: hatsukoi "first love," miren "lingering attachment," kataomoi "one-sided longing," aishiau "mutual love," fukai aijō "deep love." The court will evaluate the depth of love and proffer leniency accordingly. And so it is on this intangible value that a person's fate can rest. Love, which for so many, is a matter of life and death.

# *LIFE OR DEATH*

Do you know what a "lie question" is? Psychologists put so much thought into these, so much effort; they draw them up for lie detector tests still in use in Japan today, not yet a relic of TV. The purpose of these tests is often to exclude a subject from suspicion, but they are still important, and the first real question asked, the one that gauges the pulse, the beat of your blood, is the one that matters above all. It is the difference between the person you are and the person you would like to be.

Imagine facing the examiner. He knows your name, age, occupation, lifestyle. You expect him to start slow, but he will not. In a homicide investigation, he will go straight with a test of your nature, like "Have you ever thought of killing someone?" And there, in the antechamber of the mind, between thought and speech, is the truth. We have all thought of killing someone. The answer to this question does not allow for virtue signaling or dishonesty. We are all capable of the thought. Killing is an impulse that lies within us all.

Once more, I sat in my bedroom, blocking out the traces of my childhood and focusing instead on the tape playing on the small TV screen. Kaitarō is wearing handcuffs when he enters the interrogation room. Prosecutor Kurosawa is already seated, and there is no one else with them, no typist keeping track. Yet Kaitarō must be aware of the men behind the glass screen and all who are waiting for his testimony, for when Kurosawa walks round the table to release him from his cuffs, Kaitarō's movements are studiedly minimal. He does not rub his wrists but affects a relaxed posture, resting one arm on the table in front of him, creating his own space.

Kurosawa pushes a plastic cup of water towards Kaitarō, the gesture earning him a quiet smile, a flattening of the lips. For a moment the prosecutor glances at the camera and Kaitarō angles his body to face the viewfinder. I can see him more clearly, the lines on his face, the grooves by his mouth where his lips have learned to curve down.

"Haven't you got what you need?" Kaitarō asks.

The prosecutor shrugs. "There is more to it than just the facts."

"You want my soul? Is that why you administrative idiots are here, fumbling with my head?"

"I want to discuss something personal."

"More feelings?" Kaitarō unbends and takes a sip of his water.

"Love."

"You want me to define it for you?"

Kurosawa is silent.

Kaitarō reaches again for his water but pauses, the cup halfway to his lips. "You want to know if I really was in love?"

"Yes."

The expression on Kaitarō's face is unreadable.

"I want to be fair," Kurosawa says. "I have covered several homicides that have revolved around passion."

"Have they involved people like me?"

"No."

Kaitarō sits back, considering. "Will you argue that I was never in love?"

"Tell me about your work," the prosecutor says.

"You too, Kurosawa? You want to see me hang?"

"Tell me," he says, his voice soft, "tell me about your work."

Kaitarō leans forward and puts his face in his hands.

"Don't you care what happens to you?"

"It doesn't matter anymore what happens to me."

"I think it will help you," Kurosawa remarks.

With his fingers still pressed to his temples, Kaitarō shakes his head. "Nothing can."

"Then just tell me the truth."

The silence stretches between them. It is only seconds on the timer ticking away at the bottom of the screen, but it seems an age.

"Sometimes," Kaitarō says, "it is easier to be in someone else's skin." He flicks a glance at Kurosawa. "Have you always liked yourself? Are you comfortable in every situation? In a profession like mine and a life like yours, where you have to get close to people, you need to be a shape-shifter of sorts."

Kurosawa nods; in bemusement or agreement, it's hard to tell.

"There are jobs you don't want to do, people you don't want to meet. But, as I am sure you know, it is dangerous to show anyone—man or woman—that you don't like them. Perhaps there are times when you are safe, times when it is opportune to let your dislike show, but in my world and probably in yours too, showing your true feelings is something that is forbidden."

Kurosawa leans forward. "Did you dislike Rina Satō? You walked away from her at first?"

"I tried," Kaitarō says.

"Wasn't that 'dangerous'? Didn't it go against your instincts?"

Kaitarō smiles. "It went against my common sense and my instructions, yes, but not my instincts." He pauses. "I have worked on many cases. There are always needy people looking to add excitement to their lives, or those who want to abdicate responsibility for their choices, buy their way out of emotional trauma. The key is to be professional, to keep some distance between yourself and the part you play. You work the case as you would any social strategy. I was successful." Kaitarō adds, "There was a certain sense of satisfaction in that."

"Was it hard on your personal life?" Kurosawa asks.

Kaitarō smiles. "I didn't have a personal life, and in the beginning I didn't need one. I was trying on all those people for size, challenging myself, but eventually what was interesting and new became exhausting. It takes a lot of energy to step out of your own skin, to learn to be someone else."

"So you loved no one and no one loved you," Kurosawa says.

Kaitarō sighs. "For a lot of agents it is that way. They become wary of people, find it impossible to trust anyone. If you don't trust someone, how can you love them? These agents end up alone. But we are not meant to be alone in life, are we?"

"So you wanted companionship?"

"I wanted to be myself."

"So it was timing? When you met Rina, you needed a change."

"No!" Kaitarō sits forward. "I know what I felt. Give me credit enough to know my own mind."

"I had to ask," Kurosawa says. "It's what most people will think, that she was convenient."

"They would be wrong."

Kurosawa is silent. He gestures to the glass screen at the back of the room and signals for more water. "So, if it wasn't timing and it wasn't exhaustion, what changed you? What was different?"

"She was," Kaitarō says. "The more I got to know her, I knew that she was what I had been looking for."

"She was beautiful?" Kurosawa asks, and Kaitarō laughs softly.

"Very, but in a way that was entirely her own. She had an inner strength that I admired."

"So you wanted to push her away? In the beginning?"

"I tried," Kaitarō says. "I wanted to know her as a real person, not through my job. But the more time I spent with her—we fit. We understood each other, and I couldn't leave her to the life she was leading."

Kaitarō pauses as another cup of water is placed in front of him. He smiles wryly at Kurosawa, a small remark on the change in his treatment. "I saw myself in her; she was my mate in every way. We fought for each other, found a way to be together. I trusted her as I have never trusted anyone else."

"Did she trust you?"

"She did," Kaitarō says, his voice firm.

"And you thought that was enough?"

"I hoped it would be."

"So she wasn't a mark?" Kurosawa asks, placing a photograph on the table in front of him. It is a shot of Rina in the night market; she is just about to throw an apple into the air.

"No," Kaitarō says, fingering the photograph, "she wasn't a mark."

Alone in my bedroom, I thought about cause and effect. Judges can be in charge of more than two hundred cases at a time, and the majority of the pleas they hear are guilty, with confessions typed and signed. Still, guilt is no simple thing and neither are defendants. The judges' task is to determine the full extent of guilt, to identify the truth and apply a punishment that will correct and teach. And they must do this quickly, for the speed with which they dispatch their case load affects their rank, their chances of promotion, their future. Competence is measured by how many cases they take on, and they cannot afford to linger for long.

I had not applied for Kaitarō Nakamura's sentence, and to my growing frustration it was not in the file. Instead, I had found a handwritten list of the possible outcomes faced by him. They ranged from various forms of incarceration to the death penalty. I had assumed he would have been given a custodial sentence, as it was rare for perpetrators of only one homicide to receive capital punishment, yet Yurie Kagashima had placed a star by this final option as though she would have to guard against it and defend her client's very existence. The only thing I had to go on was the schedule of his two days in court—the first to have his case heard and the second for sentencing—and I knew from this that whatever the judges eventually decided, they did not take long to make up their minds.

Once more, my thoughts turned to the documents spread across the dining table downstairs, to the footprint mentioned in the crime scene and the DNA analysis from my mother's postmortem. The saliva found on her skin that suggested contact with another person shortly before her death. I recalled this line and thought about Kaitarō Nakamura and his sentence, about all the people who were there on the day my mother died and all the choices that can end a life.

# *Rina and Kaitarō*

## *BLOODLESS BLACK AND WHITE*

Rina stood alone by the window. The marble floor of the living room was cold beneath her bare feet, sending a chill into her blood. She leaned forward and rested her forehead against the glass, rolling it from side to side so that her warm skin left a smudge. The pain in her head was bad, and it had spread throughout her body. She had ended up drinking a lot the night before, but she knew this was not the cause. Rina pressed her face hard into the window, increasing the pressure against her head. She could fold herself into the freezer right now, press herself down between the shelves, and still the cold would not help her. Still, there would be this throbbing pain, a blinding pulse behind the eyes so that she could not see.

He was gone. She had made her choice. Only now there was nothing left. It was as if the erosion of herself had begun again and she was once more powerless to stop it—a helplessness she'd chosen for herself.

Rina turned and pressed the heels of her hands into her eyes. She saw herself as she had been a few nights ago at the gala, staring at abandoned cocktail sticks, a glass of wine in her hand. She remembered Sumiko nestling against her in the car, pressing her small face into Rina's side and then pulling away slightly at the smell of sweat and alcohol. Rina remembered the heaviness of her limbs, the desolation spreading through her, and, finally, Satō's contempt when he'd looked at her in their home, the mess of toys she'd left on the floor, the way he had snapped at Sumiko.

So many years ago she had agreed to this, and again she had made the same choice. Opening her eyes, Rina caught sight of the dining table; it had been a wedding present. Looking at the shine that spread across the glossy black surface, Rina saw herself sitting there a few years into her marriage. She had several sheets of colored tissue paper on the table in front of her and she'd been cutting them into an exact square. From the corridor, she could hear happy chatter as Sumiko played in her room. Rina had been humming softly, a young mother with a healthy child and the bloom of it in her cheeks. As she reached for the box of sweets she had put to one side, she felt Satō come up behind her. She stiffened as he cupped her shoulders in his hands, felt his lips on her neck. She flinched, a tiny movement, but he felt it. He slid his hands down, brushing them against the side of her breasts, and at that Rina had willed herself to be still.

She kept her head down, looking at the table, but Satō just laughed and pulled out a chair to join her. Rina reached once more for the sweets and placed them in the center of the sheets of tissue paper. The cellophane covering the box squeaked against her fingers as she pulled the wrapping tight. She taped one side of tissue down and then folded the other over it so the tape wouldn't show. Satō sat still, smiling so blatantly that it drew her attention.

"What's so funny?" she asked.

"You! You are so intense."

"I want to make this nice for Yoshi," she said, nodding at the gift.

"You're a funny little thing."

Rina arched an eyebrow at him, because she had never thought of herself in those terms.

"Aren't you?" he said. "Aren't you funny?"

Rina said nothing, merely gave him another small smile.

"I'd bet you'd fight though."

Rina looked up at that. She looked at him clearly, no longer smiling.

"If you were cornered," he continued.

Rina let go of the box, heedless of the colored layers that fell away on one side. She looked past him, through their living room to her darkroom, now a storage closet; her former life gathering dust. Satō took her hand in his, stroking her fingers with his own. "There's a shine to you, such poise," he said, and Rina frowned. "Beneath it, that's what I'm talking about."

In that moment, Rina wanted to rise; she'd wanted to pull her hand from his grip and tell him to back off, but she didn't.

"You're tough," he said quietly. "When you focus it comes out in your face."

Slowly, Rina tugged her hand from his grasp. She opened her mouth to make a joke, but as she did, the choices she had made up to that point rose to confront her. She wondered if she was really as tough as he said.

"Hurry up!" Satō said, gesturing to the wrapping paper. "We've got to go."

Looking back on that conversation, Rina asked herself if what he had said was true. She had been shiny once as a young girl, when they'd first met, as one is before decisions are made and opportunities are lost. She would never be that way again, but then Satō had never really believed in her shine, had he? He had seen through it from the very beginning, through her to the woman waiting, the fighter beneath.

Rina raised her head and looked at her home. She could not blame him entirely, she knew. She had not been a perfect spouse, perhaps not even a good one. She should have known that his goals and dreams could not possibly compensate for the loss of her own. It would have been better to marry with her eyes open, but whatever had gone before, how she lived now was her choice. Kai had given her that. Even if Rina kept her family together, she did not have to repeat past mistakes. For both her daughter and herself, perhaps for all three of them, she could take back her life. Crossing the living room, she felt the tension in her head ease as she opened the door to her former darkroom. She would clear it out and make room for herself once more. Stepping over a broken tennis racket and several discarded pairs of Satō's shoes, she lifted the first of the boxes.

═

The form was pink. Not completely pink, Rina could see that

now. The paper itself was white. In her shock, the rows of red characters had blurred, smudging into one another, the rose expanse interrupted by oblong squares of green. Rina looked down at the form lying on top of the box while her own heart beat and beat and beat. She reached out and then drew her hand back; some documents were too poisonous to touch.

For a long time, it was the prettiness of the form that Rina would remember: the color and simplicity of it, this symbol of all she had to fear. Rina thought of the pink kanji, the empty green rectangles for her answers, the space at the bottom for her personal seal and Satō's. What did it say about the national consciousness that something so grave would be hidden beneath a façade of order and color?

Rina thought of the mascots for each government institution: the white seal in a captain's hat and blue coat painted onto all the lighthouses in the Shizuoka Prefecture, a symbol of safety, broadcasting the success of the Coast Guard and masking the bodies of those who did not survive the sea; and Peepo, the chubby orange fairy of the Tokyo police force, his name alone symbolizing the happy relationship between the people and police. Still, however cheerful the policemen and their mascot, however neatly their guns were attached to their uniforms—like mittens so they would not forget them—the guns themselves were real, and the bullets within them were real too. The death penalty was still exercised in Japan, and her prisons were filled with people you hoped your children would never meet. Even now, each and every police officer could bring fear and pain into your life. It was the same with forms, Rina thought, sinking to the floor and taking the papers with her; it was the same with everything created by people.

As a young woman growing up in Meguro, Rina had not been able to sit still; whatever the task she had to be in motion. Many times she had discussed cases with her father while pacing the floor of his study. When she first told him she wanted to drop out of her degree they had circled each other, round and round his desk, like dogs. But now her life weighed her down, the isolation of it dragging her onto the floor where she could only sit quietly and rest her head upon her knees.

Rina looked at the papers again. Most of the form was strangely blank. Satō had filled in his name and hers, along with their address and ID numbers, and he had also circled the option that declared that they as a couple desired a kyogi-rikon—a divorce by mutual consent. There was a box asking for the agreed terms of separation, but this was not filled in; neither were several of the following sections, except for one, a section present in all the divorce forms across Japan—a single space specifying which parent would take sole custody of any children.

Here, in pencil, as though he were preparing the form in draft, Satō had left a faint upright squiggle, a question mark in the box that would determine Sumiko's life. The question mark jolted Rina out of her shock in one fluid move. She was on her feet and angry in her blood, in her bones. As she rose she took the form with her and saw that beneath it there was another set of papers, this time in hallowed white, expensively produced.

Rina noted the emblem for the Tokyo Family Court on the header and the dense paragraphs of instructions beneath. This was no divorce registration form from the local ward office; there were no sections for her to fill in, no space for private terms. This was a legal application for Satō alone, the spouse who would file a case against her for divorce, a case he would make sure to win.

Inside this form was a table with reasons for the breakdown of the marriage. In bold black type was an instruction to circle all that applied and to double circle the most applicable. Here, Satō had put pen to paper, speaking clearly and plainly, as he did not to her face. He had circled one word, round and round in black ballpoint pen: adultery.

Slowly, Rina's fingers opened and the papers scattered to the floor. He knows, she thought, and he wants to take my child.

Rina walked out into the living room. All around her was the life she'd been living, but the familiar landscape had changed. What Satō suggested was terrifying. She knew people who had been forced to go through the courts. The system apportioned blame and found fault; it ripped open the person you were and displayed all the ugliness and shame for everyone to see. From her time at Tōdai, Rina knew such divorces could take years in mediation before they even passed to family court; that mediators, august citizens from your city ward, formed panels and analyzed the bones of your marriage. People trawled through the papers of your life, yet, however hard you fought, whatever your version of events, the outcome was always the same. One parent would be granted sole custody of the children and the other would likely never see them again. Joint custody is illegal, clear as only the law can be; bloodless black and white.

In her second year at Tōdai, Rina had joined a charitable group that provided free legal advice. There she had met many parents who had been separated from their children. She thought of their hopelessness, their isolation. Once a divorce was finalized and custody assigned, the courts often termed further disputes as "family matters" and refused to intervene. Even when there had been no formal agreement and one parent simply took the child, that parent was frequently favored, possession being nine-tenths of the law.

Rina thought of the people she had met, how they had ventured to prefectures far from home to hang around the schools of their children, like crows, hoping for a glimpse of them as the bell rang, before being shooed away by an irate ex-spouse and the police.

Rina had experienced this by proxy, but the reality of it happening to her was almost beyond comprehension. She saw herself waiting outside Sumi's school, perhaps in Nagoya, or a place farther away still. She would have a photograph in her pocket, dog-eared and creased, from a birthday long past. She knew how she would stand, to one side of the gates, trying not to be noticed. Then, as the bell at the top of the school rang, the strike of the hammer resonating against the bronze, she would see her, her little girl, much changed, so different from the child in the photograph. This new Sumiko would be walking with her friends, chatting and swapping candies. Rina would try to wait but eventually she would be unable to stop herself from darting forward, running towards her daughter, scaring her. It would have been years since Sumi had seen her mother. She would be frightened and confused. Rina saw her back away, a piece of candy clutched tight in her fist as Rina trembled, the emotion on her face frightening Sumi even more. "Sumichan, don't you remember? You used to call me Mummy."

Horrified, Rina shook herself out of her reverie. Tears were pouring down her face. She placed the divorce forms on the dining table and walked into the kitchen. She'd thought to get a glass of water, but then she caught sight of Sumiko's panda bento box there on the draining board. That morning, Rina had packed Sumi's lunch in the bear box so that panda could be washed at home. Panda was Sumi's favorite. Tomorrow, Rina would fill it with colorful vegetables cut into different shapes, and balls of sticky rice. She could not be separated from her daughter, could not be left with scraps of film and paper and not a living, breathing child.

She returned to the living room and picked up the phone, but just as quickly she lowered the receiver back into its cradle. She thought of phone bills that could be put before the mediators and the court, of the evidence that Satō might already have against her. Grabbing her keys from the pink shell by the doorway, she left the apartment and ran down the stairs, not bothering to wait for the lift. She ran past the porter and out of the building, stopping only at the phone box a few streets down.

She listened to the phone ring, once, twice, and then he was there, his voice traveling down the line as he spoke into the receiver, "Yes?"

Rina was shaking. She looked out of the phone box at people passing, at anyone who might be watching her. "You're still here," she said. "Thank God you're here." There was silence on the end of the line, but she pressed on. "He wants a divorce," she said.

"What?" Kaitarō's voice was suddenly clear in her ear, present and alert. "Rina, did he say so?"

"I found the forms in the box room. I was going to . . . I wanted . . ."

"Rina," Kaitarō said, and the gravity of his voice drew her to him, to safety. "How much has he filled in?"

═

As she walked, the leaves fell from the maples and beeches, amber and vermilion. The cherry trees too had been stripped of their blossoms, revealing their branches to be nothing more than bare black sticks rattling in the wind. Rina walked briskly, her heels striking the concrete of Ueno Park. She came to the junction by the main road and saw him leaning against a telephone pole. He nodded and she turned right, walking away from him. Over the phone he had warned her that Satō might have hired photographers. They must be careful not to be seen.

Rina crossed at the traffic lights, ignoring the scowls of the other pedestrians who tutted because the light was red. She ran up to the gates of the national museum and then slowed to a walk. In front of her the great square building loomed like a fortress. Inside there were five-hundred-year-old screens of courtesans at autumnal leaf-viewing parties placed next to instruments in glass cases. To look at them one could almost hear the metallic twang of the shamisen beneath the forest canopy as it rustled and darkened in the breeze.

A group of schoolchildren chattered on the steps waiting to be let in; one of them laughed too loudly and was shushed by the teacher. The little girl smiled behind her hands and those around her did the same.

Rina headed away from the museum and into the garden at the right of the complex. It was freezing. The sky was overcast, and it rendered the stream running through the garden black as it poured over the rocks and into a large pool. No one lingered outside; it was too cold. She checked her watch, a gift from her father, and moved farther into the garden, past the squat wooden teahouse on the edge of the pond. In summer it was used as a tea pavilion but today it was all shut up, braced for winter. She moved on along the path and out of sight of the museum, stopping once she was properly hidden by the trees. The wind whispered above her, rustling the branches, and all she could hear was the steady trickle of the stream.

She was fidgeting, had turned to look up the path, when she saw him. His jacket was open and his hair flew back from his face as he ran. "I'm sorry, I'm so so sorry—" she said, but he did not slow as he came towards her. His kiss was not gentle. She tasted sweat and fear and hunger. She tangled her fingers into the hair at his nape; eventually he lifted his mouth from hers. "I'm sorry," she repeated, pressing her forehead to his.

"I'm here," he said. It was all he needed to say.

He took off his jacket, as though to spread it on the ground for her, but she had already sat on the grass, folding her knees beneath her.

"I have been so stupid. I—"

"You're not stupid, Rina."

"You don't think so?"

"You couldn't have known."

"I can't—I can't do anything right."

Kaitarō sat next to her on the grass.

"Can anyone see us?"

"No, I checked."

"Do you think he has hired someone to follow me?"

"If he did, I would find them."

"You know all the private detectives in the city?"

"There isn't much that escapes me, Rina," Kaitarō said, and the quiet bravado of this made her smile.

"Did he assign blame on the form? Did he cite a reason for wanting a divorce?"

"Adultery," she said quietly. "He is planning to sue me and he has the grounds to do so." She paused and looked up at Kaitarō. "He knows about us."

"What would he gain by taking you to court?"

"Custody of Sumiko," Rina replied. "He could argue I'm unfit to raise her, take her back to Nagoya to his parents?"

"Rina, calm down." Kaitarō reached for her, holding her hands in his. "He is not going to take her. What else would he gain from a court case?"

"There are damages for adultery, compensation, but it is not much."

Kaitarō paused. "When Satō married into your family, he was given money? He has benefited from your father's business connections, borrowed capital?"

"How do you know that?"

"I'm assuming. Am I wrong?"

"No, you're not wrong," she said.

"Are his investments in trouble? He works for a real estate investment firm, right?"

"House prices are still falling," Rina murmured. "He may not want to admit it"—she turned and bit at her thumbnail, chewing the skin at the edge—"but I don't know what he's bought or how much he's borrowed. He wouldn't discuss it with me."

"What about with Yoshi?"

Rina shook her head. "The shame, he wouldn't have—"

"And?"

"My father would have told me." Rina sighed. "To be honest, Kai, he would expect me to know, to be aware of how our money was being spent. He will not forgive me—"

"Let me find out what the situation is," Kaitarō said, taking her hands once more. "If we understand his motives, we can plan."

Rina nodded and breathed out slowly. She was beginning to calm down, returning to rational thought. "We can fight this, can't we, Kai?" When he did not reply, she glanced up.

"Rina, I have something to tell you."

She frowned; a shard of dread seemed to pierce her stomach. Kaitarō's eyes were dark, darker than she had ever seen them.

"Rina, I know him."

"What?"

"I've been following him." Kaitarō held up his hands in defense as Rina got to her feet.

"What have you done?"

"Rina, I had to."

"You had to follow my husband?"

"No." He was on his feet too now, reaching out to her, pleading. "No! I . . . I needed to know who you were leaving me for. I didn't trust him not to hurt you."

"Did you know about this?" she asked, while the horror of this new knowledge slowly percolated through her. "Did you know about the divorce form?" She was almost shouting.

Kaitarō inhaled sharply. There was a pause, a fraction of a pause.

"Did you?"

"No," Kaitarō said. "But he's been seeing someone in Nagoya."

"Oh," Rina paused, and then quite dumbly she added, "That's where he's from."

"Rina . . ." Kaitarō said. He looked as though he would like to reach for her, but something in her expression stopped him. She could see her shock and pain mirrored in his eyes and so she turned away.

She tried to focus on her breathing but all she could think of was her own stupidity, her culpability. Of course she wasn't the only one to have been living half a life. "Years ago, when Satō was drunk one night," she said slowly, "he told me about a girl he'd cared for in high school. She was prettier than me and more fun, but his family did not approve, so he gave her up. Her name was Naoko, I think." At this Rina flicked a glance at Kaitarō. "Is it her? Or am I just being naïve? A hopeless romantic?"

When Kaitarō did not reply, Rina rubbed at her arms through her coat, holding herself in an embrace. "You will never lie to me, will you, Kai?" she whispered.

"No," he said, and she heard in his harsh, clipped tone his hatred of dishonesty.

"This is all my fault," she said as the full weight of her humiliation washed over her.

"I should have known, and"—she glanced once more at Kaitarō—"I have been a bad wife."

"No, Rina! Please. None of this is your fault." She sat down on the grass and Kaitarō joined her. This time he drew her close, enfolding her in his arms.

"I am a fool," she muttered. "What do you see in me?"

"Everything," he said simply.

Rina looked at him, sure that her vulnerability was still plain because he winced at her expression. "Why didn't you tell me about all this?" she asked softly.

Kaitarō shook his head. "I don't really deserve you, Rina, and I"—he looked down at his hands for a moment before finally returning his gaze to hers—"I wanted you to choose me . . . for me."

"I do choose you," she said softly. "Surely you know—couldn't you feel it that night at the gala? I have always wanted you. I just felt bound—" Her gaze traveled over him from the frown between his brows to the line of his mouth and the afternoon beard forming on his cheeks. He swallowed and she felt him reach out to cup her face. "I am not here because I am in trouble."

"Rina, I know—"

"No," she interrupted, "you don't. I know I have put other people before us, but it turns out that I am selfish to the core because after Sumi, I just want you." She watched as his lips curved into a flicker of a smile. "Can you still love me, even if I am not brave?"

His smile broadened and he nodded.

Rina rested her head on his shoulder and nestled close. Kaitarō tipped her face up and kissed her on the mouth.

"What I have with Satō," she said, "I have to believe that not all relationships are like that, just selfishness and betrayal."

"Not us," he said.

Rina took his hand, stretching out his lean, strong fingers between her own. "Not us?"

"No," he said, pressing a kiss into her palm.

For a moment Rina hesitated and then she looked up at him. "Sometimes, I used to think about what life would be like if we were married, but now, I can't say—"

"I'll take whatever you can give," he said, and in the silence that followed she knew it was true. Rina smiled as he lifted her onto his lap, and she put her arms around his neck.

"If anyone photographs this, we're fucked," he said, and they laughed as the tension eased out of them, mingling with the breeze. They were silent for a moment, watching the wind drift up through the trees and out into the great expanse of sky.

"He is just threatening you with court. He will not take Sumi," Kaitarō said. "He wants to frighten you with the prospect of mediators and an unpredictable judge." He shifted her in his arms, making sure she was comfortable.

Rina raised an eyebrow at him. "Where did you train?" she teased, but she rested her head back on his shoulder, acknowledging his point.

"Satō wants a deal, a private settlement on his terms."

Rina looked up at him. "Custody of Sumiko?"

Kaitarō winced. "A bargaining chip. What you love most."

Rina nodded. She took hold of his hand, their fingers interlacing.

"I have some evidence against him," Kaitarō said quietly, pausing to let Rina digest this. "I will give it to you. Use it and offer him a financial settlement. With the right incentives he will settle out of court." Gently, he caressed her cheek, smoothing the tension from her face. "We will emerge from this—"

"Kai, you won't approach Satō yourself, will you? This is between him and me," she said, and he nodded in assent.

"Trust me, Rina. We will get custody of Sumiko."

She leaned back against him, but she did not smile. "I'm sorry," she said a moment later. "I'm sorry for how I treated you." His arms tightened around her and she pressed her face against his neck. "I am sorry that you are caught up in all this."

"I'll make it right," he said.

"Are you . . . are you still going back to Hokkaido?" she asked

Kai eased her away from him a little, looking at her intently.

"Can I come?" she asked, echoing his words in Shimoda.

He raised an eyebrow as Rina placed her hands on either side of his face. "I mean it," she said.

Suddenly he grinned and she did too. He bent down and kissed her hard on the mouth. When they drew apart, it was by a fraction only. "What's left of me is yours," he whispered, and she smiled, relieved, radiant.

Rina checked her watch as she left the park. She was running late to pick up Sumiko, had been late for one thing or another all year, but now she was going to put it right. Sumiko was at archery practice, only a short walk from her school. Rina imagined her daughter at the head of the line, her breath almost vapor in the unheated dōjō. Her small feet in their white socks flush to the chilled wooden floor as she grasped the bow. Rina smiled. Sumi was intense in all that she did; she had already been permitted the glove and the arrow.

Rina saw her daughter step up to draw, correcting her stance, straightening her back to form a direct line from her narrow shoulders to her feet. She inhaled slowly, focusing on each breath, drawing the air in as she raised the bow above her head and brought it down, pulling the string taut all the way back to her ear. The fingers of her deerskin glove brushed her cheek and a clock ticked in the stillness as she lifted her eyes to the target and released the shaft, confident and untroubled, as she should be.

Heading into the subway, Rina scanned the shops and grocery stores beneath the fluorescent lights. Yoshi had asked her and Sumi over for dinner, but now Rina could not bear the thought of going. She would pick Sumiko up and they would go for red bean doughnuts. Afterward, Rina would make crab with tōfu and spring onions and teach Sumi to prepare it. She loved to cook with her mother. She watched so keenly as Rina sliced potatoes at tremendous speed for her favorite Sunday gratin, crying out, "My turn, my turn!"

Rina swallowed hard, blinded by the lights of the underground, and once more she felt the fear rising up inside her for, even with Kai's help, she knew that a chance of losing her daughter remained.

# *Sumiko*

# *POSSESSION*

I remember what it was like to have both my parents at home. At night, I could hear them in the kitchen, eating udon or hot pot, perhaps the braised pork and cabbage her father liked her mother to prepare for him. Father came home for dinner in those days, and even though it was late, Mama always had something ready. She would prepare a variety of dishes too, one meat, plus a soup and a salad. I listened to them as they talked in the kitchen; sometimes the small portable TV would be on low as my father checked the news, but their voices continued above it, gentle and calming. I was almost always in bed by the time he came home. In the shadows of my room, I could see the lights of the city muted into softness through the curtains. As I became drowsy, I would watch that light, listening to the hum of the heater in the background, and with that and my family close by, I would fall asleep.

As I grew older, my father started to come home later and later, and my mother no longer went to such trouble with his meals. She stopped cooking afresh for him late at night and began to leave out a large portion of whatever she and I had eaten. This progressed to conbini bento from the store, to rice balls with cold green tea, and, finally, a pot noodle by the kettle.

There were times when I awoke in the night to an almost unnatural stillness. I would hear the deadbolt on the front door click into place, and an emptiness would enter the apartment. I would hear my mother walk from one room to the other, drawing the curtains, turning off the lights. In the living room, I would hear the TV come on, soft at first. I imagined her looking towards my room to see if it disturbed me, but after a few minutes, when I didn't call out or open the door between us, my mother would turn up the sound until it was a low steady blare, as though she didn't want to hear anything but its noise, no sound of the world outside.

There were nights when she no longer watched TV, but still she did not sleep. She walked and walked around the apartment. After she had finished checking the locks and the windows, once she was sure that our home was secure, she would pause by my bedroom door, opening it only an inch or two so as not to wake me. I longed for those moments, though when I heard her and saw the thin shaft of light dart across my bed, I always closed my eyes tight and pretended to be asleep.

One night she came in. I heard her open the door and felt her hand on my head, her kiss on my cheek. I smiled at her as she crawled into bed beside me. I giggled as she cuddled me to her, but she was not smiling as she held me tight. She wrapped her arms around me and buried her face in my neck. She was trembling. I could smell her sweat, the acrid scent of fear. I could feel a fierce energy running through her like a current, though she tried to still it. She kissed my cheek, my forehead, my hair. "It's all right," she said, "all right." That was the last night I spent at home in Ebisu.

Now I know why she was afraid. Even today, in each and every separation, one parent must accept that they will lose their children. They can decide between themselves or a judge who has never met their child will.

The principle behind this practice is the belief that divorced parents will not be able to cooperate or work together to act in the best interests of the child. So only one is granted custody, the right one in the eyes of the court.

Still, there is a choice. In that brief hiatus before acrimony and legal proceedings, parents have a chance to agree privately and informally who will get custody and to establish visitation rights and uphold them. In these cases it is possible for a child to grow up with both mother and father in their life. But, of course, trust must be maintained. Both parties must agree to put their child's interests above new jobs, new homes, new partners, old hatreds, and this is where things start to unravel.

People are ruled by their desires; they will do almost anything to achieve what they want. A spouse who is tired of their ex can move to a different prefecture or country. Even if they remain nearby, they can make it impossible for their former spouse to see the child—because of illness, appointments, unscheduled weekends away. Agreements reached privately are not enforceable, and often one spouse is left with nothing, neither legal recourse nor retribution.

Because of this every separation eventually comes down to one thing: the physical possession of the child. In matters of custody, the courts value this highly, so in cases where amicable resolution is not possible, the battle to secure the physical body of the child starts early. Grandparents can get involved and hide a child away, anything to secure it for one side or the other. As she held me in my bed in Ebisu and waited for Kaitarō's information on my father, my mother must have thought this was the last card she had to play. The next day, she took me to see Grandpa.

I remember that when we stood on the green tiled drive of the Meguro house it felt like a playdate; in a couple of hours she would come and take me home. It was only when she stroked my face and I saw the tears in her eyes, the way that she was blinking, that I realized she would not be there that night to kiss me before sleep.

"Sumiko," she said, folding me into her arms. She tucked Tora, my white tiger, between us and held me close. I clutched at her, breathing into her neck, "Mummy."

"I'm here," she said as I began to sob. "I'm here. Soon we will be together again." She took out her handkerchief and dried my face and then hers before anyone could see. "No more tears now. We are Sarashima!"

I stood watching her as she walked away from me down the drive; the banks of pebbles on either side of us glistened in the rain.

You could say I was lucky. My mother, for the short time she was with me, and then my grandfather, brought me up with great care. But this story of ours has so many sides that I doubt I will ever know the full extent of it. I will never know if my father loved me: I will never know if I was a burden to him, a pawn, or a child. I will never know what my mother was thinking as she walked away from me that day. I will never truly know what she faced or the price that was paid.

Alone in Meguro, in the home we had both grown up in, the very rooms seemed to echo with her absence. At the beginning of my investigation I had only wanted to deal with the facts. I had needed each detail to speak for itself. But the more I read of the case file, the more my memories of that last year with my mother pushed to the fore. Hours would pass when I would stare into my mind's eye, the documents before me forgotten.

One morning, as the clock in the dining room ticked past the hour, I glanced at the calendar on the sideboard and calculated the days. It had been more than a week since Grandpa had left for Hakone and soon he would be home. If I wanted to discern what had really happened, if I wanted to work without his interference, I would have to hurry.

I was looking over the pages spread out before me once more when the doorbell rang. It was the postman with a parcel for me. I took the mail into Grandpa's study and set it down on his desk out of habit, switching on the lamp. There were some bills and a large envelope that I knew contained my contract from Nomura & Higashino, awaiting my signature and seal. I could not bear to think about it and so I put it to one side. Inside the parcel was a small black box. For a moment I paused. I had been so immersed in how the law applied to my mother's life, how it had failed to protect her, that I had forgotten how it applied to mine. And so I was unprepared when the day I had been working towards for years and years and years finally arrived.

I sat for a long time staring at the box in my hands before I opened it. When I did, I found that inside, resting on blue velvet, was my attorney's badge. I tilted it under the desk lamp and the light glanced off the gold work, illuminating the finely etched petals of a sunflower and within it a tiny set of scales, the emblems of freedom and justice for all men.

I turned the badge over, reading out my personal identification number engraved on the back. These badges are symbols, not only of the law but also of power. They belong to the Japanese Federation of Bar Associations and are for the honorable and the qualified. Should you be convicted of a crime, disbarred, declared bankrupt, or die, you or your family must surrender your badge.

If you are so careless as to lose it, a new one must be made and engraved with a mark indicating whether it is your second or third—a symbol of shame and a warning. Notices of lost badges are published in the *Kanpo,* the government's official gazette, so that everyone will know of your carelessness. The power and authority conferred by these symbols must never be abused, and the law must be upheld at all costs.

Yet, as I looked at my badge in my grandfather's study and sat at the desk where we had once planned my career, I realized that my relationship to the law had changed. There were lawyers I knew who had become disillusioned quickly, but I, with all my hope and energy, had thought that if that did ever happen to me it would take a very long time. Now the limits of the law and my questions about its efficacy stood out in stark relief. The law had not helped my mother; it had only trapped her and endangered her. It had not helped me. The law as I was coming to know it did not protect. It could not reconcile or mend.

When my mother first took me to live with Grandpa all those years ago, I became so distressed that he decided we should leave Tokyo for a while. In a parody of our summer holiday, we went to our house in Shimoda, and there by the sea and in the forests of the Izu Peninsula I waited to hear from my parents and to learn my fate.

Looking down at the badge I had worked so hard for, I rotated it slowly in my hands. Then I set it down on the desk and released it with a flick of my fingers, watching as it spun like a die.

## *SEA CHANGE*

The insects were silent as I walked through the forest. Neither a hiss nor a croak could be heard over the trickle of the streams that ran through the peninsula. There was a stillness to the air. Even the water had slowed to a creeping drip in the undergrowth, while moisture, invisible and silent, seeped into the bark of the trees, rendering them black.

Above me the branches rustled, their remaining leaves so thin that I could see the sunlight shining through, illuminating the veins. We had been in Shimoda for two days but it felt far longer. Before we boarded the train Grandpa bought me new trainers; they were pink with rainbows on the side, but now they were encrusted with mud. Everyone had taken to buying me things, but I did not care for them. I wanted the familiar, a last trace of summer. I searched for what I knew—clusters of dark berries untouched by the birds, white flowers nestling beneath the ferns that sprawled in the depressions and valleys—but they were gone. Nothing grew. The ground was dense with fallen leaves, and soon the autumn fruits would wither back into the soil. Winter was coming, but not a winter like any of us had ever known; it was a winter during which the very wind would freeze.

I trailed my fingers along the trees as I passed. Their trunks glistened with moss and smeared an icy paste onto my skin, coloring my hands. I had spent a lot of time alone there that year, learning the paths above my home when no one was watching me. Now

I was alone again.

I climbed up onto a ridge of rocks, their seams dyed rust red with iron, and craned my neck beyond the trees looking for the torii that marked the entrance to the shrine. I paused, listening, waiting for the hum of voices in the air, the scrape of sandals on stone. The sanctuary was isolated, but it was then, at the end of the day, when everything else in the forest stilled, that people might be there.

The sun lowered in the sky, and I could smell frost sharp and clean on the air. In my short life there had never been snow on the peninsula, although people talked of a storm that had once frozen the sea and coated the rocky cliffs with white ice. It was a myth, a story, like the ones Grandpa had told me. Only that day, I felt it would happen.

There were many shrines on the peninsula, down by the bays and on the beaches, with bright red torii perched on volcanic rocks far out to sea. They were popular; children ran and darted between the buildings while parents paid for prayer boards, ate ice cream, and listened to the sound of the waves.

The place I sought was farther inland, in the heart of the forest. Few visited it. Sometimes people came to worship during the celebrations at New Year, but, even then, it was mainly frequented by the priests. A path had been cleared of branches and sodden leaves, and I followed it through the forest, twisting and turning, pushing against the clusters of bamboo that lined the way. The path glowed green, phosphorescent and shadowed, but only until I reached the clearing and emerged into the early evening light. The bridge always startled me with its beauty, the arching wooden planks spreading out before me, the avenue of trees waiting at its end, and beneath it all the ravine with rainwater rushing down over granite rocks. I could almost see the priests who journeyed across that bridge in their robes, praying as they crossed.

That year, as Mama and Grandpa had less and less time to play with me, I had ventured onto the hillside by myself. The shrine had become my secret, as places visited alone often do. I needed somewhere secret, a place where I might find peace and security, but that evening the woods of my childhood had changed. Summer was truly gone. I rubbed my hands together—they were freezing, encrusted with dirt and moss—and I thought of another story then, of the Yuki-Onna, a snow woman who was said to appear at first snowfall, clothed all in white, hovering just above the ground so as not to leave any tracks. It was said that each year as the new snow fell, every mother must be sure to guard her children, for if she did not keep them safe inside the Yuki-Onna would come for them and steal them away.

Alone and chilled on the hillside, heedless of the mud and wet leaves, I ran towards the shrine, but the stone buildings grew dark around me, shadows falling across the paving stones as the sun set. I entered the pavilion and crossed to the pathway that led up the hill, climbing up past the Inari's stone foxes that waited there, red kerchiefs tied around their necks.

The path was straddled by a series of torii, donated by those who were grateful to the Inari for their success in business. I climbed up, passing beneath each vermilion gateway, past the brightly painted new ones with their patrons' names clearly visible in the woodwork, past our own with the kanji for "Sarashima" peeling away in the icy wind. I shivered as I emerged into the inner courtyard. The space was flanked by stone lanterns carved from volcanic rock. On special days, these were lit and each candle glowed before guttering in the breeze. I imagined what it would be like in the snow, white icicles suspended from the roof of the honden, a fine powder initially just dusting the tiles and then settling deeper, inch by inch, until everything was buried beneath a blanket of dense white, in an empty clearing in the forest with lanterns burning long into the night.

In that moment I thought of my mother pacing the floors of our apartment in Tokyo. I wondered what was happening to her. My father was away on a business trip, but I wondered what would happen when he returned, what would happen to me. Around me, the wind grew strong, chilling my cheeks until they burned, and the air was harsh in my throat as though I were swallowing ice. I pulled the sleeves of my jumper down over my hands, my skin was red with cold. The courtyard was much darker now; no lanterns had been lit. I would not find peace there and I was not safe. I turned to go but as I did a priest stepped into the square. He moved to the water font where three bamboo ladles were set out over the flowing water. He picked one up and poured the cold liquid over his hands and face, rinsing his mouth. He did not flinch as he swallowed. I stood immobile, watching this figure gliding through the shrine; in his white robes he almost seemed to glow. Then he saw me, and at his startled cry I turned and fled.

It was late when I came in and Hannae was nowhere to be seen. "She's gone to bed," a voice said, and I jumped, peering around the door to the dining room. "This cold is bad for her joints. I sent her to rest." My grandfather was sitting alone at the dark wood table. In front of him was a bowl of soba, the steam rising in wisps from the flat green noodles and broth. There was a bowl for me too. "Come and eat, Sumiko. It's still warm." I slipped off my shoes and joined him, settling carefully into my seat, trying to avoid the creaking in the wood, the sound of the rattan giving under my weight. I watched him and waited for his question.

"Why didn't you wait for me?" he said finally. "I thought we were going into town together?" He was angry, very angry, I knew. "When I tell you to wait for me, Sumiko, I need you to do as I say." His voice was hard but also so quiet that I felt ashamed. He had been frightened by my absence. I hid my hands beneath me. I had meant to wash them before coming in, but once I had begun to run through the forest, I could not stop. I had been afraid of the dark surrounding me, of the cold, of all the things I could not name.

"Have you heard from Mama?" I asked

My grandfather sighed. I think he knew, had always known, that nothing, not even his reassurances, would help.

"Sumi, you will see her soon. Everything is fine. There is no need to run around panicking. We are all right, aren't we?" He rose and fetched a warm wet towel for my hands and helped me out of my anorak. As he took the jacket from me, he leaned down and kissed my head. I bit my lip on all the questions I had for him.

Grandpa sat down with me and took a sip of his tea.

"How long do I have to stay here?" I asked

"I will call your mother tomorrow."

"I want to go home. I don't want to be here with you!"

I had expected my last sentence to hurt him, but Grandpa just looked at me. He nodded towards my noodles cooling in the bowl.

"Eat up, you must be frozen." He turned back to his meal, and I watched him spooning long strands of soba into his mouth. "These are the best things you can eat," he said after a while. "Do you see the length?"

I nodded, dipping my chopsticks into the soup.

"Long life," my grandfather said, slurping up a few strands. "That is why these are eaten," he continued, "to preserve a long life. That is what we must pray for." As I took a bite, sucking the warm noodles down into my stomach, I followed his example and prayed for those I loved.

That night, perched on my windowsill, I saw snow begin to fall, pinpricks of white at first barely distinguishable from rain. I looked to the east, towards Tokyo, to where my mother would be. I got ready for bed and pulled the shutters closed. In a few hours the beads of moisture would merge into flakes of rime, frost would snake across my window coating it in ice, and when I woke in the morning, the ground would be blanketed white. I curled into my bed, pulling the sheets high, and as puffs of my breath crystallized before me, I closed my eyes tight.

## *PATER FAMILIAS*

Grandpa tried again to reassure me the next day. He said that he would talk to Mama and that we would return to Tokyo soon, but I didn't think so. I knew something was wrong.

When I heard the phone ring that night I crept downstairs. Grandpa was in his office and, thinking me safely asleep in my room, had left the door ajar. I slid down against the wall outside, sitting beneath the clock he had brought back from Europe. Its chimes drowned out the first part of the conversation, and I leaned towards the door, fearful of missing anything.

"What are his terms?" Grandpa asked.

I waited for what he would say next, but there was a pause as he asked my mother to hold on. I heard his footsteps and my entire body went still. I expected him to come out of the office at any moment and find me, but instead he put my mother on speaker phone so that he could pace in front of the desk.

"Rina, are you there?"

"Yes." My heart beat faster at the sound of my mother's voice. She was near—so near; I wanted to talk to her. "He's being coy," she said, and I jumped when my grandfather slammed down his fist in frustration. "Dad, don't," my mother pleaded. "He's just enjoying his position."

"Power you've given him," my grandfather snapped. I heard him take a deep breath and begin to pace again. "Where is he now?"

"He went to Nagoya, to liquidate a real estate portfolio or so he said. I think he's back in the office now, but he hasn't come home."

"Hanging out in Roppongi?"

"He's just making me sweat, staying away, so we will make him a good offer."

"What does he want?"

"I think the Ebisu apartment and a further sum in cash. Kaitarō has looked into his affairs." My mother coughed nervously. "This is what we both think."

My grandfather paused. I could hear the scratch of his pen on paper. "How much cash?" he said. "How much will he want?" For a moment Grandpa paused. "Rina, even if we pay him, what is to stop him from coming back for more? And what about Sumi?"

"I . . ." My mother hesitated. "He must agree in writing to stay away from Sumiko."

My grandfather laughed, a jagged sound, and I frowned. "You think that will keep him away?"

This time when my mother spoke she sounded exhausted. "We have to trust. I cannot . . . ensure this will go our way. If he agrees to an uncontested divorce and waives custody, that is the best we can hope for."

"He will extort us into the future," my grandfather said. "He can meet Sumi outside her school, turn up at weekends. He can make our lives hell. We will never be free of him." His voice was harsh, but I heard the depths of his anxiety there, perhaps even guilt.

"I think," my mother said, "that he will stay away. He will have a new life after all."

"That isn't enough, Rina. He is in debt, isn't he?"

There was a silence on the line and then very quietly my mother said, "Yes."

"And the money his father and I gave you on your marriage?"

"That has gone. I believe he over-invested during the bubble."

"I will need to see some bank statements before agreeing to the final amount," my grandfather said.

"He won't like it, but I'll ask him."

There was a pause and I heard my grandfather take another breath. "I'm sorry, Rina. I should have had him checked out, hired a PI."

"No—"

"I should have," he said. "I should have looked beyond his family and our friendship."

"Dad"—my mother spoke softly but there was steel in her voice—"it was my choice. I chose to marry him."

My grandfather was quiet as he stood in front of his desk. Eventually he spoke. "Shall I draft the papers for you?"

"Thank you. I'll call when I have a better idea of the terms. I—I'll see that he is reasonable."

"Okay, Rinachan. Stay strong!" he exhorted her, and I blinked at his use of the phrase because it was normally something Grandpa and Mama said to me.

"Thank you," my mother said, and I wondered if she was smiling.

"This new man," my grandfather said. "You trust him?"

This time I could hear her smile. "I do."

"I'd like to speak to him."

For a moment my mother paused; she waited and I waited with her. "Once the settlement has been agreed, we can talk about Kaitarō," she said. "How is Sumi? Is she okay?"

My grandfather sighed. "She's nervous, got lost in the woods yesterday and frightened herself."

My mother's voice was pained, almost present with us in the house, and I felt a pulse of satisfaction. "Is she all right? Can I talk to her?"

"Rina, she's in bed. Let's keep her out of this."

"Okay," my mother said, but I knew she did not agree. "Okay," she said. "About the settlement—"

"Yes?" Grandpa said.

"The research Kaitarō did on Satō is good. When I get him to the table it will be helpful."

"Does he love you, Rina?"

"He does," she said.

Yoshi sighed, and I could hear the exhaustion in his voice when he spoke. "Then I had better meet him properly, hadn't I?"

"He is a good man," my mother said. "Different from Satō."

"I'm not sure that's saying very much," my grandfather said, and I heard my mother laugh.

"Dad?"

"Yes, Rinachan?"

"I'm glad you're my father."

"Me too."

"You'll kiss Sumi for me?"

"I will," he confirmed.

There was a click on the line as my mother hung up. By the time my grandfather walked across the study, I had run up the stairs. I tiptoed quietly towards my bed, the darkness deep and impenetrable as I crawled under the sheets. Outside in the hall my grandfather stood very still, listening.

# *Rina and Kaitarō*

## *SHOWDOWN*

The cold swept through Tokyo that year, seeping into every corner so that the great glass buildings and skyscrapers seemed like an icy manifestation of it. Kaitarō stepped off the metro and into the center of Roppongi. As a hangout for rich foreigners and businessmen, he didn't have much cause to come here, but sometimes clients liked it, and the ambitious salaryman with entrepreneurial aspirations found it had benefits too. It was where Satō could be found these days, listening to everything anyone had to say.

Kaitarō walked into the lobby of a hotel and took the lift to the sky bar on the top floor. The place was packed, and they were letting in more women than men, but the guy on the door was a contact of his and let him pass. Satō was not hard to find; he was at one of the central tables with his work colleagues, a prominent place, somewhere to see and be seen.

Kaitarō strolled over to the bar. He signaled a waiter and asked him to deliver a message to Satō. "Tell him he's got a phone call."

He watched as Satō peered into the shadows and moved into his line of sight, greeting him with a nod. Then gestured to the main doors and walked towards them. Satō excused himself from his table and followed. Kaitarō felt him catch up and turned just as the other man put a hand on his arm.

"What the fuck do you want?"

"I have some information for you."

"I don't know how to say this any more clearly, but you've been fired, Nakamura. I don't need you anymore."

Kaitarō looked at the heaving bar and the table of colleagues Satō had just abandoned. "Yet you come when I call," he said.

All around them, tall glass windows provided a sprawling view of Roppongi. Kaitarō glanced down at Satō's hand where it had tightened on his arm. "Downstairs, I don't want to be seen."

"Don't you know when you're beaten?"

Kaitarō reached inside his inner jacket pocket and extracted a pack of cigarettes. "Come on," he said. "I'll thumb you a smoke." Then he jerked his arm from the other man's grasp and walked into the elevator.

Outside they turned a corner and stopped in an alley between two hotels. Satō held out his hand for a cigarette, muttering as Kaitarō lit it. Narrowing his eyes, Satō took a drag and blew the smoke out into the air.

"So you've gotten yourself a divorce form," Kaitarō said finally, "but you haven't filled it in."

"I don't need you, Nakamura. She's doing what I want all on her own."

"This has to stop."

"She's scared, isn't she?" Satō smiled, certain.

"You haven't got any evidence against her."

"That is what you think."

"I know," Kaitarō said, leaning into Satō's face. "You have nothing."

"As I said, you can't be sure." Satō laughed. "But at least you managed to fuck her. Finally!" He took a drag on his cigarette, still laughing as Kaitarō lunged and grabbed him by the throat. Satō was driven back, his head hit the wall and he dropped his cigarette, his hands were braced against Kaitarō's forearms. He smiled. "Ah" he said, "there's the violent streak I've been waiting for. What do you think this is? A showdown, like in the movies?"

"You are going to settle," Kaitarō said slowly, driving his wrist into Satō's throat. "You are going to settle out of court and give her custody of Sumiko."

Satō's breath was short but still he grinned at Kaitarō. "I don't think so, Nakamura." He shoved at the forearm restraining him but could not get free. "I think mediation is necessary." Satō pushed again and finally Kai released his grip.

"She'll fight me," Satō continued, "and think of what she'll be subjected to. The questions. Written statements scrutinized by august members of the community. All those people reading about my wife, judging our marriage. And she won't deny it, will she? She won't be able to lie to them, and she'll be known as someone who sleeps around. Isn't that what you are?"

"Rina is not in danger. I took care not to be photographed with her."

"Yes, but one or two might have slipped through the net, so this is what you are going to do for me—"

"No, Satō, this is what you are going to do for me." Kaitarō stepped up to him again; he could see the uncertainty in Satō's eyes as he brought his face close. There was a flicker of fear. "You are going to settle out of court," Kaitarō continued. "You will get the apartment in Ebisu. You will agree to a further sum of money with Yoshi Sarashima, and you will cede custody of Sumiko to Rina."

"Why would I let my daughter live with that woman? And you?"

"If you do not, I will send your family pictures of your mistress in Nagoya. I will disclose the details of your debts. I will talk to your father in person and tell him what you asked me to do, and then I will turn over all the evidence I have amassed on you to the courts. Rina may not have been building a case against you, but I have, and unless you behave honorably, you will never be welcome in Tokyo again."

For a long time Satō was silent, and then he withdrew a cigarette from his own pocket.

"I could keep her," Satō muttered, lighting the cigarette and throwing the match into the gutter. "We've both made mistakes. If I took the divorce off the table, spared us both the shame, she'd stay with me."

"But you won't see a penny," Kaitarō retorted.

"What about Sumiko?" Satō asked.

"You might be able to visit."

"I'd be at her mercy on that."

"She is kinder than you are."

"You've got it bad, boy, if you think that," Satō laughed.

Kaitarō's eyes did not leave Satō's face. He watched as this man he so despised turned his life and Rina's over in his mind.

"They'll never accept you," Satō said, but his resolve was slipping. "We're more alike than you think, you and I. And you won't make her happy." He leaned back against the wall of the alley, fumbling with his cigarette. "She doesn't really need people," he said quietly, "and when she realizes that you'll be gone."

For the first time, Kaitarō became aware of the alcohol on Satō's breath, and just for a moment he wondered if the other man was more drunk than he'd thought.

"She won't truly love you," Satō said quietly. "When you settle into a normal life, a normal routine, you'll never be enough for her."

Kaitarō would have laughed were it not for the feeling in his chest. A feeling he never expected to experience in relation to Satō. Pity. For a second that pity mingled with fear. He could not imagine living without Rina's love, but then he realized he would not have to. Kaitarō felt his shoulders ease, the tension slipping out of them as he looked at Satō again. "What was between you and Rina is your business," he said, and Satō glanced up at him.

"Squeamish, Nakamura?"

Kaitarō just shrugged.

"You tell her . . . ," Satō said, "you tell her that if she crosses me on the settlement—"

"Rina can't know I was here talking to you."

"What!" Satō laughed, his merriness resuming. "You want me to cover for you?"

"I want you to keep me out of your negotiations. Remember what I can do to you, Satō. I don't want Rina to ever know how we met. My silence for yours."

"How do you know they'll give me the apartment?"

"Rina has told her father about our affair and that you want a divorce. Yoshi will protect her. He will agree to settle."

"You've worked it all out."

"I want to finish this."

"And will you ever tell her? Eventually . . . ?"

Kaitarō was silent. He looked at Satō, who quietly began to laugh. He was still laughing when Kaitarō drove him against the alley wall and even then he did not stop.

"Don't forget what I can do to you, Satō," Kaitarō hissed, his hand tight around the other man's throat. "Don't ever forget—"

He felt Satō try to swallow but he just increased the pressure on his windpipe; he felt Satō shove against his chest, but he would not budge. Eventually, Satō smiled and whispered into Kaitarō's face, "You think you're so much better than me?"

Kaitarō stared hard at the other man, taking in the bloodshot eyes, the burst capillaries on his cheeks, and finally his eyes, his laughter.

"I do," he said, releasing Satō's throat. Then he walked out of the alley, away from the twinkling lights of Roppongi and into the night.

# *HOME FREE*

Kaitarō was waiting for her in his apartment, idly tapping a pen on the wooden surface of his desk, although he was barely aware of this as she came in, transfixed by the sight of her.

She was happy. He could see it in the tilt of her chin, the turn of her head as she closed his front door and walked towards him. Her hair, longer now, swayed against her collarbone, brushing the silk ties that held her blouse together at the shoulder. She was beautiful. Even here at the end of a long day, she was beautiful and fine. He could not imagine a time when she would be otherwise.

She reached him and perched on the edge of the desk, moving a half-filled cup of tea out of her way; it had left water marks all over the surface. There were papers strewn everywhere. He was messy, he knew, but she didn't seem to mind.

"Are you ready to go?"

"I could watch you forever."

"Why don't you watch me over dinner?"

Kaitarō smiled and dropped the pen he had been playing with onto the desk; it rolled away from him, with the slogan facing up—HONMA REAL ESTATE INVESTMENTS—Satō's firm; Satō's wife, but not for much longer. He knew that a few months ago, the sight of this pen might have caused Rina to pause, to question him, to question them and what they were doing. But that night she smiled and reached for his hand. Satō was fading from her life and she didn't give a damn.

"How's Sumi?"

"Desperate to get back to Tokyo. Yoshi says she asks for me every day, but I think she just misses her friends." Rina smiled as he pulled her towards him.

"How long do I have you for?"

"Just tonight. They're returning to Meguro tomorrow and I'll join them there."

"So soon?"

"I need to be with Sumi. I miss her."

Kaitarō handed her her handbag, holding on to the strap until Rina met his gaze.

"It's only for a little while," she reasoned, "and I'll see you in Hokkaido."

"One day I will have you forever and there will be no limits."

"Yes," she sighed, "but right now I'm hungry!"

Kaitarō laughed and let go of the purse. With an arm about her waist, he escorted her out of the building. They were nearly there; they were almost home free.

═

Later that evening, Rina sat at Kai's desk. There was a photograph in front of her, a picture of them both that she had developed in black and white. Rina picked it up in her hands, framing it between her thumb and forefinger. She glanced at Kaitarō lying in the bed asleep. For once he was relaxed, in true repose, his features smooth and slack.

She loved his openness, the way he was so unguarded with her, that he was willing to live with a woman who would point her camera at him even in his sleep. There was courage in that. Real trust. She understood the bravery it took, particularly in front of a camera.

Rina rested her cheek in her palm. She loved these moments in the quiet of the night—a recent gift for them, the chance of spending an evening together. In the past months, whenever they had been apart, Rina had imagined herself in this apartment, imagined that the small studio was her home, that her photographs clipped to the walls belonged there and that the world contained only this man and this desk and this bed. Now the fantasy had spread into reality and it would include her whole life—her daughter. Once they found a bigger place, and soon they would, they could be a family. Then Sumi would be with her always and none of them need ever be apart.

She looked again at the photograph in front of her. It was an experiment, part of a new sequence she was planning on intimacy, the layers between public and private life. The shot had been taken in this apartment, the camera propped on the very desk she sat at now. She had pointed the lens towards the bed and set the timer to take the shot in ten minutes' time. She'd sat next to Kaitarō, who was facing away from her, wrapped in a cocoon of sheets. She had been watching him when he turned towards her and his arm curled around her waist as he rolled over in the bed. Rina had looked up, just as she heard the shutter click, freezing them: she, looking straight at the camera, her eyes large and dark, the freckles on her nose standing out in stark relief and flickering over her cheeks; Kaitarō blurred, relaxed in sleep, his arm curving around her waist.

Rina loved what she had captured in this picture, the unguardedness of it. There was something predatory about it too, which thrilled her—her gaze staring at the lens capturing him, unknowing in sleep. She also loved that even in this state he was possessive, his hand grasping hers and his other arm curled around her waist, for they were both of the same mind, intertwined, each of them wearing the hint of a smile.

She had always been drawn to black-and-white photography: the revelation of it. You could see more of a person when they were staring back at you in monochrome with nothing to distract from their nature. She looked at the image of Kaitarō rolling into her like a wave curling on the shore.

Outside, dawn was breaking over the city. In the distance the monorail train rumbled past, the sunlight catching on the corners of darkened glass. Rina smiled, for the thought of all the eyes and faces within no longer frightened her. Anyone could look into her world and she would not mind. Rising from the desk, she hunted around the room for her handbag. She opened her notebook to see if she would need to pick up anything for Sumi before she met them in Meguro. Putting it back, she peeled off her T-shirt, crumpling it into a ball and stuffing it down into the bag. She stood for a moment, silhouetted in the light, the sun outlining the curves of her shoulders, her breasts small and high, the globes of her bottom in white lace panties, feet bare on the wooden floor. Rina reached up to the curtains in front of her, brightly colored squares of silk patched together, like hanging quilts. She had bought them for Kaitarō in the market. They looked good, she decided, nothing like the decor she'd selected in Ebisu. There was not a trace of beige upholstery or lacquer cabinets here, only the colored squares of her curtains and the rush basket filled with film and photographs. When they had returned from Hokkaido and had found a new place, all these things could come with them.

Behind her, Rina heard a shutter click. She raised her arms, twining her hands together above her head. The shutter clicked again and she looked over her shoulder at him, her face partly hidden by her arm. He was sitting up, the sun slanting down on his face, catching his stubble in the early morning light. He lifted the camera once more and pointed it towards her. Rina raised her eyebrow and smiled.

# *FIRST LOVE*

Kaitarō stooped beneath the wooden lintel and took a seat at one of the booths. From where he sat he could see the sea, the great gray swathe of it struck through with flashes of light. The clouds rolled in thick and dark, giving the air a twilight hue even though it was only early afternoon.

He had wanted to get there early, wanted to be prepared so as not to evince surprise when he saw her. He had memories of this place, memories of what it could do to a woman, but then Megumi loved it here and had wanted to stay. He ordered some tea and mussel tempura. He thought of what he'd said in his letter to her, how inadequate the phrasing, how brief his explanation for coming home. Still, he had learned to become distant in intimate circumstances. It was a lesson he had learned in this very town, and old habits died hard.

Megumi would tease him about the letter, he thought, but after a moment he stopped himself. The old Megumi would have teased him, the girl who had loved the barren wildness of Hokkaido, who wanted to be a fisherman's wife. It was hard to believe that the woman he was about to meet might not bear any resemblance to his Megumi at all. She might be puzzled by his letter, even annoyed. She might think him irrelevant to her life. Still, he'd wanted to warn her, to spare her any surprise when he brought Rina here. He remembered Megumi as a friend, and if there was any hurt at all, he wanted to spare her that.

Kaitarō looked up, startled, as an umbrella snapped shut by the window. He glanced outside and there she was in the rain, looking in at him, in at the café where they used to meet. Her face was the same. There were wrinkles around her eyes and her skin had thickened, blunting her cheekbones, but it was still her, and her eyes as they sought his were kind.

She crooked her finger at him, gesturing for him to join her so they could walk on the beach as they used to, over the sand that stretching out behind her, now pitted with rain. He held up the plate of tempura, the tightness in his throat easing; this was a battle they had always fought.

She gave him a small shrug and he swallowed in relief as she entered the shop. She put her umbrella in the stand and came towards him. Her scarf was in her hand as she sat down. She folded it neatly into a square and then placed it in the pocket of her anorak. It was a matronly gesture, but somehow it fit.

"Mr. Nakamura," she said.

"Mrs. Honjima."

"Can I get you anything?"

"They know what I like," she said. "They'll bring it along."

She was relaxed as she looked at him, but he knew she couldn't really feel that way.

"You are getting married?" she asked.

"You are married," he said.

"Yes." Megumi rolled up the sleeves of her cardigan, giving him time to gather his thoughts. It was unlike him to be slow and unable to ease a situation. Even so, he couldn't help but stare at her. His gaze traveled over her face, from her cute snub nose to her faint eyebrows. He noticed fine white strands mixed in with the black of her hair. Her lipstick seemed too bright for her skin. She hadn't worn any when he had known her.

"There's no need to feel bad, Kaitarō," she said after a while.

"How is Tsuji?"

"I am happy with him. Very happy. He was the right choice for me."

"I never had any doubt!" Kaitarō laughed and then paused when she stiffened.

For a moment he saw her as she had been at their last meeting. She stood on the stretch of sand that she loved and he told her he was leaving, that he was not cut out for life in Hokkaido with her. He had expected her to shout at him, to throw something in his face, but it was her stillness that he remembered. He had waited for her to turn to him so he could comfort her, had wanted to hold her, this girl who had been his only friend, but she waved him off.

She stood still for a long time, her arms crossed over her chest, looking at the sea. He had called to her as she moved away from him, but she kept on walking. She walked to the edge of the water and then on, out into the waves till they soaked her skirt. It was the last image he had of her, standing in the twilight, with the waters, gray, all around her.

"Thank you for meeting me, Megumi."

"Why have you come home?" she said finally. She pressed her lips together, rubbing the lipstick into her skin.

"I missed you."

"I'm glad!" she said, and they both laughed. She had always been honest with him; he admired it.

"Have you seen your mother?" she asked after a while.

"Yes, I got in this morning."

"She has always been strong."

"I know her strength," Kaitarō snapped, before bowing his head in apology. "And now she is alone."

Megumi said nothing. He wondered if she still disapproved of him, if she thought he had been wrong to leave his mother here, to leave them both here.

"You look well," Megumi said. "The city suits you."

The waiter approached bringing a tray of pebble-brown sweets, tea, and a damp hand towel. He smiled at Megumi and chatted with her about the day's catch and asked if Tsuji would be in later. Kaitarō thought that under normal circumstances she would have introduced him, but Megumi seemed to sense that he wouldn't stay long, that he didn't want to leave too much of an imprint.

"I wouldn't like Tokyo," she said when the waiter had left them. "I've seen it on those shows, you know. Lots of rich people in their tiny apartments."

Kaitarō smiled. "Not everything good comes from a house near the sea with three square rooms and a corridor kitchen."

She shrugged and bit into a sweet.

"What is she like, your city girl?" she asked.

"She's thoughtful," Kaitarō said. "Strong. A photographer. She has a daughter."

"Is she beautiful?"

"Yes, she's beautiful."

Megumi nodded and played with her hair, stretching out the strands between her fingers.

"When does she arrive?"

"Tomorrow."

"How long will you stay?"

"I only want to show her a few things."

"Do you want to have dinner with Tsuji and me?"

"No, thank you, I—"

"I'm glad," she said with a quiet smile.

"You'd like her, Megu, really you would."

"I'm sure."

"Perhaps we could have tea instead?" Kaitarō suggested.

"I'll meet her sometime; it's a small place, our home." She grinned at him then, knowing how he felt about it.

"I am pleased for you and Tsuji," he said. "Where are you living now?"

"We have a cottage by the pier. I love it," she admitted, and she smiled at him freely this time.

"It's not the one you used to point out to me?"

"It is actually." She was laughing. "Tsuji built a porch around it." She smiled again as she spoke of her husband, her lipstick all gone. "In the summer evenings, we have tea out there."

"It sounds idyllic."

"It is. For me, it is," she said.

"Shall I call for the bill?"

"No, no, they'll put it on my tab."

"But Megu—"

"I insist. You are my guest."

They gathered up their coats and left the shop.

"I meant to ask, do you have children?" Kaitarō asked, grinning at her and buttoning up his coat as they walked along the beach road.

"No." Megumi stopped on the path. "We can't have children."

Kaitarō paused, awkward in the silence. "I'm sorry," he said finally, trying to recapture the ease they'd just had with each other. "But you are happy, Megu?"

"I am," she said. The kindness he had seen when she'd looked in at him through the window was there again in her gaze, rueful, but there. She squeezed his hand. "I want you to be happy too, Kai."

"You know, I just might be," he said, smiling at her.

"Good!" Her answer was bright, like when they were kids. "I'll see you," she said, and she walked away from him then, down the coastal road around the curve of the bay, her green umbrella swinging like a benediction. There was no way, he thought, that he could thank her.

## *LAST LOVE*

Sapporo as they approached it from the air was not as she expected it to be. When the plane had begun its descent, flying low over Hokkaido, Rina had looked down eager to see the land of small black bears, vast ice plains, and winter breweries. But the island's capital was just another city; it sprawled, gray and crowded, tapering into fingers of suburbs to the north and southwest. Unlike the view from Narita, however, where the vastness of Tokyo stretched to the horizon, Sapporo petered out, giving way to flat plains and pine forests bristling green in the mist.

In the baggage claim, she scanned the people in the hall, looking for him. As she waited, she tightened the rainbow wool scarf around her neck and pulled it down into her coat, breathing in the scent of her daughter. Sumi had been standing by the door in Meguro just before Rina left for the airport. Yoshi had nodded farewell, but he did not reach for her. Sumi, however, had tugged her down for a cuddle and given her the scarf. "To keep you warm," she had whispered, as Rina knelt before her. Then she'd pressed a small Care Bear into Rina's hand. "He'll enjoy a trip," she said, and Rina had laughed, holding her daughter tight. "I'll be back in a few days, okay? This is important." Sumiko nodded as Yoshi moved to stand beside her and took her hand. "You'll miss your flight," he said.

Now as she waited beside her bags, her family seemed far away. The minutes lengthened as she stood by herself. Then, at last, she saw him. He was walking towards her, a satchel slung over his shoulder. So strange, she thought, that she had not sensed him this time, nor seen him out of the corner of her eye, but he was walking straight towards her—openly now—and when they met in the center of the concourse, the light in his eyes was something to see. "Rina," he said, looking at her, smiling before his lips touched hers, taking his time, savoring the fact that they could now kiss in public. Rina's hands came up to brush through his hair, and at the feel of him, the warmth of him against her, she smiled.

They drove north along the coast road, the ice of the sea breeze kept at bay by the sporadic gusts emanating from the car's heater. They drove for about two hours, past the river of Rumoi and the port there, finally stopping amid a small cluster of houses in a bay. Rina unbuckled her seatbelt and turned to look around. There was a local store behind them and further down the road, a café. Finally, she turned to Kaitarō to see him watching the small bungalow to their right. A gray trickle of smoke crept from its one chimney.

"She's in," he said, turning the key in the ignition and waiting for the sound of the engine to fade.

For a moment, Rina put her hand on his arm. "Can you believe we're here, Kai? Did you think we'd make it?"

"I hoped," he said with a quiet smile. "You scared me for a while there."

"Good!" Rina said, picking up her handbag and getting out of the car. She grinned as she came to join him.

"I'm nervous," she said, glancing at the house. The blinds were drawn and nothing of the interior could be seen.

"Don't be." Kaitarō tucked her hand into his arm and drew her to him. "We're together."

His mother was silent as she let them in. She bowed low to Rina and took her coat, offering her some guest slippers. Rina bowed too, peering covertly at the house. It was small as he'd said, and very dark because of the drawn blinds. Mrs. Nakamura walked over to the windows and pulled on the strings, letting in the light. The wintry glow of the afternoon highlighted her hair, wisps of it emerging from her bun, and the housecoat she had pulled over her trousers. She had been asleep when they rang the bell, Rina thought, as she followed her into Kaitarō's room, past the kitchen where the window looking onto the sea was now clear of all pots and plants.

Rina stood in front of that window later. There was a bowl of cold water before her and she was rinsing the rice that had settled at the bottom, swirling the grains until the water grew cloudy with starch. Mrs. Nakamura stood beside her and said little as they worked, though she glanced occasionally at Rina out of the corner of her eye, monitoring her progress. Rina smiled. She hoped her technique would win approval; it felt good to be standing in Kaitarō's home with his mother, making rice for their family.

They would clearly have a feast that evening, for the array of autumn produce on the kitchen counter was beautiful to behold. Rina said so, gesturing at the fat matsutake mushrooms, a pumpkin, and a fillet of salmon so fresh and wild that its flesh was a deep red. She was rewarded with a small nod and handed a delicate green kabosu so she could scratch the skin of the citrus and smell its zest. There would be grilled matsutake seasoned with the kabosu, she was told, and salmon nabe, glazed pumpkin, and sticky rice. Rina smiled so widely that her excitement thawed Kaitarō's mother a little more, and she invited Rina to call her by her first name, Shinobu.

They ate together that night beside the heater in the central room at a low table with blankets on their laps. Gradually, Shinobu began to speak a little more about herself, and Rina took great pleasure in the smiles she directed at her son. Kaitarō relaxed too, the tension easing from the set of his shoulders, now that they were all together in his home. Rina said little in the beginning, but then she began to join in the stories, talking of Sumiko and Tokyo. Eventually, Kaitarō began to tell his mother about the life they planned together, and in this he spoke for them both.

When they were having tea, Rina went to her suitcase to fetch the present she had brought with her. Sitting down on the floor with them and wrapping the blanket once more around her legs, she lifted the box and presented it formally. "It is not new," she said, "but I brought it from home." Rina watched, anxious and excited as the wrapping was set aside to reveal an antique miso bowl. "It belonged to my mother," Rina said, watching as Shinobu smiled.

Very slowly the older woman lifted the blanket around her

knees and rose to her feet. "I have something for you too," she said. "Well, for both of you." She went into her bedroom and returned with a key; it had a little plastic label hanging from its ring. "This belonged to Kaitarō's uncle," she said, joining them again. "He left it to me when he died. It's the key to the shed he used as his darkroom." She smiled slightly. "It meant a lot to Kai when he lived here. Perhaps he will show it to you." Kaitarō reached out and took the key, holding it in the hollow of his palm. Then he turned to his mother and grasped her hand.

═

"When did your father die?" Rina asked as they walked along the sea road the next day.

"A couple of years ago."

"And how is she?" Rina hesitated. "Without him?"

"She told me he mellowed towards the end." Kaitarō walked quickly as he drew her along the bay towards the café and dock where the fishermen were already sorting out the day's catch. "I can't believe he was the first to go," he murmured. "I always thought—"

"I can imagine," Rina said. "Is it true?" she asked. "That he mellowed?"

"She said that to comfort me," he replied.

Rina paused on the path; she wanted to ask more, but they had reached the sea and Kaitarō was already calling out to the younger men by the boats. Some of the older ones turned too and nodded at Kaitarō as he approached them and began to haggle over the catch.

"What are you doing?" Rina asked when he returned to her, his hands full of plastic bags wet with fish.

"Cooking you lunch," he said. "Come on."

They stopped to pick up some yuzu, kindling, and other bits at the local shop. Rina hung back in the aisles, taking it all in, the familiar rows of ingredients; the shop even had conbini bento in the large fridge to the side. Every now and then she caught someone looking at her, but she just smiled and turned away. Eventually, she went outside to wait, looking down the road, past the fishermen and their boats to the wide flat expanse of the shore stretching down to the sea. In that moment aerated bales, like grounded clouds, chased each other across the beach—foam from the deep seas whipped up with plankton and sand.

"We're going over there," Kaitarō said, pointing towards the wet plains and the crashing surf.

"It will be freezing!"

"It will be worth it, I promise." Rina frowned at him as they stepped out onto the street, feeling the grit of the salt someone had spread on the walkway. The path was certainly slippery in parts, and the frigid wind blew straight off the sea and into her face. "I want to get back to Sumiko in one piece!" she squealed.

"You will," Kaitarō said, taking her hand with a smile. "Come on, wild Hokkaido girl."

Rina grimaced as they left the road and began to walk out across the sands.

"There's a cove not far ahead."

In the end he was right; the rocks sheltered them from the cold, and among them was the entrance to a cave where the winds could not reach them. Inside was an old metal grill set against the wall, wrapped in a tarp.

"It's communal," Kaitarō said as he joined her at the mouth of the cave.

Rina watched as Kaitarō unwrapped the grill and cleared the old fire pit, digging out the ashes. He built the fire up slowly using the tarp as a shield, arranging the wood shavings and twigs he had bought at the shop. Eventually, he placed the grill beside the flames. Then he took a board and knife out of his backpack and set out the bags of produce, shrimp, and a whole fish with a speckled olive skin whose name Rina did not know.

"I'll be back in a minute," Kaitarō said, picking up the knife and seafood and walking down to the sea. A little anxious about the fate of their lunch, Rina watched him, but soon she smiled, admiring his skill as he slit the belly of the fish open as though slicing down an invisible seam, deftly clearing out the dark red and maroon innards and washing the blood away in the water. Beyond him, the sun began to set on that short winter afternoon and the squid fishermen lit the lamps on their boats, their lights dotting the horizon.

The fire was burning steadily when Kaitarō returned, and a

breeze prodded the flames, bending them for a millisecond and flicking them straight again. As the light began to fade, shards of wood broke away, smoldering into embers at the bottom of the pit. He'd bought a number of things while haggling, including the sweet shrimp that were in season now in the far north. She had seen pictures of them, but the ones before her were enormous, a full hand span at least, pale orange tinged with red, and so plump and meaty she could already imagine their intense flavor when roasted. Rina's stomach rumbled as Kaitarō peeled the rind of a yuzu with his knife and threaded some of the prawns onto skewers before draping them with strips of knobby yellow peel. He did the same with the translucent chunks of fish. Rina watched transfixed as he worked. She was wondering about the fish, about what it was, when he told her—a wild halibut. She had tried some in Tokyo, but when he handed her a skewer she was amazed. It had never tasted like this, so rich and firm as she placed it in her mouth, oozing with sweet liquor, which combined with the oils from the yuzu was slightly singed and bitter on her tongue. In delight, Rina sucked the juice off her fingers and then bit into the prawns, savoring the rich umami. They were extraordinary, these skills of his, and so straightforward too, so natural.

By the heat of the fire, he shed his jacket, leaving only the thick weave of his jumper and his scarf. Both were unfamiliar to her; he must have taken them from his room at home. She couldn't imagine him wearing them in Tokyo, but they suited him here, in this rough and elemental place. There were crabs in his bag, still live, and he had placed his coat on top of them. "I'll cook them when we get home," he said, though she hadn't asked. Smiling to herself, Rina reveled in this side of him, this man who could cook crab and probably lobster too, who knew the tides year-round and where to place the oyster nets in the spring. He seemed at ease here, and he became more so as Rina devoured the fish because it was so good, so fresh, only hours old. Eventually, they cuddled together, never quite warm but replete, sitting close.

"You will have to do this for Sumi," she said after a while.

He looked down at her, nestled in his arms.

"In Tokyo?"

"In Shimoda on the beach by our house. Or we can bring her here? She would like it," Rina mused. "She's a real little savage."

"Like her mother," Kaitarō said, leaning down to kiss her.

"Like her father," Rina replied, "who will teach her to fish."

Rina smiled at the strength of the emotion on his face; it matched her own. "If you'll have us," she said. He pressed her down onto the rocky floor of the cave and kissed and kissed her. Beyond them, at the far end of the beach, the tide had turned, laying bare a stretch of fine shingle where a lone sandpiper lingered, looking for food.

# Part Four

Be bad, but don't be a liar.

—TOLSTOY

# *Sumiko*

## *SHIMODA*

There are constants in your life whose significance you don't realize until they're gone. Our home in Shimoda was like that for me; it was the last thing I expected to lose. For so many years that house had been at the center of my family, a site of love and happiness. I thought of all who had lived there and what it had meant to them. As I grew up I wondered about the stories in its walls; echoes audible only to those now deep underground.

What I remember most vividly is not a picture or a person, but a sound. The sound of the clock in the living room chiming the hour. When Grandpa went down to Washikura alone, I would phone him from Tokyo. Each time I did so I would listen very carefully. I could hear the soft timbre of Grandpa's voice. If the window was open there would be the faint cheeping of birds, and through it all the clock would chime, slow musical notes. I am told this is the sound of Big Ben, the largest clock in the world, but for me it is Shimoda. From the dust and smog of Tokyo, when I heard that clock down the telephone I could see the gleaming teak floors of our home; I could feel the warmth of the sun shining into the living room. I could even picture the ocean just beyond the edge of our garden, the light catching on the waves, the ocean I had lived beside all of my life. The sound of the clock would drown out what Grandpa was saying, but for those few seconds the words themselves didn't matter; it was as though I was there with him, in the heart of our home, listening.

There are other things I remember. On summer mornings, when I had slept late and come down to find that everyone had gone out into the garden, I would stand barefoot on the pink linoleum of the kitchen, a cup of hot Milo in my hands, looking out across the lawn sloping down to the cliff's edge. I watched the sun rise high up over the ocean, illuminating the south arm—a finger of molten lava that had poured down into the sea, and the tiny white lighthouse that stood at its tip.

Some days the water was charcoal gray and choppy, heralding a coming storm. But sometimes, in bright sunlight, as I followed the path of my grandmother's bougainvillea around the veranda of the house, the white clouds on the horizon would darken and roll inland as mist, and the wind would carry with it the salt of the sea.

Grandpa taught me how to tend the bougainvillea and, year upon year, regardless of the rough cold air, the gnarled branches remained, bristling purple with a tiny white flower in each fluted cup. That last summer, when I walked out onto the grass, it had never occurred to me that there would come a time when my home, our land, and that view of the sea would no longer be mine.

I still go to Shimoda. I take the train and walk from the station up into the hills and through the forest. I can sense my mother there; I can feel her with me just beyond the curve of the trees. Still, when I venture down the slope to the bank where the tree line thins, I am brought back to reality. I look down at our house and I feel like a thief.

New people live there now. I am trespassing on them and on my own memories too. My grandfather's greenhouse, built to grow strawberries in the winter months, is gone and in its place is a plastic inflatable pool. The gardens and flower beds have been replaced by grass that is easily maintained. The old wooden veranda, which shaded the southern part of the house, has been torn up and the area is now laid with concrete and tiles. There is no bougainvillea. When I look up at the windows of my bedroom, I expect to see my tiger, Tora, waiting for me, but instead there are no toys at all. The people who live there know nothing of my family; they did not build our home, and they do not know what happened there. What was mine is mine no longer, and what was there is gone.

# *FOR THE CHILD*

What do you have left of your family? Memories, keepsakes, perhaps even some home videos or, if you're lucky, clips of loved ones on TV? I have only my Kodachrome slides and these tapes: reams of film, glossy and treacherous, like oil; recordings of a man who was charged with my mother's murder. I have watched each interview repeatedly. What haunts me is the last one and the feeling that it was always going to lead to this.

When I first watched the opening moments of this tape, there was no outward sign of what was to come. The windowless walls of the interrogation room told me nothing. I could not even see what kind of day it was—fresh with a breeze rustling through the leaves or wet beneath a sullen gray sky. I only knew that when Kaitarō came into the interrogation cell and sat before the camera, his demeanor was the same as it had been for every other tape filmed during the investigation.

Kaitarō had refused to sign the first confessions that were prepared for him by the police detectives, and there had been no sign of them since, but today when Prosecutor Kurosawa enters the room he carries a leather portfolio under his arm in addition to a newspaper. Kaitarō looks up and nods as though greeting an adversary whom one might, in other circumstances, quite like. His lips twist when he sees the folder and the confession within it, but by the end of the day he will look at it differently and he will do so under a new form of duress.

Kurosawa pulls a packet of cigarettes from his back pocket. He taps out one and then another and offers the first to Kaitarō, who lifts an eyebrow as though asking the price. Kurosawa sets the cigarette down in front of Kaitarō nonetheless and lights the other, taking a long, slow drag.

"The press are out in force," he says after a moment, "foreign boys in particular."

Kaitarō glances down at the cigarette and with a gentle flick of his finger rolls it back to Kurosawa.

"Mr. Sarashima has applied for custody of the child," the prosecutor remarks, sitting down. His posture like Kaitarō's is relaxed and friendly. "Reporters approached him at home—luckily the child was away with the housekeeper at the time," Kurosawa says, "but now he's had to pull her out of school."

"Will they go to Shimoda?" Kaitarō asks.

Kurosawa pauses. "No," he says, eventually. "The house is for sale."

"I see," Kaitarō says softly.

"Were you close to Mr. Sarashima?"

Kaitarō considers this for a moment and then shakes his head. "Only one person was close to Yoshi."

"His daughter?"

"Yes."

"Did he approve of your relationship?"

"In the end."

"You did not care for him?" Kurosawa presses. When Kaitarō does not reply, he changes tack. "What of the child? You knew her, you liked her?"

"How is she?" Kaitarō asks.

"She has lost both her parents and she cannot live in her own home."

Kaitarō swallows. He leans forward and places his palms flat on the table, looking down at his hands, his nails long, overgrown, but clean.

"The press would let up if we could proceed to trial."

"Really?" Kaitarō asks. He is still looking down, though his voice contains a thread of levity. I cannot not tell if it is wry or indifferent, real or feigned.

"Once I file the indictment, the trial will be expedited. Attention will move away from the family."

"You have your evidence."

"True." Kurosawa leans back in his chair.

"Will they be left alone?"

Kurosawa shrugs. "I cannot control the press, but media attention will shift, at least."

"And Sumiko?"

"Will grow up with her grandfather."

Kaitarō sits forward. "Has he told you what he plans to do?"

Kurosawa pauses for a moment, as though deciding how much the information is worth to Kaitarō. Eventually he says: "He has found a new school and will change her surname."

"To Sarashima?"

"Yes."

"He gave this to me," Kurosawa says, reaching into his portfolio and drawing out a photograph. He offers it to Kaitarō, who takes it in both hands. For a second I cannot breathe as I realize it is a picture of me. Very gently, Kaitarō lays the photograph down on the table in front of him, his forefingers resting against each side of my face. I am six years old, dressed in my uniform for my first day of school. I look very neat and very small. Yet, despite all the formality, you can still see the excitement in my eyes, the brightness of my smile and I am suddenly sure who the photographer is, that I am looking at my mother.

Kaitarō's finger traces the curve of my cheek, coming to rest at the dimple at the corner of my mouth. "Rina kept a copy in her wallet," he says. "She was never without it."

"This is not just about you," Kurosawa says pointedly, watching as Kaitarō's face lifts, suffused with rage and pain.

"What do you need?"

Kurosawa reaches for the leather portfolio on the table between them and draws out a thick sheaf of papers bound with a large clip. This confession is much lengthier than the ones Kaitarō first rejected. Kurosawa places an ink pad and pen next to the papers on the table.

Kaitarō takes a deep breath. "One of your flunkies write that?"

"No, I did." Kurosawa keeps his eyes on Kaitarō's face. "I referenced the tapes," he says. "Do you want to read it?"

Kaitarō sits still, thinking. He looks at the papers lying on the table and then he gestures for a pen. "I trust you," he says.

In silence, Kurosawa slides the papers towards him and Kaitarō signs where he is told. As he reaches for the pad of ink so that he can mark the final page with his fingerprints, Kurosawa offers him another cigarette. Very deliberately, Kaitarō shakes his head.

"You really don't want one?"

"I quit," he says.

"When?" Kurosawa asks

"A year ago."

"For her?"

"Yes," Kaitarō says. "For Rina."

If I close my eyes, I can still see Kaitarō's hands on my photograph, the ink pad beside him and his fingerprints on the paper, the characters of his signature. If I cover my ears, his voice remains in the darkness. From the very first moment I heard them his words stayed with me, swirling in my head: the intimacy with which he spoke about me, the softness of his voice as he said my mother's name, the confidence when he spoke of our holiday home, Washikura. He refers to it by the shorthand "Shimoda," as did my mother and as do I. He knew so much about us, was almost one of us. I remember the way he spoke about my grandfather. He called him "Yoshi," not Mr. Sarashima. "Yoshi"—as though he had the right. As I sat in my bedroom with the screen flickering before me. I realized that my grandfather too had had a complex relationship with Kaitarō Nakamura, and that the answers I sought would not be found in the defense file or in the study or anywhere in my home in Meguro.

## *AN EYE FOR AN EYE*

The road leading to Grandpa's office was broad and quiet. There were several buildings on the way, squat business centers with floors rented out to accounting firms, but it was also a residential area, a slower environment for the practice of law than the glass-towered firms in Roppongi, where I had been offered a position. As I walked, I looked up at the trees lining the sidewalk. The leaves were motionless in the heavy summer air and it was quiet, very near dusk. The sky grew hazy in the twilight, that point in the evening that mirrors the dawn, and I could almost see my grandfather arriving at the office—an old man on his bicycle, the walking stick he now reluctantly used secured in the basket. The man who had raised me. Suddenly I was grateful that he was far away, where what I was about to do could not yet hurt him.

I buzzed the intercom and took the lift to the first floor. Walking through the open pool of secretaries, I stopped beside my grandfather's PA, Auntie Yuka, who had joined the firm when I was twelve. She was seated in a small cubicle beside his office. "Sumi-chan," she exclaimed when she saw me. "Congratulations on your offer from Nomura & Higashino." I smiled and nodded, taking her outstretched hand. "Your grandfather told me before he went to Hakone. He is so proud of you!" She beamed at me and patted my arm, squeezing it affectionately. I gave her a small smile in return.

"Such a good girl! We are all so pleased."

I bowed and thanked her once more, looking around at the

office I had visited as a child.

"Auntie," I said, "Grandpa has sent me to collect some documents for him. He wishes to look over some paperwork once he returns."

"Of course, dear," she replied, taking the keys to his office out of her desk drawer. "I wish you would tell him not to work so hard. Do you know he keeps calling in for his messages?" I nodded, murmuring something about stubbornness, and she patted my arm again. "He will slow down when you join us here after your time at Nomura. We are counting on you."

"Thank you," I said, accepting the keys. My hand was on the door handle of Grandpa's office and I was about to push inside when she called to me again. "Sumichan, would you like me to bring you some tea? Oh—how was your talk at Tōdai?"

"It went well!" I said, shameless now. "Please, I should hurry—"

"Of course, dear! You must have so much to do before you start at Nomura. . . ." She was still talking as I bowed once, and then twice, and shut the door.

Once inside, I breathed in the familiar scent of the office, cedarwood and sawdust and a hint of the lemon that Grandpa liked to drink with black tea. His tea service stood on the lacquer bureau: a Tokoname ware ceramic pot with a set of cups on a fitted tray—no vending machine here. The ikebana of lotus leaves and lilies by the window was elegant and fresh, replaced every three days. Nothing was neglected, even in his absence.

I walked past his desk and headed for the cabinets and drawers on the far right of the room that were shielded by a tall ebony screen. All professional work was locked away in the firm's storage library on the third floor, but this was where Yoshi filed his personal cases. Any material he would have collected on the death of my mother and the man who killed her would be there.

Under my mother's name, I found my parents' divorce registration form and a copy of the settlement with their signatures and personal seals at the bottom. It detailed a gift of the Ebisu apartment and a further transfer of funds to my father. In the same file, dated several months later, were the sales agreement for our home in Shimoda, along with an advertisement that was featured in the local papers and run by estate agents: *A rare find! Unmodernized seaside home held by the same family for the last eighty years. Bargain price.* I glanced once more at the date and saw that this ad had been placed while Kaitarō Nakamura was still in police custody. At the very back of the file was an envelope, yellowed with age. My mother liked to seal her envelopes with stickers, even private documents that she kept for herself. She favored cranes—this one showed a bird in flight—now torn in two. I stood and traced the ragged edges of the sticker with my fingertips.

It took me a while to find Grandpa's notes on the trial. The papers were filed under "Tokyo District Court," as though my grandfather had only been able to associate my mother's death with an instrument of justice. I took these to his desk along with the small yellow envelope and opened both.

What I discovered is hard to tell. I learned that the sale of my home in Shimoda was because of Kaitarō Nakamura. I learned that my grandfather had never come to terms with my mother's death or his role in it. I learned that he would hunt her killer to the very end of life in order to extract the ultimate price, an eye for an eye.

# *Yoshi*

## *1994*

Yoshi pushed aside the sliding screen and stepped into the dining room of Washikura. Before him was a large table in the western style, commissioned at Rina's birth. Slowly, he ran his fingertips over the maple wood. He loved its texture and variety, the splinters of gold mixed with stripes of deep brown with hints of charcoal at the edges, as though the tree itself had been singed. Slowly, he slid his hand across the oiled surface and paused over a knot in the wood, a walnut-shaped whirl, a mark of its age.

He used to talk to Rina here. She preferred this room to his study, and even as a little girl he would find her sitting at this table, looking out to sea, with her books and pencils laid out before her. It was here that she told him she had finally decided to leave her law degree. Here that they had argued again and she had explained her choice. He could still hear her words, see her pacing before the window. She thought best on her feet, as he did.

People will always need photographs, she said. In the future, whatever the changes in technology, pictures will still exist and people will treasure them. This is what I love. Don't you want that for me? Looking at her, so bright and purposeful, Yoshi realized that he wanted what she wanted. Now she was gone and he had only the echo of their words around him.

It was at this table too that he had first confronted her about Kaitarō. It was during the summer—the last summer they had spent together in this house. Sumi had gone out to play in the garden and Rina, perhaps sensing the opportunity for time alone, had been making herself some tea. She was coming out of the kitchen when Yoshi intercepted her. She halted, cup in hand, and wrapped the edges of her cardigan around herself. Yoshi gestured to the dining room and, reluctantly, she followed him. They sat in silence for a few moments with only their thoughts between them. "You've been meeting someone," he said finally. Rina unclenched her hands from her steaming cup of tea and looked at him. Her expression was calm and resolute. "Just a couple of trips, it's nothing."

"Please be careful," he said, but she raised a hand to stop him. Yoshi watched as she rose from her chair. He remembered the rigidity of her stance and also, incongruously, her feet encased in white socks. It was the socks that stayed with him. She was a young woman, a mother, but still his girl, always his girl. "He is just a friend," she said, her voice firm, but not convincing. Yoshi pressed his lips together and tried not to reply, but in the end he was unable to. "You have not introduced him to Sumiko, have you? You've not brought him here?" he asked. When she did not answer he looked up at her. "No, Dad," she said then, "not here." She moved towards the door but as she passed him he felt her hand on his shoulder, the warmth of it spreading through to his skin. "I promise," she said. Now she was gone and this house was all he had left of her, one space alone that remained inviolate.

Yoshi sat at the table for a long while. It was some time before he could rise. There were times when he thought he might never get over the loss of her loss. He felt it in his body's resistance to life. His joints ached in the morning and he could not rise smoothly from his bed. He also knew that he was getting older, could feel in his bones that he was not young enough to be a father again, yet that was what he had to be: for Sumiko.

Out in the hall, Yoshi picked up his small suitcase and took it into his bedroom to unpack his things. He would stay for a few days and then send for Sumi. Hannae had taken her away to visit some relatives—to keep her away from the horror of everything and get her out of Tokyo, but now it would be good for them to be together here, in Shimoda. In the meantime, he would rest and try to find some peace; if he could not sleep at night, he would listen to the roll of the waves on the foreshore, the sound of the sea.

In the freezer Yoshi found frozen white salt-fish. He left it out to defrost and put a cup of rice into the rice cooker. He would light the wood burner in the living room and eat his supper in front of the fire. It was spring but the nights were still cold, and outside the skies were cloudy too, so not even the moonlight shone through to illuminate the darkness.

He placed the kettle on the stove and when the water had boiled he poured it into the small clay teapot to warm it. He prepared a light sauce of soy, mirin, and spring onions and steamed the fish. It was a basic meal, like the kind his father made when his mother was away and they'd had to survive as men together. When he was alone and low, it was what he liked best. When Sumiko was ready for university, he would teach it to her.

Yoshi moved into the living room to the basket by the wood burner and selected some kindling for the fire; he searched through the bundles until he found some scented applewood and loaded it into the stove with the paper and kindling. He sat there long into the night, with his meal and his tea. He fetched his father's old radio and placed it on the small side table next to his armchair. He struggled with the frequencies and wondered how his parents had managed with it in the sixties, and then, as the faint opening notes of Elgar slipped from the speakers, he closed his eyes and dreamed of the past.

Yoshi had come to Shimoda to consider what kind of life he could now lead with Sumiko. He needed time alone, to think and plan, but his grief was too raw, and the house felt desolate without Sumi in it. Its emptiness reflected his life back to him, showing him what he was: just one failed old man. Perhaps he and Sumiko could spend more time in Shimoda. He could teach her about his parents and how they used to live, tell her how the house came to be left to him and why it was so important. They could move down here; he could sell his legal practice and devote his time to Sumi. He would build the life for her that he had wanted for Rina. Keep her safe.

Upstairs in his briefcase was a set of arguments he had thought about sending to the public prosecutor leading the case against Kaitarō Nakamura. Yoshi would burn them. He would forget what he had done and what had been done to him. He would do this, he thought, for Sumiko.

The next morning, as the sun rose over the sea, Yoshi felt a modicum of his energy return. He phoned Tokyo and consulted with his secretary before breakfast. His thoughts of the new life he would build in Shimoda had given him a sense of purpose; they would help him push through his fear and his grief. He went to the market and spent a good while browsing until he found the perfect piece of halibut. He did not even haggle. At home he put the fish on the counter and set aside the herbs he would need for his supper along with a yuzu he would zest for garnish. In these fleeting moments, Yoshi felt as though part of his youth was with him again. He would cook properly and think of the future.

In the afternoon, he walked around his home with a notepad and pencil; he surveyed the house and thought of the changes he would have to make if they were to move down here. He would extend the porch so they could have barbecues. He should redecorate Sumi's room and have a new set of bookshelves and a desk installed for her, so she could study. There was also the den off the dining room. Until now, it had been a storage space, a place to keep coffee table books and garden shoes. The room looked out onto the garden and down to the sea, but it was unmodernized. Unlike the dining room, there were no sliding glass doors, only a window that leaked. Beneath the window, water stains visible in the wood, was a chest that doubled as a window seat. Rina used to sit there on the afternoons when she wanted to be alone; this was her room really. Perhaps he could convert it into a snug for Sumiko, so she would have her own space.

Yoshi set down his notebook and walked over to the chest. Over the years it had been the keeper of many things—Rina's toys, Rina's magazines, Rina's gardening gloves for the greenhouse, Rina's flip-flops and beachwear from when she took Sumi down to the sea. It would have to be cleared, and for a moment Yoshi looked at it with desolate apprehension. It would contain things of Rina's that she had touched, loved, and casually discarded, sure she could retrieve them again as soon as she needed to.

As Yoshi opened the chest, a faint odor of mold rose up to meet him. He looked down. The chest was filled with magazines that had gotten wet, Rina's old sandals and Sumiko's red bucket for the beach. Yoshi located a plastic bag and began to empty the magazines into it. The chest was not as full as he thought it would be; perhaps Rina had cleared it out the previous autumn. He found a couple of architecture books that he'd bought with Rina in Atami, years ago, when they had first thought of renovating the house. He set them aside, but as he did so the slipcover fell away from one of the books revealing the black hardback beneath. Yoshi opened the book to realign the flap but what he saw made him forget about the cover. There was an envelope wedged into the seam, sealed with one of Rina's stickers, a red-crowned crane in flight.

His hands shaking, Yoshi sliced the crane in half with his thumb. There was no note inside, no letter, only a square Polaroid that slipped from the envelope. Yoshi turned it over in his hands. The picture could have been of a much younger Rina; she was radiantly happy, looking straight at the camera. She was also wearing an oversized shirt. As he looked closely he could see it was a man's shirt, partially buttoned. Her legs, which she had curled beneath her, were bare. Around her shoulders was the arm of the photographer. His face too was young, deceptively so, and unmistakable. They were sitting in Yoshi's armchair by the wood burner. Rina had lit the fire and you could see the glow of the flames beside them. The man was dressed in khaki pants and he was wearing Yoshi's gardening fleece that had gone missing that summer. Rina must have fetched it for him from the den, perhaps in exchange for his shirt. Kaitarō was smiling as he held Rina. Their faces were close, inseparable. On the back she had written *home in Shimoda.*

Yoshi dropped the photograph to the floor. Rapidly he leafed through the rest of the book but there was nothing more. He fanned it through his fingers and lifted it up, shaking it, but there was nothing there, nothing else for him. He threw the book aside, not caring as it slid across the floor. He knelt down, looking at the picture of his daughter and the man who had killed her. As the evening drew on he did not move; the sun lowered on the horizon and still he sat. It was only when it became too dark to see that he got painfully to his feet.

Yoshi knew when the photograph was taken. Their hair was damp and there was sand in it. She had lit the wood burner to dry off, but it was summer; you could not swim in the bay much past August. He thought back to that summer, to their last year as a family in Shimoda. There were only a couple of possible dates, short weekends he had spent at Mount Fuji with Sumi, when Rina would have been alone and could have let her lover into their home. He moved towards the trunk in the den and threw open the lid. In a rage, he tossed everything into the plastic bag. These were Rina's things, but he did not care. He found a man's shirt missing a few buttons, and his grief imploded. He picked up Rina's red sun hat that she loved to wear to the beach and crumpled the red matting in his fist, tossing it aside. He kept going until he found a notebook, crisp with newness. He wanted to throw it away, but it looked innocent, untouched. She had only written on one page. Yoshi saw Sumi's name and a list of schools in the Shimoda area. Beneath this was a list of alterations to the house—

*snug for Sumi*
*barbecue pit*
*new deck?*

Rina had been lying to him for a long time. She had lied about the state of her marriage, her affair, her plans. After all he had done for her, the care he'd taken, the love—she had lied to him and not trusted him with her life.

Once more, Yoshi looked at the photograph lying on the floor. He could not bear their ease, their happiness together. Rina had brought Kaitarō here; she had been planning to live with him in their family home as he now planned to live with Sumi. She had been building a life for herself and she had not told him. She had been building a life, perhaps even without him. His throat raw with pain, Yoshi realized that she was not the daughter he knew; she had been taken from him.

It was late by the time Yoshi rose to his feet. His knees protested as he climbed the stairs, he had spent too long sitting on the floor of the unheated den. The halibut he had so carefully selected lay uneaten on the counter; the peeled skin of the yuzu had curled in on itself, dry and shrunken. Yoshi did not notice. He left everything out as he climbed into bed; it was many hours before he could sleep.

## *NO REST*

In Tokyo, days later, in the heart of his firm, Yoshi opened the cabinet in his private office where he kept his personal cases relating to his homes and his family. Yoshi sifted through the files before finding the one he was looking for. Reaching into a separate drawer, he pulled out the court guidelines for sentencing, a document he had read many times over the years. All around him were the trappings of his work: his tea set, his dictaphone.

Yoshi opened his file and set out each document. This was all the information he had amassed on the death of his daughter and the man who had killed her. One by one, he laid them across his desk. It was late. Outside he could hear the suppressed buzz of the office as the young attorneys made final calls and the assistants gathered their belongings to go home. There was the clink of crockery as one of them walked around the desks, collecting the cups.

Yoshi sat down. The task ahead of him was personal and it had to be done in privacy. Earlier, he had given several of his client briefs to the other attorneys; his secretary had been instructed to hold all calls and postpone his meetings for the next two weeks. His staff would not be involved in this case; it was a task for him alone and it would consume him.

There was a time when Yoshi had thought of burning this file. Back in Shimoda when he'd imagined that there could be a new life for him and Sumiko. But the past was relentless; it had been hiding in his sanctuary. Nowhere was safe; there was only the future and he had to finish what he had started. When he found a buyer for Washikura, he would put the funds into an account for Sumiko. He was too old to move from his life in Tokyo, too old to change course, but he could put the money aside for her. Perhaps Sumiko could start again, even if he could not.

His wrist ached as he reached for the final bundle of paper—these were his notes on the case, recommendations for sentencing, and, clipped to the front of the first page, the name and address of the lead prosecutor: Hideo Kurosawa. Yoshi ran his hands over the notes; he felt the paper under his fingers and his lips twisted. Normally, it was people with more than one death on their conscience who received the death penalty, but there were exceptions: this depended on the evidence, the motives of the killer, and the arguments prepared by the prosecution. Yoshi pulled a fresh piece of paper towards him and reached for a pen.

# *Sumiko*

# *THE TRIAL OF KAITARŌ NAKAMURA*

The lawyers of my grandfather's generation practiced across the spectrum of the law. Rather than specialize from the very beginning, as we do today, they were able to apply themselves to a vast range of cases. My grandfather lived for this work. He was an exceptional attorney and a generalist; he could turn his hand to anything, even death.

In his office, I found a case built for the prosecution. It was there in the form of a dozen letters accompanied by a log of when they were sent. Letters from my grandfather to lead prosecutor Kurosawa containing my grandfather's own legal arguments, each set out with his characteristic precision. There were no replies.

My grandfather began his case by addressing the wakaresaseya industry: barely legal, unregulated, and flourishing in Tokyo. He outlined the absence of any legislation or statutes to govern the industry (not even a license was required to work as a private detective or agent), and summarized the dangers this line of work presented to the public. He drew particular attention to the freedom these agents felt they had to manipulate the lives of ordinary people, and how their actions often led to deeds that were against the law. Grandpa argued that because there was no strong evidence of psychological damage in Kaitarō or a previous history of violence, his manipulation of my mother and subsequent assault on her were both self-interested and calculated. He emphasized that a hard line was needed to crack down on the industry and communicate a warning, an example to those who might follow in the footsteps of Kaitarō Nakamura.

Grandpa wrote at length about my family, but not in the way one would expect. He added to his case by setting out the details of our life. He described his personal wealth, the financial protection he had provided for my mother. He listed the bank accounts in her name. He illustrated, clearly and concisely, the financial motive Kaitarō would have had for staying with my mother and all he stood to lose if she left him.

Grandpa took pains to highlight that within months of meeting her, Kaitarō had been fired from his job and was forced to live with no real source of income, save sporadic earnings from his photography. It was clear, my grandfather said, that Kaitarō had invested a great deal of his life and his future in my mother, and that this was what was at stake.

Finally, Grandpa researched and cited several homicide cases in which the murderers were driven by selfishness and financial motives. He profiled the victims and the accused and detailed each of the sentences imposed, establishing a pattern. He chose trials that were as recent as possible. In all of them the courts had been unforgiving.

I have described to you how a prosecutor will present his view of a case to the court, and how an attorney will prepare a defense. So too do the courts establish a narrative of their own. The purpose of these narratives is to get to the heart of the events, to understand the true motivation of the accused, whether he has lied to the state or not, and the extent to which he feels any remorse.

When Kaitarō Nakamura was tried, it was not one judge who presided over his trial, but three. Public juries were not part of the legal system at that time, so the court's interpretation of events, the verdict and sentencing, relied solely on the men at the head of the courtroom, seated in ascending order by age and experience.

The youngest would have been just like me, a protégé fresh out of the Supreme Court training facility in Wakō. He would have been tasked with drafting the initial narrative and proposing a verdict and sentence. His work would then be revised by the second judge, a man in the middle of his career, perhaps on a three-year rotation to Tokyo. Finally, the dossier would be edited and approved by the third judge—a senior member of the establishment, there to represent the institution of the law.

My grandfather was well aware of the judicial temperament. Judges are human, just as a public juror would be, but they are not as unpredictable. Immersed in the system, reliant on prosecutors, and in charge of hundreds of cases at a time, judges mostly preside over guilty pleas. Their courtrooms become places where bad people are tried and their job is to root out the liars, to teach and correct. The role of the triumvirate still exists today, and it is in place to provide consistency in judgments—to ensure that the unilateral values of the legal system are upheld. Grandpa understood this. He knew that patterns of sentencing are set down much like patterns of thought. The more these patterns are repeated, the more their worth is reinforced. Judicial opinions evolve slowly. They do not shift much from generation to generation, and they can be predicted and tracked. By a skilled prosecutor they can be shaped, and that was what my grandfather aimed for.

Within Grandpa's papers was a sense of regret. Regret that he had arranged the match between my mother and father. In their divorce settlement my grandfather paid my father to get out of my mother's life. And it appeared that this money bought Yoshi one more thing.

Among the witness statements given to the prosecutor about Kaitarō Nakamura was a voluntary deposition written in the hand of Osamu Satō. He did this at my grandfather's urging, but also to spare himself the public shame and spectacle of being questioned before the court. In his testimony, my father admitted to hiring Kaitarō Nakamura. He said that he asked Kaitarō to seduce my mother and provide him with grounds for divorce. He described Kaitarō as a man who was difficult to control from the outset—a renegade who exceeded his brief from the very beginning and who later both stalked and threatened Satō.

It was clear, my father said, that Kaitarō had his eye on my mother's fortune; he said he loved her, but he had moved in with her so that she could support him. At their last meeting, my father stated that Kaitarō had shown every intention of continuing to deceive Rina and her family into the future. My father claimed that he had wanted to speak out, but that having hired Kaitarō he felt too ashamed. He said that he came close at several points to telling the truth but that Kaitarō had blackmailed him, threatening to expose him to his family. My father attempted contrition. He said that he could not forgive himself for his selfishness, his cowardice. He concluded that if Kaitarō and men like him could be prevented from doing any further harm, then my mother would not have died in vain.

The court gave my father a civil responsibility fine for his actions, but the prosecutor chose not to press charges. His deposition was filed away to form part of the overall narrative, and when Kaitarō Nakamura confessed, his statement became the most important testimony. So my father, who began it all, was free to go. Justice in the eye of the beholder.

There was no sign of what Grandpa really thought of my father's statement or his escape, but as I read on I could see that he used this deposition to reinforce his portrait of Kaitarō as a man whose refusal to speak to the police once in custody demonstrated his disregard for the truth and his lack of remorse. Grandpa stated that Kaitarō's delay in signing the confession presented by the prosecution had drawn out the misery of those he had already hurt and opened them up to the persecution of the press. He was a man who did not understand love or family and would never repent for what he had done. The emergence of an eventual signed confession did not indicate repentance, but rather a tired, guilty man's acceptance of the inevitable.

If confessions are a measure of "correctability"—an offender's potential to be educated and reintegrated into society—then my grandfather was determined that Kaitarō should not be rehabilitated. Redemption was and is reserved only for those who display genuine remorse. By detailing the absence of it in Kaitarō, my grandfather hoped to draw down the harshest punishment upon him, to ensure his death.

Capital punishment can take years to enact. It occurs without warning. People spend an eternity in cells waiting for the axe to fall, and then one day it does. Only when a person is dead will the family be notified and invited to collect the body.

This procedure has remained unchanged for many years, except for one amendment. When the treatment of forgotten parties was finally revised and the Victim Notification System introduced, victims' families were allowed to sign up to receive information about the criminals who had harmed them; they were entitled to know of their fate. So I realized the significance of the phone call I had received from the Ministry of Justice and what it had meant for Kaitarō Nakamura and me.

At the end of my grandfather's file, there was one more document: a personal statement written by my grandfather. I could see him, still seated at his desk after the legal arguments were done, finally removing his jacket and tie and draping them over the back of his chair. His tea, untouched while he worked, had developed a thin film which brushed his lips as he sipped from the cup. The liquid was cold, sharp, and he was glad of it. Before him was a clean piece of paper, but his hand shook; his fury was spent. The familiar cedarwood scent of his office enveloped him, reminding him of the trees lining the hills above Washikura. He could hear Rina's footfalls as she ran between them. It was as though she was there with him now, watching him. And there was nothing, no legal arguments, no precedents, only overwhelming grief. He had lost the person he loved most in the world, the person he had failed to protect. Yoshi knew that he was alone in his office, that Rina was not really there, and the only thing he could do was write the truth as he saw it. The truth had to be enough.

## STATEMENT OF YOSHITAKE SARASHIMA

My daughter, Rina, was my life. She was, until the birth of my granddaughter, my sole reason for living. There are so many things you fear as a parent; it is a state of almost constant terror. From the moment they take their first steps, you watch over them so carefully. You shelter them whenever possible. Your first urge is to protect them. As they grow up, you want to make sure their lives are perfect, that they will never face the hardships you have suffered, never be confronted with pain, never make your mistakes. And even when they make mistakes of their own you still want to catch them, no matter how old they are.

Rina is dead. I will never hold her again. My girl is gone and through no fault of her own. We did not always see eye to eye, but she was a wonderful daughter and a wonderful mother. She loved her own child so much that she was trying to do what was best for her when she was killed.

Kaitarō Nakamura took her from us. He put his hands around her neck and strangled the life out of her. This was not a woman caught out late at night by a mad man in the street; this was a mother in her own home, recovering from a divorce and choosing to put her daughter first. She wanted to leave him; she wanted to start again and remove her child from the influence of someone she could not trust. She wanted to make her world safe, and for that he took her from us.

I have many memories of Rina; they haunt me in the night and through every minute of the day. I am changed without her, broken. I will never hear her voice calling me through the rooms of our house, never feel her kiss on my cheek as she calls me Dad. I will never again watch her tucking Sumiko into bed at night or teaching her how to paint as my wife used to do with Rina. I cannot walk on the beach in front of our holiday home because with every step I expect to hear the click of her camera behind me, the fall of her footsteps as she runs across the sand. She will not age. She will not grow old with me. She will not see her daughter graduate from school or celebrate her coming of age day. She will not be there at Sumiko's wedding, and, most likely, neither shall I.

We lost my wife to cancer when Rina was just fifteen. It was a loss she felt keenly. She knew what it was to grow up without a mother. She would never have wanted such pain for Sumiko. She had such hope for the life her daughter would lead and all the experiences they would share together. She would have wanted Sumiko to know how much she was loved, but this is something I cannot even express.

I hope that Rina knew she was loved too. For so long it was just the two of us. I tried my best to raise and guide her. I tried and failed to be both mother and father to her. Now history has repeated itself and I must be both parents again, for Sumiko, if I can manage it.

I cannot escape the fact that I too am guilty. I will never forgive myself for the role I played in arranging Rina's marriage. I will never forgive myself for allowing her husband or Kaitarō Nakamura into our lives. I should have protected her. I should have saved her.

Incredibly, there are still moments when I experience happiness. I find myself smiling at something Sumiko has said or enjoying a simple task, a meal. These are things I cannot forgive either. I cannot forgive that I am alive and Rina is not, or that she is dead because of me. I dream of her spirit in the rooms of our house, and I hope that she forgives me. I will raise her daughter in the best way I know how.

And I know this: Rina would not forgive the man who willfully took her life, the man who did not love her enough to let her go. The man before you is a man who entrapped her, lied to her, and finally killed her. He knew what he was doing. He has destroyed all our lives. I implore, I beg you, for the honor of my daughter and the faith I have in the justice of these courts, to impose on him the only sentence you can: the sentence of death.

I sat alone at his desk, alone as he was, and the only thing that separated us was that the ink of his statement had long dried, and the paper I was holding was a photocopy, which my meticulous grandfather kept on file. I was crying. I had lost her all over again, and my grandfather's despair had morphed into my own as though it had always lived there in the fabric of this room waiting for me to find it. There was nothing left, only the remnants of those I loved. I tried to hold my memories of them close, but I could not; they had changed.

I thought of my grandfather, enjoying the hot springs, safe and warm in the comfort of knowing that I had secured my future; that it was all he had planned for me, that it would be bright. I thought of the man who taught me about justice, who held me on his lap and read me all the stories he knew. The grief of that man was as unfathomable as mine, but it had changed him. I could no longer see the person I knew. I could not understand how his grief and perhaps even his feeling of culpability had led to this.

As I sat alone with his papers, my fingers tracing them sentence by sentence, I wondered what else lay beneath his words. My grandfather had met Kaitarō Nakamura when he was free, when he had lived with my mother and loved her. Grandpa had known him, seen him through my mother's eyes, and glimpsed, however fleetingly, the life they were planning with me. He had accepted Kaitarō into our family, and the more I read over his statement and the case he had built against him, the more this intimacy bothered me, until I wondered if there was something else there too, a demon driving my grandfather harder than grief.

When I looked up from his desk, the room was dark. The sun had set while I was reading. I turned on the desk lamp and began to gather up Grandpa's papers and notes, putting them back in the file. It was then that I noticed the clear plastic folder beneath them, and the sight of it, jarring amid all I had read, actually made me smile. The label read: Yurie Kagashima. If my grandfather had prepared a case for the prosecution and supporting documents for Prosecutor Kurosawa, then he had also anticipated the defense. There were only a few pages inside and a typed letter.

I thought back to my first meeting with Yurie so many years before, when I'd been just a child. I still remembered her kindness, her eel bento and the Shogi set, but of course these memories had changed too, transformed into something else by my knowledge of events. Yurie Kagashima had met me, she had seen and touched my mother's body, and she told me herself that she had spoken with my grandfather. She had in fact approached him several times.

There was something about this case that made her do that, something beyond the evidence and even the videotapes. She had met Kaitarō Nakamura in the flesh as I never would. She had sat with him, looked at the scars on his face and listened to his tale, before they took him back to the cells and set a date for his trial.

Her sympathy for Kaitarō enraged my grandfather, but it did not dilute his understanding of her case. By the time I encountered his papers, I had read over all the evidence that had been amassed. I wanted to evaluate the documents for myself, read through the details closely and privately as the judges would do. I did not need the smoke screen of other people's opinions and agendas. Because of this, although I had looked over all the documents Yurie Kagashima had referenced and used, I had not yet read her personal notes or her summation—the written opinion that she would submit to the court. When I finally did later that evening, I was surprised by how accurate my grandfather's assumptions had been.

The young Yurie Kagashima was shrewd, but she was not as bold as her older self would be. It would take her twenty years to develop the confidence to act beyond the law as she had in giving me the files. During the trial, she accepted Kaitarō's guilty plea and the prosecution's case against him. Hers was a sympathetic but traditional defense. She spoke at length of his deep remorse, which she concluded was genuine. She repeated that he had loved my mother more than anything in the world. She repeated his claim that he did not want to live without her.

She knew what would appeal to the court, so she documented Kaitarō's offers of financial reparations to my family, all of which had been refused. She spoke of how Kaitarō had tried to set aside my mother's belongings from their home on the night she died and had asked for them to be returned to the Sarashima household and kept, for me. How he had gathered her photographs, her work, together in a duffle bag. She spoke of his lack of criminal history and former convictions. She grouped all of these factors together in an attempt to convince the court of his better nature, to reduce his sentence and save him from death.

Finally, she argued that the catalyst for the fatal events on March 23, 1994, was my mother's discovery of Kaitarō's true profession. At the heart of her case was the fact that Kaitarō had truly cared for my mother, loved her, but that once he started their relationship with a lie he had become trapped in a situation from which he could not extricate himself. His was not an act of cruel premeditation, but one of a desperate man who found his back to the wall. She described how my mother and Kaitarō were together, their mutual love and dependence. She wrote about the life they had planned together, of his intention to marry my mother and adopt me, and of his acceptance by my family.

Here, in his notes on Yurie Kagashima, my grandfather circled around and around this final point. So I discovered something as I had read over his personal statement and these papers that made my doubts and fears make sense. Yurie Kagashima was not imaginative, but she was thorough. She had the measure of my grandfather in a way I never have. She wrote to him, and this was the letter that I found in his file. It was a final petition to meet and discuss the compensation Kaitarō Nakamura had offered him. She said that in the interest of full disclosure, she should tell my grandfather that she had learned something about him. She knew he had hired a PI to investigate Kaitarō Nakamura and that he had been aware of his true profession and his role in our lives. She suggested that Yoshi's decision not to tell my mother the truth supported his acceptance of Kaitarō, and that if he had embraced him as a son once and forgiven him for past sins, could he not do so now?

This knowledge about Kaitarō had come into my grandfather's possession months before my mother's death, but he had never told her what he knew. There are phone records indicating that he called her in the week before she died, witness statements that he had visited her with springtime sweets and some of my things in preparation for the move. He who could perhaps have broken the news to her most gently, who could have prepared her and helped her see past it, had chosen to remain silent.

# *THE SUNFLOWER AND SCALES*

The Tokyo District Court is a sterile, dispassionate place. The sound of the hundreds of feet that pass through each day are muted by the gray linoleum floors, and the halls are filled with the somnolent whir of the ceiling fans. The rooms themselves are white chambers, an extension of the cells in which Kaitarō was interviewed, where the bare strip lighting bleaches the skin. Even the air holds no trace of life; recycled through the vents it remains the same temperature from the sultry heat of summer through to the frigid chill of winter—dead and artificially generated for a waiting room between one world and the next.

Of course, my grandfather attended the trial. He was no ordinary forgotten party to be kept away by ignorance or information denied him. As a legal professional he knew the system and was more than capable of ascertaining the court's schedule. Indeed, he understood the effect his presence at court would have. He would have counted on it. He would have used his presence as the father of a murdered woman, the grandfather of an orphaned child, his status as a respected attorney in Tokyo, to hold a mirror up to the law and keep it there.

There is only one homicide statute in Japan—Article 199 of the Penal Code. It states that "a person who kills another shall be punished." There is nothing more. The distinctions between calculated homicide, a crime of passion, or manslaughter are applied by the panel of judges as they determine the sentence. In 1994, they did this alone in a closed room accompanied only by the paperwork of the trial. My grandfather would have used his presence in court to highlight the seriousness of the crime and the consequences, to keep Kaitarō's profession and the brutality of Rina's murder at the forefront of their minds.

I have attended plenty of trials so I can imagine it all too clearly. My grandfather would have been unyielding as he sat before the court, firm in his silent condemnation, his fury. He would have shown no sign of knowing Kaitarō Nakamura, no empathy, no compassion. If he did, it might have undermined the case—it might have set Kaitarō free, and so he campaigned doubly hard for his death.

When Kaitarō entered the courtroom he was clean-shaven, his hair and nails cut and clipped by the state. He wore the regulation beige shirt and matching trousers. His hands were cuffed but he was also bound with a thick orange rope, which wrapped around his waist and was held by the guards who stood on each side of him; tethered like an animal in our gleaming modern city. He wore plastic slippers on his feet to further impede escape.

At the head of the courtroom on a dais sat the judges, swathed in their voluminous robes, the high black backs of their chairs rising above their heads. They did not stir as Kaitarō was brought before them. Flanking the judges on a lower step were five trainees in their navy suits, hands folded in their laps. On the left and right sides of the court, facing each other at parallel desks, were Prosecutor Hideo Kurosawa and Defense Attorney Yurie Kagashima.

The junior judge, a thin young man with an unfortunate scattering of acne across his cheeks, spoke first. He read out Kaitarō's name, address, and the crime he was on trial for: the homicide of Rina Satō. The judge asked Kaitarō if this information was correct, and he confirmed it with a simple "yes"; it was the only thing he would say throughout his trial.

Prosecutor Kurosawa rose to read the indictment concluding with the charge: murder. For a few seconds the court waited in silence. The junior judge glanced at his superiors and, after a nod from them, leaned forward towards Kaitarō. With each guilty plea a defendant is given the opportunity to speak to the charges and perhaps attempt to soften them. But here, Kaitarō, after a small shake of his head, said nothing.

An officer of the court approached Prosecutor Kurosawa, who handed him a thick paper file containing the signed confession. As the file was passed to the most senior judge, the prosecutor spoke: "Saiban-chō, the state regards this crime as one of the utmost brutality. Although you will read my opinion in the report I have submitted, I wish to emphasize at this point that Rina Satō died by suffocation as a result of being strangled.

"Such a death is singularly long and painful. The victim does not ever completely stop breathing, and so it requires a great deal of physical force over several minutes for cerebral hypoxia to occur. The defendant would have had to persist in the strangulation against all the victim's attempts to fight, the moments when she struggled and gasped for air. This in itself shows how malevolent her murderer's intent was, how strong his need to kill her. In those long, sustained moments there would have been no mercy or hesitation, only his will to take her life.

"We know that Kaitarō Nakamura is a supremely selfish man. He worked in a profession that is fundamentally destructive. He was paid to break up families and preyed upon a couple's unhappiness. He took this young woman away from her husband, her father, and her child. Their lives will never be the same.

"Although Mr. Nakamura's relationship to Rina Satō and his emotional attachment to her have formed a basis for speculation at the heart of this trial, I am of the opinion that there was no love in his history or his actions. He is a killer and a danger to society, and we believe the most appropriate penalty would be the sentence of death."

Kaitarō, standing in the middle of the court, suddenly turned looking not at Kurosawa and the team for the prosecution but at Yoshi Sarashima, sitting in the front row of the public gallery. Kaitarō's look was long and direct, and Yoshi did not disappoint; he matched him gaze for gaze.

With a slight cough, the defense counsel stood up to speak. Young Yurie Kagashima was dressed simply in a white shirt and black cardigan. Her hair was long and pulled back from her neck in a ponytail. She was holding in her hands a piece of paper from which she read.

"Saiban-chō, my client signed a full confession and agreed to the charges," she said. "Today he is here to be judged, and I would ask you, with your indulgence, to peruse the material I have compiled on my client's remorse, his genuine atonement for the grief he has caused Mrs. Satō's family, his relationship with members of that family, and the further circumstances of this case. In light of this material, I ask for a more lenient sentence than that proposed by the state."

The clerk crossed to her and she passed him a file and three videotapes. Every eye in the courtroom followed this file up to the high bench where it joined the case for the prosecution. The middle judge placed the files before him, one on top of the other. "The court will review the evidence and reconvene for sentencing in three weeks—Monday June 6," he said, and with that the three judges rose and filed out, with the clerk carrying the paperwork behind them. The prosecution exited through a door on their side of the court, and the public, having been suppressed into silence, burst into speech. As Kaitarō Nakamura was once more bound in rope, cuffed, and led out by his guards, my grandfather turned towards the gathered press. Yurie Kagashima, the young defense counsel, sat still at her table and watched.

═

A clock ticked behind me as I sifted through Grandpa's papers, scattering them into disarray, searching for the final court judgment. I combed through his file again and again but there was nothing. Judgments are not published or distributed. My grandfather certainly would not have been sent one, but then, having attended the trial, he would have known its outcome.

I thought of how neatly everything had been filed away, a matter accomplished. I thought of my grandfather's energy in raising me, the power of his will, his desire to exact revenge on Kaitarō, and I knew that between us all that was left for me to do was to wait for him to come home and ask him what it was like to kill.

Alone in his office, I picked up the envelope my mother had

sealed with a red-crowned crane all those years ago. Lifting the flap, I pulled out the Polaroid picture within. There they were: young, in love, so happy. Two people frozen in time. Two people, now dead.

Slowly, I began to put the files back together, reordering everything page by page. Yet, despite all I had lost and found in those documents, none of them answered my main question, which was how had it come to this? The facts remained before me, immutable and clear; I was just waiting for them to click into place, and somehow I knew, with a dread that did not waver, that soon they would. Once more, I went over the details of the case in my head. I thought of my grandfather, of his silence to my mother before she died. I thought of the footprint in the apartment that did not match the size of his shoes or Kaitarō's. The unidentified saliva on her body. I thought of my father, who had started it all and had retreated to a life in Nagoya. I thought of Kaitarō, who after his initial silence had wanted his story to be heard. And, finally, I thought of my mother, hoping for a new life. I thought of everyone who had been involved that day, in the last hours of her life as I pulled open my grandfather's filing cabinet and pushed back the other hanging files. And there, lying flat at the bottom of the deep drawer, in an envelope marked with her name, was a tape.

I remember reading the label several times. It did not make much sense initially, but eventually I realized with a pain that punched and twisted in my gut that it could only be one thing.

It was a security tape. The name of the bakery on the label was unfamiliar, but its location was in Shinagawa, and the footage was recorded on the day my mother died.

And so it turned out that what had haunted me all along—the fear that every member of my family would be tarnished by the events and changed beyond recognition by them—was true. Not only were we all involved in my mother's death, but each and every one of us was guilty, even me.

# *Rina*

# *THE TRUTH*

Rina pulled open the blinds, allowing the morning light to flood into her new home. It was March, the month of new life, and as she looked at the sun pouring across the floor she remembered the moment this place had truly become her home, when she and Kaitarō had first been given the keys.

They had lain side by side in the empty apartment. It had been warm enough to slowly strip the clothes from their bodies, to lie in the sun shining in from the windows and look at each other. The completeness they had found in Hokkaido was there with them as they lay on the bare beechwood floor in Shinagawa.

"Will it do?" Kaitarō asked, looking around at the empty space, the blank walls and stripped kitchen.

"It's lovely."

"I've some ideas for Sumi's room. I should show you—" he said, moving to get up.

"Not yet," she replied, tugging him back down to her, and he acquiesced without complaint. Rina nestled close, running her hands over his stomach, savoring the texture of him, the smell of her own skin mingling with his. She played with the smattering of hair on his chest and bit him idly. He turned and hugged her, pushing her onto her back. Through the clear windows, naked without their blinds, the light moved across their skin in bright, wet splashes with nothing to cast a shadow upon it.

Rina smiled at the memory. They had a thing for floors it

seemed, how embarrassing. She placed her fingertips on the glass window in front of her. Far from the tall, wide views that she had in Ebisu, this window was a rectangle set into the wall, revealing the chunky concrete apartment blocks and external staircases of Shinagawa. One of the things she liked most about this apartment was its position near the top of the building and the light this afforded them—this, and the fact that there was not a modern condominium in sight.

Rina turned back to the apartment; it was almost finished. The furniture from her marriage had been given to Satō along with the place in Ebisu, and in the months before she and Kaitarō had found this place, she had returned to Meguro to live with Yoshi and Sumiko. Now though, after so much preparation, their home was nearly ready, and she and Kaitarō had finally started their own small photography firm.

One of their first projects was a portrait service they offered to the neighborhood. When Rina looked back, she was amazed at the transition in their work, in how it had evolved from landscapes to themselves and now to this. She and Kaitarō had such responsibility behind the camera, but they found that they enjoyed the trust given so freely to portrait photographers; it was something they treasured. Most days they worked together, managing the orders, but they also alternated so that they each could work independently. While one was out at shoots or in the local communal darkroom developing, the other kept house, shopping at the market or browsing second-hand stores for furniture. Everything was coming together in this one small space that was finally theirs alone.

Along one side of the living room, Rina had placed a sideboard with cupboards for storage; these contained blankets and a portable heater for the colder months. At the far end was a tiny kitchen, and just before it, a square black dining table, low to the ground and surrounded by cushions on four flat seats. Rina thought of all the things that would happen at that table—family meals, Sumi's homework, Rina's sewing and the creation of costumes for local festivals. Perhaps, in time, another baby would come and Rina and Kaitarō would sit up late there going over the accounts long after both children were asleep.

Off the living room was a short corridor leading to the two bedrooms and a family bathroom. Rina had dressed the opening of the corridor with a noren, a silk screen made from a vintage kimono she had found in the Ichiroya flea market. The kimono was part of a wedding trousseau, an item that had been kept in the same family for decades, but it had been damaged in a fire and the material sold on. She loved markets and all the unexpected things you could find there.

As she worked with the fabric, Rina had been careful to preserve the central panel across the back, cutting only one slit in the silk, allowing the picture to remain intact, while providing a route through to the private areas of the flat. Now the embroidery shimmered in the morning light. In the middle of the panel were trees, their jade and emerald leaves spreading out in broad fans. Above this in ascending stripes were the golden tones of the sky and then, where the clouds should be, a flock of cranes in flight, their wings delineated in red, cream, black, and brown. Rina loved how the colors of the screen complemented the room. She had thought of it that morning while at the florist and had brought back a selection of flowers now wrapped in brown paper on the sideboard.

She walked into the kitchen and fetched a small crystal vase (a housewarming present from her father) and also her scissors. She was not trained in ikebana, was self-taught, but she preferred it that way. In the tall condominiums of Ebisu, floors and floors of women would join together for flower arranging mornings, boasting to each other about which instructor they had managed to secure, but Rina had never felt able to join them. Now she did not have to. First, she selected a green chrysanthemum with a long thin stem; each of its petals at once distinct and part of the group. Next was a bird of paradise flower with its red sheaves of flame tinted orange and yellow at the edges and finally, a branch of palm. Pressing her nail against the base of the frond and having made a small cut, Rina peeled it away in a long strip of green. She did this three times and wound the strands around the other flowers, creating a diagonal sash that held the stems upright, secured and still.

The ikebana complete, she placed it in the vase, smoothing out the strips of palm so that they stood tall and striking against the red and lime green of the bouquet. Then she smiled. It would be perfect for when Kaitarō came home, a vibrant welcome.

He had left early that morning and would be out all day photographing children's birthday parties. Her task was to finish painting Sumiko's room and affix the remaining silver star border to the walls. It was Sumi's last day at school before spring break. Rina had so much planned for them in the weeks ahead, including moving her daughter into their home. Yoshi wanted them to take it slow, to let Sumi stay a while longer with him, but Rina would not permit it. She and Kai had waited long enough. She would finish Sumi's room and as soon as everything was ready, they would finally live together as a family.

Rina changed into some old dungarees already smudged with paint and picked up the phone to call Kyubey She would pre-order bentos to be delivered, and then when Kaitarō finally came home they could spend the evening together. As she was putting down the phone, a knock sounded at the door. It was loud and startled her. The apartment block was old, and unlike her former home it had no porter; anyone could walk up unannounced. The bell was currently broken, so people had no option but to thump on the door, but this was something she hoped to fix. She saw him through the spyhole just as he called her name.

Satō smiled when he saw her, but it was not a real smile, and he did not remove his hat. "What took you so long?"

"Nothing," Rina murmured. "Why are you here?"

"Not going to invite me in, wife?"

"Ex-wife," she said, turning and allowing him inside. She did not offer to take his coat; he was not staying.

Satō removed his jacket and draped it over the bureau by the front door. He kept his shoes on and wandered into the apartment, hands on hips, looking around.

"It's not what you're used to," he said with a small smile. "Paying for it yourself, are you?"

Rina nodded and did not elaborate.

"Where's what's-his-name?"

"Kaitarō is out."

"On a case?" Satō was still smiling.

"What's it to you?" She moved to stand in front of him, in front of the silk noren, so that he could not go into the bedrooms.

"Is my daughter's room through there?"

"My daughter."

"Ours."

"Not anymore," Rina said. She was angry now, her initial shock at seeing him ebbing away. She stood her ground, squaring up to him as he continued to stare at her. He was not overly tall, had never been imposing, but he had just enough height to look down on her.

"What does Yoshi think of this arrangement?"

"We are getting married."

"Yes," Satō said, his eyes taking in the room, the low traditional table, the ikebana waiting to welcome Kaitarō home. "I had heard that."

As he said this, Rina took a step back. The look on his face did not bode well. "I want you to leave."

"No tour?" Satō said, crowding her. "No explanation of how my wife and child are going to live?"

"We are not—"

"We didn't part that badly, did we, Rina? I gave you everything you wanted."

"Why are you here, Satō?" she asked.

"I—"

"*I* never want to see you again," Rina said clearly. "I do not want Sumiko to see you, and I will not be persuaded otherwise." As she said this Rina smiled, a small, gentle smile. "We both know the law, don't we? We know what I can do and what you cannot. You have lost the power to challenge me."

"There she is," he said, "the fighter."

"Get out."

"So he's to be her father, is he? He'll raise her. Sit her on his knee?"

"He'll be a better father than you."

"Glad to have him in your life?"

"Evidently."

"Well, I put him there."

Rina turned away from him and walked over to the window.

"Honestly, Satō, get out, I don't have time for your games. I'm done playing with you."

"Has he told you about his work? His cases?"

"I am not going to discuss my future husband with you."

"Where do you think he is right now?"

"He's working."

"And where the fuck is my daughter?"

"With her grandfather." Rina looked up at Satō. "And he will make sure, as I will, that you never see her again." Rina pushed away from the windowsill and came towards him. "Don't think you can come here. I will bury you. I know all your secrets, and if you threaten me I will destroy your family and your life."

"I hired him, Rina."

"You are a liar."

"This family you have, this new life, your new marriage, it's because of me."

"I despise you."

"You think I couldn't tell you the truth if I wanted to?" Satō asked.

"You can't even be honest with yourself."

Satō's hand went to his mouth whether to stop himself from saying something or to affect a dramatic pause, it was unclear. Then he turned and picked up his coat. Rina breathed a sigh of relief, but she did not follow him to the door; she did not want to be near him.

"He's a wakaresaseya," Satō said adjusting his hat.

"What?"

"He breaks up other people's relationships for money."

"He's a photographer and you were leaving."

"Ask him."

"I shall do no such thing."

"Ask him how he knew to find you at the night market last year, when Sumi was so conveniently with Yoshi, and again at that photography lecture. When he took you to the nature reserve near your family home, did you think it was a coincidence? That he just happened to know the things you loved, could seduce you with nostalgia?"

Rina said nothing; the relief that Satō was leaving was fading away, replaced by something else. Still, she fought him. He had his coat on now and was coming towards her. He reached for her and she evaded his grasp, moving away until she felt the windowsill at her back. He joined her there and curled a finger under the shoulder strap of her dungarees, pulling her against him. Suddenly, she smiled. "Did it not work out with Naoko?" she asked and felt a pulse of triumph at his narrowed eyes. "Is that why you're here?"

Satō leaned in. She could smell whiskey, sour on his breath. He ran his fingers up her throat and into her hair. He lowered his head and brushed his lips across her neck, licking her rigid skin; then he covered her mouth with his, pushing into her with his tongue. Rina bit down, hard, until she tasted blood. She grimaced as he jerked away from her, glad when he stumbled. She felt her lips curve up as he patted his pockets for a handkerchief, his hand still over his mouth. "I am very pleased that this is the last time I shall ever see you," she said.

Satō wiped his lips and walked over to the sideboard. "This is the agency he works for," he said, placing a business card and some papers on the flat black surface. "Ask them for your file or ask him." He gave her a slow forced smile, though she did not move and her expression did not change. "Ask how much I paid him to fuck you," he said. Then he was gone and Rina stood alone, unmoving, in the hall of her home.

# *ESCAPE*

Rina ran her hand across her mouth scrubbing at her lips, rubbing away all traces of his blood—though the taste of him, smoky and metallic, remained with her. It was not true, she thought, it could not be true. For a moment, she contemplated going into Sumi's bedroom and starting on the last wall to be painted. Satō was controlling, and this was very like him. If life didn't hand him the endings he wanted, he got angry. Most likely Naoko had dumped him or found someone else.

Rina went into the kitchen and splashed cold water on her face. She rinsed out her mouth and poured herself a glass of chilled tea. "It's nonsense," she said aloud, but as she returned to the living room, she saw the business card and papers still lying on the sideboard. It would be better to rip them up and throw them away before Kaitarō got home. There was no room for anything of Satō's in their life.

She picked up the card. On the front was the name of Kaitarō's former boss at the detective agency. It didn't mean anything, Rina thought. Satō could have found out where Kaitarō used to work and obtained a business card. She ripped it in half and then looked at the folded piece of paper beneath it. It was one of Satō's credit card statements with several payments to the agency listed from May to September of the previous year, something Rina could not ignore.

Stapled to the bank statement was a leaflet. Rina read it slowly; it described the agency's services, the traditional private investigator offerings and some extras. The language was suggestive and discreet, but the implications were clear. Beneath this was an invoice. It detailed expenses incurred over the summer (train tickets, car hire, a motel room in Atami), and at its base, in black and white, was the name of the agent who had filed it: Kaitarō Nakamura.

Rina dropped the paper to the floor. She could feel the blood pounding at her temples. For a moment she remained very still, as though if she did she could pretend this had not happened, that her life was as it had been, as she wanted it to be. But this new information would not be held at bay, and the transformation it wrought was relentless. Images flew across her mind's eye at furious speed. She thought of Kai, of all the months when things had so blissfully come together, each look, each kiss, each moment—all of them now, faster than she could imagine, were being rewritten.

They had been through so much together, some of the darkest and also most wonderful moments in her life. And Kaitarō was at the heart of it all. He had truly known her, understood her. She could still remember the anguish she had felt when she thought she must walk away from him, the guilt and the longing. The terror of possibly losing Sumi resonated still, yet he had been like a savior then, helping and guiding her. He could not be part of a trap, a deception. Instantly, she was transported to that autumn day in the museum gardens, her relief at being with him and no longer alone, the way she'd asked if all relationships were just dishonesty and betrayal and his calm, clear answer: *Not us.* He had promised never to lie to her, yet, surely, that was all he had ever done. But then, because it was without mercy, her mind presented her with memories of Hokkaido, how he had taken her to his home and laid himself bare; she thought of how he'd held her in their cave, the warmth of his arms around her, the bliss of being with him in Tokyo, working with him, living with him, and it hurt so much she could not breathe.

Rina walked into their bedroom, the room she shared with Kaitarō. The bed was made, the coverlet pulled up tight, but just beneath it their pillows were slightly crumpled from sleep. If she picked one up, it would smell of him. Slowly, Rina backed away from the bed. What was it that her father had always told her? That the very best lies are close to the truth.

Next to the bed, lined up against the wall, were the flattened boxes she had just unpacked. She would have to fill them again. Sumiko could not live here. At the thought of her daughter a desperate grief overwhelmed her. She ran into the room she had intended for Sumi. The walls were a cold, pale pink. The stepladder stood by the paint cans, waiting for her to finish. Rina thought of all she had done, all she had planned in this room, and one thought dominated the others. If she had not been so stupid, if she had not been selfish and delusional, she could have been with her daughter. Her marriage might still have broken down, but she could be in Meguro, living with Sumiko, and they need not have spent any time apart. She had left her child to play house with a man who had been deceiving her.

Rina returned to her bedroom. At the top of the closet was a leather weekend bag. She dragged it down, heedless of the towels and scarves that fell to the floor with it. She threw in underwear, shirts, a jumper, her jeans, one on top of the other. She added her toothbrush and toothpaste and reached for her camera, but as she did so she paused. It was the camera he had given her in Atami, the one she now carried every day and used for work. For a moment Rina did not know what to do, and then her gaze lit upon a shopping bag by her bed. It was a present she had bought for Sumiko, an obi, for Shichi-go-san. Now that Sumi was seven, she could wear her kimono with a formal obi instead of childish ties. Shichi-go-san would be her first step towards adulthood, and even though the ceremony was not for months, Rina had not been able to resist. She wanted everything to be perfect when they went to the shrine. Dropping the camera into her holdall, she reached for the obi and laid it flat on top. She would take everything that was hers, every part of herself, she thought, sealing the bag.

Next, she reached for the phone. After two rings Sumiko picked up and Rina breathed in a sob as she heard her daughter's voice. "Darling, it's Mummy," she said. She smiled as Sumiko squealed and began to talk about her day. "Darling, shhh—Sumi, I am coming to get you." There was a brief pause on the line as her daughter digested this. "Ask Hannae to pack some overnight things for you.

I will be with you in an hour, and we will go to Shimoda." Rina listened to the wonder in her daughter's voice, the excitement. Tears welled and overflowed down her cheeks as Sumi chattered down the line. "Yes, darling," Rina said. "I promise, I am coming." Rina rubbed at her eyes and nose, wiping away the tears. "I will come and get you, and I will never leave you again." There was a silence on the phone and Rina called out softly, "Sumi, did you hear me?" She smiled at the joy in her daughter's voice as she heard her shout, "Yes!" "Sumi, I'm coming, tell Grandpa to expect me."

Rina carried the bag she had packed into the living room. She thought of what else she would need for Shimoda and remembered the train. She glanced at the clock. Sumi would have had lunch at school, but it was a long journey to Shimoda and she would need a snack. She could not come empty-handed; she must bring a treat, something Sumi would really like. Grabbing her keys, she ran down the several flights of stairs and out into the narrow street. She walked to the bakery on the corner and shivered as the cold air raced up her arms. She realized that she was standing outside in a T-shirt and her paint-stained dungarees. Several of the customers looked askance at her, but she ignored them and walked up to the counter, pointing to a box of freshly made manjū. "Red bean, please," she said to the girl behind the counter. As she waited Rina rubbed her arms and took a deep breath. It would be all right. As soon as she could get to Sumi, she would make everything up to her. Rina glanced up and saw the store security camera pointing down at her. She had not lived in the area long, but she came into the shop nearly every day; she thought of all the versions of herself this camera must have seen: the woman in love, planning a new business, setting up house with Kai, to the person she was now.

At the checkout Rina noticed some boiled cherry blossom sweets and added them to her manjū; then she returned to her apartment, running up the flights of stairs as though they were nothing. She was gathering up her things when she heard a knock at the door. On the threshold was the delivery man from Kyubey with the bentos she had ordered. For a moment it was as though she had returned to that morning and the day she had planned was proceeding as it should—before Satō had destroyed everything she loved. Nodding to the delivery boy she took the boxes and gave him his money, telling him to keep the change. She carried the bento to the dining table and set them out, one in her place and one in Kaitarō's. Normally, she would have chilled them in the fridge until he came home and then fetched him some tea or a beer while she made a salad, but none of that would happen now. Exhaling slowly, Rina left the bentos on the table and picked up her bag. Then she heard his key in the lock.

## *THE KILLING*

He was smiling as he entered. His eyes were bright, his expression so happy it could almost have erased the day. He was breathing heavily, theatrically, one of their jokes about all the stairs they had to climb. "You had to pick an apartment on the sixth floor!" he said, shutting the door and coming forward to kiss her. His camera bag was still in his hand, and he lowered it to the ground as his lips touched hers. Kai was here, the warmth, the taste of him as he enfolded her into his arms. He was home.

Rina looked up at him. She was still in shock. It was impossible that he was looking down at her as though nothing had changed, as though their lives were still the same. He smiled in puzzlement before seeing that she had an overnight bag on her shoulder and her handbag with it, that her grip on the leather straps was tight and unyielding.

"Rina, what is it?" he asked, laughing as he tried to pry her hand from the bags. She stepped forward and rose on her toes, pressing a kiss to his forehead. She felt his skin beneath her lips, the softness of his brows. This was something she did often—when they sat before the television together wrapped in blankets, or in their bed when she woke to find they had been sleeping nose to nose. She always kissed him. Only now, she was saying good-bye.

"Rina?" Kaitarō frowned. He stepped back to look at her and his gaze followed hers. He saw the papers scattered on the floor, the business card, now torn in two, the leaflet, credit card statement, and invoice beside it.

"Satō was here," she said, watching as the full implications of this played across his face, turning his skin white.

"I will kill him," he said softly.

"No Kai," she said, and he turned to face her. She was as surprised as he that her voice was still calm. "He told me the truth."

"What truth? Rina, whatever he said, whatever he claims, it is not true!" He walked away from her and then pivoted, coming back. "It has nothing to do with us, who we are—nothing! He is just a spoiled and bitter man."

"He has spoiled us too," Rina said, picking up on his words. "And you let him," she said.

"No!" Kaitarō's gaze darted around their home, as though it might help him. He spotted the bento she had placed so carefully on the dining table. "Darling, let's sit, let's eat, we can—"

"We are finished," Rina said, her voice low, and something in her tone, the certainty of it, seemed to reach him.

Kaitarō grasped the strap of her bag at her shoulder and pulled it from her hands, throwing it clear of both of them. "Stay with me," he said. "I have always protected you. You and Sumi." He stood before her, blocking the front door, vibrating with energy. Rina turned and walked away from him into their bedroom. She took one of the flat packed boxes against the wall and folded it into shape. She opened the closet, ripping her clothes out by the hangers, throwing everything inside until the box was stuffed. Then she picked up the ball of string on her bedside table and tied the box tight.

"Rina . . . please think about what you are doing."

"I have thought, Kai," she said, and the endearment was strange on her tongue, as though it was fighting her and what she had decided to do. "You have had months, a year, to tell me the truth. You could have made this right." She pulled out another box and headed for the chest of drawers.

"Rina, I couldn't. Look at what we have. I didn't want to lose you. I was trying to protect you. What does it matter how we met?!"

Rina lifted out a row of folded clothes and lowered them more carefully into the box this time. Then she turned and Kaitarō stepped back at the pain in her eyes.

"You were protecting yourself," she said. She picked up the ball of string again and held it in her hands. "I was never the person I wanted to be with him, you know?" she said, and then suddenly she laughed, "Yes! You do know, because I was myself with you." She watched as Kaitarō took a step towards her. Rina was gripping the string now, pressing it into her fingers as the grief surged through her. "You are not you anymore. What we had was not real." Her voice was soft, nearly a whisper. "I thought that we were honest with each other—about everything."

"We are!" Kaitarō pleaded.

"No," Rina said. "You don't value me. What am I really? To you? To Satō?"

"We are not the same—"

"I am just a stupid woman who can be betrayed, twice. A woman who can be lied to. I was raised better."

"Rina, Yoshi and I—"

"Don't," she said. "Don't talk about my father." Kaitarō stared at her, and the misery on his face pressed her back, back, until her knees stopped at the edge of their bed. She sat down and looked away from him. He was worried, she thought, very worried, but he was glad that she was not screaming. Perhaps he believed this could be salvaged, but it was not so; she would make sure of it. Kaitarō took another step towards her and she held out her hand to ward him off. She was speaking softly, not because she was calm, but because she was broken. She was broken and weak, as she had been for many years. She thought of Sumiko. What would her daughter think if she could see her now and what she had become? Rina imagined Sumi, older, on her coming of age day, watching her as she sat on this bed. She would despise me, she thought. I am not fit to be her mother. I left her because I wanted to play with a lover. I could not tell a lie from the truth. Slowly, she lifted her eyes to Kaitarō, and this time there was fury in her face.

"You have taken everything from me," she said, hurling the string at him and then the clock on her bedside table, her books. Walking towards her, he caught some of the missiles and let others fall to the wayside. He grasped her hands.

"Rina stop it," he whispered.

"No!" she screamed, finally hitting out at him. "You have destroyed me."

"Rina . . . Rina," Kaitarō said; he could not stop saying her name. He took hold of her arms and pressed her down into the mattress of their bed. She pushed against the strength of him all around her, his weight; he was trying to subdue her, and the only thought that Rina had was that once more she was being overpowered and handled.

"I love you," he said, wiping at the tears running down her face. "I love you more than life." His words, when they reached her, caused her to fight back. She wrenched her hands free and gripped the sides of his face. They were close, very close, nose to nose; she could feel his breath on her face.

"I don't know you," she said. "And I don't want to know you." She shoved at him, just as he tried to press her back onto the bed. She kicked out trying to catch him in the groin, but he was too strong, too heavy. With one hand she reached up and dragged her nails down his face, watching his skin bead with blood. The second man she had made bleed that day. "I don't need you," she said, looking him straight in the eye "I will be better on my own."

He tried to grab both her hands and pin them together as they writhed on the bed. She managed to hit him again, smacking his bloody cheek, and suddenly Kaitarō screamed loud and high, a scream of despair, full in her face. The force and volume of it terrified her.

Rina thrashed frantically and kicked him, causing him to lose his balance. Scrambling to her feet she ran down the corridor into the living room; she could feel Kaitarō close behind her. He grabbed her by the back of her dungarees and pulled her to the floor. Rina gripped the sides of the door frame but she could not hold on and fell hard, smacking her chin. She tasted blood in her mouth and kicked out at him, trying to crawl towards the phone on the bureau or the front door—whichever she could reach. For a second she could move freely and then she felt his whole weight come down upon her, pressing her into the floor of their home, crushing her against the wood. She tried to shift him. "You are nothing!" she screamed, and as she did so he reached beneath her and turned her to face him. "Nothing but a whore!" Kaitarō knelt above her. He held her wrists in one hand and the string in the other. He shook out the twine, ready to wind it about her wrists and secure her in place, but his focus was on her hands. Rina kicked upward fast, kneeing him in the balls, crushing the sacks up into his groin. As he recoiled in pain, his grip slackened and she was free. She turned over, crawling fast, knowing that she had to get away from him, that this could not be saved. Yet as she rose to her knees he looped the string around her, catching at her shoulders and drawing it around her neck. "Stop it!" he screamed just as Rina lunged forward choking, gasping, feeling her nails lose purchase on the string. She clawed at his wrists, his hands, scratching and scratching. "Just listen," he was saying. "Listen!" Blood filled her face; she could feel it pulsing beneath her skin. She could not breathe, could not breathe. She kicked and kicked, but he just pulled harder. She tried to gasp at the air but there was nothing in her lungs. "Rina . . . please stop," she heard him say, almost pleading. She weakened, falling to the floor, and he turned her to face him, his grip on the string loosening.

Her first breaths came in wisps but then the air was like lightning and Rina inhaled deeply, feeling the oxygen coursing through her. It was painful but she could breathe and it gave her strength. "Stay with me," he whispered. He was stroking her, smoothing her hair from her face, massaging her throat, pulling the string away. Rina looked up into his eyes and the sight of him, the knowledge of his lies, of the life she had loved and lost, broke her heart anew. "Stay with me. I am nothing without you," he said. She watched as a tear rolled down his face and it was this, his weakness, a weakness that mirrored her own, that filled her with rage. Even now, she could stay with him, cling to him, instead of finally relying on herself. "I don't need you," she said.

His hands, which had been stroking and soothing her throat, paused. He shook his head. "I don't want you," she said, pushing away from him. "I will be better on my own," she shouted, grappling with him as he threw her back onto the floor. Her head hit the wooden boards hard and his hands gripped her neck, tightening. Rina tried to break his hold, clawing at his fingers, but he was too strong. She kicked, kicked again, but she had lost one of her shoes and her stockinged foot just slipped along the floor. Fighting to breathe, Rina's chest swelled and contracted. The pressure around her neck intensified, his finger pressing down hard on her windpipe as the pain returned and she was robbed of air. Once more, she tried to push against him, but her vision blurred and there was only the violent pulsing of blood in her head and weakness spreading throughout the rest of her. Rina writhed, keening, squealing against the loss of her life. She kicked again and again until she could no longer tell if she had truly moved or imagined it. Kaitarō was crying, sobbing in his grief, pressing her down into the floor of their home. Beyond his shoulder, she could see the ceiling, the hanging screen and the corridor to their bedroom, the cranes in flight. This is it, she thought; all I will ever be. "Sumiko—" she whispered, but she could not speak. She tried to say the name and though her lips moved, nothing else did. There was no sound. "Sumi, Sumi—"

# *Part Five*

Everything has been figured out, except how to live.

—ATTRIBUTED TO SARTRE

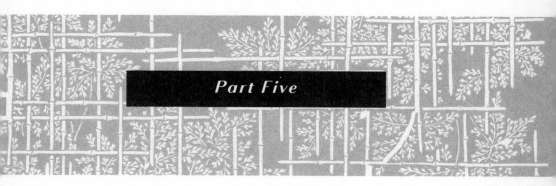

# *Sumiko*

## *BREATHE*

All through the day I watched as dark clouds massed over Meguro; the air was hot and heavy, as though packed with too many particles. The storm, when it finally came, was sharp and sudden, a cacophony of raindrops, hard, fat pellets that clattered across the streets and washed everything away. Now, as I looked into the garden, the air was fresh and clean and the plants shimmered in the twilight.

Night was falling when I settled into Grandpa's chair; the leather creaked and stretched, accepting my familiar shape. I turned on the reading lamp beside me, leaving everything else in shadow. On my lap was the velvet box that had accompanied me through this journey. It was open now, the petals of the badge gleaming gold around the tiny embossed center: the sunflower and scales. Justice for all men. Through the open shutters came the steady whine of the cicadas from the garden. The reverberating chirrs started in the grass and then rose up into the air, louder and louder, amplified by the darkness of the night, as so often our thoughts can be.

I listened, waiting for the metallic clink of the gate, soft footsteps on the tiled drive. And then there it was, his key in the lock. "Sumichan!" he called. I heard the slap of his shoes on the marble as he changed into his slippers in the hall. The light from the study would have been visible to him. I imagined he saw it and smiled, believing me to be working, perhaps finishing up one of my extra cases, or preparing to start work at Nomura & Higashino.

"The abalone was so good, Sumichan!" he called, moving into the kitchen. "They packed some for me as I left. Shall I prepare it for you?" I heard him setting out plates on the dining table. I imagined the thinly sliced abalone fanned out across a platter of ice. "You should eat more!" he said, breezing into the study. He beamed as he saw me sitting in his chair. "You work too much," he said. "Come." He held out his hand to me, relaxed and vital, refreshed by the hot springs.

He was no longer the man who had drafted a case for the prosecution against Kaitarō Nakamura. His hair, which was black then, only lightly interspersed with white strands, had faded to gray. His limbs were thinner, smaller, as though he was shrinking. But his face was still strong, his brows dark, the wrinkles and folds in his skin the result of his many facial expressions. His eyes narrowed and he smiled at me. Then he cocked his head to one side as though solving a problem. It has been twenty years and he still looked at me that way, as though I was a child he could tease out of every mood.

His gaze lit upon the box in my hand and he grinned. "It has arrived!" he said, his voice filled with satisfaction.

"I found this," I said, removing a square of paper from beneath the box. It was a newspaper clipping, like so many of the ones he had given me over the years. In the seconds after he took it, Grandpa did not seem either surprised or alarmed. Then he unfolded it and read the story, those few lines that summarized each one of us.

"Sumiko—"

"I found it in a police station in Shinagawa," I said. Yoshi frowned as he absorbed this, his mind working quickly. Before he could say anything, before he could create another tale, I spoke once more. "And I found your file."

My grandfather was silent. He rubbed a hand across his mouth and turned to the bookshelves surrounding us.

"My file?"

"Your file on Kaitarō Nakamura. In your office," I said, wanting to leave no doubt between us. Slowly, I rose to my feet.

"Sumi," he whispered my name, as though if he spoke softly enough we could return to a time before. I gestured to the now empty armchair, inviting him to sit.

He moved forward in shock. I could see him trying to school his features into impassivity, to exert his familiar self-control, but his hands were shaking as he placed them on the arms of our chair.

"You lied to me."

He looked down at the carpet, turning from my gaze.

"You have lied all my life," I repeated. "Your stories, taking me to visit the motorway in Shinagawa—" I broke off at this, at the veneer of our shared history.

My grandfather shook his head once more as though that might reverse what had occurred, but it was futile. I wanted answers, and he knew how relentless I could be. After all, he had taught me to argue himself.

"I found her. Did you know that?" he said eventually. His cheeks trembled, but he did not cry, and I noticed then how thin and papery his skin had become, how frail he actually was. "She was lying on the floor," he continued, "still in those stupid dungarees." He reached into his jacket pocket and brought out his handkerchief, stretching it between his fingers, and as he did so, I could feel his devastation, his guilt that he should have saved her, guilt he carried to this day. Guilt I now shared. Ever since I had found the security tape I had wondered if she had not gone to the bakery for me, if I had told her to hurry home, to just bring herself, whether she might still be alive. Yoshi clenched his jaw and took a deep breath. "He was kneeling beside her," he said, and he did look at me then. He met my gaze steadily as we finally spoke of the man at the heart of our grief. And there was no more fragility in my grandfather's expression, only a candid and dark reality.

"Would you have wanted to grow up with this? Would you?" he asked, holding out the newspaper clipping, and it was my turn to look away, for I could not answer him.

"I know what he is," I said avoiding his question. "I know what he has done, but you should have found another way. . . ." I paused as my grandfather snorted in disbelief. He stared at me with parental disdain, and, although he had wronged me, I felt ashamed. His look seemed to say that I was a child, a silly girl who was refusing to understand.

"I have watched the interrogation tapes of him," I said, and his eyes widened. "I have read the defense files and your notes, as well. You took these events from me, but they were mine to know. They are mine to know."

My grandfather took a deep breath and released it slowly.

"You have curated her life and mine, created a memory you wanted me to see," I said, my voice rising with exasperation. I thought of my mother, the woman I still longed for, and all the ways she had been taken from me.

When I first obtained the case file, I had thought only of her. I had not cared then what had happened to Kaitarō. But as I watched him, read about him, I realized that he had known aspects of her that no one else would, and my thoughts had turned to his sentence. I had begun to fear for him, a fear that had grown and solidified as I read my grandfather's notes.

"What is it like to kill?" I asked quietly.

"What?" At this my grandfather's eyes narrowed.

"He is dead, isn't he? That is what the Ministry of Justice called to say?" I stood quite still, staring at him, but I stepped back when my grandfather gave me a quiet smile. "I can understand why—" I began, but I was all the more shocked when he laughed.

For a moment I paused. "Did Yurie Kagashima's defense save him?" I asked, thinking of the woman in court with the ponytail who had once held me on her lap.

"What do you think, Sumiko? Have you thought about your role in this too?" my grandfather asked, rising heavily to his feet.

"I don't understand," I murmured, torn between my wish to go to him and the sudden anger in his eyes. Anger that had lain dormant until now.

"Have you thought about where she got the idea that we had accepted him as part of our family? You may not have known what was happening, but you were the one who told her that he was a nice man," my grandfather said. "A good friend who liked your mother very much."

"So her argument that he loved her—"

"Won out," my grandfather said. "The court believed he truly cared for your mother and that his remorse was genuine. They concluded he had committed a crime of passion and could be reformed."

"But Prosecutor Kurosawa?" I said, thinking of the photograph of me that Grandpa had given him, the force of my grandfather's arguments, the trial I had imagined so clearly. But then I remembered the taped interviews, the measured demeanor of the prosecutor, the relationship between him and Kaitarō that I could never quite gauge. Despite my training, I had jumped to conclusions, and along with this realization came something else, a feeling as strange as it was forbidden: relief.

"Kurosawa didn't respond to my letters," my grandfather said. "In the end he called for a long custodial sentence with labor."

"So the phone call from the Ministry of Justice?"

"Kaitarō Nakamura is alive," Yoshi said, "and about to be released."

I took a moment to process this, and at once I saw how my grandfather must have been reduced to a forgotten party after all, abandoned and alone, his professional expertise unable to affect events. Still, as sorry as I was for him and all we had lost, one thought remained at the forefront of my mind. "Where is he?" I asked.

"Don't be stupid, Sumiko."

"I want to see him."

"He killed your mother!"

"I want to talk to him," I persisted. "He can tell me about her."

With surprising speed, Grandpa strode towards me and took hold of my arms. His skin was wrinkled and fine, but his grip was hard. "*I* have told you about her," he said, bringing our faces close. I looked back at him, wavering, trying to match his gaze.

"I have done my best, Sumiko," he said, still holding me tightly.

"It is not enough," I said, twisting away from him, stumbling as he suddenly released me and turned away. And even though he stood with his back to me, everything he had given me, my childhood, his protection, his love, hung in the air between us.

"I don't think I can work for Nomura & Higashino."

"Nonsense," he said, glaring over his shoulder.

"I mean it," I said softly.

"Don't do this, Sumiko. If you're trying to punish me . . ."

"I'm not."

He turned to face me once more, shaking his head. "But you've signed the contract—"

"I haven't."

"This will damage your career—irrevocably."

"I don't want to specialize in corporate law," I said.

Grandpa's expression softened and he extended his hands to me, taking my fingers in his. "Sumichan, you've had a shock. You don't know what you want." I stiffened and his grip on my hands tightened. "This is grief, Sumi. You're not being rational."

"Before you came home," I said, "I opened the contract. But I can't sign it. . . ."

My grandfather set his jaw and let go of my hands. "I did not raise you to be like this."

"Is that what you said to my mother?" I asked.

"Rina failed to accept her responsibilities."

"And you think I am the same?"

"You are well trained, disciplined. You can be everything she was not."

"I will be myself," I said, watching as he realized what I was saying. "As she was."

"She is dead," he said, walking away from me. "She left you to grow up without her."

"I want to see him," I insisted, and he stopped, suddenly still, his lips stretching into a line of frustration.

"You won't reach him in time," he said.

I tried to remember the details of the phone call I had received, calculating the notice period the Ministry of Justice would have used. It could not be that I was too late, that he had been released. After a few moments, it became clear that my grandfather was bluffing, and he saw that I knew.

"They won't let just anyone in," he said. "What are you going to do? Pretend to be his lawyer?"

"There's no need," I said.

"The irony of it, the final use of your training," my grandfather sneered.

"I'm not going to misrepresent myself," I said.

Grandpa stood facing the bookcases, our collection, an amalgam of all our work to that point. "Their rules are strict. Only relatives may visit."

"What class of inmate is he?" I asked, but my grandfather wouldn't answer. I wondered if he had received reports of Kaitarō's behavior during his incarceration and his subsequent classification. The higher the designation the more visits and letters a prisoner was allowed. Such a report would have been Grandpa's right to receive as a forgotten party. under the new ruling.

"Has he had any visitors?"

"No," my grandfather replied as we stood together in his study, a few feet apart, unable to reach for each other.

"Not one?" I asked

My grandfather looked back at me with tired eyes. "He has no family, not anymore."

"Where is he?" I asked

"Sumiko, don't do this," he said, finally pleading.

"Where?" I repeated.

"Chiba," he said, closing his eyes so he could not see me. "What will you say your connection is?" he asked as I paused in the doorway, thinking of the man who said he loved my mother and killed her.

"Kaitarō Nakamura was to be my stepfather," I said. "I am his family."

## *SADAME*

On the train to Chiba I was unable to sit still, so I wandered through the carriages. I stood in an enclosed corridor between them, amid the noise of the churning wheels, and leaned against the door. I could see my reflection in the window—a small woman in leather boots and a navy shirt dress, belted tightly at her waist. My fingers gripped the steel rail beside me, encircling it, my nails pressed into my palm as though they might anchor me.

When Grandpa and I went skiing in the Japanese Alps we had traveled on small local trains. They moved so slowly that you could see the rows of bamboo swaying in the breeze. Like ostrich feathers they bowed in the wind, clustered along the train tracks and riverbanks. Each detail was clear: the dark poles stretching towards the light, topped with a plumage of jade leaves. On this train, the outer world was a delicate blur. In the distance, the caps of the mountains gleamed like opalescent pearls strung across with telephone wires, and the isolated houses and fields of the countryside coalesced into stripes of color until the world flew by so fast that it looked as though it was running away from me, heading over the tracks and back to Tokyo where I belonged.

Only it was too late for me to stay home where I and those I loved might have been safe. As we neared Chiba, fear, angular and ugly, rose within me; the train slowed and the outer world crystallized into the hard edges of the station platform.

I was nervous as I walked towards the prison gates. What I

had not acknowledged in the study was that I might not be able to see Kaitarō Nakamura. My grandfather was right when he said the rules were strict. I could try to argue that I was a relative, but there was something beyond my control that would stipulate whether or not I was allowed to see him. My course had been determined twenty years ago, in how Kaitarō had viewed me as a child.

Even today, when a prisoner first enters Chiba, all potential visitors are registered with the front office. Those who are not named then will not be granted entry.

My hands were shaking as I withdrew my ID documents from my bag; my driver's license stuck in my leather wallet and I had to tease it free with fingertips slippery with sweat. I bowed to the guard as he gestured for me to wait and walked to the booth next to the perimeter fence. I watched him reach for the telephone. He held my driver's license in front of him, reading out the details. I waited as he paused and listened; eventually he nodded and spoke again. It had begun to rain, and the air filled with faint drizzle, practically mist. The guard quickened his steps as he returned to me. "The prisoner is at work," he explained, "but there is a room where you might wait for the next half hour."

He gestured to the main building one hundred yards away, an imposing concrete block with black glass doors. I had assembled so many arguments in my head, anticipated so many problems gaining entry (I had even brought my badge) that for a moment I did not understand him. The guard wiped the moisture off his face with his sleeve and frowned at me. "Ms. Sarashima?" he repeated. "I need you to fill in a form," he said, glancing up at the sky and the rain that was beginning to fall in earnest. As dense drops splashed onto the tarmac around us, he took my arm and steered me beneath the bright yellow awning of the prison shop. There he handed me his clipboard and a pen. "Please fill this out," he said. "You must be precise." I nodded and took the form from him, fumbling a little. "He registered me?" I asked slowly, looking up once more. "I am on his list of visitors?" The guard frowned and narrowed his eyes.

"Sorry," I murmured quickly, bowing my head. There were questions about my background that I answered swiftly and then a large empty box: *Please state the topic you wish to discuss with the prisoner.* In small print below this the text read: *Please do not deviate from this topic or your meeting will be terminated.* I paused, the pen nib resting against the paper. Then I wrote down three words: *my mother, Rina.*

The guard looked down at the paper and nodded. Then he took the form from me and ran through the rain to his booth. Alone under the shop awning, I glanced at my watch and noticed the drops of water scattered over my arms. I brushed them away, shaking the rain from my hands, and entered the shop. The air inside was cold, blasting from the air conditioners, chilling my skin. There was no one else inside, only aisles filled with the items produced by the prisoners.

It is the duty of every prisoner to work. Even those on death row who live in solitary confinement work alone in their cells. The rest spend their days in the prison factories fulfilling contracts to make branded department store bags and chopsticks. When these orders are complete, the prisoners are trained in a craft, and the products they make are sold in the prison shops.

The room before me was large, vast even, like a warehouse. Strip lights spanned the length of the ceiling, and the walls glowed white. There was a carpeted space at the end of the room showcasing a velour sofa and a clear glass coffee table, alongside traditional chests made from red elmwood and black ironwork. Arranged in front of me were low tables topped with wicker baskets full of foil packets of green tea and clay models of the gods. Along the walls were racks of men's leather shoes in black and brown. There was an arrangement of ties and walking sticks and then, in a glass cabinet, tie pins of black lacquer with silver and gold metal work—a golden carp swimming in a dark pool or a silver peony against the black night sky.

As I walked around the room, I thought of the men who had made these items and what their existence was like. Life in a facility like Chiba is largely silent. Prisoners are not allowed to talk to one another or look at each other. During exercise, bathing, even prayer, communication is prohibited and punished. In the factories, each man may focus only on the work before him. He cannot glance at the guards or other prisoners, check the time, or look out the window. Permission has to be sought before he wipes his face or blows his nose. It is a world where men have little control over their minds and bodies; the only things they can influence are the products they create.

I thought of Kaitarō as I had last seen him, the man in the videos with his despair and defiance. I saw his face framed by long dark hair, his eyes gleaming at the camera, and I wondered which of these items he had made. I wondered how he might have changed in this world where for years he had been told exactly how to sit, stand, even sleep. I imagined him in the factory every day, inured to the routine body searches that took place before he entered the canteen or his cell block, looking at nothing and no one, moving to the sound of chimes. It was possible that I would be the first person he had really seen in twenty years. I wondered if he would be able to look me in the eye.

The door at the back of the shop opened and a sales assistant entered. She walked quickly in her flat shoes, wiping at the corners of her mouth with a handkerchief. She smiled and beckoned me towards the till. "Have you seen these?" she asked gesturing to a stationery rack on the counter. It contained the usual notebooks and writing paper with cherry blossoms, paper drinks coasters patterned with autumn leaves, but next to this, in a stand of their own, was a set of notebooks featuring Kumamon, the black bear of the Kumamoto Prefecture. This mascot is so endearing that he has gained nationwide popularity; his picture is even featured on babies' milk bottles and instant noodles in supermarkets. On this notebook he wore the hat and uniform of a prison guard. There was a smile on his shiny black face, and bright red circles of health in each cheek. One paw was raised in a cheerful wave. Beneath him in bold green characters were the words KUMAMON'S MEMO!

The sales assistant looked at me expectantly and I gave her an enthusiastic smile. I knew people who collected these notepads; some would even be jealous if I bought one. I opened the front page and saw a slip of paper inside. *Do not eat this,* it said. *Do not use this as a weapon.* And finally, *Do not throw it!* I thought of the rows of men sitting in the factories, the tensions between them, the silence. The whir of the machines as the notebooks were assembled, one by one.

Outside, I stood in the rain before the gates, waiting to be let through. Reaching into the pocket of my dress, I drew out the newspaper article that I had kept there. I had found it on Grandpa's desk that morning, abandoned in the gray light of the dawn. I unfolded it and read once more the words that were so familiar to me, the story of each of us. I stretched the article between my hands until it was so wet it seemed to seep into my skin. As the gates opened before me, I crumpled the paper in my fist and dropped it into a bin.

The soles of my boots squeaked on the jade linoleum as I was escorted past the waiting room with its white walls and long wooden benches. I was shown into a meeting booth no more than six feet wide. It was divided down the middle by a glass partition pierced through with tiny holes. It would be impossible to reach out to someone through the glass or even to touch them. Only the air might travel between us.

On my side of the partition was a desk and a brown plastic chair in which I sat down to wait. I waited and waited. I waited until I thought he would not come, until I thought that he could not face me. The instructions taped to the wall at my side stated that I was to speak exclusively on the subject matter specified at the gates and to do so quietly and calmly. I was not to communicate with the prisoner in foreign languages or gestures. Any contravention of the above rules would result in the meeting's immediate termination.

I dropped my gaze, thinking of how I would speak to Kaitarō Nakamura. How would I be quiet and calm? Would I even know what to say? We had little time. Prison visits last for fifteen or twenty minutes at most. On his side of the glass partition were two chairs: one for Kaitarō and one for his guard, who would monitor and record what was said, but the seats remained empty. There was nothing else, only the silence, a silence that lengthened with the ticking of the clock.

I was breathing slowly, shallowly, when I heard it, the slap of his slippers on the linoleum. I hesitated, unwilling to look up. It had been days since I had last watched him on the screen in my bedroom, and finally there he was. The guard entered first, followed by a small man in a gray jumpsuit. They had shaved his head, but now so close to his release the hair had been allowed to grow back. It protruded from his scalp in a salt-and-pepper halo. His shoulders were hunched and his face was turned away from me as he held his hands out, waiting for his cuffs to be removed. With his head down, still refusing to look up, Kaitarō reached for the chair and sat down, moving with small economical movements. If there was a time for pity, it would have been in the prison shop, when I had braced myself for meeting someone who had loved her and lost her too. Now all I could see was my mother lying on the floor of a foreign apartment with deep purple bruises around her neck.

The man in front of me shifted in his seat, and I felt a jolt of shock as he raised his eyes to mine. His gaze traveled over me, from my hair held back from my face with clips, to the crisp collar of my shirt dress. Very slowly, the corners of his mouth curved up into a smile.

"You look like your mother."

We have many words for fate. Some are sentimental; others carry energy within them, cycles of luck and choice. The word that occurred to me as I sat in Chiba prison was old, archaic even, but the most appropriate: sadame. A resigned fate that must be accepted because it cannot be changed.

Kaitarō's face eased into a placid, neutral expression. Still, a light remained in his eyes as he looked over me, cataloging my features in agile glances. The guard took a seat behind him and sat with his pen poised above a pad of paper. Eventually, Kaitarō's gaze stilled and settled on my face. The knowledge that he had expected me, had registered me as a visitor twenty years ago, hung between us. Had he known I would come? Or had he only hoped that I would? I had been raised by my grandfather; I might never have known about him at all.

Kaitarō leaned forward slightly in his seat. "You're a lawyer," he said.

I looked down at my clothes, at my black boots and dress, the casual nature of them. Then I remembered the portfolio I had brought with me in case all my familial arguments at the gate had failed, and the small round badge I had pinned to its rim. It lay on the desk in front of me. I nodded and again he smiled, slowly, wonderingly. "Like your mother," he said.

"I qualified recently."

"You are registered with the Tokyo Bar?" he asked, his eyes never leaving my face, and I nodded in reply.

"Your grandfather tried to have me executed," he said.

"I know."

"Do you wish he had succeeded?"

The blood rushed to my face as I thought of all the things I had experienced in the past weeks. Certainly, there were times when I had wished him dead. "Not at the moment," I said.

"Do you blame him?" he asked. And I thought of Yoshi at home, mourning the life he had created.

"I might have done the same," I said, referring to my grandfather's attempted revenge and not his secrecy with me.

Kaitarō nodded, accepting my answer. "What will you do now?" he asked.

"The statute of limitations has long expired."

"You are a resourceful family," he said, and I almost smiled. He did know us.

"Are you glad that you are alive, Kaitarō Nakamura?" I asked, my voice audible but low. The guard behind him leaned in to hear, his hand paused above his notebook. I looked at Kaitarō but he remained silent, his eyes cast down, and I wondered if he was remembering my mother. I wondered if he could visualize, even now, the smile she would develop when some small element of life pleased her. Finally, he looked back at me.

"I am the only one who remembers her," he said.

The rage that rose within me was black and choking. I looked with hatred at this sad, thin man. "You are not the only one!" I hissed, my voice loud in the tiny room. I leaned towards him, my breath condensing on the acrylic partition, pushing at the tiny holes between us. The guard stepped forward and placed a hand on Kaitarō's shoulder. He had risen to meet me and now he was shoved back into his seat. The guard gave me a stern look and I sat back, bowing my head in apology. The seconds ticked by and I kept my head down, contrite. I was running out of time.

"Sumiko."

I looked up as Kaitarō said my name. He reached forward, his fingers touching the glass, covering the porous holes.

"I am not the only one who remembers her," he said. "But there is no one who knew her as I did."

"My grandfather knew her," I said.

"Does he talk of her?" Kaitarō asked, smiling when I said nothing. "If I died," he said, "so would she and everything she was to me."

I curled my lip, my anger plain for him to see, along with the knowledge that he was right.

"I have something for you," he said as I tried to compose myself. He ran a hand over his stubbly hair, more white than black.

"I don't want anything from you, Sumiko Sarashima," he said, and I started at his correct use of my name. "But I want you to have my memories." I frowned at him, and the silence stretched between us.

"I have been writing to you," he said with a wry smile. "One letter a month, seven pages each." Against my will my lips twitched at the thought of the prison regulations, enforced even for unsent letters. "Every month," he said, leaning in to the partition, "I wrote a letter to you, in the hope that one day you would read them."

"You are a murderer. I should burn them," I said.

"True," he acknowledged. "But there are some other things that I saved from our house." I had been staring at him, unwilling to give any quarter, but I flinched at his choice of pronoun and the life he had shared with my mother. "There isn't much," he continued. "Only what I gathered up on the night she died. It was taken into evidence. Your grandfather was the guarantor of our lease," he said gently, "all of the furniture, most of our belongings, were disposed of by him."

"What do you have?"

"Photographs of your mother in Hokkaido with me," he said. "I grew up there."

"I grew up without her. You can never make up for that."

"No," he said simply. Behind him the guard rose; our meeting had come to an end. Kaitarō turned and held out his wrists to be cuffed once more. I looked at him, at his dry, flaky skin and hollowed cheeks and tried to see if there was any trace left of the scratch she'd given him, the bloody scab on the videos. I looked and looked but his whole face was pale, the pallor of a man kept indoors for twenty years with only thirty minutes a week outside. As he moved towards the door in spite of myself I called out to him. The guard looked at me in annoyance, and I put out a hand to stay him. "Please," I said. "Please will you let me have the documents and photographs he mentioned?"

"They will have to be assessed, Ms. Sarashima. Our censor comes on Fridays." I saw Kaitarō smile a little, the action so slight his guard ignored it. As the door was opened for him, Kaitarō looked up at me. "Sumiko," he said, and the warmth in his eyes stayed with me, "Burn them if you like."

# *WHAT IS IN A NAME*

My grandfather avoided me after my visit to Chiba. He barely acknowledged my presence in the house, refusing to speak. We did not eat together, and I am not sure that he ate. It was as though in uncovering our past I myself had changed and the sight of me pained him. Still, I approached him every day, unable to stay away, and eventually I forced the issue by asking about the one thing he would discuss: my father.

He told me that they both attended Kaitarō Nakamura's day of sentencing at the Tokyo District Court. My grandfather was early, but my father arrived late, hoping to slip in unnoticed and stand at the back. When the verdict was announced he fumbled with the door and ran down the main stairs, rushing across the marble expanse of the lobby and out into the rain. My grandfather followed, sure of what he would do.

My father walked away from the courts and down the street towards Kasumigaseki Station. On the corner was a phone booth, gray with the dirt and marked with footprints from other people's shoes, cigarettes, and sweat. He opened the booth and quickly shut the door. Then he hesitated for a moment, staring at the receiver, before finally reaching for it and dialing a number.

The air inside the booth was hot and condensation formed on the glass. My father's face was just visible as he lifted his head and smiled. He spoke rapidly into the phone. There was a pause on the line and he waited, waited for someone to come to the phone, the person whose approval he needed most. He was holding the receiver in both hands and you could see his mouth frame the word "father." In seconds the smile fell from his face; he bent his head, listening, and then slowly he lifted the receiver away from his ear. He stared at it for a moment before replacing it in its cradle. A small queue of people had begun to gather outside, some of them reporters, others waiting for the phone. A man stepped forward and rapped on the glass, startling my father, who nodded and quickly left the booth. He pushed through the people on the pavement, waving away the reporters who tried to speak to him. He could not help them, he shouted; he was not the man they sought, not Osamu Satō.

As more people gathered around him he was driven back towards the concrete edifice of the courts until he could go no further. A few yards ahead of him on the path, my grandfather waited, sheltering beneath an umbrella in the rain.

My father was not charged with a crime, though he was ordered to pay a civil responsibility fine for his actions. His family were not hounded by the press. Even so, the Satōs cut him from their lives, but they did not do this because of how he had treated my mother or even because of her death. It was the full catalog of his offenses, collected and assembled by Kaitarō Nakamura, that drove them to it. The details of their son's life reached them in a brown paper parcel tied with string.

The report detailed Satō's business dealings, his drinking, his debts, the loss of the money given to him by Yoshi on his marriage, his dismissal from his firm and his pursuit of the woman in Nagoya. Finally, his actions to obtain a divorce were described, as well as his treatment of my mother. In all this, the murder of a young woman was but the final straw. I asked Grandpa if Kaitarō had sent them the file, but in the gloom of our dining room he pursed his lips in a tired smile. "I sent it," he said.

He knew my father would not contact us again and he had not. The last communication I ever had from him was a birthday card, sent shortly after the divorce when my mother was still alive. I had been sitting on the floor of the living room in Meguro, opening my pile of cards, when I found it. Inside he had written his address in Nagoya, another home I would never see, and enclosed a photograph. The two of them were standing outside an apartment block on a thin strip of grass. I must have held it for a long time because Grandpa came in from the other room. "Aren't you finished yet?" he asked me. "Are you counting the love letters from all your admirers?" He stopped when he saw what was in my hand, and he came to sit beside me on the floor.

"Who is this?" I asked.

"Your father's girlfriend."

"She's hideous," I murmured as he took me onto his lap.

She wasn't hideous, but she wasn't anything like my mother. Her face was broad with a heaviness to her cheeks—a woman no longer young. There were lines at the corners of her eyes and mouth; they creased around her tight smile. My father had his arm around her and his expression mirrored hers; I could not tell if they were happy.

I remember that I turned my face into Grandpa's neck. He had risen to his feet, lifting me with him. Then he set me down and bent towards the pile of cards I'd left on the floor, gathering them all together in his hands. In that moment he started a tradition that would extend to my adulthood: he arranged all the cards in rows across the coffee table, one by one, so that they covered it completely. "Look how special you are," he said.

We put the photo away in one of the family albums, and in the days after my return from Chiba prison I found it again. It had not changed; the figures on the grass were just the same, frozen in time. I had learned so much about my father and his role in my mother's death, and I knew, looking down at that picture, that I would not go in search of him.

═

For a time perhaps, the knowledge of my father's fate helped to heal my grandfather. Though he grieved deeply for my mother, in knowing his enemies had been punished he was able to put his rage aside and look to the future. In a cocoon of silence, he rebuilt the world around him. All that was lost he re-created and invested in me.

I know that I am lucky. My childhood was safe. All through my life my grandfather has supported and guided me. His mistake was in thinking that the world lay within his control, that his version of events could be read as law. The law itself does not protect; it is often inadequate in the world we face today. What matters most is knowledge—of ourselves and others. What I learned from my mother changed my life.

Grandpa did not understand. He sat in our home and looked at the house as though in his absence it had betrayed him. Gone were our evenings in the low light of his study; he no longer cut out newspaper articles and handed them to me each morning. Not only had I defied his judgment; I had changed his reality, his present and his future, and that he could not forgive.

As the summer drew on, moving closer to the date of Kaitarō's release, I came downstairs early each morning to check if his letters and photographs had arrived. I wondered if he had changed his mind and decided not to send them. I wondered if he had been indiscreet in his composition, criticizing the prison or its guards, causing the letters to be withheld. And all the while, the contract from Nomura & Higashino remained in the study. I still had not signed it, and each day I grew more uncertain about what to do. Finally, I visited my mother.

═

The road twisted ahead of me, rising with the terrain, each new curve revealing a new facet of our neighborhood—a shrine, a park where children played, a tea shop, a hairdresser, a funeral parlor where the dead could be prepared and revered in peace. White houses crouched low on the slopes with miniature topiaries in the front gardens, potted persimmon trees or bushes of natsumikan, and all the while telephone wires wove between the houses with crows perched upon them, as though threaded through the neighborhood. They were always watching and waiting for a fresh rubbish bin or a small child with treats.

I stopped by the florist, where there were several traditional bouquets of chrysanthemums standing in blue buckets of water, but I chose a bunch of hydrangeas instead for the flowers that would be blooming on the hills of Shimoda.

The road crested a rise and then sloped down, leading to a steep set of stairs where the gradient proved too much even for the locals to walk unaided. At the base of the staircase was a playground my mother used to bring me to. The swings and seesaws there were much more colorful than the ones I used to play on, and there was a sandpit with a panda on springs embedded in the middle. All was deserted and quiet as I passed through. There was no trace of the busy expressways, offices, and tower blocks in central Meguro. There was only the light slanting across the telephone wires and shining through the trees and, at the end of the street, the temple where I had been given my name and where my mother was buried, our local temple, the site of our family tomb.

Inside the complex, I did not climb the steps to the main hall, but instead followed a path that led around the building to the small cemetery at the back. My grandfather and I had been there together only weeks before, when we had lived in a different world.

It was during the festival of Obon when the dead are said to return home and the chanting from the temples can be heard long into the night. Grandpa and I had brought dishes of ohagi, rice covered in red bean paste and wrapped in cellophane. I knew that soon the temple guardians would clear away the food before it began to rot or draw the urban foxes in the night, but when I visited that morning our offerings were still there, and so were those of other families, the beribboned boxes placed neatly before each grave.

At the far end of the cemetery were the family water pails, our crests painted black on the pale bamboo. I looked for the Sarashima symbol: three balls suspended in the center of a pentagon. Then I filled the pail with water and lifted the smooth weight of it in my hands.

There were many generations of tombs. Some were old, with lichen creeping over the stone; others were new granite, which gleamed in the morning light. But there were no monks that day, nor worshippers to pay their respects, only the crunch of the leaves as they crumbled beneath my feet.

Plots like these were hard to find. They became available only when a family was forced to move further out of the city. Then they took their dead with them and their land was sold on. These "new" plots were seized as soon as possible. When my mother was young, with the strength of the Japanese yen and the influx of foreigners into Tokyo, the value of land had risen with intoxicating speed. Pressure was put on temples to release their burial grounds, and so mausoleums emerged, buildings several stories high with floors filled with private altars and a cupboard for your family ashes. It was the modern way: skyscrapers filled with the dead, while the living longed for the past.

My mother once told me a story about Grandpa and this graveyard, how as a boy during the Second World War, he had been caught stealing rice cakes from tombs, seeking refuge amid the bombed-out streets and starvation. She wanted to remind me of how lucky I was, and she succeeded. But I also remember being stunned. It was so hard to imagine my grandfather in that position. He was so upright and dignified, comfortable and well fed, and in his hands the story morphed into a humorous tale of a greedy boy with no respect for his ancestors, even though his desperate reality was clear to see.

Looking at our history through the prism of his, I saw that my grandfather had witnessed the collapse of his nation and the legal system. He had lived through the American occupation and the change it had brought. What then must he have thought of the mad prosperity, the bubble era that had occurred when my mother was still alive and when I was just a child? What did he think of the rising stock markets, the property speculation, that brief period when Tokyo was the wealthiest city in the world, and the crash that followed? What did he think of the world we lived in now?

He must believe as I do that whenever a haven presents itself it must be treasured, for we humans are consistent in our desires, and because of this we are never safe for long. It was not lost on me that the rise and fall of the markets that had so captivated my father had caused a crash that lasted for twenty years following my mother's death and is known, even today, as "the lost decades."

My grandfather valued peace and I had disturbed his. But I also wondered if his anger stemmed from the fact that I was not taking advantage of current prosperity, that I was veering from my career path as my mother had done. Yet knowing her story and his, I felt so much closer to them and those buried beneath me, our history. That morning, standing by my family tomb, I waited for the cycle to repeat itself, knowing that it would, and knowing too that now the question of how to live was up to me.

Setting my flowers on the ground, I knelt and pulled the withered stems of weeks ago from the metal vases and refilled them with fresh water from the pail. Then I arranged the hydrangeas on each side of the tomb, ensuring they were symmetrical. For a while, I lost myself in the work, ladling fresh water over the stone, washing away the dust and wiping the granite clean with a cloth from my bag. Our plot had been paved over entirely so that no weeds or detritus would mar the memorial. It was practical but also strange since my grandparents had loved nature and the natural order, had known every flower on the Izu Peninsula. This was even represented on the tomb itself, for when his wife died Grandpa had her favorite sketches etched onto the granite—the strawberry plants from the winter hothouse in Shimoda, an azalea in full bloom—her most treasured memories carved in stone.

My mother had also contributed to our tomb; she supplied our name. By the time she reached adulthood my mother was an accomplished calligrapher, skilled enough to merit her own artist's title, but as a child she had only her enthusiasm and fledgling skill. She had drawn the name "Sarashima" on a sheet of rice paper in Meguro, and Grandpa had that transferred to the granite. Now I read those same characters carved vertically before me. Her own artwork on the tomb beneath which her ashes lay.

Wiping away a last trace of dust, I settled my fingers into the deep grooves and slashes of our name, tracing the strokes of each character, following the path of my mother's brush. The Buddhist names of my ancestors were further up. But that day I was only interested in our mortal name, our family name, the name my mother loved, that I have now chosen to keep.

Sitting beside her in her final resting place, I thought of the contract I had neither signed nor returned to Nomura & Higashino, the path that had been laid out for me. I had been fully prepared to take it: to do an apprenticeship of sorts in corporate law and then to use the experience and contacts I made to grow my grandfather's business. He deserved the rest and to have the burden lifted from him. Still, that morning I realized that I had changed my mind. When I thought over all I had uncovered, I wondered if my life and the knowledge I had so painfully acquired could be put to better use.

The law has moved on a great deal since my mother died and my grandfather became a forgotten party—a role he fought against, going to extraordinary lengths to be heard. There is greater support for the families of victims now. They can sit next to the prosecutor in court and give testimony, even question the perpetrator and perhaps move towards some form of closure. But there will always be crimes, and the law will have to evolve with them, for the question of what we can do to each other will never be settled.

My grandfather distrusted humanity. He strictly controlled what was allowed into his life and had retreated to corporate law where he himself could be private, protected. I could do the same, or I could apply to my tutors from the Supreme Court and find a position working with the victims of crime.

Drawing some sticks of incense from my bag, I lit them and placed them in the burner before the grave. Then I stood to pray. At my naming ceremony, my father had insisted that I was called Sumiko Satō. But my real name, the one I bear now, that my mother first compiled so that the strokes of each character would add up to an optimal number and that remained on the altar of our family temple, combines the characters of my given name—celebration, beauty, child—with our surname—absolute island. There are several combinations that form the name Sumiko Sarashima, but those were mine. My grandfather had been so pleased when he'd first seen it. He said it was everything he hoped I would be, a fortress, a bastion of strength. I love my name and my family, but I did not want to be an island anymore.

At home, as I opened the gate and walked up the tiled drive I saw my grandfather's bicycle leaning against the house. I swallowed and braced myself for a confrontation within, even if it was only so he could see me and turn away. I unlocked the front door and peered into the front hall, but all was quiet and still. It was almost as though a sense of peace had settled upon the house. Grandpa had opened the window shutters wide and light poured into the rooms and over the desk in his study. As always, when I entered my home, I went there first. My grandfather was nowhere to be seen, but for a second my heart lightened as I saw he had left something for me on his desk. A large brown paper parcel, pristine and unopened, that had come that morning in the mail: the letters from Kaitarō.

## *WHAT I KNOW*

In the end I followed them to Hokkaido. I don't know what I'd expected when I got there, certainly not the heat. I had always thought that summer so far north would be cool, perhaps even cold to the touch. My skin was moist with sweat as I wound down the windows of my hire car and drove up the coast. I passed several kombu farms with their bamboo poles and ropes of kelp submerged beneath the waves and the rocky shoreline stacked with produce, laid out to dry in the sun. The breeze was rich and salty, the air infused with the scent of the sea.

I stopped to read the directions I had been given and struggled with the Ainu place names on the road signs, the last remnants of a native people who had been colonized and killed. I listened to the language in the ports, noting the muscular consonants of the Tōhoku and Hokuriku regions, the influence of settlers from the mainland. I ate fried oysters and corn on the cob and watched the fishing boats sail out into the bay with names painted on their sterns in both Japanese and Cyrillic.

I had read Kaitarō's letters, but they had not prepared me for the tiny hamlet where he had grown up, the single street by the bay and the run-down family store in the center, next to the café with the broken neon *é* that might never be fixed. I parked my car at the edge of town and walked along the sea front. People stared at me, surprised to see someone new. Some of them waved, but when they tried to speak to me I turned away, uneasy in this land that had meant so much to Kaitarō and my mother and yet was foreign to me.

I looked in at the café but it was closed. There was no hostel or inn, so I would have to drive to the nearest town by nightfall or sleep in the car. I walked down to the beach and paused by a ledge of rocks that jutted out into the sea. Beyond them the curve of the bay continued, ending in a series of caves. Their cave would be there, I thought, looking out to the water that ebbed and flowed in front of me, water that would travel all the way down the coast to Shimoda. For just as people in this world do not pause or even exist for long, so the water before me was not the water that had been.

I turned my back on the beach and walked up the sea road until I found Kaitarō's bungalow. This too surprised me. It was like all the others with their bleached walls, chipped paint, and flapping outer doors, each one separated only by a tiny alley filled with cracks where lilac wildflowers grew and shivered in the blowing wind.

Kaitarō's mother was long dead and a new family lived there. In the backyard was a small trampoline wet with rain, and the windows of the living room had been left open, revealing a young woman inside. She caught me snooping and although she smiled and gestured for me to come over and talk, I shook my head, suddenly shy. There was no traces of Kaitarō or my mother there, but perhaps I could still find the small shed where once they had taken photographs of each other.

On the night my mother died, Kaitarō had piled these pictures into a duffle bag. Now I held them in my hands. Although these pictures were not part of the investigation for long and were Kaitarō's property by right, he had not been allowed to see them while serving his sentence. Inmates are not permitted to have keepsakes in their cells. When the photographs reached me they arrived in their own sealed police pack, so I wondered if I was perhaps the first person to actually look at them in twenty years.

Our word for memory is kioku; a record or document is kiroku. These words are so close to each other that only one sound divides them. Just so, a photograph is not merely a means of documentation but also the creation of a memory—a place where the human spirit and the physical world can combine.

At the edge of the settlement, beyond the cluster of outbuildings, sheds, and a few straggling vegetable gardens, was a field of wildflowers that lead to a forest. The trees before me were verdant and full, bristling with greenery. There was only a trace of yellow at their edges, a tiny sign that soon they would turn gold, red, and brown. When my mother was here it had been late in the year and the momijigari, the wave of autumn leaf viewing, had already swept through the islands. Still, there had been some leaves on the trees amid the black branches, patches of umber and vermilion.

The view before me was familiar as I walked towards the trees and took the pictures from my bag. In the first one she was wearing boots in the long grass and looking towards the forest. The collar of her shirt had been pulled up to cover her neck, protecting her from the cold, and her face was in profile. She was slender and still as one of the trees. The photograph had been shot in color but underexposed so that the figure of my mother blended into the landscape—elemental in a northern frontier land.

In the next photograph she glanced back at Kaitarō, and the mood of this one was completely different from the last. She was facing the camera, looking into the sun, and the late afternoon light was soft as it touched her face, illuminating her features, her large dark eyes and the glow of her skin against the shadows of the forest. She was smiling, and she looked young and free. Alive.

The following pair of photographs were clearly taken on the outskirts of town, near the outbuildings, one of which might be the shed Kaitarō and his uncle had used as their darkroom. In the first shot my mother was inside the shed. She had opened the shutters of the single window, and the winter light glanced off her profile. The picture was in black and white, emphasizing the clean lines of her face, the elegance of her form. The accompanying one was much more playful as she turned in the room, touching the vats and an ancient hand pump that drew water from a well. The slow shutter speed had blurred and enhanced the twirling speed in her motion, the joy in her face.

In the last photograph he had joined her. They had set the timer on the camera and placed it within the darkroom, looking out towards the entrance, so that the two of them were framed in the doorway. She was teasing him, her hands messing with his hair, and he had lifted her off her feet so that her fur-lined boots were just clear of the grass. She was laughing, her eyes shut, but he was looking at the camera and he too was smiling; one of his last photographs as a free man.

These are not family photographs of relatives in a row smiling stiffly, where no one moves beyond formality. These pictures were like a conversation, a dialogue between the two of them, from a time only they knew.

I turned with the photos in my hands and walked through the long grass, trying not to crush the wild orchids as I went, looking for the spot where she had stood. But in the late summer sunshine the birds in the forest, the wild herbs and the tiny flowers, told me nothing. There was only the sound of the leaves rustling in the trees.

I thought for a time that I would stay in Hokkaido and seek them further. Perhaps in the following days I could walk into the town again and talk to the people there, but as I reached my car and sat within the muggy stillness, I knew I would not.

In the package I received there was one more photograph and it was of me. I was standing on a rocky shore, perhaps near our home in Shimoda, perhaps up the coast in Atami. My mother was shooting into the light so that the rocks and I, even my white T-shirt and red shorts, were in shadow, silhouetted against the indigo of the sea. I was standing in profile so that only part of my face was visible. Still, she had caught the moment when the breeze lifted my hair and the light touched my face as I looked out over the waves, and in that look was a world of possibility.

As I held this image, the only trace of my mother's last project, taken during our final summer in Shimoda, I tried to remember being there with her. I could feel the breeze cool on my face, the cold shock of the water, the slip of my sandals on seaweed as I climbed among the rocks. Perhaps there had been a trip to a harbor to see the yachts, the sound of my feet on the concrete as I ran and ran, and later, a cone of ice cream and strong arms lifting me into the air for a photograph beneath the sun.

What I realized is that I am all that is left. All of these stories, photographs, and facts reside within me. There are tangible things that remain: the stub of her plane ticket to Hokkaido, her shoes, her packets of scent, his letters. These things tell the story of a life, of many lives intertwined, but I am the point at which they meet.

═

On the tarmac in Hokkaido in the glow of the dawn, I stared out of the airplane window, waiting. The engines vibrated as the stewardesses shut the lockers overhead. I bit my lip, impatient, longing for that moment when the plane would taxi down the runway, for the punch of acceleration in my back as we were propelled into the air with no turning back, only flight or destruction.

I knew that I would keep Kaitarō's letters, with the imprint of his pen clear on the paper, and I would not burn them. I could not. I would always be connected to my mother and her lover, but the rest was up to me. As Sartre, whose writing my grandfather introduced me to once, said, freedom is what you do with what's been done to you. I had to build a future for myself, a life.

As the plane finally rose into the air, I looked down to see the airport and then Sapporo shrinking beneath us. Soon we were gliding away from Hokkaido's volcanoes and lakes and its long stretches of isolated coast. We skirted the edge of Uchiura Bay and crossed the Tsugaru Strait and the churning blue sea. Leaving the white-capped water behind, we returned to the island of Honshu, gliding over the forests of Aomori and mountain ranges so steep that any town or city was like a pocket of civilization that had settled in the cracks.

The land flattened as we crossed Fukushima and the golden rice fields of Tochigi, stretching out into a kaleidoscope of color from the green swathes of woods to the burnt ochre of harvested soil and the patchwork of crops still ripening in the sun. For a long stretch there was the silver glint of industrial greenhouses where tomatoes and cucumbers were grown, interspersed here and there with blue tiled roofs and dusty provincial tracks, small settlements that nestled on the banks of rivers. But, as we crossed the plains, the villages grew once more into towns, the towns into cities, finally evolving into the great sprawling metropolis that was my home.

I felt the plane shift and tilt. I saw the wing tip arc against the sun, and beneath it the land flowed out before me, the edges of Tokyo blending and spreading into Chiba. One concrete expanse melting into another, a forest of steel and glass and progress.

I looked down and tried to find the train line I had taken only a few weeks before, following it in my mind's eye to the station and the great square edifice of the Chiba Prison. I could almost see the guard outside with his morning Styrofoam cup of coffee directing visitors to the car park, handing out forms, and in the town and schools beyond the complex, people going about their business. I glanced at my watch, noting the time and particularly the date. Only a few hours more and a new member of the public would walk out through those tinted glass doors, for it was the final day of his sentence and soon Kaitarō Nakamura would be free.

Since meeting him I had often thought about what he would do once released. In the tapes he had claimed that he did not want to live without my mother, so I wondered if he would end his life. Would he drive out into the countryside to a ghostly stretch of Suicide Forest and lie down to die? I did not think so. I thought that like me he would live with my mother's memory. He would live with what he had done.

The plane turned towards Narita, and as I looked outside, searching for the airport in the distance, my whole view was filled with Tokyo. Gazing down at my home, I could almost see each of the old boundaries of the city, still there within the fabric of the metropolis, like age rings within a tree. Once on the ground I took the express train to Shinagawa, a former outpost now at the heart of the city and the site of my mother's last home. As I made my way through the underground corridors of the station, the endless tunnels of flashing neon posters and signs, I thought of all the things this place had once been, from a small village to an outpost of Edo to what it was now: the international gateway to Tokyo and the rest of Japan. From all over the world people were channeled through the airports in torrents towards Shinagawa. Nearly a million a day passed through these halls, the floors polished to such a high shine they mirrored us back to ourselves.

It was after rush hour but still busy as I made my way up the escalators and through the turnstiles before coming to a stop beneath the station clock. It was nearly time, the second hand ticked relentlessly on, and I imagined Kaitarō walking down a corridor, still handcuffed, towards the exit of the prison. I saw the guards readying his belongings—a bag of his clothes, the few items he had kept, and an envelope filled with the money he had earned in the factories. I saw them signing papers, unlocking his cuffs, and then as the clock struck nine with the tick of a pen and the swipe of a card, the doors opened, and calmly, if slowly, Kaitarō Nakamura emerged, blinking against the sun.

A tingle of fear danced along my spine, for now it was my turn to do the same. In front of me was a final covered walkway. At the very end I could just make out the intersection and the hordes of people crossing there, all heading to the embassies, hotels, and vast office complexes that surrounded the station. I looked up at the clock again and my breath caught in my chest. It was well past nine but it was as though my life stood waiting. I could sense all of humanity outside beyond the arch, and I could either retreat from it and hide away or embrace it. I shifted my satchel on my shoulder, thinking of the photographs of my mother within and also the picture she had taken of me, and suddenly my choice was clear, as perhaps it always had been. Clasping my bag more securely, I started towards the exit, moving swiftly up the walkway and stepping out into the light.

# *Acknowledgments*

This novel was inspired by a real trial in Tokyo that occurred in 2010, but it is a work of fiction. For the purposes of my narrative I have changed the time period, location, characters, and all the lives and choices depicted are entirely of my own invention. What fascinated me about the real case was the humanity of the original story, how we love, and what we are capable to doing to each other for love, and this is where the novel began. This book has been many years in the making, several of them spent traveling and researching in Japan with the aid of organizations there and in the U.K., and it is now my great honor and privilege to finally acknowledge all the incredible individuals and institutions who have supported me and *What's Left of Me Is Yours.*

I must start by thanking Richard Lloyd Parry, the Asia editor of *The Times* who covered the original case in Tokyo and was kind enough to share his articles on the trial and insights into the Japanese marriage-breakup industry with me. I am particularly grateful to him for his advice over the years as well as his extraordinary *People Who Eat Darkness,* which introduced me to the Japanese legal system.

Many sources contributed to my research on Japanese law, foremost among them the Embassy of Japan in London and the prosecutors who have served as First Secretary of Legal Affairs there: Fumihiko Sakamoto and Naoya Maeda. I am also indebted to the attorneys in Tokyo who spoke with me about their training, careers, and the evolution of the law: Masako Suzuki, Aiko Koma, Chie Komai, Fuki Iwai, and Tomoko Kobayashi. Thank you for your enthusiasm, candor, and generosity: 今度東京に行くときは一杯おごらせて! I am also grateful to the legal professionals of the British Japanese Law Association (BJLA) who shared their expertise with me, and I am honored to have been made a member of the BJLA.

For their scholarship on prosecuting crime in Japan, the significance of love in Japanese law, divorce law, child custody, and child abduction, my sincere thanks to David T. Johnson, Mark D. West, Takao Tanase, Malcolm M. Feeley, Setsuo Miyazawa, Masayuki Murayama, Matt Antell and David Hearn. I was not able to access a prison in Japan, but I am deeply grateful to the Human Rights Watch Prison Project for their report "Prison Conditions in Japan," including the "Handbook for Life in Prison" from Fuchu Prison in 1994, an invaluable resource and contemporaneous to Kaitarō's story in the novel.

So much of my research would not have been possible without the British Association of Japanese Studies and the Toshiba International Foundation which awarded me a Toshiba Studentship for my anthropological work on *What's Left of Me Is Yours* and facilitated further fieldwork in Japan. I am also deeply grateful to all the wonderful people across Japan and particularly in Tokyo, Atami, and Shimoda, who invited me into their homes, showed me around their neighborhoods, and were so generous with their hospitality and time. To Masami Nakamura, Nori Tsuchiya, Sumiko Itagaki, Chie Matsuda, Henry Onodera, Yoshikuni Nakamura, Yumi Fukui, Yasuko Norita, the Family Ushirosako, and the staff and students of Den-en Chofu Gakuen, thank you for welcoming me into your lives and treating me as one of your own.

To my "Japanese family" in London, in particular, my dear friend Sumiko Sarashima, thank you for the gift of your beautiful name and for all the years of "Niku Nights," encouragement, and friendship. Thank you also to Otosan, for all the bubbles that have kept me sane, and to Sayuri and Takumi for reminding me that dinosaurs—particularly stuffed ones—are far more important than anything else. I am honored to be your godmother (although if you are reading this before 2030, you are too young!).

For the regular late-night discussions, much-needed advice, assistance with translation and writing in Japanese, my thanks to Asuka Isono, Kaori Maeda, and Kazuko Yoshida. My work would also not have been possible without the online Monash University Japanese character dictionary.

On all matters anthropological, I would like to thank Joy Hendry for her endless patience and for coming to my rescue on crows and time. I am grateful as well to the works of Melinda Papp, Peter Wynn Kirby, Dorinne K. Kondo, Yoshinobu Ashihara, Alex Kerr, Inge Daniels, Christopher Tilley, David Lowenthal, and Nam-lin Hur. For their assistance in medical, forensic, and psychological detail, I am indebted to Jill Harling, David Neaum, Justin Parker, and Leigh Curtis.

For their extraordinary photographs, articles, and insight into Japanese photography from the 1970s to the present day, my thanks to Masahisa Fukase, Yurie Nagashima, Shomei Tomatsu, Shoji Ueda, Ryuji Miyamoto, Masafumi Sanai, Seiichi Furuya, and Daido Moriyama. For their expertise in all technical aspects of photography, I am indebted to Holder Pooten of the London Institute of Photography, and Debbie Castro. I am also very grateful to the Arvon Jerwood Prize for Literature, The National Writing Centre "Inspires" Award, the A. M. Heath Prize, and the Literary Consultancy / Peggy Chapman-Andrew Bridport First Novel Award, for seeing merit in the early manuscript and providing the financial support, encouragement, and writing retreats I needed to complete it. Everything I got right is because of these incredible people and organizations. All errors are my own. 感謝してもしきれません.

*What's Left of Me Is Yours* would never have gone out into the world without my wonderful agents, Antony Harwood and Grainne Fox. Thank you for believing in me and for prying the manuscript out of my hands! I am also eternally grateful to my editor, Margo Shickmanter. Thank you for loving these characters as much as I do and for pushing me to make the novel the best version of itself. Your insight and rigor are an inspiration. To Federico Andornino and everyone at Doubleday and Weidenfeld & Nicholson, *What's Left of Me Is Yours* could not have found a better home, and I am thrilled to be published by you. Thank you for making this book, my dream, a reality.

I am very fortunate in the writing community I have around me, but I would not be here today without Louise Doughty. Louise, you gave me the courage to take myself seriously as a writer and to write professionally. I am more grateful than I can ever say. My thanks also to Richard Skinner, the Faber Academy, and the staff and students of the Creative Writing M.St. at Oxford University, in particular, Clare Morgan, Jane Draycott, and Frank Egerton. I owe profound gratitude to the many mentors and friends who have supported me over the years: Nikita Lalwani, Liz Jensen, Jacqui Lofthouse, Nicola Upson, Tessa Manisty, German Munoz, Guinevere Glasfurd, and Patience Agbabi. Thank you for your natural brilliance, endurance, invaluable insights, and gin. You are my heroes.

And last, but never least, I would like to thank my family. To Mum and Dad, everything I am today is because of you. Thank you for always believing in me and for supporting me through some pretty crazy decisions—like leaving a job in finance to write. Thank you for never wavering in your faith. To my husband, Tom, I could never have written this book without you. Thank you for the endless cups of tea, for reading and rereading my drafts (even when they just looked the same!), and, most importantly, for marrying me. You are my everything.

## A Note About the Author

STEPHANIE SCOTT is a Singaporean British writer who was born and raised in Southeast Asia. She read English literature at the Universities of York and Cambridge and holds an M.St. in creative writing from Oxford University. Scott was awarded a British Association of Japanese Studies Toshiba Studentship for her anthropological work on *What's Left of Me Is Yours;* she has won the A. M. Heath Prize and the Arvon Jerwood Prize for Literature and was runner-up in the Bridport Prize Peggy Chapman-Andrews First Novel Award for an early draft of the manuscript. *What's Left of Me Is Yours* is her first novel.